PROMISES
IN THE
DARK

STEPHANIE TYLER

A SHADOW FORCE NOVEL

A DELL BOOK
NEW YORK

A Dell Mass Market Original

Copyright © 2010 by Stephanie Tyler
Excerpt from *In the Air Tonight* by Stephanie Tyler copyright © 2010 by Stephanie Tyler

Published in the United States by Dell, an imprint of The Random House Publishing Group, a division of Random House, Inc., New York.

DELL is a registered trademark of Random House, Inc., and the colophon is a trademark of Random House, Inc.

ISBN 978-0-440-24597-1
eBook ISBN 978-0-440-33972-4

This book contains an excerpt from the forthcoming novel *In the Air Tonight* by Stephanie Tyler. This excerpt has been set for this edition only and may not reflect the final content of the forthcoming edition.

Cover design: Lynn Andreozzi
Cover illustration: Blake Morrow

Printed in the United States of America

www.bantamdell.com

2 4 6 8 9 7 5 3 1

For the men and women of the United States military.

"We sleep soundly in our beds because rough men stand ready in the night to visit violence on those who would do us harm."

—*Winston Churchill*

ACKNOWLEDGMENTS

As always, I have many people to thank.

My editor, Shauna Summers, for her unwavering support, and everyone at Bantam Dell who helped during the making of this book, which includes Jessica Sebor, Evan Camfield, Pam Feinstein, and the art department, who rock my world with their covers.

My agent, Irene Goodman—for believing and for listening.

Larissa Ione, because I could not do this writing thing without you.

My amazing support system of Lara Adrian, Maya Banks, Jaci Burton, and Amy Knupp—you guys help keep me (semi-)sane. (I know, who am I kidding. . . .)

All my amazing, wonderful readers, who make my day with their e-mails and letters and blog posts and shout-outs on Twitter and Facebook. And a special shout-out to the Writeminded Loop!

And always, for Zoo, Lily, Chance, and Gus.

The past is never dead. It's not even past.
—William Faulkner

PROLOGUE

17 years earlier, Freetown, Sierra Leone

*O*hmohs... *Ohmohs?*
How much?
The incessant calls echoed in his ear, a mix of Krio and English he wouldn't soon forget as he ran through the crowded marketplace along the narrow streets by the harbor. He'd long ago grown immune to the noise, the dust, the bodies that passed too close. Learned how to be invisible so he could steal food, clothes and whatever else he needed to survive in the busy place. Even pickpocketed the occasional tourist.

To blend in, he'd covered his head so the blond hair

wouldn't make him stand out more. Rubbed his face with a fine dust and kept his eyes averted because there was nothing he could do about the blue color, which got more intense as his skin tanned under the hot sun.

He would not get stolen or sold again.

He remembered the last town he and his parents had traveled to. The soldiers had come in one night, and if he concentrated hard enough, he could hear his mother's voice, begging, *Don't hurt my son.*

He hated that that was the only thing he could recall of her now, the rest overshadowed by the horror he'd seen. And they had hurt him, dragged him away from his parents and put a cloth over his mouth that made him sleep.

When he'd woken up, he was with a new family.

Udat wan ehn uswan yu want?

Which one do you want?

He'd lasted for a day before he'd escaped, even though there was no one to go back to. He'd found a deserted alley to sleep in for a few nights until some other boys found him. Some American, some African.

All had the same story. And so those friends he'd made here became his family. Together they stayed free, and he lost track of the long days that stretched into even longer nights.

There were five boys altogether, the oldest being twelve.

He was eleven, but felt so much older. He ached in a way he shouldn't, because he knew too much.

The oldest boy taught him, kept them all moving from place to place. Recently, they'd crashed in an abandoned warehouse that seemed promising for longer than a few nights. Plenty of spots to hide.

There were rumors of a place close by that helped kids, but the oldest boy warned that he'd just be taken and sold again if he told his story.

No one wants to help us.

He didn't feel well, hadn't wanted to go hunting through the stalls for something to eat, but the rest of the group was counting on him. His stomach burned, tight from hunger. He'd never get used to that, the gnawing feeling that he would never be full or comfortable again.

Even after he ate, he felt sick.

That didn't stop him from grabbing bread filled with fish and rice. The tourists haggled, the locals smiled and the music pounded in his ears.

Today was easy—it was packed and the small fight that had broken out helped him. He moved past the chaos toward his escape route.

"Boy." A man clapped a hand on his shoulder and spoke loudly. "You shouldn't be alone."

The feeling closed in on him again—he was too small, too weak. Suffocating under the disguise. He opened his mouth to say, *I'm with my mother,* to point to some unsuspecting woman who would not claim him, but nothing came out.

Instead, he jerked away from the man who no doubt had seen him steal one of the day's prizes and ran down the alley. No one followed, and he considered it a victory, stuffed some of the bread into his mouth and chewed, the roiling in his stomach abating for the moment.

He would go back to the warehouse and share the rest.

But as he slowed to a walk, a bag went over his head,

blocking both light and air. He struggled, but the body against his was bigger and stronger.

Later, he would learn not to struggle, found that going limp was actually a better strategy. That a swift skull to the attacker's chin with the element of surprise was damned effective.

But then . . . he'd known next to nothing except for the fact that no one would ever get the best of him again.

When he opened his eyes, he was in a drug-filled haze. It might've been minutes later—or hours or days—and he knew it didn't matter anyway.

A man and a woman stood over him. They looked concerned but he had to get away from them.

Panic turned to terror, even as the man held him to stop him from shaking and the woman spoke of home and brothers. School, play and *nothing bad will ever happen again under our watch*.

This time, he didn't have the strength not to believe them.

CHAPTER

1

17 years later, Kambia, Sierra Leone

This was the place—the small house with the light purple facade that looked like every other tin-roofed pastel-colored one that lined the wide dirt road. The market that ran nearly down the center, allowing a small area for cars to lumber through, teemed with people, none of whom seemed to notice or care that it was hotter than hell at 0800. Music blared from one of the opened windows, an incessant fixture, as if it covered the violence and misery and fear and lightened the worry.

Maybe it worked. This area was more prosperous than

most and the feeling of hope remained here. Or maybe that was his own projection.

From out of his pocket, he took the picture—worn from carrying it around for the better part of six months—and shoved it at the African man who waited at the door.

The man stared at it, frowned, then nodded. "Yes. I've seen her."

"Where? Show me."

"She is there." The man pointed to a spot on the equally worn map that was held out to him, then took the money—American dollars—pressed into his opened palm. "You are military? Soldier?"

"Just a tourist. Here for the scenery."

The man furrowed his brow, not believing a word of that. "You are not the first one to look for this woman today."

But I'll be the first one who gets her, Zane promised himself. It was the third town he'd visited in less than twenty-four hours. He'd done this one on foot because the last driver refused to come this far out into the bush. But he'd known he would hit pay dirt here.

The man stepped back into the shadows after drawing a crude map of the exact location Zane needed, even as the children who'd been eyeing him from afar ran past when they thought he wasn't looking and then circled around to approach him.

One of them didn't turn away when Zane eyed him. The brave one, who'd lost his fear years earlier.

Zane recognized the look, chin jutted with bravado—real or faked, it didn't matter—it was an *I'm not scared of you* attitude.

"Money?" he asked in English as he held out his palm, defying Zane to say no.

Zane dug into his pocket, pulled out some crumpled bills and watched the kid's eyes widen as he handed them over. Then he turned and walked away.

Stick with those you can save, because you sure as hell can't save them all.

He stood taller than most here, looked over the crowds as the smell of cooked fish and rice floated through the warm air—women and men tried to sell him everything from carvings to homemade falafel. Even weapons were fair game, with those vendors whispering to him from darker corners as he strode past in search of any kind of god-damned vehicle to take him farther in-country.

He'd have to pay in order not to have a driver, but he didn't need the added burden of another person. And when he found an old Land Rover, he bargained with the owner until he was able to drive away alone, kicking up dust behind him, his roll of money a lot smaller.

But he had cans of gasoline and the engine was decent. With the windows rolled down and his weapons hidden under a false third seat, an added bonus, he was prepared for various checkpoints and other assorted fun times in this country.

He should check in with his brother Dylan, would when he got farther along. Right now, there was nothing to report other than he was closer to his goal.

They'd been *closer* to the doctor for months now. Frustrating as hell, and Zane wasn't about to jinx it.

When Dylan had told him about this newest intel on Olivia, Zane had taken leave and insisted on going to West

Africa. Didn't give a fuck that Dylan and Riley couldn't join him immediately.

He wouldn't waste a day waiting for backup. Not in this case.

If Dr. Olivia Strohm had truly spent the last three months successfully evading DMH—an extremist group with terrorism ties and businesses all over Africa, ranging from skin trade to black market weapons—rescuing her was something he could damned well do on his own.

We'll meet you in seventy-two hours, Dylan had promised. *That should give you plenty of time.*

He would meet his brother at the port in Freetown. A place he'd never thought he'd go to again.

In his time with the military, he'd traveled to many cities along the western edge of Africa, including in the Ivory Coast and Liberia. Freetown was always avoided, mainly because it was a major port—too crowded for stealth.

The crowds had been the thing that saved him once. Now, the thought of going back made his blood run cold. The Kambia District was close enough, the market smaller than he'd remembered and far more dangerous than he could've known when he was merely a boy.

Thank God for small miracles.

His life had been built on small and not-so-small miracles, from his adoption to his live-for-the-moment lifestyle that had worked really damned well for him. For Zane, time off had always equaled trouble—he liked to keep busy, keep moving, and when he was on leave, his brother, the spy for hire, could always find him something to do. Black ops, gray ops, it didn't matter, and he'd been on as many missions with both the SEALs and his brother in an unofficial capacity. But this was by far the most important one he'd ever done.

The party facade he'd built up like brick walls around his past crumbled down last year with no warning and he'd barely had time to roll out of the way and avoid the fallout.

Most of it anyway.

Maybe if he found Olivia, things would go back to normal. *His* normal. So he took the leave because his brother promised they were close to finding her, since finally, after three months of dead fucking ends, they had a bead on Dr. Olivia Strohm.

Which would've been great if it hadn't been a possible death report.

"A clinic was bombed in Morocco. No patients died, but DMH staff did," Dylan informed him. *"The papers said it was a suspected illegal clinic. There was no note—no one ever claimed responsibility for the bombing."*

"That's strange." Groups who did shit like that always wanted to take responsibility. It was what they did—they wanted the notoriety, making a name for themselves was a huge part of their deal.

Then again, no group would be stupid enough to go after DMH in that capacity. No, most of them wanted to work with them.

"Rumors were that the clinic was involved in black market organ trafficking," Dylan said. *"All the staff was identified—all except one. A female."*

Zane shook his head hard, as if Dylan were right in front of him as opposed to across the line—and the continent.

Zane. That's what Mom and Dad named him in the hotel.

Dad was a huge Zane Grey fan. Wanted his new son to have a fresh start. "Olivia didn't deserve what she got."

"Most of the good ones don't."

But then, just last month, reports started trickling in, that DMH had been offering rewards for the capture of a woman. That she'd been spotted in different African villages and towns. Some called her a healer, and some a killer, but they all agreed on one thing—she was American and danger surrounded her.

Now he planned on following that lead, no matter where it led him.

S ome people might consider this place hell, but Olivia Strohm knew it wasn't. No, Kambia was far from it, and since she'd been to hell on earth twice already, she considered herself something of an expert.

It was nearly dark, but the heat wasn't retreating. Wouldn't.

She wrapped the rag around her hair and rubbed another cloth over her neck. She took a long drink of water because her body demanded it, even though she'd long grown used to ignoring most of her body's needs in exchange for freedom. She had work to do, and that superseded anything else.

She hadn't needed much money here. No, with her services, she'd been able to barter for the more important staples, like food and clothes and places to stay. This house was hidden behind two others, abandoned long ago. But the women she'd met had hustled her back there and helped her settle in without question.

Later that first night, they came back. Shy. With questions, with medical problems, some she could help with and some she couldn't. There was a clinic twenty miles away that she could refer some of them to. For women like Dahia, who'd lost her child to typhoid two months earlier, Olivia had to be the one to reiterate to her after an exam that more children were impossible, just like the midwife had.

Sometimes, she felt as if she did more harm than good, but Dahia brought her cassava and bread later as a thank you.

For the last two days, there had been ripples of gossip in the small village that a pregnant woman was looking for help and running from an important man who followed, intent on taking her back.

Olivia had run too, and she'd learned that no man was that important.

In the past months, she'd killed several men—on purpose—and in the aftermath, struggled with her conscience. Wondered if she could even function back in the real world, and decided no.

She was safer here. Alone, with no real ties. And even though the local women insisted that she shouldn't get involved with the pregnant woman heading her way, that the men who ran the human trafficking ring would take her away and lock her up—or worse—she didn't listen. Told them her home was open to give shelter to whomever needed it.

She'd survived so much already—she would not let the threat of a random stranger take her down or destroy her will.

Outside the small, three-room house, she heard a rustle

in the bushes. It could be an animal...or it could be a woman, too frightened to come inside.

She'd left a candle burning outside—*a signal,* Ama once told her. Ama, the angel who'd helped her for a month after she'd escaped and taught her some of the ways to survive this harsh place.

Ama, who had not deserved what had happened to her.

The lump rose in her throat but she pushed it down ruthlessly. *No, not now.*

She grabbed a heavy iron skillet before she stepped outside onto the creaky porch and stared out, unable to see anything but shadows.

"Come, come," she said, her voice low and urgent in the dark. She repeated herself in Krio as well, *kam naya,* to encourage the woman to come forward.

You can't save them all. But you can help some.

Those words from her first year of residency rang in her ears more often than she'd like to admit.

And so she waited, impatiently shifting from one foot to the other, fighting not to let her nerves get the better of her. But it wasn't a woman who came forward. No, it was the outline of a man. She saw the fatigues and the guns and thought it might be one of the soldiers coming to try to close down her makeshift office.

She would have to pay—or close up and move. Or possibly fight for her life.

She tightened her hand around the cold handle of the skillet held behind her back and waited for the bark of an order.

But this man stepped into the light with his hands in view, free of weapons. Blond. Blue-eyed. Face of an angel and the devil mixed, and the throb in her belly overrode the sudden, sharp fear.

She was being rescued. And that was the worst thing that could happen to her now.

"Dr. Strohm? Olivia?" The voice was deep and dark, washed over her like a sudden rain.

He knew her. But she'd never seen him before in her life—she would've remembered. "What do you want?"

He came closer, through the tangle of bushes and up the small red dust path to the house she'd taken over. She'd moved in, swept it out and cleaned it as best she could. It didn't matter what it looked like. It was temporary.

Everything about her life now was temporary. "Who are you?"

"I'm Zane Scott. A friend of Skylar's."

Skylar. Her former patient. Her friend. One of the reasons she was in this mess to begin with, and yet she felt no malice toward the woman. Only the hot stab of fear at being found. "What are you doing here?"

"I'm here to help you."

There was a calm in his voice that nearly mesmerized her. He'd gotten close now, was in front of her and had extended his hand toward her. When she glanced down, she saw that she was actually holding out her free hand as well.

She pushed it down by her side again.

"Has anyone else come here tonight?" he asked.

"No, you're the only one." Her voice came out more softly than she'd intended. Fear, she told herself. Nothing to do with the contact with someone who might be from her not so distant past.

The wind rustled the bushes again, and when Zane

turned to check that no one was behind him, she struck, surprised him with a blow to the side of the head.

He sank to the ground with a heavy thump and her heart beat wildly because she had no plan. There was nowhere for her to go tonight. No, she'd have to wait until morning to leave, to escape this seemingly well-meaning man.

Which meant she'd have to keep him with her.

Zane Scott was tall—over six-foot-three—and heavy with muscle, although he wasn't overly broad when he'd stood in front of her. No, he was just right.

It took all her strength to get him inside the door and close it behind them. She stood, panting, realized that she'd only been here for three weeks.

How had she been found?

Trouble comes in pairs, Ama used to say. A warning for Olivia that just because one bad thing had happened, she was not to let her guard down against the possibility of more.

That was rare. Even her sleep was broken and uneasy. Dreams replaced by nightmares. If she could physically do so, she'd stay awake all night, every night. As it was, the few hours cost her. Her hands shook and her focus was off.

Good thing the medicine she practiced here was battlefield, because oftentimes, it wasn't pretty.

Zane was wearing green jungle print camouflage. Military. He appeared to be alone, but he wasn't the only one who knew where she was—he could have reinforcements that would come to help him.

Has anyone else come here tonight? She rifled through his pockets, bypassing the weapons, until she pulled out a roll of money. A further search yielded nothing—no dog tags, nothing that would identify him as military beyond his clothing and weapons, nothing that told her anything... until she checked the pocket by his thigh.

A note, written by Skylar. *Zane is one of the good guys. Trust him,* she'd written, but for all Olivia knew, it was penned under duress. Yet it was written on Skylar's personal stationary, and she recognized the signature, since Skylar had signed all of her books personally for Olivia.

Behind the note was a photograph—well worn and instantly recognizable. It was from her apartment back home in New York.

It was a picture of her and her mom, taken in Central Park. She'd been laughing. If she turned the picture over, she'd see the handwritten note from her father.

Zane really was here looking for her. And something in addition to Skylar's letter told her that he wasn't DMH. No, those men would not talk to her the way he had. They would just take her, like they'd done before.

Zane stirred and she froze. But he only woke for a second, just long enough to open his eyes and stare at her.

He murmured, "*Beautiful,*" and passed out again.

The only mirror she'd seen in the past months was a small piece of glass that had remained in the frame, long after the rest of the oval piece was shattered.

She wondered if maybe she'd hit him harder than she thought. Because beautiful was not how she felt. Ragged, but not beautiful.

She no longer resembled this picture... couldn't recognize herself no matter how hard she stared.

No matter how hard she tried, she couldn't remember

the last time she'd laughed. Not since DMH had kidnapped her from the parking lot of the hospital in New York.

Escape from the extremist group had been easier than she'd thought and to this day she still questioned whether her conscience had been destroyed along with that clinic.

She went back and forth, feeling a cross between anger and pity for the staff who were killed. Transplanting illegal black-market organs was a lucrative field and the doctors working there absolutely knew what they were involved in, and had admitted as much to her when they thought she'd begun to believe in the process as well. The patients knew it—they were paying through the nose, but she bet they had no idea that some people were being killed for their organs and others had them taken out against their will.

Maybe those who paid the high price for their new organ wouldn't care. Faced with death, their survival instinct had gone into overdrive, pushing them to risk everything, even jail, to save their lives or the lives of their loved ones.

Olivia had done her share of survival long enough to understand their reasoning.

And she had more names—of doctors, both in the States and Europe, who were part of DMH's illegal operation. She was valuable to DMH and the only way they would leave her alone was when she was dead.

Now she slid the stiff rope around her rescuer's wrists, tying them awkwardly behind his back and then went to work on his ankles. She took his weapons and placed them out of his reach. Stared at the guns and the knife and re- membered how she'd had one of each when she'd left the clinic, how they'd stayed by her side while she lay on the floor of Ama's house and gotten the drugs DMH had been feeding her out of her system.

The withdrawal had been the worst. Olivia could still feel the bile rise thinking about the hours and days that blended as she writhed in pain on the floor. Sweating. Shaking. Alternately praying for death and wanting to get strong enough to take revenge on DMH.

Bastards.

Her fists clenched, and she knew the hatred had been the only thing that had gotten her through that terrible time. That and Ama, who Olivia discovered had been tortured to death after Olivia had left, and only because she'd helped Olivia and refused to tell the men from DMH where she'd gone.

All because of you.

So much death and destruction, all on her hands—her soul. She'd had it before she'd been captured, for sure, but even then, all her patients had been consenting.

Ama hadn't consented to being beaten senseless.

And no matter how many times she'd told herself that she'd been forced to remove the organs and transplant them, that it had been a combination of fear for her family and the drugs, she knew she wouldn't forgive herself. Couldn't.

But she could attempt to make amends. And she could even pretend that it might be enough.

CHAPTER
2

In his dreams, the rescue did not go like this. Not at all.

Zane kept his eyes closed. Although she hadn't hit him hard enough to knock him out but rather stun him momentarily, his gut told him to play along. She'd been through hell and if this got him in the door—which it did since she'd literally dragged him inside her house—he'd deal.

Now he just had to convince her he had nothing to do with DMH.

He'd heard her sharp intake of breath when she'd found her picture in his pocket.

And when he'd opened his eyes and told her she was beautiful, he'd meant it. She was. Tanned. Wild.

She'd survived against all the damned odds, and asking

if anyone else had been there looking for her had simply served to freak her out further.

But she was in imminent danger and it was time for him to get her back in the game. He opened his eyes and stared up at her, his hands tied tightly, but not all that securely, behind his back. He could get out of this easily—if and when he wanted to.

Now was not the time, not when Liv still had that fierce look in her eyes and the heavy skillet in her hand, and fuck, his head was going to hurt like a mother for days.

She looked a little remorseful. But still angry. Her dark hair was longer, framed her face now that she'd taken it down from the cloth she'd had wrapped it in earlier, but her eyes still glittered.

It was so much fucking better than a photograph. "Olivia, I'm a friend. I'm here to help you. You need to come with me."

"You're not exactly in the position to tell me what to do," she pointed out.

He shifted on the dirt floor so he was up on his elbows. "I'm not going to hurt you—you know that."

"Either way, you're not doing me any favors. In the morning, I'm leaving, but not with you."

"What do you mean?"

"Do you not understand English? I don't need your help, if you're really here to give it."

He blinked in disbelief. Shook his head even, as if he wasn't sure he was hearing correctly, then looked around the small house with its bare walls and lack of windows, plumbing and other niceties. "I know being captured can fuck people up."

"You've been captured?"

He didn't answer and she probably took that as a resounding no.

"You were saying something about how you think I'm fucked up," she continued.

"I didn't say that."

"But you didn't know me before, so how can you tell if I'm different?"

Okay, yeah, the woman had a point. But who the hell would want to stay here? "Your parents are—"

She held up a hand. "Don't tell me—worried sick?"

Of course they were. He'd hated going to the house, speaking with them. The police and the FBI had already been there, as had the CIA. But Zane had been the only one whose hope they'd clung to. "They miss you. They want you home."

She was shaking her head, her eyes not meeting his, and something was really wrong. He'd rescued many people before and all of them were happy to see him.

This couldn't be Stockholm syndrome, since she'd escaped from her captors already. "We've been looking for you a long time—since the beginning."

"Why?"

Why? Because he'd heard her yelling and had been helpless to stop her from being taken. "I heard you scream the night you were taken from the house in Minnesota by DMH's men."

She flinched as if he'd slapped her.

"We didn't have enough manpower to save you then. I wasn't at the house, but if I were, I would've tried."

"You're absolved of your guilt."

"What?"

"I forgive you." She dismissed him with a wave of her hand, turned her back and walked through the open doorway to another room in the small house.

She was packing.

"You're coming with me, then?" he called.

"No, I'm shifting locations so you won't keep bothering me. Someone will come by and free you when I'm gone," she assured him.

He lowered himself back down to the ground, his head throbbing from both the blow and frustration. He hated the idea of rescuing her against her will, but he'd do it. When they got back to the States, a psychologist could help her deal with everything that had happened.

It wasn't every day a woman blew up a clinic. God knows what else she'd been made to endure. Everyone had their breaking point. But Olivia didn't seem broken. No, she seemed . . . determined.

And then he stopped thinking and went still, his instincts screaming.

Someone was outside the house.

In seconds, he was out of the bonds and moving across the floor slowly, his weapons back in hand from where she'd left them.

He moved silently into the bedroom, where she was still throwing clothing and supplies into an old bag. Pressed his body to hers and put a hand over her mouth so she wouldn't scream.

"It's just me. Don't make a sound," he whispered against her ear and then moved his hand from her mouth. She turned, looked stunned that he was free.

"Stay here. Don't move," he told her. "There's someone outside."

She nodded, fear in her eyes. He moved out the back door and wound around to the front, using the thick brush that surrounded Olivia's hideaway for cover.

There were three other houses in front of hers—making it impossible to see from the road. You wouldn't know her house was even there unless you were told specifically where it was.

The bushes tangled around his legs, forcing him to move more slowly than normal. His night vision was pretty good, developed from years of missions that forced him to depend on his own senses, rather than equipment that was heavy to carry and could break easily.

The air carried the scent of aftershave his way. He pulled his knife as he got closer to the spot he'd checked out earlier—the perfect place to watch the comings and going from the small house.

A man was there, waiting in the dark, watching the house, wearing night vision goggles, and Zane wondered what had taken him so long to get from the other village to here.

But he didn't stop to ponder that for long. Debated the merits of capture versus kill and decided on the latter. Getting Olivia home was the mission—everything else would follow once she was safe.

Closer...closer...he came up behind the man, who didn't notice a thing, so intent on checking the house and playing with the BlackBerry he held in his right hand that he made Zane's job a hell of a lot easier.

He dropped on his knees and had the man in a headlock before he could make a move to fight back.

"Coming in second does have its benefits," Zane growled, right before sticking the KA-BAR into the man's carotid for a silent, fast kill.

The man's head dropped forward and Zane left him there, to scout the area. He found the man's car parked close. No signs that he'd brought anyone else with him, and what the hell was that all about? If he was with DMH and they wanted her back that badly, why hadn't they sent in a team?

He went back to the dead man and rifled through his pockets. Found no ID, but several weapons, and the Black-Berry, which was high grade, an international phone with a high-powered camera. When he scrolled through, he found pictures of both Olivia and himself, taken earlier on her porch. Saw that they'd actually been sent to an encrypted e-mail address.

They were watching Olivia. Waiting for . . . something. But what?

Whoever this man worked for had pictures of Zane now. He was as marked as Olivia was—and if his picture leaked to DMH, he could be as good as dead.

Olivia swore she heard a soft groan wafting through the humid air and she waited by the front door, her own weapon in hand, watching the darkness where Zane had disappeared.

He might have just saved her life. Or he might not have survived, and the tension squeezed her head like a tight band.

"Come back, please come back," she murmured, well aware of the irony of what she asked, when moments earlier all she wanted was him to be gone.

The sounds got closer. She squinted and saw a figure—Zane—coming around the back of the house.

Relief flooded through her, but it was short-lived when she noted he was dragging a man behind him up to the back door.

If Zane was part of DMH and wanted you dead, you'd be dead by now. The thought was oddly comforting.

"I can't leave him out in case he's being followed," he explained. "Do you recognize him?"

She stared down at the dead man. He looked to be in his early twenties, a kid. A kid with weapons strapped to him. Caucasian, red-haired. Dressed similar to Zane. "No. I've never seen him before. How did you know he was here?"

"The man two villages over who told me where to find you said I wasn't the first to ask."

The picture. She'd forgotten about it, had shoved it back into Zane's pocket in order to pretend it didn't exist. But no doubt he'd shown her picture and of course the locals recognized her. She was an anomaly and not all of them necessarily wanted to help her.

It hit her then, that if Zane had the picture, he might know about her past, because she'd tucked the newspaper article, written years earlier about her, in the frame. She blanched at the thought of being more exposed than she already was and wondered how far she'd get if she ran out the back door and kept running until her legs gave out.

But he was behind her now, holding her up.

She hadn't realized her legs had sagged.

"When was the last time you ate anything?"

How long? "I'm not sure."

"Come on, lie down, Liv."

Liv. Normally she despised the shortening of her name like that from a stranger, but hearing it from him, it felt right. As if he'd been doing it her whole life.

She'd been without food longer than she'd thought if she was thinking like this. Ridiculous. She wasn't sentimental. Needy. No, she was logical. Serious.

God, she was so confused. And so she listened to him, lay down on the bed while he did God knows what with the dead body and then came back in. He'd washed up from the pump at the side of the house.

With his blond hair slicked back from his face, his cheekbones appeared even more chiseled.

He strode into the kitchen area like he owned the place, came back to her with bread and chicken and soda she kept in the ancient icebox.

She ate in silence for a bit, sitting up with her legs crossed Indian style. Zane remained standing where he had a view of both front and back doors. When she finished, she walked past him to put the plate and the bottle back in the wash bin. "Are my parents okay?"

"Yeah, they are."

"Good, that's good." She'd worried that they'd be in danger, whether or not she was in touch with them, but her gut had told her that no contact with them would be best, no matter how painful it might be for them.

Zane was next to her then, handing her an envelope she hadn't found when she'd searched him earlier. It was from her parents. Written in her mother's handwriting . . . and there was a picture of her parents standing with Zane. They looked fine. Not like they were under duress at all.

"I couldn't think of any other way to get you to trust me," he said after a few minutes. "I didn't know if it would work, but I figured, between that and the note from Skylar..."

He trailed off and she wiped a tear away with her fingers and looked up at him. All she could do was nod.

"I hated giving them false hope, but they understood. Look, Liv, we're leaving in a few minutes. DMH typically sends in men alone, but they're usually much better trained than that guy. It's tripping all the alarms in my head that he *wasn't* working alone, that backup's not far behind."

She knew she didn't really have a leg to stand on anymore. No, she needed him, and while she didn't like that at all, she appreciated it. "I'll go with you tonight, yes. But tomorrow, I'm going off on my own again, so you can call off your team."

Zane's expression hardened. "I'm not prepared to negotiate. And it's just me."

That stopped her in her tracks. This man had come here by himself. For her.

"Who sent you? Was it my parents?"

"They didn't hire me."

"I don't understand... you're doing this all by yourself?"

Zane took a step toward her, a grim pull to his mouth. When he spoke, his voice held a barely couched edge of anger. "I've got some help, but for now, we're on our own. You need to follow what I say so I can get you to a safer place."

"But you are with the military, aren't you?"

This time, he simply nodded.

"But you're not here in any kind of official capacity."

He didn't answer her question and she continued. "You said before, you've been looking for me from the beginning. And the picture . . . you found it?"

"Yes."

"You were in my apartment, then. You took my picture from the frame all by yourself," she heard herself whisper, and he confirmed that with a nod.

Yes, he knew. Everything. She hated that and she hated him all at once.

It was his turn to speak. "I know about the bombing of the clinic. I know you're wanted in conjunction with that—both by law enforcement and DMH. You have to come out of hiding to explain. Talk about what you know—it's your only chance."

Yes, she had chances—knew things that could both help her and hurt her at the same time. What kind of odds were those?

And Zane, done answering her questions, told her, "Let's go, Olivia," in a tone that was at once controlled and commanding. Made her want to follow him.

She realized he would not let her win this one. He'd also brought too many links to her past for her to ignore him. But if anyone stayed with her, they would die. She would not be responsible for more innocent people's deaths.

She stared between him and the open door just beyond him as the tension mounted between them, the air heavy with it.

"Don't even think about it. I'll have you pinned before you even get close."

His words were both a threat and a challenge. She was prepared for either extreme.

All she could think to do was run, which she did, out the front door.

She made it as far as the porch, and probably only because he'd allowed her some rope before he'd made a move. He tackled her, but somehow gently, and because she'd turned to fight him, she ended up under him, his body on hers.

God, he was so handsome—and a thrill ran through her, coiled and unfurled deep within her.

Here, it was all about saving lives. Looking for mercy.

It would be so easy to give in . . .

His breath was warm, her body, weighted with his, legs tangled under the night sky.

"You. Are. Coming. With. Me."

She didn't argue then, simply wound her hand into his hair and pulled his mouth to hers. Because it felt right. Because it was inevitable.

Because it was all she could think of to do.

He responded without hesitation and it was better than she could've hoped for—the best, actually, like a million sparks catching dried brush to start an unstoppable fire.

She'd thought she was dead inside. Feelings, urges, shut down.

But now all she wanted was her would-be rescuer right where he was, wanted him to pull her clothes off and take her until her cries pierced the night air.

When he pulled back, she heard herself murmur, "*please.*"

She had not begged once for anything in the past six months. She was begging now.

L iv's body was warm and welcoming, pressing up into his, and Zane would be kidding himself if he said he'd never thought about this, about what kissing her might be like.

The reality was far better, and normally he wouldn't have stopped, despite the circumstances.

Resisting her whispered invitation would kill him, especially when her hands traveled along his shoulders and then massaged the back of his neck in a way that made his body tingle with need. Except, her sleeping with him, it would be like her dismissing him. What had she called it? *Absolving him.*

For some odd reason, rather than comforting him, it pissed him the hell off. He propped on his elbows but remained on top of her as he spoke. "You've suffered through terrible things. And you're scared, but—"

"But what? You're going to tell me it's okay? And if I go back, then what? DMH will magically leave me alone?" She waited patiently for his response, and damn, why did she have to be so logical?

"There's protection. Official protection."

"So I'll be on the run. Looking over my shoulder. Tell me, how's that different from what I'm doing now?"

"You'll have running water."

A small smile played on her lips. "It's harder for them to find me here."

He ran a hand through his hair in frustration, his body still keeping hers in place. His head ached and he was sleepy.

She reached up then and touched the side of his head. "I'm really sorry I hit you."

"Makes me feel good you can protect yourself," he admitted. "But it's not enough."

He debated the merits of kissing her again, when he heard a rustle in the bushes just off the porch.

It was where he'd hidden earlier, and he quickly brought up his Sig, pointed it in the general direction of the noise and prepared to pull the trigger.

"No." She held his wrist, attempted to pull his arm down so that his gun wasn't pointed in the direction of the bushes. "Someone's coming to see me. A patient."

"You never said you were expecting anyone."

"I wasn't expecting that man—but her, I was." Just then, a very pregnant woman emerged, holding her belly in obvious pain and walking toward them. Zane still kept the gun out, but at his side as he let Olivia scramble out from under him.

This was not good.

And still, he let the women go into the house together while he waited outside, scanning the area.

It was all quiet, but he had a feeling that wouldn't last long.

After about ten minutes, Olivia came back outside with a large pot in her hands, practically running.

"Are you going to hit me again?" he asked.

"It's tempting. But I need your help more."

Finally, she was seeing the light.

Except, she shoved the pot in his hands. "Fill this. Then heat the water—warm, not hot." She barely glanced over her shoulder at him as she walked away. "I've got a baby to deliver."

Son of a bitch. He'd been on countless missions in many hot spots, and a single woman was going to be his hardest one yet. "We've got to get out of here now."

"She can't travel—she won't make it."

"We don't have the time for babies, Olivia."

There was no answer.

"Seriously, we need to move out."

This time, a scream answered him. Not Olivia's. No, the mom to be's. And it didn't sound like a cry of happiness.

CHAPTER

3

Olivia wiped the sweat from her brow with her forearm and concentrated on the woman in front of her.

Ida was dilated to seven centimeters and the baby was breech.

She hadn't told Zane that she wasn't sure Ida would make it even with them staying put. The woman had waited too long, traveled too far—and maybe none of that would matter in the end, but the heaviness in the pit of Olivia's stomach told her otherwise.

The labor was moving quickly. She'd have to turn the baby or attempt a cesarean, although that choice rarely worked, especially here. If the blood loss didn't kill Ida, the infection that was sure to follow would.

She comforted the woman in a low voice to reassure her, just as the sounds of gunfire slashed through the night. Ida screamed.

"No," Olivia whispered fiercely. "Not a sound." She pushed a towel into Ida's mouth for the woman to bite on and Ida nodded, understood, bit down hard on the cloth in fear and pain.

A hand on Olivia's shoulder made her whirl sharply.

Zane didn't say a word, just surveyed the scene in front of him, a heavy machine gun in his hand and another hanging from a long strap across his body. Where he'd gotten them from she had no idea, but she was grateful when he handed her one.

He held the pot of water with his other hand, and he placed it on the floor before he motioned to her to come closer.

"Tell me what the deal is with this woman," he growled.

"What do you mean?"

"There's a small army coming this way. I'm assuming it has something to do with your guest."

Before she could answer, there was more gunfire—this time, not as distant. She stifled her own scream and swallowed the bile that rose in her throat. "She's the wife of a warlord. She was sold to him."

"And he's not happy she left him," he finished, his brow furrowed in concern, although it seemed more directed at Ida and the baby than the soldiers that were coming toward them. "I'll take care of it."

"All by yourself?"

"I know, doesn't seem fair to them, does it?" He didn't smile when he spoke. "Take care of her."

He was going to leave her alone in here and she fought the ridiculous urge to beg him to stay.

What had she gotten them both into? She grabbed his arm when he began to walk away.

"You can do this, Liv," he told her, and she let go of him. But he didn't leave then; instead, he pushed the heavy wooden table over onto its side, and then he picked up the mattress, with Ida on it, and carried it, placing it behind the cover of the table and away from the doors and windows.

"Stay low," he told Olivia. And then he was gone.

She heard male voices—shouts in Krio, and English. And then there were screams—women from the village. Some bullets ripped through the thatched roof and she threw her body over Ida's, who'd passed mercifully into unconsciousness.

When the firing stopped momentarily, Olivia checked on Ida's progress. Nine centimeters. The baby would have to be turned now, or neither mother nor child would have a chance.

As the fighting picked up again, she urged the baby to turn, her gloved hands working as if guided by some unknown force. The room had become stifling, almost unbearable, and the constant firing was impossible to block out.

Ida woke briefly, stared at her with a look Olivia knew all too well.

She wasn't going to stay and fight.

Olivia couldn't blame her, but the baby still had a chance. She took off the gloves, wiped her hands and waited as she took Ida's hands in hers. "It's okay, Ida. You can go."

A small moan and Ida was gone. Now that the woman

would feel no pain, Olivia cut and pushed and pulled, knowing what little time she had left was crucial. The smell of blood overpowered her, her ears rang and the room began to spin as she heard screams.

She was certain some of those screams came from her.

The baby was finally out and she held the boy for a moment before a cry tore from her throat. Rage and frustration boiled over, and she took a deep breath to push those emotions back before she lay the baby down on the bed next to his mother and unwrapped the cord from where it had wrapped tightly around his neck.

She reached into her bag and used the instrument she'd gotten from a local clinic last month to clear his mouth. Nothing.

She had failed. That had happened more often than not over the past months. DMH had taken something from her, more than she'd wanted to admit.

The hand was on her shoulder again but she was busy wiping the baby down with the warm water, would not leave him like that.

And then suddenly, she noted that the infant was stirring with tiny breaths.

Minutes later, he gave a healthy cry and she realized tears streamed down her face as well.

When she turned to Zane, she swore his eyes were wet too.

"I think you might be my good luck charm," she told him, although she could barely get the words out.

His smile was small, but it was there. "We still need to leave, Liv. It's going to be tough going for a newborn."

"I know just where he'll stay." Dahia's faced flashed in

front of her as Ama's words echoed in her ears—*When something is taken away, something is always given in its place.* "I know someone who will love him. Keep him safe."

"That's all anyone can ask for," he said. He moved forward to cover Ida's body with a sheet, gently. Respectfully. And then Olivia let him guide her out of the house, the baby in her arms.

The doctor is still in-country. Our source panned out."

Elijah lay back on the bed in his house in Marrakech, listening to Ace report the news through the intercom as he pushed the woman who'd been between his legs away. She looked hurt and he had the urge to slap her, but instead, he pointed to the door, watched as she hurriedly gathered her clothing and left, pulling her dress over her head even as she went into the hallway.

He'd never bothered to learn her name, but he remembered Olivia Strohm's. It haunted him, as did her large, dark eyes that had stared at him with a mixture of contempt and pity.

Now her eyes were haunted. The hair was longer and the body thinner, but it was most definitely Olivia on the screen of his BlackBerry, standing on the porch of a small house.

His man, Kieran, had transmitted the pictures and the report and hadn't been heard from again since nine P.M.

Kieran, his twenty-three-year-old cousin who'd flown to Africa to work and train with Elijah. Kieran, who believed in DMH and looked up to Elijah.

"What happened to him?" Elijah demanded.

"Give me a minute—I think I know," Ace said.

Elijah put his feet on the floor and began to pace the bedroom. He'd thought Kieran was ready. Wanted him to be. But now the feeling of dread grew with every passing moment.

As the head of DMH, he'd been making a major name for the group in recent years. DMH dealt in terror camps, drug trafficking, black market weapons, black market organs, skin trade, human trafficking . . . and the list went on.

Elijah's problem was getting Dr. Olivia Strohm back—and under control. He now had her entire file, things he hadn't known about Olivia Strohm when he'd had her in his grasp.

Until recently, he'd believed her dead, killed in the clinic bombing. Had believed the override destroying the building had been a mistake.

He should have known better. Olivia was smart and strong. Perfect for him. And she knew far too much about the operation. Knew key names. Doctors from major U.S. hospitals who were involved in the black market organ operation. And because she knew, they were all compromised. It was threatening to grind the operation to a halt, because the doctors were afraid they would be exposed—or killed, as Olivia had pulled the switch to the bomb in the clinic in Morocco, killing most of the staff and exposing the illegal nature of the operation.

So far, Elijah had managed to do enough damage control that the organ trafficking at the clinic seemed like an isolated incident. But if Olivia talked to the CIA, DMH would be in some serious trouble. It could devastate that branch and potentially cripple the rest of the organization for a time.

He'd gotten far too invested in this woman for his own good, but would admit that only to himself.

"This man is what happened to Kieran—picture number four," Ace said tightly, a definite sense of blame in his tone as he pressed a button on his phone that transmitted an e-mail with pictures attached to the large screen of the computer in front of Elijah.

Elijah flipped through the rest of the e-mailed pictures quickly until he got to the one that interested him—the man in the combat fatigues, turned to stare directly into the camera, Olivia standing behind him.

"Find out who he is. Now," Elijah barked to Ace. "I don't care what it takes. Run his picture through the military databases—use our sources. Check the CIA and FBI as well."

But the man was military—Elijah could smell it. He had the cocky look of someone who was trained well and could handle anything.

Almost anything. This man would regret getting involved in DMH's business. Elijah would make sure of it.

CHAPTER
4

Zane had won this battle, but only for the moment.

He'd had the element of surprise on his side—it wasn't necessary but always appreciated. He'd taken out two of the four men heavily armed with AKs—loud mean fucking guns perfect for ruthless country like this—before the second two could react.

They'd taken more ammo to put down. The next four—well, that had nearly cleaned him out.

Granted, now he was the proud owner of all their ammo and their guns. Spoils of the victor.

"Zane—I want to wash my hands before we bring the baby in to Dahia," Olivia whispered. She'd stopped at the water pump along the side of the house. "You need to hold him."

He freed his hands by placing the weapon and bags on the ground next to him and took the baby—impossibly small in his hands, and so damned helpless.

And sleeping. Soundly.

He looked away from the tiny face to watch Liv shove her hands under the pump to scrub the mess of childbirth from them. The baby's blanket was dense but soft and she'd cleaned him off well; his skin shone with health.

Again, total and complete chaos had followed Zane. He'd grown up in it, at least for the first eleven years of his life, and was surprised he was still drawn to it, moth to flame, Icarus burning his wings, in spite of the memories it dredged up.

Memories that remained hazy, no matter how hard he tried to put a straight edge to them.

He could've done more about the atrocities that happened to him and the other boys he'd known when he'd come of age. Gone back to the scene of the crime, searched people down. Demanded answers.

Thing was, he was pretty damned happy with who he'd become.

But the thought that there could've been grieving parents out there, still mourning for him . . . well, that knotted his gut almost as badly as knowing Olivia had still been out there.

The infant stirred in his arms and Zane brought him closer against his chest so the baby could feel his heartbeat—Chris, his SEAL teammate and the team's medic had taught him that. Zane had been on the receiving end of a few deliveries by Chris's side. Granted, those always ended in a moment of joy between the baby and the parents.

When he'd gone to see Olivia's parents, he'd expected anger and grief, but not the raw pain that had given him a brutal slam to the chest. If he hadn't already been committed to this journey, meeting them would've sealed the deal.

"I'll take him now, Zane," Liv whispered, and he surrendered the bundle to her, snapping to and rubbing his face hard, to wake himself from the reverie. Now was not the time to take a walk into the past.

And he refused to think of Olivia as the past. No, she was present and future and there was no way he would leave a woman to wander around in chaos.

Within minutes, they were at the back door of a mostly hidden house. Zane remained outside, listened to the urgent, whispered Krio, the tears, the thank yous.

When Liv came out she was smiling with tears in her eyes again.

"Ready? We'll have to go on foot."

"What about the car?"

"They blew the tires. And the engine," he said. "Probably figured it was yours."

"Damn."

"I'll get us another as soon as I can. We're probably safer not driving tonight anyway."

"My neighbor about a mile down the road has a truck— maybe we can borrow it?"

"She'll most likely never get it back," he said.

"I'll make it up to her somehow. I'll leave her money to buy a new one," she urged.

Grabbing her bags and the old rifle she'd been using, he

led her along the back of the houses in the dark—swift and silent, prepared to carry her if she couldn't make it.

But she was all one foot in front of the other, no stopping. She moved like a machine, but not like she was heading to freedom. He had a sinking feeling he was nowhere near done attempting to convince her that she needed to leave this place. Even as the nagging in his gut told him she was not safe—and never would be as long as DMH existed.

Now he was in the thick of it.

Identifying him would be easy if they had access to classified military files. And somehow, he knew they did.

The woman wasn't naked but she might as well have been, since the sports bra and tight workout shorts fit her like a second skin. And Caleb should probably feel like a dirty old man—more than he already did—but he justified the spying since he was sanctioned, and paid, to do it.

He was hiding in the bushes outside the house in the dark, using binoculars to hone in on Vivienne Clare doing yoga, through the opened shades of her living room. Wondering if she'd strip down anytime soon to shower. Hoping anyway . . .

"Are we enjoying the view?" Mace, his Delta teammate spoke into the mic in his ear with a drawl, something Cael had never understood, since Mace had spent his formative years in upstate New York, not North Carolina. His friend had been yanked from that state when he was ten and sent to live with his grandparents. That's where he now owned the inherited bar and land, and where Cael spent much of his free time.

Cael didn't answer him directly, but didn't stop looking at Vivienne either. "What are we supposed to do? Watch her for the next twenty-four hours in hopes someone from DMH stops by for coffee?"

"Nope," Gray piped in, Cael's other teammate, who waited in the car down the street with Mace. "Just got word we're supposed to bring her in. Kind of in the unofficially official capacity."

Mace started swearing and Cael just sighed. They'd do their jobs, of course, because they trusted their immediate superior, who'd issued the order, but the unofficial missions always held a good deal of risk.

Cael had known this particular job would prove to be shitty, had felt it the instant Mace briefed him on it this morning. Before he'd had coffee. Or actual sleep.

No, he'd spent the past days in a prison called SERE, where he survived, evaded, reconned and escaped with the best of them, and had a split lip, a severely bruised sternum and a qualification for continued service checked off in his file to show for it.

He took immense satisfaction in that, because damn, training was fucking brutal. You were beaten and frozen and yelled at; every attempt to break you was made.

Gray had taken the worst of it—he'd been sick the week before and it had gotten worse during SERE. IV antibiotics had taken care of it quickly and now he had only a hoarse voice—and multiple contusions.

Before SERE, he and Mace and Gray and the rest of their Delta team had been chasing their tails for weeks, running from one location to another as Army Intelligence attempted to find the next U.S. location DMH—aka Dead

Man's Hand—planned to hit with one of their attacks. And just as Cael left SERE and headed to his evals and the doc, Mace called him with the breaking news, straight from Noah's mouth.

"We have reason to believe that DMH received a software program that was supposedly designed to protect nuclear facilities, but can be used to disable existing systems and render the facilities susceptible to sabotage."

Reason to believe *meant chatter from Homeland Security. And things that sounded that big usually panned out.*

Mace continued to give him the information gleaned from the report. "Vivienne Clare—she goes by Vivi—hasn't received any recent payment for the program that we've been able to track. It hasn't been confirmed as to whether or not she knows the software was taken from her."

"Wait—she?"

"Yes, she. Remember women, Cael?"

Cael sighed, because he remembered. Mainly, they were trouble. Always wanted more than he could give. And really, there was only so much a man in his position was willing and able to give.

Not just willing—a woman needed a major security clearance before he could even think about revealing his Delta status to her.

Sex was easier. "So we don't know if she's in danger—or if she is *danger."*

"Right. It's undetermined if she sold this program or if it was stolen. Gray said that if her computer was unprotected, someone could've gotten in and copied the program without her knowledge. Here's the background—Homeland Security's had an eye on her for a while because of her father. Lawrence Clare used to work for the government as a software developer. Apparently, one of his programs was hacked, causing a major problem with the electrical grid on the West Coast. He claimed that a co-worker sabotaged the system, but was never able to prove it. He was fired but, according to our sources, continued to create security programs for private companies. Vivienne was twelve at the time the hacking occurred—when her mother and Lawrence divorced, Vivienne stayed with her father. At the time of his death, he was working on a program for a private company that owns nuclear power plants. Never finished it, but somehow it's been leaked."

"And we think Vivienne sold the program her father was working on to terrorists?"

"She worked in private security software development with her father. In order to live up to the agreement on this contract with InLine Energy, she'd have to finish the program—at least that's what she's on record as telling InLine. She took over the responsibility of finishing the program since, apparently, her father had been paid over half the money on the contract. If she can't finish the program, she's supposed to return the money. Her house is in foreclosure, her bank accounts are desolate and it's six months later."

"A desperate woman in desperate times," Caleb said.

"And get this—her most recent security system that she's developing is targeted for use by the U.S. military."

Would she then have the balls to attempt to sell one system to the U.S. military and another to a terrorist organization?

No one was that stupid—or that smart.

Hell, he guessed they'd find out soon enough. And while he hated to scare a woman the way he was about to, he reminded himself that she was a possible traitor to her country.

Years ago, that wouldn't have seemed right at all, thinking this fresh-faced woman could be responsible for helping a terrorist organization, but times had changed.

He tuned out Mace and Gray's conversation with their other teammates, Reid and Kell, and focused on their soon-to-be non-virtual prisoner.

Vivienne, their great white software hope, was five feet five inches tall. Curvy.

She wasn't classically pretty. Her face was a little too angular, almost asymmetrical, her hair was in a messy blond cut, heavy bangs, and the ends of her blond hair were dyed bright blue.

He couldn't see her eyes—the file said they were hazel—but from the picture he had, they were catlike.

If Cael were sketching her, he knew it would take him a while to catch the nuances of her face. She hadn't broken a smile yet, not even the hint of one. She seemed agitated, angry almost, and if he drew her, he wouldn't get the animation correct without concentrating hard.

And still, it wouldn't do her justice.

She was on the phone now, cradled between her shoulder and ear. She talked with her hands, didn't even notice she did, probably, but tying her hands could effectively render her mute.

"She doesn't trust," Noah had told him earlier, right before they'd left to find her. "Consulted attorneys about her options with InLine Energy and her possible contract with the military. Looks like she put her own program on hold to try to deal with her father's."

She'd been smart to consult with attorneys. In today's climate, separating yourself from the terrorists wasn't always easy for those involved in the fight. Suspicion ran high—security was tight as hell and everybody could be the next traitor, especially when she was dealing with such sensitive, and potentially explosive, matters that InLine Energy handled.

"So the program she's been working on for the military hasn't been leaked?" he asked.

"As far as we know. Right now, the InLine software is of major concern because it has a much greater potential to harm than her own program does," Noah answered. "In the right hands, it will provide intense security. Vivi's father was some kind of genius. He was also a conspiracy theorist. She got his gift for numbers, but not the crazy theories," Noah had continued. Basically, Vivienne was raised unconventionally, and what was happening to her was her father's worst nightmare.

But damn, she was young—looked like she belonged at a rock concert, not hacking computer systems.

The house was run-down, but there were some flowers planted along the front porch. The windows were clean and the lawn was mowed.

Someone was trying.

He recalled the picture he'd seen of how the house had looked just a few years earlier, when Vivienne had gone off to college and her dad had been left all alone. It had been in a state of total disrepair and Lawrence had been issued multiple citations.

Instinctively, as if she felt Cael's eyes on her, she reached for the hoodie that was thrown across the back of the couch and pulled it on. Three laptops held court on the large coffee table. Several cell phones were strewn about as well, and Cael figured he'd have to take all of that when he took Vivienne . . . whether or not she wanted to go.

No, this had long stopped being about choice.

"Who's going to break the bad news to her?" Gray asked.

"I'll do it," Caleb heard himself say.

Reid and Kell, who'd remained mostly silent in his ear until now each gave a quick, "Roger that." Both men were the more taciturn ones of the group, loners, and somehow best friends who half the time could barely stand each other's company, let alone any of the others', who they deemed too damned talkative. They were listening though, Caleb had no doubt, both of them in the truck, Kell working on the crossword puzzle and Reid reading the Westerns he liked so much.

They'd sweep her house efficiently while Caleb and the others escorted Vivi the few hours to post.

Now Caleb slid the binoculars into a pocket of his cargo pants while debating between explaining first or simply taking her and dealing with her fallout later.

When he saw her move toward the back door with a watering can in hand, phone cradled against her ear, he figured *now* worked better than later.

Dressed in black, he moved silently around the house toward the back and struck pay dirt with the complete privacy of her enclosed backyard.

It was time to get some answers.

Your card has been declined." The robotic message echoed in Vivi's ear and she spoke back, trying not to spill her water as she walked.

"Not possible. Stupid, stupid computer." She hung up, aware of the ultimate irony, since she was surrounded by open, lit laptops, which appeared to be mocking her.

"I wasn't talking about you guys," she said, as if to appease the fickle beasts, hoping to mollify their tricky motherboards into submission.

She'd deal with the credit card mishap later, because she'd paid that bill—the minimum anyway. She had more important things to do, most especially dealing with the software her father had been working on for InLine Energy. If she couldn't produce a working program, they'd demand their money . . . and she didn't have it to give them. She'd lose the house for sure.

And, judging by her lack of progress over the past months, it looked like that might happen sooner than later.

She'd begun to split her attention so she could finish up the code for the new software prototype she was designing with the Army in mind, a hybrid of her ideas and her father's, taken from memory, because in the end, he'd been so paranoid he'd refused to put anything in writing.

The contract should come through any day now, the lawyer representing her side of the deal had promised. It was hard for a civilian to break in, but her lawyer had some pull, knew a general who knew another general who'd downloaded a sample of her newest security system and had thankfully been impressed.

Her father's notoriety—and now hers—certainly hadn't

hurt, as the FBI had been quietly trying to recruit her into their cyber crimes division. Truth was, if she was to continue to create this type of software, she needed security. But when the offer had been extended last year and then again two months ago, she hadn't been ready to think about working for the FBI.

God, her father must be rolling in his grave at the mere thought of his kid even considering working for the government after his experience with them. And even though she never bought into his conspiracy theories, jumping into working for Big Brother didn't sit comfortably with her.

She threw the phone down on the couch. It missed, fell to the floor and the back and the battery fell out, and no, exercise hadn't helped her shitty mood one bit.

She opened the sliding glass door and stepped outside, stomped around the back deck, pouring water over the stupid, stupid plants that mocked her by dying every single year.

Normally, it didn't bother her that much. It had been the family joke when she was growing up—*Vivi kills living things.*

Yeah, ha-ha.

This spring, however, making sure these damned things lived meant something.

She almost added, *if it killed her,* but couldn't stand the irony. "Live, dammit," she muttered as she poured water onto the still green plants she'd bought last week, a yearly ritual that Vivi re-created in hopes that she could change her luck.

Didn't matter that she could program software better than any Ivy League–educated man or woman in the country. The fact that she could kill a cactus was what would end up on her gravestone.

At the thought of gravestones, a chill shot up her spine and she instantly chided herself for her silly superstitions. Step on a crack, break your mother's back, black cats in her path and Friday the thirteenth were things she took seriously. It didn't make sense in her otherwise logic-filled, live-by-the-numbers life, but she'd had them for as long as she could remember.

She shivered again, feeling the sensation she'd had earlier of being watched. She finished watering and then, thoroughly spooked, turned to walk back into the house, when a hand clamped firmly over her mouth. An arm wound around her midsection, pinning her arms to her sides, and the watering can clattered to the wooden deck.

The hold left her legs free to kick. Which she did, but barely made contact before she was tilted on her side, suspended in the air and carried away along the side of her house, down her driveway and into the backseat of a waiting SUV.

It took off as soon as the door shut. At that point, the grip eased—she jerked away from her captor, stunned and scared, heart pounding.

She expected to see a gun pointed in her direction. Instead, she found herself looking into the calm face of a handsome man dressed all in black.

He was all dark hair, with even darker eyes. Piercing eyes, like finely polished stones, but somehow not cold. And he was broad—so very broad and ripped.

So very military.

Had she breached something? Sometimes, during

development and testing and implementation, her father would accidentally go too far. Given his government background, she'd been privy to the soldier-at-the-door scenario happening in varying forms. CIA or FBI agents. The police. But it had always ended easily, peacefully.

Her father had never been taken from their home in secrecy.

She opened her mouth to speak, to yell, to do something, but the man held up his hand. "Vivienne, we'll explain everything shortly. You will not be harmed. This is for your immediate safety."

Then again, the times she'd been escorted out of her home in the past, the men had always identified themselves immediately. Not like this.

These men could be the ones who'd stolen the program.

She wanted to yell. Kick, scream, throw herself out of the car, which wouldn't happen, with two men on either side of her. There was nothing stopping her from leaping into the front seat and trying to disable the driver, though.

Never let yourself be brought to a secondary location. Do whatever you need to stop that from happening.

Maybe her self-defense classes had actually paid off.

Without waiting, she lunged over the seat and grabbed for the driver's head. The car swerved, the driver cursed a blue streak and hands like iron grabbed her.

In seconds, she was back in her seat and handcuffed to the man next to her, the car was on the correct side of the road and all three men were deadly silent.

The man she was handcuffed to was the one who'd taken her from her house. He'd handcuffed his wrist closest to the door to hers so she was basically leaning across him, unable to do anything but attempt to balance as the car took a sharp turn.

"That was really stupid," he muttered.

"Who are you people?" she demanded, because really, she had nothing to lose at this point. "Where are you taking me?"

No answer.

She attempted to shift and his hand went to the back of her neck, touching a pressure point that left her unable to do anything. She felt dizzy, but it wasn't uncomfortable, and then she was vaguely aware of her head falling forward into the man's lap as her eyes shut in induced sleep.

Olivia's neighbor agreed to the deal. The old truck was worth far less than they paid but there was no getting around that.

She'd also had to pay so the woman would never tell who she sold the car to. Par for the course. Money meant nothing to Olivia now, and it meant everything here.

Now the truck jolted along the road, the muffler loud. At some point, they'd have to abandon it, but right now, it was their BFF.

They went at least an hour in complete silence. Everything had moved so quickly tonight and yet it had seemed to span days upon days, as if it all happened in slow motion.

And she was on the run yet again.

You never stopped.

"Thanks for everything back there," she said finally.

Zane's only response was a nod, and yes, she knew she owed him more. But for now, it was enough.

"You seem to know this place pretty well."

"We're about to find out," he muttered, and they both winced as he hit a particularly nasty hole in the road. She shifted and held on to the bar over the window so she wouldn't hit her head on the roof again, as he asked, "How long have you been here?"

"A few weeks."

"Before that?"

"Does it matter?"

"They're tracking you—the places you've been are probably being heavily watched. So cut the tough girl crap and tell me."

It came out harsher than he'd intended but that rendered it more effective. Liv told him where she'd been hiding and for how long, and he traced her footsteps in a mental map.

She'd covered a lot of ground—whether DMH had been following her the entire time or only relying on local intel regarding her attempts to dig in and stay in one place, it confirmed what he'd suspected.

They were screwed. Getting her out fast would be difficult. Slowing down could prove deadly.

But most of all, he needed Liv's cooperation, no matter how pissed at him she got.

"You did good back there," he said. She didn't answer, and he accepted the stony silence. "Skylar says you're an excellent doctor," he continued. "She said you saved her life."

"Is she in good health?"

"Yeah, she's doing great. About to get married."

"To who?"

"The man who rescued her from DMH," he said, felt

her eyes boring into him. He refused to take his off the road.

"Good for her," she muttered. "I hope you're not expecting me to be swept off my feet by you."

"Wouldn't dream of it."

Yeah, the bonding moment around the birth of the baby was most definitely over.

They rode for another long while in silence.

Finally, he found what he was looking for—an old shed where he could hide the truck. It was about a mile away from the house he'd scouted coming in as a just-in-case hideaway if they were forced to backtrack, but this was as far as the old girl would take them. She'd overheated half a mile back and he'd rather be able to park her in a hidden spot so tracking them wouldn't be easy.

He got out and opened the doors to the shed, then walked around to her side and opened the door. "Might as well get out here, rather than in there."

She didn't argue. The dark, dank shed was no doubt a great hiding place for all sorts of creatures. Not that the tall grass she stepped into wasn't, but she had a flashlight and a machete and could run more easily out here.

Once he pulled the car inside, retrieved all their belongings and locked it up, he grabbed his own light and began to move forward slowly.

He wore heavy boots and didn't have an extra pair for her, but if he went first, he'd take the brunt of any angry snakes. He encouraged her to hang on to the back of his pants with a free hand so he wouldn't have to worry if he was accidentally moving too quickly for her.

He'd traveled like this many times before—night, stealth.

Danger. It was always a goddamned rush. The thrill that normally coiled deep inside him knew it was time to unfurl and enjoy.

Tonight was really no different, although he swore he thought it would be, should be, really, with Liv keeping up pretty well behind him. There were no complaints from her, and there should have been. This was unforgiving country under the best of circumstances.

And finally, over the rise of a small hill, he shined the light onto the path ahead of them and saw the house they would stay in—long abandoned and no amenities other than a tin roof. A deserted house, no doubt used by squatters. Not the best place, but there were certainly worse.

The big problem was that they'd been forced back in the other direction from where he'd originally come—hours farther from the meeting place than they'd been before. On this terrain, that could easily add half a day to their liaison.

You've got her. That is all that matters.

And a bonus—a working water pump outside. It was perfect.

They approached the house cautiously. He shone the light inside—they'd gotten here an hour or so before sunrise. Deeming it safe and solid, he motioned for her to come inside.

But she stood there, at the threshold, peering in with an odd look on her face. She shone her own light around, checking the corners, the ceiling. Did that three or four times and remained there as though her feet were glued to the spot.

Maybe she was in some kind of delayed shock? He wanted to urge her inside but he knew that wouldn't work.

Instead, he began doing what he needed to, creating a perimeter outside the house, and then creating another with a wider border.

She waited outside the doorway looking inside the entire time. When he finished, he stood next to her for a few seconds.

Finally, she said, "Will they find us?"

"Look, the front's wired. So's the back, except for this." He moved past her to the interior, pointed to a small section that resembled a crawl space. "If they come here, head for this. Fast."

"You'll be here to remind me, right?"

"Couldn't pry me away," he told her.

For the second time since he'd met her, she smiled. He took that as a damned good sign.

It was an even better one when she walked inside and pulled the door closed behind her.

CHAPTER
5

Four hours ago, Vivi had awakened to find herself face-down in her kidnapper's lap, which was embarrassing enough. Since then, she'd been walked into this drab room with the two-way mirror and the hard chairs and the even harder-looking man, who sat across from her.

He wasn't one of the three men from the car. Interestingly, no one hid their faces from her, which relieved her slightly.

Unless, of course, they didn't care if she saw them, since they planned on killing her. Which was something she was trying hard not to think about.

This stone-cold man who sat across from her wore all black, could easily be part of the military. Or not.

The thing was, she'd been answering all his questions, and in return he'd answered none of hers. She was pretty sure they'd taken all her computers and were now pouring over both her current security program as well as her father's flawed one. She'd asked in short order for her attorneys and her contacts at Homeland Security and was given nothing in return except more questions.

Most of them centered on her father's ill-fated software security, which had ultimately gotten him fired from his government job, and about the InLine Energy project. Every now and then, the man would ask her about her own new program, to which she would reply, "It's a work in progress. It's unfinished and the first person to see it when it is complete will be the U.S. Military and Homeland Security."

Now she had to pee. And her mouth was dry. The water in front of her looked so inviting, but she crossed her legs and stared at her interrogator again.

She'd asked to use the bathroom three times. Each time, she'd been told, *In a few minutes.*

A full bladder wouldn't be enough to induce her to spill secrets, if she had any, which she didn't.

Finally, the man whose lap she'd slept in stuck his head in the room and said, "Come with me."

Without a second glance at the man who'd been questioning her, she followed and almost sighed when he pointed to a door marked restroom.

After she'd used the facilities, she washed her hands and glanced in the mirror.

Dark circles. Pale skin. Ugh. And, God, she needed a shower.

She turned and walked out. Right into the big man. "Sorry."

He didn't say anything, kept a hand on her to make sure she'd regained her footing. And continued to hold her arm even after she stepped back away from him.

The memory of being handcuffed to him was far too fresh in her mind. And despite the fear uncurling in her belly, there was something else there, making her throat tight and heat flood her face.

Maybe it was the way he studied her—not the cold gaze like the other interrogator. No, there was heat in his eyes, and it made her uncomfortable to even think about her kidnapper in that way.

"Are you all right?" he asked.

"Do you really care?" He raised his brows but didn't answer and she realized that she needed to get him on her side, not piss him off. "Do I have to go back in there?" *God, please say no, please say no...*

"Yes. But first, I'd like to hear more details than what you've given."

He'd obviously been listening in, must've been watching, noticing her discomfort. "I don't know what other details you're looking for. I've freely told the other man everything he's asked about. If there's something wrong, can you please just tell me?"

No answer.

Someone had to believe she spoke the truth, or else.

Or else.

She was in trouble but good.

Finally, he spoke. "So tell me again, Vivienne." He still

held her, his body blocking her view down the hallway. And yes, anything to avoid that other room.

"It's Vivi, please," she said absently. "Do I ever get to know your name?"

He paused for a second, and then, "It's Caleb."

Caleb. The name fit him. Strong. Old-fashioned. He was seriously dark and deadly. And he had her in his sights. As did the rest of his mystery organization.

She had to convince him she was telling the truth, and fast. "Look, I've been developing security software since before college. I dropped out my freshman year because my dad..."

You will not choke up. You will not. "My dad needed my help," she finished.

"Was he sick?"

"He never functioned well in the real world," she said truthfully. "We worked together on private security programs from the time I was fifteen."

And still, there was never enough money.

"What about the program for InLine?"

"I've been working on it."

"What's the problem?"

Should she tell him? Up until this point, she'd simply been insisting the program was unfinished. That wasn't a lie, exactly—in her eyes, it *was* unfinished.

Never one to trust, her father had installed a crucial safeguard into the program that would give him the ability to shut it down if one of the nuclear plant's alarms was turned off illegally.

The problem was, although the program was complete for all intents and purposes, the safeguard wasn't working properly. She couldn't fix it as of yet and she did not want to be responsible for what could happen if she handed it over as is. She was sure her father would not have wanted that either. Not after what happened when he was working in software development for the government, when a program of his was nearly used by a homegrown extremist group to trigger explosives in an office building in two major cities in California. Thankfully, the FBI had managed to stop the bombing, but after the dust cleared her father had been fired, even though he swore he hadn't been the one to tweak the program to allow the sabotage. He cited a co-worker as the saboteur but had no evidence.

From that day onward, his distrust of the government grew a thousandfold and continued to fester until the day of his death. So even though his programs were created to be secure enough to prevent any break-in, Lawrence Clare never took chances.

She was for sure her father's daughter, and yet, going against her instincts she took the chance and told Caleb about the safeguard—why it had been placed inside the program and how she hadn't been able to get it to work.

"So you'd be able to shut down InLine's computers with that?" he asked.

"Yes."

"But let me guess—you wouldn't dream of doing that, you're just doing what your father would've wanted for the good of the country."

She flushed. "I'd be more than willing to hand the safeguard information to InLine and Homeland Security. Monitoring them is not a job I would want. I don't think the program is affected if the safeguard isn't functioning, but I have no real way of knowing. But this is an important project—I have a real problem handing something over that isn't perfect."

"You had no problem taking InLine's money." Caleb gave a small smile as he spoke, but his eyes were pure ice.

Now she struggled, repeated the words she'd told the man interrogating her over and over: "As I've said, at the time I didn't know that my father took half the contract's money for the program. We didn't work together on it. If I had the money, I would return it, but I won't hand over incomplete software—it's far too dangerous."

Cael shrugged, unconvinced. "If that helps you sleep better."

"I don't sleep well," she shot back. It was only then that the man, the one she would reluctantly call handsome, even though at the moment she hated his guts, released her.

Not that there was anywhere for her to go. But still, the small taste of freedom energized her. "I've told you exactly what happened with that software. You can verify it with my lawyers. They know everything—and Homeland Security knows about my current project in development. I haven't done anything wrong."

Caleb didn't say anything but his smirk seemed to say he wasn't buying it.

"Call them." She rattled off the attorney's number. "The same information's in my BlackBerry—the one you confiscated."

He didn't say anything, simply walked her back down the hallway and opened the door to the windowless room.

It was, thankfully, empty, but that didn't mean getting

locked back in there was any easier. "Don't I at least get a phone call?" she asked before he closed the door.

"You're not under arrest."

"So I can go?"

"No. And trust me, you're going to wish you were under arrest."

With that, the door closed and she let her head sink into her arms on the table in front of her. But she refused to cry and she held that victory tight.

After he'd watched Kell interrogate Vivienne and get basically nowhere—a rarity for Kell—Caleb decided to do some interrogating of his own.

He was glad he did, had a feeling she would open up to him, despite the fact he'd been the one to kidnap her.

Armed with the new information regarding the safeguard on the software, he headed to Noah Wright's office to share the news.

As he knocked, he thought about Vivi's head in his lap for the entire two-hour ride. How Mace couldn't stop laughing and Gray tried to keep a straight face while he drove, but Cael saw the smirk anyway.

Fuckers, both of them.

He rubbed his wrist that was marked from the cuff, letting go to push open the door when he heard Noah's "Enter."

As usual, Noah didn't waste time. "If Lawrence Clare's systems for InLine Energy is as good as Homeland Security says it could be, DMH is holding a ticking time bomb."

"I've got some news on that front." He repeated what Vivi told him about the safeguard.

Noah sat back and tapped two fingers together thoughtfully. "So there's a back door into the program that can be accessed remotely to stop an attack on InLine's system if need be. Lawrence thought ahead."

"Sounds like Lawrence was paranoid as shit," Cael muttered, and Noah nodded.

"I'll have Gray look at the safeguard. Did Vivienne give any indication as to whether or not the software could be used successfully without the safeguard working?"

"She's pretty sure it could, although she's not willing to stake her life on it."

"Smart girl," Noah conceded.

"What we need to find out is if DMH has found the safeguard—and whether they're hesitating to use the program because they don't realize the safeguard is useless."

"Useless right now." Noah sat forward. "Vivienne needs to fix that safeguard. She also needs to tell us everything she knows about the program—how it can be utilized. I need every possibility and I want to hear it from her. She'll do it under your constant watch. And she'll do it fast."

Caleb should've seen that one coming. "Wouldn't Gray be better off taking the lead on this one, given his proclivity for this kind of op?"

Noah crossed his arms and stared Caleb down for questioning his order with a look that would normally have Cael shitting his pants. "Gray can work the program from here. But she responds to you. You can't deny that."

"Stockholm syndrome," he muttered.

"It's all we've got right now." Noah's voice remained steely. "We're keeping her on-post so she'll be safe."

Caleb caught himself before he snorted. Yeah, Vivi would surely feel safe after being kidnapped and then shoved into a house and told to work on a program in order to save her life. "She acts like she doesn't know the program's been stolen. She's insisting that she told InLine Energy the program was unfinished and that they want their money back because she hasn't honored the contract. She acts like she's still working on it. She contacted attorneys about what the next steps should be."

"I heard all of that, yes."

"Do you believe her?"

"Do you?" Noah asked.

Cael hesitated briefly before nodding. With that, Noah slid the laptop across the desk and motioned for Caleb to sit and read.

Cael did. Noah had run a check on the lawyers' names that she'd mentioned—and had come up empty. "What the hell?"

"According to Mace, who went to pay them a visit, the lawyers are gone—no sign of files, no sign she'd ever worked with them."

"You think DMH—or whoever stole the program—did that?"

"I do now, based on the intel you've received regarding the safeguard."

"They just realized too late that they'll need Vivienne to bypass it." A chill ran up Cael's spine and he realized that his team had probably gotten to Vivi just in time to save her life. The last screen on the computer proved it—a live feed run from Vivi's house by Gray, which showed a group of men ransacking it just hours after Cael had taken her out.

Ransacking and looking for Vivienne.

Whether it was DMH or not, those men had been planning on grabbing her. And she might've had no idea.

Or she might know everything and this could be some elaborate scheme to keep the military and Homeland Security off the scent of a totally different but equally destructive plan to hurt the United States. "Any other family of Vivi's we need to worry about?"

Noah shook his head. "Both parents are dead. There are some of her mother's ex-husbands, but Vivienne lived with her father after the divorce. Looks like her house is currently in foreclosure—it's been that way for quite a while. She's been attempting to make payments but she's got a lot of debt."

"DMH would pay a lot more than the United States for her programs," Caleb said.

"Homeland Security's aware and involved. The FBI has been interested in having her work with them in the cyber crimes division, so I'm hoping they'll get off their asses and help." Noah slid a set of keys across the desk. Private quarters. "For now, Delta's involved, charged with keeping her safe. Whatever you need, I'll get it for you."

Caleb stood, pocketed the keys. "Do I tell her all of this?"

"Yes. She needs to know, has to know the extent of the ramifications, whether she's responsible or not," Noah said before he dismissed Cael and picked up his phone.

Caleb left, closed the door behind him and stood there for a few moments to let the weight of all he'd learned settle in. In reality, Vivi could well be in collusion with DMH, yet he couldn't reconcile that with the earnestness of the woman he'd spoken to earlier. They would believe her with a great deal of caution. And then he headed back to the room Vivi was being held in.

Mace had joined Gray at the door, and both men were waiting silently for his return.

"I'm taking her to one of the private quarters. Which I'm sure you already know," Caleb said, and Mace nodded.

"It's spooky, man. The lawyers' offices were stripped bare. There's no record of either attorney," Mace said quietly, although there was no way Vivi could hear anything. "Kell and Reid dusted her house for prints earlier—Noah sent them back for another round to see if the guys who broke in left any behind."

"Think she's got any idea of what's happened?" Gray asked.

Cael could see through Vivi the way he could see through glass—she was telling the truth. Had no idea that the lawyers she mentioned were gone and that her father's software had been stolen out from under her. "I think she's clueless."

But not for long.

Gray shrugged. "If someone had access to her computers, they could've copied the program. I'd go with that rather than a hack—she'd be protected from a hacker. But she lives alone, has no real social life. She wouldn't be expecting someone to sit down at her computer and download from it."

"How do we know her staying here doesn't put the post in jeopardy?" Mace asked.

"DMH would be crazy to try to grab her here," Caleb said, although that didn't convince any of them—if DMH needed her that badly, they would go to any lengths. But Noah had to have weighed both the risks and the consequences before making his decision.

"What about clearance protocol?" Mace asked.

"I'm keeping her computers here—I'll give her a couple of brand-new ones with a program installed that lets me monitor what she's doing. I'll give you a copy of her program on a Zip drive for her to load. Put her on a separate network and you're good to go," Gray explained.

"She could still hack into the base's security, if she's as good as you say," Mace argued.

"She's in a shitload of trouble. She's going to cooperate if she wants to get out of this mess," Caleb said grimly.

"If she's not DMH's decoy," Mace muttered, and if Vivi wasn't, for sure she had a large target painted on her back.

Reid and Kell had spent half an hour going through her place, gathering all the computers and files and backup equipment. Everything electronic. They also found a lockbox that contained her birth certificate and social security card, passport too, and they'd grabbed her purse, with her wallet and checkbook.

But they'd left everything else behind. And, from the looks of the surveillance tapes, they'd gotten out with little time to spare. Better not to let the enemy know what the military was up to. As of now, DMH had no idea that Delta had taken Vivienne out from under them.

"You ready?" Mace asked.

"Yeah, you guys can go," Cael said, but before he could enter the room, his phone vibrated in his pocket.

He pulled it out. His older brother's name flashed on the screen. He flipped open the phone and Dylan was talking before Caleb could say anything.

"Cael, have you heard from Zane?"

Those words hit Cael like a punch to the gut. "Not for a couple of weeks. Why?"

A pause, and then, "He's missing."

Cael turned and put his forehead against the file cabinet, the cool metal soothing him. Even though the door was closed between them, he kept his voice low so Vivienne wouldn't hear anything. "He's MIA?"

A long silence and then his brother Dylan admitted, "It's not an official mission."

Excellent. Even worse. "Tell me everything."

"He went to get Olivia."

"The doctor? D, that was your mission." But even as he spoke the words, he knew that wasn't true. Zane had been as much a part of Dylan's search, if not more so. But this was beyond.

"He wanted to go in and get her so we wouldn't lose her while I was delayed tying up some loose ends in . . . well, that's not important. Look, I'm sure he'll check in—probably just got a little off course."

"*Off course* and *DMH* don't go in the same sentence." Cael had followed the intel on Olivia through Dylan, knew about the clinic bombings and the woman's possible escape. "What's his last known location?"

Another unnaturally long pause. "He's . . . ah, near Freetown."

Freetown. If Dylan were here in front of him . . . "He's back in Africa by himself?"

"He's been before."

"With his team."

"He's the one who insisted, Cael. I didn't force this on him."

Caleb broke out in a fine sweat. As many bad dreams as Zane had experienced in his first years with the Scott family were as many waking nightmare scenarios Caleb thought about when it came to protecting his younger brother. "Find him, D."

"I will. I'll keep you posted. Call me if you hear first."

"Same." Cael shut the phone, knowing arguing would get them nowhere. Dylan's energy was better spent looking for Zane.

He leaned against the outside of the locked door and wondered if he should be as worried as he was about Zane.

His gut told him yes. Definitely yes, if past experience played any role. Zane could find trouble more quickly than anyone he knew—and Cael knew a hell of a lot of trouble-makers, present company included.

He also knew how shitty this trip could be for Zane's psyche, because as well as his brother hid it with an "I don't care" attitude, Cael knew differently. Zane wanted to believe in something, wanted to belong so badly and for a long time refused to let it happen.

Cael believed in God and country and the Army, knew that his parents loved adventure seeking and that it was in his blood.

So far, he got his adrenaline pumping the legal way, through Delta Force. And then he came home and he acted domestic, tried his best to keep track of his youngest brother because he'd lost that fight with Dylan years earlier.

"*Leave the boy alone.*"

"*He's not a boy and he's better off working for me than the other trouble you know he'll find,*" Dylan told him. Dylan, who was running some bullshit operation like spies for hire. "*I'm not a spy,*" Dylan would tell him through gritted teeth, "*And you're just pissed Zane went Navy instead of Army.*"

Well, sure, he was damned annoyed at that, didn't understand why Zane had to break the family tradition.

Bad enough Dylan had gotten out so fast, but at least he'd served. Zane was breaking a tradition of years of service to the Army—dating back to their great-great-grandfather.

"*Maybe Zane didn't feel as connected to our traditions,*" Dylan reminded Cael. "*Or maybe he knew you wanted him close—to keep an eye on him.*"

"*Someone had to. You were gone,*" Cael pointed out, going for the jugular, because that was always most effective.

"*Yeah, getting a job, dammit. Or else we couldn't have stayed together. You and Zane rode roughshod over Aunt Lynn.*"

They had. Their aunt, and only living relative on Dad's side, had been like one hundred and nine when they'd moved in. She'd nurtured them but never worried about things like homework or curfews.

It had been up to Caleb to keep Zane in line. And he had, barely. Most of the time it was like balancing a fine tightrope.

Zane always had a wild streak, coupled with an inherent wariness, because of the way he'd lived until Mom and Dad brought him home.

For a while, Zane was almost . . . feral. Living off instincts and fear. Not wanting to hang out with the family.

Not trusting. Hoarding food. And it continued for the better part of two years, until Caleb decided to follow him home from school one day instead of hanging out with his friends the way he normally did. He witnessed at least ten boys circling Zane, knocking down his books. Taunting him.

Zane had done nothing but stand there and take it.

"Why don't you fight back?" Cael asked his brother after they'd gotten home.

Zane had stared down at the ground in their front yard, kicked the dirt and didn't answer. Cael figured he was embarrassed that his older brother had seen what happened.

"Zane, I'll teach you how to fight," he'd offered, and Zane finally looked him in the eye.

"You think I don't know how to fight, asshole? I could kill those motherfuckers. That's why I don't fight." And then he turned and walked away.

Cael left school early the next day, and he lay in wait for Zane's bullies. And because Zane wouldn't touch them, Cael had. Beat them up and told them if they ever touched Zane again, they'd regret it. And then he'd taken the blame, refused to say why he'd done it.

That night, Zane sat at the dinner table with them for the first time.

From that day on, Zane and Cael had an uneasy truce. Cael still bugged his brother far too much. Zane pretended to be less annoyed than he really was, and for the most part, it worked. Dylan definitely balanced them out.

This was the worst possible time for Zane to get himself in trouble. Caleb had his own brand of the stuff waiting behind that door.

The faster Vivienne got the safeguard on the security program working, the faster he could help Zane out.

First, he had to figure out whether or not Vivienne Clare was in danger—or worse, if she *was* the danger.

With that in mind, he unlocked the door and stuck his head inside to take her from the interrogation room. Little did she know she was about to be out of the frying pan and walking directly into the fire.

As the sun came up, Zane attempted to keep them comfortable. He'd spread out the blanket on the floor—it was made of a material that thankfully helped them remain cool. Within a few hours, they would be roasting in here anyway.

He'd boiled enough water in the large pot he'd taken from her house to fill both canteens. While she'd tended to the baby, he'd grabbed a few threadbare towels as well, plus homemade soap and all the food she'd had in the house.

Most of it would go bad if they didn't eat it soon, and so Olivia unpacked it and spread it between them. They sat across from each other—she picked at the food while Zane ate with the vigor of a man who viewed food as fuel.

It inspired her to choke down more than she normally ate. And when the food was mostly gone and the water finished, he said, "I still can't believe..."

But he stopped, shook his head.

"What?"

"A baby. In the middle of all that, a baby was born." He looked stunned as he thought about it.

"Yes, well, their timing is usually pretty impeccable,"

she said wryly. She looked down at her hands again. They'd stopped shaking from the adrenaline a while ago, but they still felt like they were moving without her direction, the way it sometimes happened when she was lost in a big surgery.

Zane was right. The baby was a miracle in hell. They didn't happen often and most of the beauty was in the un-expected.

The look on Dahia's face when Liv handed her the infant and told her to go and hide—well, it was indescribable. It gave her chills just thinking about it now, even as a thin trickle of sweat made its way down her back. "I was scared to death."

"You got the job done." Zane stripped his shirt and lay back on the cloth, hands behind his head. He wore no dog tags, had a few telltale scars . . . and he looked so good.

She forced her eyes away and pulled up her borrowed pants.

"You should take those off instead."

"What?"

"Take your pants off before you overheat."

He was right—it would get hot in here, despite its shaded location. She shimmied out of them and lay like Zane was, the T-shirt coming to the tops of her thighs.

She wouldn't look at him to see if he was looking at her, but saw out of the corner of her eye that he'd already laid down on the blanket.

Now, their bellies comfortable, they rested, although neither was fully relaxed. Both on guard, she mused. So many damned enemies. "No one's tried to hurt my parents, have they? No threats?"

"They wouldn't be that stupid. Your parents are too visible. It would be too much of a risk," he said.

Thank God for that. Her father was part owner of an NFL team, her mother the daughter of something akin to the closest thing to royalty America had as the daughter of a beloved actress and philanthropist. They'd been together for thirty years, a golden couple, marred by the tragedy of what had happened to their daughter when she was young. They were constantly written up in the society pages—and they'd employed security since that fateful day she'd been kidnapped at nine years old. "They've believed I'm alive the whole time, haven't they?"

"Yes. Your dad told me that you're a fighter." He touched the side of his head where she'd beamed him. "I didn't know he meant literally."

"I didn't hit you as hard as I could've, you know."

"Trust me, I do."

She packed up the remains of the food carefully, sealing it back in the bag, and felt the tiredness spread over her body along with a strange sense of peace. Odd, because she knew Zane was waiting for her to tell him about DMH. He'd probably also like to know about her near panic attack at the door earlier, but he wasn't getting that.

It was as good of a time as ever. *Never* was the optimal time, but that wasn't happening. "You want to know about DMH."

"I have to know, Liv," he said quietly. "Big difference."

Somehow she knew he wouldn't force the memories from her unless they threatened national security. Her stomach roiled from the small amount of food she'd eaten and she sat up and soaked a towel, put it on the back of her neck and breathed in deeply. She would not get sick in here, not now.

She would not be weak.

Maybe telling him would help. It couldn't make her feel worse, for sure. "I don't know how helpful I can be."

"Don't bullshit me, Olivia. DMH doesn't come after people for nothing. They wouldn't waste time on you unless you know something."

"That makes sense, yes. But I figured, because of the clinic thing, they want me out of a need for revenge."

"Could be part of it, sure."

"They told me that if I tried to escape, they'd find me. Hunt me down like a dog in the street."

"They won't find you."

"Maybe not, if I stay lost. If I go back home and talk to the CIA, I'm vulnerable. I know too much about their operations. Names. Dates."

"Can you tell me?"

She could, because she could still leave Zane behind and not feel the consequences of her spilling this intel. And so she did, rattled off names and descriptions and numbers and he took notes on his phone as she talked. She'd memorized everything because she'd never had a safe place to write it all down.

And when she was done spewing out the information to him, she remained silent for a while. Zane wasn't pushing her, but he also didn't tell her it would all be okay, didn't tell her not to cry . . . all he did was reach out and touch her arm lightly, but there was so much strength in that. So much comfort.

It would be so easy to fold into him, to roll with him on

the soft dirt and cry out his name, the pleasure sweeping every other thought from her mind.

Too easy. If it was easy, it couldn't be right.

In the OR, she used to waver between surrendering control and trying to retain all of it. But in the end, she knew she could do everything right and it was up to the human body to decide whether or not it would all work together.

She truly believed it was up to the will of the person on that table, and there was little more she could do than attempt to influence it with her scalpel. In her personal life, control was imperative. "What else do you want to know? You want to hear everything those men did to me?"

His jaw clenched for just a second and then, "When did you escape from them?"

"It took over two months." It all felt like it happened to someone else, as if she'd simply been observing. And then, when she'd escaped, the drugs wore off and she'd realized . . . it *had* been her. And all those people . . . the things she'd done during that time . . . the things they'd forced her to do . . .

No. No one had forced her. She'd had a choice, could've refused and been killed. And she'd lived with the fallout.

"How did they treat you?" he asked after a few minutes passed.

"Did they torture me, you mean? Yes, but not in the way you think. I mean, the drugs were one thing. I've always hated them—the loss of control—but that was the easy part. After that first day, no one hit me," she said tonelessly. "They just kept me in a room alone and the drugs took the edge off everything. It took me weeks to build up a tolerance but I continued faking the symptoms so they wouldn't up the dose and I wouldn't become even more addicted. I heard Elijah talk about the different operations of DMH. He wanted me to know about them. It was his way of bragging, like he'd hoped I'd be attracted to all the power he had." She stared down at her hands. "He told me that my hands held equal parts healing and destruction, and that I had a power I could use to further my own career."

She glanced at Zane, wondered why him, why she was able to reveal all of this to him.

Nevertheless, she did. She'd never been one to dwell and she didn't see a reason to start now. "They never had me harvest the organs. But when I tried to refuse to do the transplant operations, they would put me in a room with a timer, the organ and the recipient. The patient was usually close to death and it was like, *How can I do that?* Whether the recipient was guilty or not, I couldn't stand there and let another death happen on my watch."

"I'm sorry, Liv. I know that doesn't mean much, but I am."

"It helps." She played with the edge of the borrowed T-shirt she wore, fraying the hem a bit with her fingernails. "That's how the other doctors began to trust me, because I started performing the transplants. I pretended that I understood what DMH was doing—that it was free-market enterprise, that we were saving people's lives. It's why the other doctors told me things about DMH's organization. I mean, Gabriel Creighton—Skylar's father—had told me some when when we were locked up together. It was enough to know what I was up against, that they had a long reach."

That night she'd been dragged onto the plane, she remembered screaming until her throat was raw and she was sure she'd damaged her vocal cords for good.

Her throat had been sore for weeks after that. She closed her eyes. "They first took me from my car. I called Skylar."

"You were right to do so. It was a better move than calling the police."

"If you say so. When I woke up in that house, Skylar's dad was brought in to me and I tried to help him. But they were torturing him. He told me he was ex-CIA. Said he might not survive. And then he told me that I might not either."

She bit her lip and wondered why this all seemed so fresh, as if the wound had opened and begun to bleed again. "Elijah would try to have philosophical conversations with me," she said. "He wanted to know if I thought the future of organ transplants should be a buy/sell deal. He asked me how it felt to know one person's death meant another's life." She shook her head slowly. "He's a really smart man. Scary smart. With the right intentions, he could've done so much good."

"He's a psychopath."

"Probably." She shrugged, dipped the towel into the water and rubbed it along the back of her neck again, since the nausea came back just thinking about him. "He told me about DMH. How it started. He was so eager for my approval. And things might've gone easier if I'd given it, pretended I admired him. But I couldn't. He was...being in the same room with him, I always just felt cold."

"What else do you know about him?"

"He called me Mariana a few times and didn't realize it.

It's not like I corrected him," she said. "He wants me because I resisted. Because I got away. He can have almost anything in the world and what he wants is someone he doesn't think he can have." She paused. "It was always very important to him that I thought he was smart. I think he has a learning disability—dyslexia. I recognized some signs when he made me spend time with him."

"You'd be able to recognize him if you saw him again?"

"I would recognize Elijah anywhere," she said, her body shuddering involuntarily. "He loved to spend time with me. Would say things like *You could be my equal.* Like I wanted to be anything to him—or like him."

Zane's face tightened. "Just the thought of you spending time with him makes my fucking skin crawl."

Hers too. But it hadn't been the first time she'd been too close to evil.

Would she be that lucky if it happened a third time?

She glanced into the concerned eyes of the strong man who sat next to her and looked away, drew her knees to her chest, whispered, "I feel like they're coming for me—I feel it all the damned time, Zane. And I don't think they'll stop until they've got what they want."

Elijah had no choice but to let Kieran's parents know about their son's death, could still hear his aunt's muffled scream, and then her persistent, *No, no no . . .*

They would blame him—the family always did. Not more than he blamed himself, although he knew that collateral damage couldn't be helped.

Recruiting family was the best way to keep DMH alive

and running smoothly. Perhaps Kieran hadn't been ready for such responsibility, but he'd been young and strong and reconnaissance was the best way to learn.

Elijah had no idea there were military men in the area, and while he stared at the picture of the blond-haired man and waited for his information to process, he knew that this mess... all of it was because of Olivia Strohm. She'd escaped, done damage to DMH by destroying the clinic and now, if not recovered soon, she could easily fall into the hands of the CIA.

He'd been playing cat and mouse too long, pawing with her, enjoying watching her think she'd escaped his reach. Now he realized that she, like Mariana, had become his weakness.

Mariana, his former lover, mother of his child, had taken his son from him; Olivia, his cousin. Losing the two family members so close together caused a pain in his heart he never thought he'd be capable of feeling. Hadn't, since his older brother had been killed in combat.

His brother's death had been the original turning point. From that moment on, Elijah had thought of nothing else but taking the DMH operation global—and of getting revenge on the USA and its military.

He couldn't get revenge on Mariana, as she was already in her grave, but the doctor was still out there, ready to disseminate information about his operations.

Maybe he'd gotten too far removed from the game. In the beginning, he would've been the first one with a pistol in his hand, ready to defend the then small, essentially unknown organization with his own hand, had been willing to give up his life for the cause.

Kieran had reminded him so much of himself at that age, full of bravado, ready to take on the world. Elijah had taken him under his wing, shown him the ropes, even gave him a seat at the poker table, an honor Kiernan understood.

Now that would never happen. He'd given Kieran the best training he could, but his cousin had been no match for this man, this...Navy SEAL. Zane Scott. Elijah stared at the serial number and the official picture of the Navy SEAL who was supposed to be invisible to most of the population.

Thanks to a key player in Homeland Security, Elijah could get any information he wanted. And still, that couldn't ensure that DMH wouldn't crumble like a house of cards.

Ace walked into his office without knocking, the familiar sneer on his face. By rights, the son of Elijah's father's best friend was second in command—would take over operations completely if Elijah was killed.

Lately, Ace had been looking at him as if he wanted to do that job all by himself.

"You weren't supposed to allow the program to go online. Now it's leaked that we're the ones who have possession of it." Ace stared at him, the contempt undisguised. "We've got a major problem."

"Then fix it."

"I was trying to. I've taken it offline, so all we have to deal with are the rumors, which are enough. You need to focus on your own problems, not mine."

"I am."

Ace stared at the picture of the man named Zane Scott

sitting on the desk. "Meddling in military business is not helping us."

"My source is secure."

"You wouldn't need to use the source if you'd taken care of Dr. Strohm properly in the first place," Ace sneered. "You had to bring in another woman to screw things up. Couldn't let it rest."

Elijah resisted the urge to bite back. Being called stupid—even inferentially—was something he was used to from his younger years. But he'd learned to compensate for the dyslexia, and ruled an empire in the making with DMH.

Years ago, it had simply been a dream.

Now Ace was telling him that it was crumbling, and Elijah refused to believe that, to buy into the other man's panic. "You need to deal with your own situation, or our plans will be irrevocably ruined. Make it work, any way you can."

He didn't point out that Ace's recent attempts to grab the creator of the software had failed miserably, or that he'd been right to tell Ace to kidnap the woman at the same time he took the software. No, Elijah wouldn't say a word, would save that ammunition for another time and place.

"I'm taking the jet," Ace announced.

"I'll join you in a day." For his plans, Elijah would need cooperation both here and in the States, and he had the perfect contact to make sure neither Olivia nor Zane Scott survived for much longer.

CHAPTER
6

Zane hated to keep pushing Liv for intel but he had to. And he wouldn't risk sending it to Dylan in a text or e-mail. No, he'd tell him when they spoke next, a call he was putting off as long as he could.

"You can't run for the rest of your life, Liv. Not like this—and not all by yourself."

She nodded as if she knew that. She was too smart to think she could, but she was in full run mode still. "If you give the CIA the information I gave you, I can stay here until they do something with it."

"That could take a while. No one wants you out here unprotected. And I promised I'd get you back."

"To what, Zane?" There was no pity in her tone, no *woe is me*. Only steel.

Strangely enough, the expression that she made was so strong it made him want even more to pick her up and cradle her. "There's a lot back there, Liv. A lot of people you can help."

"I can help a lot here too."

He sighed. The argument was going nowhere. "Want to tell me how you escaped? I'd like any tips you can give me."

She didn't laugh, but she wanted to, despite the inappropriateness. She'd always appreciated gallows humor.

She shifted, leaned her back against the wall as fat drops of rain began to splatter against the roof and the dry ground beyond. "There was a fail-safe security system that locked us in and everyone who wasn't supposed to be there out. And in case of emergency, we were to evacuate immediately and the building would . . . take care of itself."

"The building was wired to blow?" Zane asked.

She nodded. "Funny, but it didn't seem to bother anyone but me, you know? And we all learned the system—we had to be able to activate it. We were one big damned team. There was a woman there—another doctor, a third-year resident. She'd failed all her exams but DMH hired her for an insane amount of money. It was her first day on the job. I knew the body thing would confuse them, as she'd arrived at the clinic a day early, before the new patients were scheduled to arrive. I was the only one who knew that, shuffled her into the break room, activated the bomb and left the building, saying I needed a cigarette. By that time, the guards knew me well enough." Her voice trembled, her body shook as she relived that day. "The doctors were all so greedy. Ignoring their oaths. This wasn't about people consenting and selling their organs. That's an altogether different debate. No, this was murder in some cases. I'm just grateful I was the one doing the transplanting and not the harvesting."

"You went through hell."

She turned away. "Maybe I'm no better than any of them. I had no right to be judge and jury on those people."

"You did what you thought was right at the time," Zane told her. "Whatever happens after that—"

"Is on my conscience," she finished. "I made sure there were no patients in the building. Not one."

"The two doctors who died in that bombing, they'd both been doing illegal organ harvesting for years. They weren't forced or drugged. They lured people into their offices. It was greed. Murder. Just like you said." His voice was fierce when he told her that.

She wanted to believe that with every fiber in her being. And couldn't. "Sometimes I wonder if I should've stayed inside that building too. I almost did."

"Liv, no . . ."

She stared at him, her eyes crystal clear. But she didn't say anything else.

"Did you hear about any other clinics?" he asked.

"There are two more. I was never able to find out their locations. The one I was in was the biggest, from what I gathered."

She paused and then, "Am I in trouble for blowing it up?"

"Yes. And no." Zane ran a hand through his hair. "It's the least of your problems, Liv. That can get sorted out."

She almost snorted, but raised her eyes to his face at the last minute and was stunned by the sincerity in his eyes. There were no lies there.

He meant what he said, and she wasn't sure why that scared her so much, more than it should.

"Is there anything else you need to tell me?"

DMH was like an insidious poison she wanted out of her bloodstream. Maybe the more she talked, the faster it would leave her. "One of the doctors, he would check out the girls who'd been kidnapped and sold. They were mostly American girls. Young—between eighteen and twenty, he said—lured at the idea of being models or actresses or meeting rich men abroad. He would get them ready. Make sure they were perfect."

She stopped then, felt drained. Her head began to throb.

Zane simply gathered her against him, paying no mind to the heat. "It'll be okay, Liv."

But it had never been okay, not really, since that horrible day twenty-five years earlier. She'd always suspected that had been a warm-up, some kind of taunt from the universe. Had prepared for it since then as if it had been fact and not simply theory and speculation. Had waited for it, trained for it. And then it had come true.

And when it had, she'd fought like hell to get away again.

"It's over," Zane continued to murmur. But no, Olivia knew it was just beginning.

When the alarms rang out as he was readying to move into the new quarters with Vivi, Cael assumed it was a drill.

Training on-post had stepped up immeasurably in past years, and so he automatically reached for his phone to double check with Noah before he went back to Vivienne Clare.

But it was far from an exercise.

Security had been breached and the post was on instant lockdown. Caleb's orders were instantly changed, via Noah.

Get her the hell out of here and use a secure line only.

Vivienne was to be taken to a safe house off-post in order to make the software safeguard usable in order to stop DMH from using the program. Even though the area where Delta comms were housed was infinitely secured, Noah decided that keeping Vivienne Clare there was too much a threat to the rest of the families in the immediate vicinity.

"You really think this is all about her?" Mace asked in between the blare of the alarms. He'd come into the hallway while Cael was on the phone with Noah, prepared to help his teammate.

"You saw the video feed from her house," Cael said as he handed his first line gear to him. "DMH needs her."

"Maybe. But why didn't they kidnap her when they took the software—cross their *t*'s and dot their *i*'s and all that shit, you know? They're not known for being sloppy." Mace still didn't trust any of this—out of all of them, he was the most suspicious, the one who asked so many damned questions that sometimes they wanted to strangle him.

Most of the time though, they were damned grateful for the way his mind worked.

"Things change. They're getting nervous."

"Don't trust her, Cael. Not yet," Mace warned, and

dammit, Cael wasn't the trusting type, but he did live and die by his instincts.

"I don't," he said shortly. But he did—why, he wasn't sure, beyond a gut reaction.

The possibilities of what cyber warfare could do to the infrastructure of the United States was no longer just theory—no, in fact, hackers had threaded their way in far too often—and easily—over the past years. So far, the government had been able to keep it quiet so as not to alarm the American public, but news outlets were leaking information faster than the government could plug the holes.

Vivienne Clare could be a part of the problem as easily as she could be part of the solution.

What bothered Cael more was the intrusion on a secure post. "If this is for Vivi, how the hell?"

"We weren't followed back here," Mace muttered, but that didn't matter now. Gray had Vivi's computer equipment in a truck waiting out front. Mace headed out with the gear. All Cael needed now was Vivi.

Even if this current threat could be neutralized quickly, it didn't mean there wouldn't be more. Taking down a power plant—or several—could simply be the beginning of DMH's plan, and the extra security now in place to stop an attack wouldn't hold forever. They had to disable the program, one way or the other.

Caleb stared at the door for a moment, knowing that Vivi would have to know everything sooner than later. How she would react to the pressure, he couldn't be sure.

His hand was on the knob when Gray came barreling down the hall.

"They put tracking devices in her computers," he said.

"I'm running tests now, but I've given you new computers to take so she can keep working. I'll bring you hers when they're clean."

"Shit. At least we know how they found her," he said. "Takes a set of balls to break in here, though."

Gray nodded. "Noah said to go now—back gate. He'll get the word out that you can leave, but you might get there before he can do so, given the current confusion."

That meant Noah was basically giving him permission to break out of the post if orders didn't filter down fast enough to the MPs who guarded the gates. Keys in hand, truck packed, he needed to grab the most important part of the equation and make tracks.

Vivi tried the door when the alarms first started ringing, worried that there was a fire somewhere and she was trapped. But there was no smoke she could smell and she'd been forced to wait at least five excruciating minutes until the door opened and Caleb walked in.

Her heart thudded hopefully, because he was alone, and then hope shrank because of the look on his face. Tight, and not all that unreadable. There was a major problem. The tension between them was palpable and the alarms were louder now.

"You need to come with me. No questions," he said, his voice abrupt, and she didn't argue. Her feet moved despite the fact that dizziness from rapidly dropping blood sugar made her off balance. It didn't matter, since Caleb's hand closed around her arm, the other held her lower back and ushered her out a door and into a waiting black truck that could've been the same one she'd ridden in earlier.

She strapped the seatbelt on as Caleb did the same in the driver's seat. When he pulled away, she realized they were alone in the car and headed away from the sirens.

No questions.

As she stared out the window, she caught sight of her surroundings. She couldn't be sure, since the truck was moving fast, but it looked like a military facility.

She turned her attention from the side window to the front one and nearly screamed, because the gate they were rapidly approaching was indeed closed. She shifted in her seat to get a better look, saw the soldiers in front of it, waving Caleb to stop.

"Not a word," he warned.

She nearly bit her tongue off as they got closer, and maybe this was some kind of test of her courage. She wanted to close her eyes but couldn't. Instead, she braced herself and stared straight ahead.

And prayed a little.

Caleb muttered something—a curse maybe, or perhaps a prayer of his own—and his arm shot out protectively across her chest.

The men moved out of the way at the last minute, opening the gate as they did so, and the truck was able to continue barreling down the road at top speed.

Relief washed over her and she released a breath, hadn't realized she'd been holding it and gripping her hands together tightly.

His arm moved away and he ran a hand through his hair.

"Can I ask a question now?" she asked finally, and so much for following the rules.

"We're on lockdown," he explained. "No one's allowed on or off post."

"Except you."

"Looks like it took them a few seconds too long to get the orders." He gave a small smile and Vivi realized he liked trouble, judging by the way he'd been ready to crash through the gate without attempting to slow down.

Well, at least she knew she had been on a military base... and that the man next to her was a soldier of some sort. Army... Army had posts, Navy had bases. One of her stepfathers had been a History Channel buff.

Obviously, getting her off-post was extremely important. A wave of fear washed over her, made her throat dry. She managed to croak out, "Was that... about me?"

"Maybe."

She realized she wouldn't get more than that, supposed she should be grateful for that bit of information, but it only made the dizziness worse. "Is there any water in here? Or soda, because..."

She was aware her voice faded a bit and felt Caleb's hand on her cheek and then her forehead. "You're burning up. How long have you been sick?"

"Um, the last few minutes?"

She heard the crack of a soda can, although the truck was still moving fast. "Here, drink this—I'll hold it."

There was even a straw, miracle of miracles. And she took long pulls of the sugary drink until the dizziness lifted somewhat.

"Are you diabetic?" he asked.

"No."

"When was the last time you ate?"

"What time is it?"

He cursed loudly, and then in a much gentler tone than he'd used since she'd met him, he said, "Vivienne—Vivi—I'm taking you someplace safe. You'll be comfortable there."

"You're staying with me, or will I be handed over to some other man in black who won't answer my questions?"

"You'll be with me. And I've answered a few."

"The devil you know," she muttered, and heard him snort. "I didn't mean to say that out loud."

She grabbed the soda can from him and drained it, the sugar working to clear her head. "How long will I be there?"

"That depends."

"On what? Who's after me, Caleb? I have a right to know why I'm in trouble."

He was silent for a long minute, and then, "It's about your father's program."

Something had changed in Caleb's demeanor. There was an urgency—as if he wanted to continue believing her but was torn and he was looking for assurance. "What are you talking about?"

"You need to fix the safeguard so it works."

"InLine Energy sent you to collect the software?"

"No."

The thought of her constant failures in trying to rectify the safeguard was enough to tie her stomach into knots again. She didn't like failing.

When it became obvious Caleb wasn't going to tell her more, she finally said, "I'll work as hard as I can to fix it."

He nodded, obviously pleased with her answer. "Tell me

something—isn't the point of the program itself to be unbreakable?"

"My father didn't take anything for granted. He didn't trust anyone."

"Not even you?"

The question was like a knife to the heart; the answer, one she knew all too well. "Not even me."

After she said that, she heard Caleb swear under his breath and she didn't want to ask or answer any more questions.

While she stared out the window, lost in her own thoughts, Caleb drove them north on the highway for maybe an hour through North Carolina before exiting and cruising through a residential area she wasn't familiar with.

He pulled into the garage of a house on a typical suburban-looking street, let the garage door come down before he said, "Wait here. I'll check out the house."

Alone in the garage, in the dark, she started to panic a little. The dark had never bothered her before—although she now realized that most of the time, she wasn't in total darkness, but rather, bathed in the comforting light of a computer screen.

Finally, after what seemed like an hour but was no doubt closer to five minutes, Caleb came back to the garage and to her side of the car. He opened her door for her.

"All clear."

She climbed down with his help and entered the house. The soda's sugar rush had helped her feel less shaky, but he kept a firm hand on her arm. Earlier, she would've assumed that was to keep her from making any false moves, but now the touch was gentler.

He was making sure she didn't fall. When she got inside, she noted that the house was clean and well furnished. And no doubt secure.

"Have a seat," he told her, and she did, sinking gratefully into a kitchen chair while Caleb went back out to the garage.

He returned less than a minute later, carrying a large bag and two laptop computers she'd never seen before.

"Can you get started setting these up?" he asked as he placed them on the kitchen table. "They're brand new, should be fully loaded. I've got your father's program saved."

"What about the wireless system? I don't need to go online, but for security purposes, it needs to be protected."

"It is. Your IP won't be detected."

"Where are my computers?"

"They're being checked by Grayson—one of the men you met earlier," he said as he rifled first through the freezer and then the fridge.

"Checked?"

He ignored the implied question and instead held another soda out to her. "I hope you're okay with pizza."

She nodded. It didn't matter what she ate. She just needed fuel so she didn't drop from the combination of exhaustion and fear. Her body and mind were essentially numb and she didn't feel like she could process light conversation, never mind complicated software conversions.

Discovering she'd been on a military post eased her fears somewhat, but she knew she was in trouble. She'd seen her father get railroaded when she was younger—he never got over that. It was the beginning of a long, downward spiral that left him bitter, and Vivi cut off from much of the world.

She'd just started to live for herself, and now she was being drawn back into her father's problems. Truth be told, she'd never actually gotten out from under them, but finally taking time to actually date someone, even if it hadn't worked out—and then nearly selling her own system to the military—had been a big step forward.

When Caleb sat down next to her, she readied herself for more questions.

And two steps back.

Talking about all of this was a good first step for Olivia to take. Zane had always known that catharsis was good for the soul, even if he didn't believe in it for himself worth a damn.

But for Liv . . . now that some of it was out in the open, she slept.

He knew her conscience should be clean, that she'd never truly been given a choice by DMH, but he wondered if she'd ever feel the same way.

When the sun went down, they'd travel for as long as they could manage. But he had the uneasy feeling that Olivia wasn't nearly as convinced as he was that she needed to leave this country and get herself into some serious protection for a while.

He moved toward the window and looked up at the sky. It had clouded up nicely, dissipating some of the heat. A nice soaking rain for the rest of the day would be helpful, but it would suck if it continued through the night.

Just then, one of his two phones rang, a low staccato echoing from deep inside his pack, where he'd stuck it hurriedly last night, along with the DMH guy's cell.

Keeping his voice low, he greeted Dylan with, "What's up?" And then he moved to a far corner and listened to Dylan's fluent string of curses.

He used the time to wonder if D had told Caleb. Probably.

"Where. Are. You," Dylan said finally.

"We're . . ." *In the middle of the goddamned jungle, with soldiers and DMH on our ass, no transportation and no foreseeable way out of goatfuck central.* "We're just fine."

Dead silence on the other end, and then, "What. Did. You. Do."

Saved Liv's life. "We're fine. Might be a little late getting to the LZ."

"Zane . . ."

"I had to double back," he said, explained to Dylan about the DMH flunkie. And admitted to being caught on film.

There was cursing again. More this time, and Zane checked out the flash of lightning across the sky, counted the seconds until the rumble of thunder followed.

The storm would be here soon. "D, man, it's all right. We're only behind like twenty-four hours." Maybe. "Olivia gave me intel about some of the doctors who worked at the clinic."

He ran down what she'd told him, knew Dylan was recording all of it.

"So Olivia can make Elijah. And she stole this intel from him. Blew up a clinic." Dylan gave a long whistle.

"He won't like being made a fool of above all else. Until he finds her, he can't restore his pride."

"Then we kill him."

"Easier said than done."

That was true. Even though Liv could identify Elijah, there was no way in hell Zane would let her get even remotely close to him again. "We're moving out tonight—we'll go as far as we can and then I'll be in contact. She doesn't want to leave, but I'll make sure she gets to Freetown and on the boat, if it's the last thing I do."

No point in mentioning the drug lord baby thing, because he was sure Dylan would jump through the phone.

"It better not be the last fucking thing you do, Zane, or I'll kill you," Dylan said warningly before he hung up.

"Yeah, yeah," he muttered to the phone as another flash of lightning lit up the small house and the floor shook with the rolling boom that came right after.

He turned to see if Liv was still sleeping and saw she was awake, watching him. By the look on her face, he could tell she'd heard every word he said.

Shit.

"That was Dylan," he said by way of explanation. "My brother . . . he was the one at the house last year, the one in Minnesota."

"I never knew that's where I was. I'd think DMH would pick something a little more exotic for a kidnapping." She was half joking. But there was a fire in her eyes pointed directly at him.

I'll make sure she gets to Freetown and on the boat, if it's the last thing I do.

She felt far more vulnerable than she should because he

already knew so much about her. All she knew about him was that he wanted to drag her, kicking and screaming if necessary, to a place she didn't want to go.

And now she had complete confirmation he'd never planned on giving her a choice in the matter.

"Am I your prisoner?"

"What the hell are you talking about? You know you're not, or I would've had you in cuffs and back in the States already, dammit."

"Are you going to arrest me for bombing the clinic? Are you planning to take me home against my will? Because don't think I won't tell the first person I see that I'm being kidnapped."

"Liv, look," he started, and then realized there was no way out of it. "I meant what I said. I can't apologize for it."

She stood then, felt her temper rise and any good feelings she'd developed toward him were quickly forgotten.

She should've known no one could be trusted. No one. "I don't want your apologies—I just want you and your do-gooding to stay the hell away from me."

"I can't do that. Won't.

"Why do you care so much? Is it an ego thing? They got away before you could stop them and now you've got to prove that you're a big bad soldier?"

"No," he managed through gritted teeth. "And I'm a SEAL. Navy. Not a soldier. I've spent months of my life looking for you, worried you were hurt. Alone. Scared. I don't know why the hell you affected me so much, and I don't give a shit about your ungrateful attitude or your inability to listen to reason."

She let out a short, humorless laugh. "Oh, I get it—

you're all warrior tough and you don't want people to think badly of you if you don't bring back the woman. This is just another mission to you, an adventure, but this is my life," she lashed out at him. "You have no idea what it's like to feel so lost, to have no one to turn to. To not want to turn to anyone. So please, just take your plan and get the hell out of here."

He didn't respond, but his eyes darkened, his jaw tightened and an emotion she couldn't quite place flashed over his face for a brief second before he walked out the door and into the pouring rain.

In turn, she sank down to the floor and began to sob. What the hell had happened to her? Had she really allowed DMH to turn her into someone she didn't even recognize?

CHAPTER
7

His anger barely contained, Zane walked out onto the wet dirt. Although it was just noon, the storm darkened the sky so it looked more like early evening. The rain came down in sheets—he could barely see the trees in front of him and still he stood and tilted his face up to the sky, let the water pelt him as Liv's words echoed inside his head.

Why do you care so much? Is it an ego thing? They got away before you could stop them?

He couldn't tell her that her screams haunted his dreams. How he'd been forced to stand helplessly in that motel room, listening through headphones and unable to help. Sacrificing her for the greater good of the mission.

How he'd been unable to think of anything else for months because he knew she was still out there.

Think, Zane . . . remember, you didn't want to be rescued either.

But he'd been much younger. Olivia should be smarter than he'd been.

She's fucking scared to death.

He sighed and the anger began to dissipate. She could push him, lash out at him, and it wouldn't matter. He couldn't let it. Because he understood.

So he had a few weapons, could escape the drug lords. DMH might be more of a problem. He was a day behind getting to the harbor at Freetown, DMH had a picture of him and Olivia still refused to agree to come to the States.

And her arguments to that effect were so damned logical . . . but Africa was not the place to keep her safe.

Whatever else she'd been through when she was younger didn't matter. The serial killer who'd kidnapped her then—he was gone and it was over.

Or at least the danger was. He was pretty damned sure you never got over something like that.

Still, DMH was bigger. Wouldn't go away—at least not easily. And Zane didn't have answers for Liv—in his line of work, there rarely were any and he'd gotten used to it.

"What was your plan?" he heard Liv demand from behind him, turned and saw her also standing in the pouring rain, the T-shirt plastered against her body, molding her breasts. Her legs were bare, her eyes fierce, her chin raised proudly. Stubbornly.

He could just imagine the hell they'd put her through to force her to do the transplants. And even having relived the memories, she still looked formidable—shoulders squared—but her heart was broken.

"Come back home with me, Olivia." His voice sounded different . . . raw. "Let me take you out of hell."

"Don't you see—it won't matter." She put a fisted hand to her chest. "It'll always be with me. I'll always carry it with me."

Yes, he understood, better than she knew. He'd lived with it, shoved it down, pretended it didn't exist.

His parents had wanted it that way. Thought that by changing Zane's location they could change his life. And it had most definitely changed for the better . . . but his past was still there, always threatening to bubble to the surface.

"You haven't answered my question," she told him, pretending she wasn't affected by what he'd said about getting out of hell. And maybe she wasn't. Maybe nothing but saving people could get through to her these days.

Maybe nothing got through to him but that either. *Fuck.*

"My plan was to grab you, get you to Freetown and onto a ferry," he said through gritted teeth. "My plan involved saving you. It didn't involve having the person in danger hit me with a metal frying pan—then tell me to stay the hell out of her life and her business."

She didn't bother to look or act contrite. "I never asked you to come," she said again—her refrain. Her goddamned mantra.

That was it. He closed in on her with three steps. All he could freakin' think to do was kiss her, and so that's exactly what he damned well did, hard and fast, without giving a shit what she wanted right now.

But she did want—he could tell by the way she molded

against him. She tasted soft and sweet and spicy all at once, like cool rain and the kind of hot summer sun that let you know all was right with the world, and his body enveloped hers, the way he'd wanted to from the moment he'd seen her on the porch.

When he pulled back, she kept her eyes screwed tightly closed as if she could make it all—including him—disappear.

He murmured in her ear, "Open your eyes, Liv. I want you to know my name. To know me—to watch me when you come."

His voice sent a visceral reaction, a blast of heat, as if she'd been licked by fire, and she wanted to go back and walk through it again and again.

She also wanted to slap him, and both urges were of equal strength. She finally did open her eyes, and pulled away at the same time, then yelled over the sounds of the storm, "I don't need you. I can give myself an orgasm. Several, actually."

He grabbed her wrist, held her in place. Although his voice didn't raise, there was no mistaking the utter and complete command in it. "That's nothing compared to what I can do for you."

She shuddered then, ready to come from his words alone. Her body was responding whether she liked it or not, and dammit all to hell, she liked it. "Damn you. I was okay before you got here."

"I wasn't. And when you stop bullshitting yourself, you'll realize you weren't either." She thought he'd walk away then, but instead he wound a hand through her hair and brought her face close to his again. Kissed her hard and well enough to make her respond almost instantly, his mouth a hot contrast to the cooling rain. His tongue dueled with hers—the kiss was half fight and half victory, and although she wasn't sure who the victor was, his kisses were the best she could remember.

Her hands grabbed at the slick skin of his shoulders—his arms remained firmly wrapped around her waist so their bodies molded to each other.

Would he take her right here, in the rain, on the ground? It was so primitive and primal and it felt so right. She wanted to rip her shirt off to feel her breasts rub against his bare chest.

She wrapped her body around his, let his hands roam, tugging at her wet shirt until they were skin to skin and she was hot with need.

They kissed until she couldn't breathe—until she didn't care that she couldn't—and then they kissed more, ignoring the storm, the roll of the thunder rising with their lust.

When he broke the kiss, he pulled her body from his, covered a nipple with his mouth through the soaked fabric, sending a jolt of white hot intensity straight to her core. Her moan was lost in the rain, even as she wound her hands in Zane's wet hair, because she wanted more.

She wanted everything. His hand traveled between her legs, stroked her bare sex, and she nearly came at that touch, a jolt of sexual awareness washing over her, reminding her what she'd been missing, what she'd been denying herself.

She wanted him to take her—in the dirt, the wet, it didn't matter, she wouldn't stop him. Couldn't. Right now, she needed him as surely as she needed air—her body ached, strained against his, sealing the kind of violent, pleasure-filled release she hadn't had in forever.

This was her white flag. Her surrender. And she knew that she needed it to survive, needed lovemaking as violent as the storm, as violent as what had happened to her. Somehow that was exactly the way she needed it to be, to draw out the old, and usher in the new under a cleansing deluge…under a man named Zane, against his damp, hot flesh, with a passion that was savage and lethal all at once.

Zane had been holding back for so damned long, he knew his reaction to Liv would be fierce. Primal. One he'd be unable to control if she didn't stop him, stop this immediately. And he waited for her to, but she didn't do it.

When he'd first come to live with the Scotts, he'd had a lot to learn about impulse control. For a long time, there had been no limits or boundaries, and even though he'd had plenty of proof to the contrary, he'd needed to discover that he wasn't invincible.

No one was.

But here, with her, with the storm a shield from danger, Zane felt pretty damned bulletproof. His hand remained between her legs, forcing them open as she held his shoulders for dear life.

When his fingers stroked her, she moved with him, her hands circling the nape of his neck as she struggled for bearing.

There would be none—not out here, not with him. And as his finger slid into her hot flesh, her moan rose up, would've been loud as anything if the storm hadn't caught it as part of its fury.

A second finger joined the first and she was riding his hand now, her lips parted, eyes closed . . . smile on her face.

He never wanted to see that smile fade, would work on that all afternoon.

He watched her reactions, felt her shudders, heard her moans over the rain, and he was so goddamned hard he could cut glass. But he shoved his own desires down in favor of fulfilling all of hers.

He felt her orgasm approach—her legs stiffened around his hand, her mouth dropped open farther and she went so still that for a second, he didn't think she'd let it happen.

But she did, the release making her knees buckle. His arm tightened around her waist, pulled her close as her climax swept her away, felt her bite his chest as though she was trying to keep from screaming.

She was so slick, it would take one stroke to fill her, easy enough to lay her down and let her clench around him so tight . . .

He needed to stop thinking with his cock for a second, he realized—they needed to be inside, out of range.

Maybe he should even goddamned stop this. But thinking ceased again when she pulled her T-shirt off, let it slap to the ground, because holy fuck, she was gorgeous. Curvy. High breasts with dark pink nipples that he could taste. A small triangle between her thighs.

Her cheeks were flushed, her eyes bright . . . her body open to his appraisal. And her eyes held a dare.

———

Zane unzipped his pants and Olivia's mouth dropped open again at the sight of him.

It wasn't that she hadn't known he'd be beautiful. When she'd watched him earlier, the rain streaming over his face and chest, she'd felt a tug between her thighs, a feeling so powerful it propelled her out the door to him.

But now, the lethal savagery of his looks hit her—the savagery that had been almost hidden behind the all-American-boy looks—but not well enough. His eyes glowed, his hands clenched into fists . . . and the massive power between his legs made her mouth go dry.

She waited for him to approach her, but he didn't.

"They didn't . . . Fuck, I should've asked already." He shook his head.

"They didn't what?" She saw the look in his eyes, the sudden hesitancy. "No, Zane, they didn't hurt me like that. They did it in other ways."

He continued to watch her, unmoving until she said, "Please, I want this. I need this. You're not taking advantage of me. If anything, it's the opposite."

Naked and wet, he enveloped her, carried them both into the shack and lowered them to the waterproof sleeping bag on the floor, then rolled so she was on top of him.

And then he said, "Take it away, Liv."

She did. Her hands went to his shoulders first, and she paused for a moment to stare at the broad, muscled chest and cut abs again before her eyes moved lower, as did her hand, slid along the hard muscles as he held his breath.

He remained still under her exploration, but she knew it was only a matter of time before he took over, wrapped her in his arms and rolled her under him. And she wanted that as much as she wanted control.

No, it was time to let her guard down, to prove to herself once and for all that she could.

She'd never wanted to be the type of woman who didn't trust anyone. Doing so would mean that her kidnapper all those years ago had won.

Not trusting now would be letting DMH win. And that would never, ever happen, not as long as she had breath in her body.

She bent her head and pressed her lips to his chest over the mark her teeth had made earlier. He drew a quick, sharp breath and his arousal, which had been jutting against her from the first kiss, grew harder against her palm. She trailed her tongue left, captured a nipple between her teeth and simultaneously licked and tugged, heard, "*Damn, Liv,*" as his hips rose upward in a bucking motion, his erection pressing her sex, and she swore. Just a few more times like that and she could come, break apart and fly away. Forget where she was . . .

"Open your eyes," he growled, and she did, mainly because she was surprised at his sudden change of tone, her body pulling away from his. "I want you to know who's doing this to you."

"I know," she whispered, but he shook his head even as he drew her back down.

His gaze was locked on hers, a storm behind his eyes that was ready to release.

And she did watch his face even as his fingers slid down and found her core, gasped, open-mouthed, and got a small smile of satisfaction in return. "You like that."

She nodded, forced herself not to grind against his hand; although that was all she wanted to do.

He was going to make her come—over and over—and the thought of that was enough to push her over the edge a second time. His name on her lips, eyes on his, and the relief washed over her along with the rolling rush of pleasure.

Her hands twisted in his thick, blond hair, and she forgot the heat, the trouble, let go of everything but the feeling of Zane Scott and his heavy arousal between her legs.

Her heart drummed, her belly tightened.

With that, she let go, her third climax pulsing through her like a freight train, full speed, with no chance of stopping.

After the first, she hadn't thought that would happen again—not as intensely. She'd known she was carrying pent-up frustration, but this—it was like her body would never stop shuddering, the release making her see stars, her toes curling.

And Zane wasn't done. He waited patiently, watching her. Enjoying her.

"You were right. You do it better," she managed, although her throat was raspy, her breathing barely under control . . . her body lighter than it had been hours earlier.

He smiled then, his eyes darker with desire. "All three times?"

"Yes, dammit, all three times."

He laughed then, softly. "Then you'll like the fourth even better."

Her body tingled with anticipation and she wondered how he could bring her nerve endings under his control with simple words.

Because he's lived up to every promise he's made so far.

She heard a rustle and saw him rolling a condom on himself.

He must've seen the surprise on her face, because he said, "Always prepared," and she knew she would've let him inside her anyway, because all her caution had been tossed to the wind a long time ago.

She pulled him down to her, brought his face close to hers for another kiss, because he hadn't kissed her again since they were outside and she wanted his mouth on hers. Wanted to see if it had been the storm, or her hormones—or something else entirely. And when his tongue played against hers, she knew she actually still had the ability to feel.

As he kissed her, he shifted his weight over her and she spread her thighs to him, letting him know that she was ready for him. When he took her, it was with one swift push, filling an urge so necessary she gasped against his mouth in what would've otherwise been a scream.

"Tight, Liv . . . tight, wet for me," he murmured, paused as if attempting to gain his composure.

And then he gave up, drove into her with her legs wrapped fast around his waist, her hands gripping his back, and all she could do was hold on and let herself go.

It was all she wanted to do.

The pizza was frozen, courtesy of whoever stocked the safe house. Cael slid a plate next to Vivi and she picked at a slice absently while he polished off the rest for lack of anything better to do. And then he simply waited, restlessly.

He hated not doing. Sitting. Watching.

He'd always had situational awareness in spades. It helped him in so many ways throughout his life and never more than in his military career.

It was goddamned exhausting being that aware all the time, but he couldn't turn it off, no matter how hard he tried. He was always intense. Appeared hard-assed, even when he was attempting to be gentler.

He was never more on than now. And it was a huge part of the reason he couldn't sit still, was firing on all cylinders, and there was nothing he could do but sit and watch Vivi.

According to Gray, the MPs had detained two men with no ID or authority to enter the post and contained them. Of course, they weren't talking, not even with the encouragement of Noah and Mace.

Their names were run through the databases and came up empty. That meant nothing—DMH was notoriously insular. Except for Elijah, who appeared to love seeing his name in print.

Homeland Security scooped them up and now Delta would be hard-pressed to get any further intel—until, of course, the nation was at risk.

To top things off, he still hadn't heard from Dylan regarding Zane.

"Stop," she said suddenly.

"Stop what?"

"You're pacing. Driving me crazy. Stop."

"Yeah, sorry," he muttered, hadn't realized he'd been up and moving. "Look, I'll be right in the next room."

She didn't make any move to let him know she'd heard. As he passed, he saw lines of code filling up the space on the screen and made a mental note to bring Gray to see if the man could figure out if Vivi was making any progress or just bullshitting all of them.

But she hadn't triggered his bullshit meter once. Other things, yes. Noah was right that Vivi responded to him, but he wondered if his CO had noticed the reverse was true as well.

You're getting soft, Cael. Soft and stupid.

Damn, he wished he was doing more than bodyguarding.

He could hack marginally well but Gray was the real geek of the group.

Judging by Vivi's rep, she would outstrip Gray of that title. She'd gotten in trouble in high school for hacking into the school's database—not that she'd needed to change any grades, because her GPA was near-perfect, remained so through college. At least the first year she was there.

If Vivienne Clare dated, it wasn't frequently—she spent most of her time working.

As he remained on the couch facing the double-paned, bulletproofed window, he could still hear the tap of the computer's keys as he dialed Dylan.

His brother picked up on the first ring. "Cael, what's up?"

What's up? Jesus, Dylan and Zane spent far too much time together. He barely kept his voice controlled when he said, "You tell me, D."

"Zane's got the doc. They're a little off course right now."

"And you're headed in to get them on course, correct?"

Dylan cleared his throat. "It's not that simple."

No, with Zane it never could be. "D—"

"He says he's okay. He sounds okay. I'm headed to Free-town now to wait for him."

Cael hated hearing the name of that damned place, and when Zane was safe and sound, he would kill Dylan for this. Really and truly. "After all is said and done, DMH still wants that doctor."

"Yeah," Dylan confirmed, and Cael's head began to throb. Again.

If Vivienne could stop DMH—well, it would certainly help Zane peripherally, if nothing else. And it beat sitting here feeling damned helpless, as well as wanting to wring his little brother's neck and hug him at the same time.

So he made an executive decision—one that Noah had put on his shoulders anyway. Vivienne deserved to know what she was up against. "D, you call me when you hear anything, understand? Anything."

"Will do. Try not to worry." Dylan hung up before Cael cursed at him and then moved on. It was time to fully work his angle.

The biggest problem now was, his angle was currently crying.

Shit. He couldn't stand a crying woman. Mainly be-cause he wasn't any good at comforting. You needed some-thing done, you came to him. You needed comforting, you were shit out of luck.

But there was no one else around.

Maybe he was wrong. Maybe she was just breathing heavily or something. He moved a few silent steps toward the kitchen, and yep, there was no doubt about the crying, although it was quiet—dignified even.

For the most part, Vivi had remained calm and cool, even under interrogation. The irritability she'd shown was mainly due to low blood sugar. Even the initial grab and the fact that he'd had to hustle her off-base hadn't seemed to throw her.

She'd been collected enough to pass a lie detector test as well, although Caleb knew he could pass one when lying through his teeth, too.

He wondered if she ever truly let go. Then again, he'd been asked the same question, albeit mainly by Zane.

For the record, the answer was *Hell yes.* Especially in bed. Because there was a time and a place, and bed was the time and the place. Well, so was the floor. The table. The car . . .

Yeah, time to get his mind back in the game. "Vivi, is everything okay?" Possibly the stupidest question ever, but hey, better to start somewhere.

She nodded, wiped her eyes and cheeks with the pads of her fingers. "What do you think?"

She didn't want to know, but now seemed as good a time as any to tell her. "I think I have some more questions for you."

She shrugged like she'd expected it, like none of this was a big deal. She was far too open to be holding any real secrets, as he'd suspected, but Mace's suspicious nature had grown on him over time.

Still, he'd thought it best to get her on solid, safe ground before he spilled what he knew to her. Having her flip out in the car wouldn't have been good for either of them. And still, Mace's distrust weighed heavily on him, and so he decided to give Vivi one last chance to come clean.

He grabbed a soda from the fridge before he sat down next to her, his hands wrapped around the cold can of Coke. "Why is your house in foreclosure?"

"I inherited a mess from my father," she explained.

"Legally, you're not responsible for his debt after his death."

"I am if he opened up credit cards and equity lines in my name," she said tightly. "I've thought about declaring bankruptcy but I'll only do it as a last resort. I thought, with the new contract, I could at least keep the house."

That was pretty damned responsible, although from the brief look he'd had at her financial records, it was also a pretty pipe dream.

The Army's contract would've helped, but... "For a guy who lived off the grid, what the hell did he need all that money for?"

"To live." She shrugged. "He was never going to collect a pension, even though he'd worked for the government for over twenty years before he got fired. After that, he had no benefits and he refused to work for anyone, stayed self-employed. Software security's not an easy business—programs sometimes take years to develop. I helped with them and worked part time outside the house through junior and senior years of high school, but it was never enough." She paused. "I've lived with a lifetime of bad news, Caleb. And I have a strong feeling you've been holding back."

"There's something you need to know. The attorneys you said you hired to advise you on the InLine thing... they're gone."

"What do mean, gone?"

"They're missing. Completely. Like they never existed."

She furrowed her brow. Her hair was loose, a tangle of blond and blue tips that framed her face softly. She looked vulnerable, and more than a little afraid.

He didn't blame her. And it would get worse when he revealed just how out of control her life had gotten. "Is there anyone you can think of who knows about your father's program, beyond the attorneys and InLine?"

"No." She gazed at him. "There's more, right?"

"We have reason to believe that your father's software program's been stolen."

"What do you mean? I was working on it this afternoon before you kidnapped me and you said you pulled a copy off my computer."

"It was copied, not wiped."

"What proof do you have?" she demanded.

"Homeland Security heard chatter that a terrorist group has a program designed for InLine Energy that can be utilized to work their system at will. When questioned, the InLine execs mentioned your father's name. They also gave the agents from Homeland a copy of the sample of the prototype your father had created for his proposal when he got the contract."

"Do you know who stole the program from me?"

How was he going to explain all of this to her?

Gently, he supposed, and that wasn't his typical way. "We have an idea, yes."

"Just tell me, okay?" Her eyes were already wide with anticipation.

"It's a terrorist organization, a group called DMH," he told her, and she shook her head. Didn't know them. Or she was a damned good actress, as Mace would suggest.

He dismissed that thought and filled her in. Told her things she'd probably never wanted to know, that yes, although they were once homegrown U.S., they now worked with many countries who hated the United States as often as possible.

"This can't be happening. It can't. My father's work—he would never want this, no matter how angry he was about what happened to him," she whispered, right before she ran to the bathroom and slammed the door shut behind her.

He went after her, waited about ten minutes after hearing her get sick and flush the toilet before opening the door.

She was lying curled up, facing the wall. When he leaned over her, she was sweating, pale and shaking. He grabbed a washcloth and soaked it in cool water before running it along her forehead.

Her eyes remained straight ahead, practically unblinking.

"Is that everything?" she asked, her voice hoarse.

He thought about lying, because *Christ,* there was more, and maybe she shouldn't know the *more* part yet.

But, then again, perhaps she needed to know everything in order to understand that her entire life was on the line here. "Yes, there is."

She didn't move, simply said, "Tell me."

"Someone broke into your house looking for you. It was about an hour after we took you away."

She nodded slowly, as if it had been something she'd thought of briefly but discounted. Now the truth was right in front of her and she had no choice but to accept it. "DMH?"

"We believe so, yes."

"Then they must know about the safeguard," she said

quietly. "They think I can override it, and the irony is, even I can't figure out how to make it work."

"You're going to have to try."

"I know. Because I know what they can do. This program was developed to protect nuclear power plants from being hacked into and remotely set to melt down, but it can also be used to *do* exactly that. And it will be, from what you're saying."

"We're doing everything we can to prevent that from happening. You worked closely with your father for years—he didn't talk about this program at all?"

"He didn't share this development with me, no. This was his baby—he didn't want me touching it, and so I didn't." She shook her head. "I'll do whatever I can to help. I'll do everything I can."

"Good girl," he said, surprised by the softness in his own voice. Couldn't help but touch her cheek, and was rewarded with a small smile from her.

"I need a toothbrush. Mouthwash," she murmured.

"There are supplies in the cabinet."

"I'm going to clean up some more. Is there anything else I can wear?" She motioned to the yoga pants she'd been wearing since he'd grabbed her from her house.

"Yeah, I brought in some sweats." He motioned to the cabinet next to the sink and she stood, ignoring his offers of help. He waited outside the bathroom, with the door partially open in case she fainted or something, while she freshened up.

She's got to know the extent of the ramifications—whether she's responsible or not, Noah had told him.

And now she knew.

When she emerged about twenty minutes later, her hair damp, the sweats hanging on her slim frame, she looked less pale, but he could tell she was still stunned. "Sorry. It's just... I have no one."

"You have me, Vivi."

The words slipped out before Cael had been able to help himself. She stood there in front of him like she wasn't sure what to do next. And although she tried to stop her eyes from welling up again by closing them, she couldn't. She took deep breaths, her hands fisted at her sides, and he did the only thing he could think of: He hugged her, and felt her immediate reaction of surprise, until she accepted the shoulder to cry on.

She didn't cry though, just buried her face against him while he rubbed her back. Her breath hitched a few times, but he could practically feel her inner strength building.

When she pulled away, he saw exactly that in her expression.

Vivi had no one... and she wasn't lying. He'd stake his job on it.

She felt so good against him, warm and soft—and damn, this was really wrong... the wrong time with a woman he shouldn't be getting involved with.

But how the hell was anyone supposed to get in if he never let the gates down?

"Caleb... Cael," she whispered. "Make me feel safe."

He wanted nothing more than to do just that.

"Make me forget..."

"Vivi—"

"I get it. This is for tonight. Or however long I'm here, in trouble. No strings attached."

Her face was so close, her breath warm, her lips pink and sweet, and falling into her, doing this, would be the best way out of thinking—worrying—for both of them.

Instead, he put his hands on her shoulders and gently pushed her back. "No, Vivi."

She nodded, flushed. "Sorry. It was stupid and I—"

"I won't take advantage of you, not after everything that's happened today."

She gave a wan smile. "I guess I wanted you to."

He wanted to tell her he wanted to as well, but she turned away, and he waited a beat . . . and then the moment was gone.

The driver was arguing with the men pretending to be police—men who'd set up a barricade in the middle of the road and wanted money . . . or to kidnap an American for ransom.

Rowan did not like the way they were eyeing her, especially since she was the American in question.

The country reminded her of Iraq—the war—except things were quieter here. Beyond the jostling around the harbor, once she found her ride and got on the road, she felt more at peace than she had anytime in the last six months.

Of course, that wasn't saying much.

The driver was polite, had driven expertly through the crowds at the harbor and navigated the tough roads with ease. He'd provided her with water, told her they would be to the camp within a few hours and then turned on a tape of

African music he played over and over again, until she knew the songs by heart.

And even that hadn't been enough to make her sleep. She was too restless, wondering what she was doing coming here, if it was too soon.

If anything would ever feel normal again.

You didn't have to say yes, she reminded herself. She could've shipped stateside and gotten a job as an EMT somewhere.

Somewhere. That was the rub. *Somewhere* was *nowhere* for her. At least here, she was wanted. Or rather, her skill set was. Blood and medicine.

The rain splattered the first fat drops on the windshield half an hour earlier and then it quickly became a deluge—the driver had slowed, visibility was nil and the urge to tell him to turn back had grown stronger with each passing minute.

And then the roadblock had forced them to stop. She checked the bag she'd kept with her in the backseat—it contained her gun, an old Sig Sauer she'd bought when she landed in Sierra Leone. She bypassed it in favor of cash, which she handed to the driver. "Just give this to them—tell them that's all they're getting and we're moving on."

The driver repeated what she said and the men who'd been arguing actually had the temerity to smile widely, like they'd just found Christmas.

She hadn't made it through all these years of combat unscathed to be killed on some road in Africa for the lack of ten dollars. Being practical like that hadn't been her strong suit but she'd absorbed a lot of what Dan had taught her.

Her husband, killed on 9/11 in the North Tower. Most days, she could barely remember what he'd looked like without the aid of a photograph, and that was far too painful for her to look at. If she concentrated really hard though, she could hear his laugh, a low chuckle, the one that told her everything would be okay.

Until it wasn't.

She could remember the abject terror of that day, but that was all. The rest was a blur of scattered information that brought smatterings of hope. A hope that faded as the day waned and was finally smashed to pieces by a phone call and a subsequent visit to the morgue too real for her to continue suspending her disbelief.

After the funeral, she went from EMT on the city streets to medic in Iraq. For a while, she was simply numb.

When she woke up, it was two years later and she was wearing full battle rattle.

But then it was too late for all of them.

She'd left because it was either move forward now or never. She didn't consider enlisting a step forward. No, that had been more of a sidestep, a way to skirt the horrors of her reality with another horror. A distraction, a way to be useful when she hadn't been able to on that fateful day.

But the distractions had failed to work lately, and she'd needed another option.

Doc J had promised that, contacted her with a letter through her CO several months earlier. He wrote that he ran a clinic, worked with missionaries, and he needed people with both medical training and combat experience. People who could handle themselves.

It's a beautiful place, he'd written. *A good place to come down from war.*

"If it's so good, why do I need combat experience?" she'd asked her CO.

"Always a good idea in a third world county. Not a place for wimps—or the unarmed."

"How did he find me?"

Her CO had shrugged. "He's got a lot of friends around here—including me."

An ex-Ranger running a clinic-slash-mission in Africa. Well, stranger things had happened and even though she didn't think she needed religion or that it could save her, she was intrigued.

She'd needed the change, she knew that. But as she looked around, she realized that a change would've been full-on civilian life. Coming here kept one foot that much closer to battle, but considering what she'd gone through before she'd enlisted, she knew she couldn't have it any other way.

When the driver finally stopped, she unfolded from the backseat, grateful to be able to stretch, even though the rain was a soaking one. She felt vaguely seasick, like the earth was still moving beneath her, and figured it would take a while to get used to all of it.

If she stayed long enough for that to happen.

Then again, going home wasn't exactly the best option for her. There was nothing there—nothing and no one.

The driver was dragging her bags out of the back of the Land Rover and across the wet dirt toward a small overhang, where she joined him. "Doc J is coming, okay?"

She nodded, turned to see who he was pointing at and barely heard the car pull away from behind her.

The man who came with a swift jog across the compound to meet her was tall. Broad. Intimidating. And when he got close, she noted he had the strangest-looking eyes she'd ever seen—more yellow than green, pale, with a dark ring around them. She'd bet they would be almost translucent in the sunlight.

His dark hair was tied back. His face was deeply tanned, grooved along his jawline, cut by a deep scar. His nose looked as if it had been broken, maybe more than once. He was anywhere between forty and fifty, although she'd guess closer to forty.

Far too young to be her savior.

"I'm Jason. Most people call me Doc J."

She shook the outstretched hand. His voice was deep and calming, but instead of soothing her it had the opposite effect.

Immediately, she withdrew her hand from his rough one and stuffed it into her pocket.

He noticed, of course. He was the type who would notice everything and it took the last of her resolve not to run after the car that was now too far down the road to save her.

She wondered how much the man with the fantastic eyes knew. No doubt he had every detail. She'd been told there was a careful screening process, that they needed *stable, committed people.*

Perhaps they'd mixed that up with, *needs to be committed.*

When that thought made her smile on the inside, she knew she'd be okay, at least for a little while.

"I'll show you where you'll be staying," he called over his shoulder, because he was already walking toward the small houses across the large dusty center of the clinic. Hurriedly, she grabbed her two large duffels and dragged them behind her.

There was only one bed in the room—a row of windows on either side that were covered by mesh only, and a single lightbulb in the middle of the ceiling. Beyond, a small table with a single folding chair. That was it.

"It's primitive, but you'll have privacy," he told her. "The head and the showers are out back—there are two of each. Generator goes off at dusk. Actually, it tends to go off whenever it feels like it."

She couldn't even bring herself to smile at his joke. She was much closer to hyperventilation.

And then he said, "I need your help."

He didn't wait for her answer, was already walking, assuming she'd follow. His words were an order and although neither of them was in the military any longer, the inherent instinct of *obey equals survival* still ran strongly through her.

She grabbed her medic bag out of one of the larger duffels and caught up with him.

"There's a woman—sick. I thought it was malaria, but now I'm not so sure," Doc J explained as they walked, giving no indication as to why the patient wasn't housed with the rest.

"So you must think whatever she has is contagious."

"Not necessarily." He swung open the door and let her inside the small, freestanding building.

The windows had been covered, so the breeze was minimal. There was a cot in the far corner, where the patient lay, surrounded by a man Rowan assumed was the woman's husband, and two children, both of whom appeared to be between eight and ten.

The woman maintained her calm, trying not to worry the kids. The husband was attempting to do the same, and not succeeding nearly as well.

It was hard to watch those close to you suffer.

It was only then Rowan realized that Doc J had remained outside the tent and closed the door.

She moved forward with her bag. "I'm Rowan," she said to the woman, but she made eye contact with the rest of the family too.

"Julia," the woman whispered. Her lips were dry; skin, clammy and pale.

"I'm Randy—her husband. This is Jocelyn and this is Jimmy. Come on, guys—let's move aside and let Rowan look at Mom." The man smiled tightly at her, moved the kids across the tent and began talking to them, presumably so they wouldn't happen to overhear anything.

Rowan knelt on the floor by the woman's bed, pulled out her stethoscope. "How long have you had your symptoms, Julia?"

"About a week or so. Not as bad—I thought it was just malaria. I've had that more times than I can count." A small wheeze as she drew in a breath before continuing and Rowan noticed the tinge of blue around her lips. "The trouble breathing started about a day ago. I was so wrapped up in what I was doing I didn't notice."

"You've never had that symptom before?"

Julia motioned for her to come closer. "I have a bad heart."

Rowan bowed her head, closed her eyes and listened to the chest sounds for a few minutes to be sure. And she didn't like what she heard, mainly because it was consistent with what Julia had just told her.

When she looked the woman in the eye, she didn't need to say anything. Instead, she excused herself and walked back out to Doc J to consult, wondering why the hell there wasn't an actual doctor here.

Granted, without the necessary equipment, like a new heart, there wasn't anything anyone could do.

"Pneumonia," she confirmed to him. "Could be secondary to the malaria. Also, the heart rhythm . . ."

"I heard that too, was hoping it was due to fever."

"It could be," she said, but her instincts told her it wasn't. She'd learned enough in Iraq, worked so closely with the doctors and nurses that she'd often been treated as such.

She'd never taken that responsibility lightly either. Because she *wasn't*—she was simply damned good at her job as a medic. Read, learned and listened.

Right now she was listening and learning about Doc J.

"Can't travel," he murmured thoughtfully, almost more to himself than to her, but she answered anyway.

"I wouldn't recommend it. Not until she gets antibiotics on board, which might not even work. She's pretty far along with the infection." She paused. "Will there be antibiotics?"

He smiled. "Yes. I don't give them out unless absolutely necessary. IV will work faster. I'll get the supplies."

"We're doing this in the treatment room, correct?"

"Here."

"What's going on?" she asked.

"You work for me, Rowan. You'll do as I say. The procedure will be performed here, and if you can't do it, I will."

She clenched her jaw, felt the familiar tension rise up the back of her neck. It was a damned IV, for Christ's sake. But the woman shouldn't be kept in a small, dark space that didn't exactly seem sanitary. "I'm capable of following orders, sir. I just didn't realize I'd be doing it blind. If I'd wanted that, I'd have remained enlisted."

She moved to march back into the room and wait for him to bring the necessary supplies, the lack of trust smarting, although it should have been expected. She'd been there less than an hour.

But Doc J caught her arm. "Soldiers are looking for her because she and her husband spoke out against the local government. They're lurking within a fifty-mile radius, if not less by now. They're sniffing, and the locals will only do so much before they'll tell what they know."

Rowan knew Julia wouldn't make a car trip, and she guessed that, even with Doc J's connections, bringing a plane or chopper in would be like skywriting *The family's here* to the men after them.

So this entire place was painted with a giant bull's-eye and she was smack-dab in the middle for now.

"I'll explain more later, but she's out of sight with her family for their safety."

"What about mine?"

"You wanted safe, you shouldn't have come here."

"In your letter, you promised me—"

"Peace," he said softly. "I promised you peace. Once you have that, you won't worry so much about the safety part."

She wanted to tell him that was bullshit—that she'd

never be able to find peace, that her heart had been torn out and stomped on and now she was simply numb and battle-scarred.

But she didn't. Instead, she felt the familiar anger rise up inside of her—except she couldn't be sure who it was directed at, Doc J or herself.

CHAPTER

8

Zane woke as dusk fell, aware of Liv's warm body spread beneath him, one bare leg still wrapped around his calf.

They'd fallen asleep less than an hour ago, unable to stop pushing and pulling each other, at the most base, physical level. And somehow, it was far more than just the physical between them—he felt the emotions breaking through the surface, especially when she kissed him.

And she'd kissed him a lot.

She didn't stir when he shifted away from her. He hated to do that, but he needed to keep a watch, even though the rain still pounded around the house, which kept things dark and cool. He yanked on his still-damp pants, grabbed his gun and took a walk around outside, his footprints quickly and efficiently washing away behind him.

Of course, that meant anyone tracking them would have the same luck. But his instincts weren't triggered, the perimeter wires hadn't been breached and, when he was satisfied they hadn't been found, he went back inside.

And Liv slept on.

He wondered when the last time she'd really slept had been and decided it was at least six months ago. And he liked that she'd been able to let down her guard with him.

He stripped off the pants again, wrung them out and hung them before walking back over to her. The blanket had moved when she shifted positions and she was partially uncovered. He had no problem taking a long look at the woman who'd cried out his name an hour before.

During sex, everything had been filtered through the haze of lust, but he'd have to be blind not to have noticed the tattoo that swirled across her abdomen. It was an odd place for a tattoo for a woman, but it looked good on her. At first, he'd thought it was simply an intricate swirl of design, but when he allowed himself to look closer, he saw it spelled out the word *strength* in a thin script.

Well, everyone needed their juju, he supposed. This was something she could never lose.

He mentally calculated the ammo he had left. Thought about the satphone and the backup battery for his GSM cell phone, plus the emergency number that could bring members of his SEAL team to help, if necessary.

Dylan was waiting. Caleb was already pissed about this whole undertaking—Zane could practically hear his brother's vibes from here.

And then he looked at Liv again. She was still resistant, no matter how willing she'd been in his arms.

Baby steps. It was nearly time for them to move out, get them one step closer to Freetown.

He didn't want to consider why he felt like that step would make him lose her completely.

Zane was looking at the tattoo. Under her lashes, Olivia watched him watch her, and for once she didn't mind the gaze that lingered over her abdomen.

After all, she was the one who put the tattoo there in the first place, knew it would draw attention from her lovers. But those had been few and far between . . . and she hadn't had more than a passing care about any of them. They'd filled a void, scratched an itch—no matter how crass that sounded, it was the truth.

"Do you like it?" she heard herself ask in a voice that was slightly husky from sleep.

His eyes lit. "I like it. All of it."

She didn't think anything could make her blush again, but that did, creating a warm heat that spread from her cheeks to her toes.

"I had it done when I was sixteen," she said, ran her hand over it, enjoyed seeing the heat rise in his eyes.

God, the man had the ability to make her forget everything, even the reason she'd gotten the damned thing in the first place.

And it wasn't an easy reason to forget. But the urge to push him away, thoroughly disgust him, still plagued her. She owed him a lot for saving her, owed him even more for searching for her all this time. He deserved to know, to understand, why the thought of going back, of being vulnerable and out of control of her life, scared her so badly.

But she wasn't ready to talk about all of it, could still hear the echo of him whispering, *Liv*, urgently in her ear, like he'd had the most important question in the world for her to answer—and he continued to ask, with his mouth, his hands, his tongue. She'd answered with a tug to his hair when his mouth found her breast, a low groan when his lips brushed her sex . . . a cry when he filled her.

She thought about the picture of her he'd carried with him for the past six months. Thought about the way he watched her so carefully, like he knew things she hadn't told him yet.

The room remained dark as the rain intensified. She lay on her side, curled toward Zane, sated but not thoroughly spent. The air had cooled incrementally, and her time with DMH had stopped replaying itself like a bad movie inside her head.

"God, I could go for a margarita," she murmured.

Zane was sweating, but still somehow managed to seem impervious to the heat's other effects. He wasn't slow or sluggish. His eyes were bright and alert and he handed her the canteen.

"This is the best I can do for now," he told her, and she took it and drained the last of the water. "You'll have to wait a few days before I can grant you your margarita wish."

"I'll hold you to it."

"You can hold me to a lot of things, Liv . . . I'm more than willing to let you have your way."

He shouldn't be able to make her tingle like that, but he did. It would be so easy for her to lose herself in him again. Easy, but not what she needed most.

Instead, she told him, "There's a man—a medic my friend Ama told me about who runs a clinic for missionaries and locals too. I want you to bring me to him."

She swore she saw him flinch before he answered, "No way."

"Then I'll find my own way there."

And just like that, the closeness they'd shared disappeared. *Good. Don't get attached, Liv.* "Ama said it's a camp for people who need a specific kind of help."

Zane raised his brows but didn't say anything, gave nothing to indicate if he would agree to go there or not.

"It's on the way to Freetown," she continued.

"Yeah, on the way," he said finally. And she could tell he knew what she was thinking.

But Zane wasn't on a suicide mission either. "You've got coordinates?"

"I've got better—a phone number."

"Give it to me."

She found the paper inside the black medical bag Ama had given her. "It's run by Doc J."

He grabbed the phone from his bag. "I'll call Dylan about him. See what he knows."

With that, he walked out of the house, leaving her alone, wondering why he was suddenly taking her seriously. Was it a trick, or had she worn him down?

She'd picked the fight, started the battle and had a real chance of winning the war. Why did she feel so disappointed?

The rain hadn't abated at all. Zane remained close to the house so he wouldn't get soaked again. Reception was better than he'd expected but still spotty enough that he used the satphone to dial his brother.

"I need you to check on someone for me," he said without further introduction when Dylan answered with a muffled curse. He didn't wait for his brother to say *Go ahead* before he gave him Doc J's name, location and satphone number. "I'm hoping you know him—or of him."

"Hold on," Dylan said, sounding like Cael, and Zane heard typing in the background, Riley's murmured voice and then he heard Dylan speaking with someone.

Liv remained inside—probably listening through the window.

She'd spoken so calmly. Like she'd thought all of this out. Like, when he was holding her this afternoon, she hadn't been relaxing, but planning.

What the hell was he doing, in this country, risking his damned life to save a woman who didn't want to be rescued?

Then again, what had he done for years after his rescue, but push everyone who tried to love him away? In many ways, he still did by not having anything close to a serious relationship—or any friendships. It was his brothers, and his team when he was on a mission, or else he was alone. By choice or because of his past, he still wasn't sure. Who knew who he'd be if he'd remained in Africa, if his biological parents hadn't been killed . . . if everything had stayed perfect.

He started, because it was the first time he'd thought about his early years in the missions as perfect.

"Okay, Doc J is Jason Berent—he's ex-Army. Ranger, not Delta, but he was in when I was. He's been running the clinic for the past five years. He was a good guy—my sources say that hasn't changed. He could be a good stopping place on the way to Freetown," Dylan confirmed, breaking into Zane's walk in the past and cementing his next move.

"The doc doesn't necessarily want it to be a stopping place."

There was a deadly silence on the other end. Because Dylan tended to give Zane a lot of rope to hang himself most of the time, he'd forgotten how badassed his brother really was. There was a reason people feared and respected him.

Zane respected him, but the fear had never been there.

"Give me your damned location, Zane," Dylan finally growled in his ear, and Zane felt the tension mount between them.

Dylan never demanded things from him. Caleb did, but Dylan . . . "No. I'll get her to the clinic and then—"

"And then what? She's leading you around by the balls, letting you risk your life."

She didn't appear to be in shock, but she had to be severely traumatized. And as badly as he didn't want anything to do with a camp for missionaries, he couldn't abandon Liv now.

He would stay with her, take her where she needed to go; he knew she would come to her senses at some point. She had to.

"That's just it, man. She wants me to leave her so I stop risking my life, okay? She's scared. She thinks she's doing the right thing by staying on the run." He didn't bother to add that he knew what that was like, because Dylan was a smart man, even when he was being an asshole. "I'm guessing Cael knows."

"I had to tell him."

"Did you run any of that intel Olivia gave me, about the doctors?"

"I did. I checked out the names with some of my sources and they're already known in some circles as being willing to do anything for a price, medically. Now I have to figure out what to do with what I know, and you need to get Olivia out."

"She'll come around, Dylan. Let me take her where she wants to go. This is a journey back for her—I can't rush it. I understand that."

And with those words, the tension broke. "Just be careful, Zane. Please, just be fucking careful with this one."

Zane wanted to tell his brother it was way too late for that, but he didn't.

Rowan Moller was twenty-eight, looked much younger, even though her eyes held a deep knowledge of someone much older. Maybe she could be helped and maybe she couldn't, but none of that was up to him.

Jason had been thinking on it while nursing a beer for the better part of an hour. Dinner was long ready, but he wanted her to wake on her own. The dark circles, the more than slight panic in her eyes could be sleep dep...or it could be something worse.

And she was looking to him for salvation. They all were looking for that from Doc J.

He'd heard himself called Doc J for so long that he'd stopped thinking of himself as anything but, stopped thinking of himself as a red-blooded, forty-six-year-old American man with needs and wants and desires.

He was far from a saint, certainly never thought of himself as a religious man and yet everyone seemed to buy it. He liked helping the people here, liked helping the men he'd recruited and trained for mercenary work even more. Yes, he brought help and consolation to the weary and chronically unprotected, and most of the people who passed through the camp never realized what it actually was.

The medical staff never did—he'd made sure to keep them separate. Most of them were savvy enough to know that the men who passed through weren't simply men passing through.

In truth, he was looking for a permanent medical staffer and had been unable to find the right candidate. The men got restless, the women scared, and in all truth, sometimes this place was too damned good at healing people.

Doc wanted that for everyone, sure, but he also needed to find someone who loved this place as much as he'd come to.

Rowan Moller's tough as shit, calm under pressure...and she's got some pretty high walls no one here's been able to scale. Not easily intimidated, but she's skittish at the idea of making connections, her CO, and Doc J's friend, had written.

He had people counting on him left and right, money piling up in an overseas account he'd no doubt never touch, and he knew he'd never be done here, despite the ten-year plan he'd promised himself.

Then again, what did he have to go back to?

Concentrate, Doc.

There was too much going on at once—and that was always a harbinger of bad things. First, the family he'd hidden away, then Rowan's arrival. Coupled with the phone call from a man named Zane and his imminent arrival—well, things were going to hell in a handbasket soon enough.

"Hey." Tristan settled next to him, bottle of water in his hand. "New medic?"

"Yes." He stretched his hands. The arthritis was better here in the dry heat, but his hands would never function the way they had when he was twenty-five. Combat—different kinds—harsh environments, life experience, they all showed in those tanned hands. A map of his life until now, with no hints of what was to come.

"I hope you don't expect me to, like, help her."

"God forbid," he said wryly.

It was the first time Tristan gave anything close to the hint of a smile in weeks. Sometimes the stretches were longer. When the younger man had first arrived, Doc J swore it took six months. Now Tristan was his right-hand man, had been for the past three years. He nodded in the direction of where Rowan slept. "She's bad off?"

"No worse than you." Doc J gave him a sideways glance and Tristan snorted.

"Then she's screwed," Tristan stated. "Is she having flashbacks?"

"She doesn't have PTSD."

Tristan looked at him quizzically. "Then why the hell wouldn't she just go home? What's her deal?"

It was the first time Tristan had asked about any of them. And so Doc J answered. "She lost her husband in the towers. Enlisted soon after." His voice was brusque, and he heard Tristan muttering something about *feeling like an asshole now.*

And still, they both knew that Rowan had a less than five percent chance of making it here. Very few lasted longer than a month. Longer than that, they tended to stick around, if not here, then at another mission or wherever they were needed.

Jason ran into them, on radio or infrequent trips to town. Most often, it was when they'd motor in, and then they'd sit around and drink warm beer and talk about the good old times they'd had together, which by definition were neither very good nor all that long ago.

But none of them would ever cop to it.

He'd seen it all between the Army and here—worst of the worst, best of the best and most of what was in between.

"Think she'll make it?" Tristan asked him, his demeanor calm and unassuming, but Doc knew better. Tristan had his back, was ready to strike at a moment's notice if needed.

The man was Irish-Cuban; he had fled into the Army and then fled from it. Then he'd come here and he'd stopped running, but Doc J was damned concerned, because the boy had never really settled.

What was here for him, beyond backbreaking labor and very few means of thanks? Would he ever be ready to take over this place alone? Would he want to? He was never fully unpacked, like he could leave at any second without so much as a good-bye.

Speaking of leaving... "You've got a pickup to make. Early morning." Doc J rattled off the coordinates and saw Tristan's small nod. Paper was in short supply here and the men got used to memorizing what they needed to know.

"How many?"

"Two. A female doctor, and an active-duty."

"Great," Tristan muttered. "Better not be a fucking know-it-all."

"I'm sure you'll set him straight." Doc J paused. "The doctor's a friend of Ama's."

"The same friend who got her killed?"

"You might not want to mention that when you meet Olivia."

Tristan shrugged, like he couldn't commit to that either way, and ambled off without another word.

Doc J stared up at the stormy sky, swore he could hear the voice from long ago, telling him, *When your prayer is answered, you take it. It's that simple.*

Nothing was that simple, but it had been a start.

Caleb sat quietly in the next room scribbling something furiously—Vivi could hear the scratch of pencil to paper, and she still felt her cheeks flush, the way they did when her mind wandered back to their embrace.

When she'd torn herself away from the comfort of his arms, she'd felt more naked in the sweats than she had in her workout clothing, which was ridiculous. Maybe it was the way Caleb had looked at her when she'd pulled away from him. It was strange, but her first impression would've been... lust.

But men like him didn't fall for women like her. This was simply a case of babysit the geek, play nice and make her do what you want. She'd been there her entire life, had fought the stereotype and then had simply given up.

Still, when she'd glanced at Caleb again and his expression hadn't changed—but his eyes, oh his eyes, dark and fierce and locking her in their scope—it had made her shiver.

Well, at least now she knew the look had most definitely been pity. She'd been a fool to beg him to kiss her.

At least he'd given her space for several hours. Now it was well into the early morning hours, and even though Vivi was tired, there was no way she could sleep. No, the stress kept her moving forward as her eyes blurred and her fingers ached, but she was no closer to finishing the program than she'd been hours before.

What did you do, Dad? Why couldn't you have let me in?

Lawrence Clare had been a certified genius, so much so that he seemed to live in another world—and often, he did. Most of the time he forgot he had a family, which she knew was the reason her mom left them. Vivi stayed behind because, even at twelve years old, she knew her father needed help.

There was no way he could have survived on his own. Beyond that, the relief in her mother's eyes when Vivi insisted on staying was apparent.

Even as a child, Vivi had been almost as good at reading people as she later was at interpreting code. Besides, Vivi had a lot of her father's qualities, and she figured her mother wouldn't want to put up with two of them cut from the same cloth.

Like her father, Vivi could be forgetful, distracted, and so she wasn't allowed to ride her bike or walk alone, because she'd do things like wander into the street. She'd finally learned to harness all of that distraction though, something her father had never really been able to do.

He'd do things like put water on for tea, then forget about the pot and nearly burn the house down. Most of the time, he forgot to eat—or to buy food.

She understood that her gift for numbers came from him, and he'd always told her to use her gift for the common good, not to be ashamed of her intelligence.

Not to hide behind it.

She wasn't ashamed, but found it was a problem for making friends. Although not on the same plane as her father, she'd still found herself without common ground with the kids around her. She would often zone out, planning mathematical possibilities in her mind. Would rather spend time with her computer on Saturday nights than anyone else.

Contrary to popular belief, a laptop did keep you warm at night.

"Dad, you have to help me out here," she muttered and, not surprisingly, she got no answer in response.

She attempted to get the feeling back into her hands, rubbing them together roughly, attempting clumsily to massage one with the other.

That's when she saw Caleb from the corner of her eye, hadn't heard him move from one room to the other, wondered if that stealth came naturally or if it had taken practice.

He didn't say anything, just sat next to her and took one of her hands in his and began to work it between his own. He stared at her hand intently, doing something with trigger points, something she'd attempted to read and forgotten about in lieu of work.

"Better?" he asked after a few minutes.

She flexed her hand, although truth be told she'd been reluctant to pull it away from his. "Better."

He went to work on her other one, while she rubbed her eyes with her free hand.

"You've been working non-stop."

"I figured you would like that."

He laughed—a short one, but it helped. "The faster you work, the faster we can make headway, yes. But sometimes walking away for a little while helps you solve the problem. It's always worked for me when I've been too close to something."

The thing was, his problems dealt with the safety of the world, so really, he did understand. Except . . . "Caleb, what if I can't do it?"

"In my world, we don't use that word. There's no *can't*. You'll pull it out of the fire. Maybe you should take a short nap. You're tired."

"You must be too."

"I can handle long nights," he said easily, letting her hand slide between his again.

"Right." She wanted to pull it away and turn back to the computer, because that's what she understood—it was safe. It needed her to work, and with the right kind of coaxing, she could get it to do anything she wanted.

Staying away from the computer meant spending more

time talking to him, and that in itself was confusing. He was still looking at her with the same intensity in his eyes... and she was still confused as hell.

"Why didn't you accept the FBI's offer?" he asked finally.

"I considered it. I still am, I guess. But it's a huge commitment. I don't know if I'm any good working for other people. I think I lived with my dad for too long."

"It must've been tough growing up like that."

"People just saw the crazy. They couldn't see beyond that to the genius." She paused. "For a while, I tried to fit in, but it never worked. I followed in his footsteps—I'm a computer geek and I'm really good with numbers, but I'm nowhere near my father's level. I use what I know for practical purposes."

"So there's never been anyone in your life—boyfriends?"

Her stomach got those nervous butterflies she'd heard so much about but never actually experienced. Now she understood. They got stronger when she forced herself to look directly into his deep, dark eyes. "I dated a couple guys when my father was alive—nothing too serious. And then he got sick and I put all my efforts into making sure he was comfortable. After he died, I dated one guy for a while... it was serious, I guess. As serious as I'd ever gotten."

"We probably should check all of them out, just to be safe."

"I'm sure none of them knew what I was doing, job-wise."

"What did they think you did?"

"I told them I was in IT. It was much easier that way. It's what I tell everyone," she said. "The first two were just some casual dates here and there. One guy was an auto mechanic. Kind of a bad boy, motorcycle-gang type."

Cael stared at her. "I know. Not the best choice," she told him. "The other was a guy I'd known from my classes freshman year in college. We kept in touch and he told me he'd wanted to ask me out for a while, but then..."

"Not a bad enough boy?" he asked.

"No, he was seeing a lot of other women and I just wasn't into that. I didn't know what I was into. But right after my father died, that guy took me to a lecture at the college—as friends. That's where I met Dale. He's an archeologist—and a professor. He traveled a lot."

"Last name and address."

"Dale Robbins—247 Lakeshore Drive, Apartment 4C. That's about half an hour from my house," she added.

He committed that to memory because he didn't want to stop working on her hands to write it down. She shifted as his touch began to make her feel...warm. Watching his big hands stroke hers, the difference in the skin color, his tan to her paler skin, highlighted by the closeness.

"How long were you guys together?"

"We dated for six months. In the beginning, I thought it was going to be perfect, but it didn't really work."

"Why not?" His voice caressed her—it was deeper now, even as his hands continued to massage hers, working the pressure points on her wrists, and she fought the urge to squirm in her seat.

No one had ever done this for her, had worried about her hands cramping or her wrists hurting. Caleb made this seem like far more than a job to him.

"It was more me than him. I mean, Dale came into my

life at the right time. I was more alone than ever, distrustful of everyone. He said the things I needed to hear. He made me feel like someone finally had my back, and it was really nice." Nice, but no fireworks, at least not the kind she'd read about, or seen in movies and on TV.

Not at all the way she felt around Caleb after less than forty-eight hours together. "He needed me. He wanted me around. But he worked a lot and so did I." She paused. "I was waiting for it to grow into something it never did, so I ended things. He wasn't happy about it, showed up at my house late one night asking for another chance. I let him in and we talked until I was too tired to argue more. I went back to sleep, he stayed on the couch, and when I woke up in the morning, he was gone. *Work,* he'd written on a note he left in the kitchen, and I knew that things between us wouldn't change. Apparently, he realized it too, since that's the last I heard from him. I'm afraid I didn't handle any of it very well, not the relationship, or the breakup. He was intense at times . . . and it was all so new to me."

"At least you realized early that Dale wasn't right for you. There are people who live their whole lives in bad relationships and refuse to let themselves see it."

"So I'm not doing badly for a reforming recluse?"

"Not bad at all."

She liked the way he talked with her. Talked to her. She believed what he said and even though that might make her naive, her instincts were telling her otherwise. "I never thought I'd be able to fall for someone. My father always said that love is the ultimate weakness, that when you let your guard down, you lose all perspective." She paused. "Sometimes I think he was right."

"So why date at all? Why even bother to try?" He wasn't goading her with the question. Rather, he really seemed to want to know—and she wasn't even sure *she* knew.

"I didn't want to spend the rest of my life living under my father's influence of distrust. I wanted to be part of a regular couple. I didn't want to be the poor girl who lived with her recluse of a father." God, she sounded defensive. Probably because she knew she'd been acting stupidly. Naively. But since then, she'd toughened up. She'd learned.

From this experience alone, she'd learned.

"Give yourself some time, Vivi. You can't blame yourself if you weren't feeling the relationship."

But she did. Because the sex part hadn't been good at all, and from everything she'd read, you could have great, even amazing sex with someone you didn't love. Granted, Dale had been her first and she was nervous, but he'd done nothing to reassure her, which made the entire experience fall into the not-good category.

"We, uh, slept together, but it wasn't very good. I wasn't very good," she blurted out, wondering why she couldn't have just stopped while she was ahead with this true confession.

He stopped his massage cold. "Is that what he told you?"

She hesitated and then said, "He told me I was young . . . that it would get better as I got older."

"He's a fool," Cael growled. "It's his job to give you pleasure, especially if you were a virgin."

How did he know that? And furthermore, why was she talking about this with him? "I suppose things would've been different with you."

He nodded, slowly, raked her with his eyes in a way that

made her shiver, as if she were naked in the middle of an open field. "Don't suppose. *Know.*"

"You stopped me before."

"I didn't want to take advantage of you."

"And now?"

He simply smiled, and God, he looked good when he smiled. But Dale had smiled too.

Dale never made you feel like this. And still . . . "What if my father was right? What if I shouldn't trust anyone at all?"

"You're going to have to trust someone along the way," he said quietly, and anger surged through her, fast and furious, her emotions bubbling with a fury she'd never expected.

"Sometimes, I felt so used by him. And that's horrible, because he was my father."

"No offense, but it sounds to me like he was the child in the relationship."

She nodded. "Yes, that's true. And with Dale—the boyfriend—I followed the same pattern."

"Maybe it's time you broke the pattern, tried something new," he suggested. "Pick someone . . . random."

"You don't know anything about numbers," she said. "Or randomness."

He stopped any more words with a kiss. It wasn't gentle, but hard, almost punishing, and enough to make her forget about numbers and patterns and Dale.

When he tore his mouth from hers, she felt flushed, her lips bruised, and as she touched them he said, "That's what it should be like."

"I'd better . . . ah . . . I mean . . ."

His ringing phone saved her and he smiled like he knew it before he turned away and answered with a sharp, "What's going on?"

What *was* going on? She'd never thought she could feel so strongly for someone, and so quickly. She rubbed her bare arms and then grabbed the blanket from the bed to wrap herself in.

What made her think she could trust him?

He saved your life . . . twice.

His job, she argued.

But the kiss . . . she was pretty sure that wasn't a part of the job at all. Then again, it was obvious she knew nothing at all about love and trust. Or kissing. Or life.

And she was trapped—cut off from her former life and completely unable to help the military, stop DMH from using her program.

As much control as she'd fooled herself into thinking she had over numbers—or anything—she now realized she barely had a grip on anything.

And this man . . . he could swallow her whole in one bite . . . and something trilled inside of her, as if to let her know if that was to happen, she would enjoy every second of it.

He looked completely in control, and her life had been so utterly the opposite when her father had been alive, she longed for stability.

Dale had seemed to understand her need to mourn her father.

It hurt to admit that during the last years of her father's life she'd been very close to hating him.

He'd left her with a mountain of debt, shitty credit and

a general distrust for most people. Of course, on that she had to agree that he'd been right.

She'd let her guard down with Dale—she should've known better. The relationship didn't devastate her, but it left her far more wary than she'd already been. She'd waited a heck of a long time to give her virginity away to someone far more interested in his own pleasure. But, just the way she'd taken care of her father for years and gotten so little in return, she'd continued that pattern—although not consciously—and much to her dismay when she finally had realized it.

Now there were firewalls around her heart.

Why did she feel like Cael could breach them with a single touch?

Why did she want him to try?

CHAPTER
9

Olivia saw that the dark had finally come and so she washed up quickly using the rest of the water and a bandanna Zane lent her, dressed in her now dry borrowed T-shirt and pants. Wished she had different shoes. "God, I hope no one took the truck," she muttered to herself.

She was packed and ready by the time Zane came back inside. "Dylan got in touch with some of his contacts—it seems that the missionaries in the areas around Freetown know Doc J well. Apparently, they use a lot of former Army to protect their clinics and camps."

"Do you think DMH can track me there, the way you just tracked Doc J?"

Zane's jaw clenched and then relaxed. "I'm sure they

could—but the missionaries wouldn't reveal that intel to just anyone. Dylan served with the guys who provide the protection, that's the only reason they revealed anything."

She nodded, having no choice but to trust that. She knew Doc J had a former soldier who indeed worked inside the clinic, providing protection and shuttling visiting doctors and such back and forth to the harbor and into the main parts of town.

"My brother's making arrangements with Doc J," he said, had flipped his phone open again and was punching in a few numbers. He spoke quickly and she caught a couple of words, like *transport,* and then there was only silence, deep and dark. The pit of her stomach ached again from fear and she hoped this would work out.

When he hung up, he said, "Someone from Doc J's camp will meet us. There's a place an hour from here. More like three, the way we're traveling, but we don't need to be there until first light. We should have plenty of time," he muttered, more to himself than her, and then, "Why the hell are you trying to get rid of me?"

"I'm not, Zane. I just want to make sure you're safe. That if I stay, you'll get out of this country unharmed."

"Too late, Liv," he told her. "DMH has my picture. I'm in this as deeply as you."

"What are you talking about?"

"I found my picture on the guy's phone—the one outside your house. He'd transmitted it already."

Ama's face flashed in front of her eyes. Ama, who'd gone to the States for medical school and then come back to Africa in order to use what she'd learned to help her own people. The woman had taken Olivia in, cared for her, didn't worry about her own safety.

There's no safety in Africa, she'd said. *There's no safety anywhere, Olivia. Fear isn't going to help you.*

Now Ama was dead. Tortured. And even though Olivia hadn't been there, hearing what had happened from Ama's friend had been horrifying.

"When?" she demanded now of Zane.

"The night I came to you. That guy arrived right after I did—or before, I'm not sure." He ran a hand through his hair.

"DMH knows who you are?"

"By now they've got a pretty good idea," he said. "I'm not telling you to make you feel guilty. You just need to know that I'm a target too."

"And what are you going to do about it?"

"I'm not going to hide, that's for sure."

She bristled. "I can do a lot of good here."

"If you weren't scared for your life, sure."

She hated him then, because he'd basically told her she was a coward. She'd fought for so long to be anything but, and in the end it didn't make a damned bit of difference. "I can't get taken again."

He didn't say anything right away, continued to watch her with those eyes that told her he knew everything she was going to say, every argument and justification, and he'd still wait patiently and listen anyway.

Having people who helped her getting in major trouble had become a pattern she did not want to repeat. "Why didn't you tell me earlier about the picture?"

"Everyone needs their secrets." He shouldered her bag along with his own. "Ready?"

Caleb hadn't wanted to be interrupted, had wanted to keep kissing Vivi as she melted against him, wanted to kiss her silly and erase memories of that asshole ex-boyfriend.

But it was Dylan on the other end of the line, who didn't even give him a chance for more than a fleeting hello before he said quietly, "Cael, we've got a problem."

"Tell me."

"DMH has Zane's picture."

Hearing that was truly like getting socked in the gut, and both he and Dylan remained quiet for a few moments, the severity of the situation weighing heavily enough for Caleb to feel the need to sink into the nearest chair.

Dylan spoke first. "He's okay. He took the guy's phone, but the picture had already been sent—I didn't know if you guys could do anything with the e-mail addresses."

He rattled off the address and IP and Caleb wrote them on the legal pad he'd been drawing on. "I'll pass it along to Gray."

"Good. Zane's headed to a clinic with Olivia. She's not ready to come home yet. He said he's giving her some rope and letting her run herself out."

"Give her some rope," Cael repeated. "What the fuck, Dylan?"

"He's playing it right. The doc's worried about coming home. Thinks that she'll bring retribution to anyone close to her."

"Yeah, that's my big goddamned concern as well. So we're on the same page."

"He'll get through it, Cael. He always does."

"How many chances does one guy get?"

"As many as he deserves," Dylan said before he clicked off.

Cael sat holding the phone. Sat and stared at the four walls that felt like they were closing in on him.

Someone had to talk some sense into Zane.

Someone needs to let the boy run free. That's the way he's happiest. The way you're all happy, his mother used to say, without anger or judgment. In fact, out of all of them, she might've been the one who needed to run the most, and she'd found the perfect match in their father.

As he heard Vivi tapping on the keys, he texted the information he'd gotten from her about the three men she'd dated—putting extra emphasis on Dale—to Mace. Mace texted back that they were still waiting for the fingerprint IDs they'd taken from Vivi's house, both before and after the break-in.

Satisfied with that, Caleb then texted Gray the intel he'd gotten about Zane, and received a terse *I'm on it* message back. Now he just had to try not to jump out of his goddamned skin while he waited to see exactly how far DMH would go to trace Zane.

It took them less than an hour to get to the shed where he'd parked the truck. The only reason he was going back to it at all was because of Liv, and mainly because she moved too slow for his comfort.

Not her fault, of course, but Zane's goal was to get them to the mission fast.

She was moving as quickly as she could, her head down, but every step seemed to echo in the early evening quiet. He ground his teeth together and said nothing.

Short of carrying her, that couldn't be helped.

He was also pretty damned annoyed with her. Felt like she'd fucking used him.

You slept with her pretty damned willingly.

Because he'd been thinking of nothing else for six months. Maybe Caleb was right, maybe it had simply grown into an obsession born of guilt and pride.

And maybe Zane knew that he'd fallen damned hard for Olivia Strohm—and he didn't want to come down from that just yet.

"Stay here, out of sight," he told her, handed her a rifle. "I'm going to stake out the truck."

She nodded, the strain evident on her face.

He resisted the urge to kiss her. Which seemed really hard to do, and so he turned away fast and made his way toward the shed.

Once in position, he got down on a knee to scan the area. Noted that even though the shed was closed, the grass that surrounded it was tamped down far more than it had been earlier—and not because of the rain. No, there was a path from the other side of the clearing, clearly man-made.

They were here, waiting for them to come get the truck. Which *they,* he wasn't sure, of course, so why tell Liv any of it and scare the shit out of her.

Instead, he went back and lied.

They weren't alone.

Olivia hadn't realized it until what was likely the last possible minute, but judging by the way Zane had maneuvered them for the past twenty, he'd been in *better safe than sorry* mode for quite some time.

She'd been sorry ever since he'd come back and told her their truck had been stolen, had been deep in thought for the hours they'd been walking, trying to figure out what she was doing. Her mind tracing circles around everything that had happened to her over the past months . . . and still, her body was prepared to do anything to get back underneath Zane again.

Her mind, her heart, wouldn't let it be that easy though.

Zane was so hard, dangerous—and he moved as if he belonged out here, blending into the backdrop of this wild place with his own primitive nature.

Moving like this with him, she could appreciate that, for the first time since her escape, she wasn't flying blind. Wasn't completely alone.

As uncomfortable as his agenda made her, she was still grateful. Never more so than now as she waited behind his tensed body, so stock-still that she was barely breathing.

They were close to the meeting place—or at least they should be. She didn't know if Zane had circled them back in an attempt to throw people off their track.

People. Soldiers? DMH?

"Run," Zane whispered against her ear and the command—and the fear—broke her stillness.

She did, aware that she was jerked in every direction by

the thick brush, the hidden ropes of vines along the floor of the forest, the wet ground spongy under her feet.

She was happy for the darkness even as she was bruised and scratched and poked, even as her legs began to protest and her breath came in short wheezes. But she wouldn't stop. Her life depended on it, and the renewed strength from that thought pushed her on for the next while, legs moving seemingly of their own accord, hands fisted, shoulders tensed.

She bit her tongue at some point, the metallic taste of blood sharp in her mouth. And she was back in the woods, nine years old, scared to death.

The feelings were just as intense now, surged through her with an extra burst of adrenaline even as the tears began to course down her cheeks. She hadn't realized she'd slowed, but Zane had, and she let herself get half dragged along next to him. By the end, he was practically carrying her, until they came to a halting stop, where she tried to catch her breath. There was a stitch in her side, and dammit, she was so out of shape, had never been this weak before, this unable to keep up.

She was jealous of his conditioning, that both his physical and mental strength seemed endless, while hers appeared to be sliding away.

She'd been fine until he arrived . . . or at least she'd gotten really good at pretending.

Now there was no more fooling herself. She was in trouble.

She *was* trouble.

Zane didn't let her inner pity party go on for long before he pushed her to the ground without warning and lay on top of her. Facedown, he lightly covered her mouth to remind her to quiet her breathing.

She squeezed her eyes shut as she waited, aware she was trembling. And then she heard muffled shouts, footsteps. How many men, she couldn't be sure, and she stayed under Zane, his heart beating against her back as the men ran by. And she prayed.

They remained in place for at least fifteen minutes. She'd counted every single second until things got quieter. Until Zane shifted and urged her to turn over and face him.

DMH has his picture—because of you.

She hoped for the best, that they were simply off course, but safe now.

She couldn't see his face at all to reassure her, and she still knew that they were anything but.

It didn't take long for Gray to get the intel. When Cael picked up the phone, Gray said, "Grab one of the computers and check your e-mail. It'll be secure, encrypted. It's a picture that one of the DMH guys had on his phone—a recent transmission that came from a provider in West Africa."

Caleb's gut roiled and he forced himself over to one of the two computers, jerked it away from Vivi's view and opened a new browser. Tried to ignore that she looked at him oddly, tried to forget the fact that the normally chatty Gray hadn't said a word, just remained on the line.

"I'm in," he said finally, clicking on the e-mail Gray had sent and saw the picture load in front of him. Fought the urge to throw or smash the computer—or call Dylan and completely curse him out for all of this. Again.

It was one thing to know the picture existed, but another to have it in front of him, made it too damned real.

Zane's face stared back at him from the screen. The picture was taken yesterday and it was obvious Zane had no idea he was being photographed.

Kid, you let your damned guard down. Because of a woman.

The same woman that had been throwing his brother off his game for six months. The same woman who'd also been captured in the picture, her face slightly more hidden.

"Cael?" Gray prompted.

"Yeah, I see it. Was DMH able to find out any intel on him?" Zane's file should be locked up pretty damned tight, especially from prying eyes of terrorists. But still . . .

"I'm sending Mace to Zane's apartment now to see if they went there," Gray assured him. "But you and I both know that if they were able to gather any intel at all about who Zane is, DMH is into the military's infastructure."

When Caleb didn't say anything, Gray continued, "Is Vivienne making any progress?"

He glanced over at her fast-flying fingers, the notes strewn everywhere, and he knew that although Vivi was trying, she wasn't nearly far along enough.

Which meant he was her protection. Her watcher. And unable to do anything to help his brother at all until she fixed the safeguard on the software. "She's trying."

"Keep us posted," Gray said before hanging up.

Vivi turned her full attention to him as soon as he cut

the line with Gray. "What's the matter, Caleb? Is there another threat? Do we need to leave?"

He hadn't realized how on edge she was, because her concentration had been so fierce. "Everything's fine.

He managed to choke out the lie, not caring if she didn't believe him, as evidenced by the look on her face. He logged out of his e-mail and turned the computer back to her before he left the kitchen.

"Caleb?" Vivi's voice was tentative; he didn't turn around, just said, "What?"

"I think I might've figured something out with the safeguard. There's another code buried inside that I hadn't noticed and I think I know how to fix it. I just wanted you to know." He heard her padding back to the kitchen and then she returned. "Caleb, is there anything I can do?"

He turned finally. "My brother might be . . . no, he *is* in trouble. Just the way he likes it."

"I've never liked being in trouble," she said honestly. "I'm sorry about your brother."

"He'll be all right. Has to be, or else I'll kill him."

Her mouth curved in a soft smile, and damn, his heart thudded an extra beat.

He'd always been about right versus wrong. It wasn't that he hadn't fallen into the wrong category at times, it was simply that he believed gray areas were things that hadn't been thought through enough.

In life, in his line of work, you needed to pick a damned side and stay on it.

He'd picked his side for sure.

When he looked at her, he noted her attention had been diverted to what was on the couch next to him.

He hadn't realized he'd been drawing again, tended to do it only in times of high stress, because that's when the creativity snuck out, when his defenses were too low to shove it back down in the pursuit of other, more serious goals.

It was on the back of a yellow legal pad he'd found on the table—a sketch in pencil...Vivi, in profile, hair falling around her face, her lips pursed against a pen she'd held to her mouth.

He'd been thinking hard about her while he'd drawn it, concentrating on the way the light hit her face, wondering what it would look like if he'd had any charcols with him, what he could've done.

Wondering what she was thinking while he'd been drawing her, spying on her.

Hell, you kidnapped her. Spying is actually a step up.

She was still staring at it, her mouth curved slightly. "That's really pretty."

"You are really pretty," he responded gruffly, wishing he could just turn the pad over. Instead, he ripped the cardboard from the rest of the pad and stood to hand it to her. "You can keep it if you want. Or not."

He'd gotten close, maybe too close...could practically feel the magnetic draw between them.

She took the cardboard from his hand and didn't back away, but glanced at the drawing for another second, and then looked back at him and whispered, "Guys like you don't go for women like me."

Was she kidding?

No, the look on her face was dead serious. "How do you know I'm a guy like that?"

She shrugged. "I just . . . I mean you're . . . probably beating women off with a stick."

Okay, maybe. But that didn't mean she wasn't his type. Or that he hadn't been about to kiss her when she made her little proclamation. "You know, I don't think I like being told what my damned type is."

She shrugged, her shoulders bared by the tank top she'd stripped down to. It was black and slightly clingy, showed off the fact that she wasn't wearing a bra, and yeah, he made sure she knew he was looking.

Jesus, he'd never had to work so hard to prove his attraction to someone in his life.

"I don't want or need your pity." She pushed past him. "That's what this would be, right? What you'd call a pity fuck? You probably drew this so you'd have a sketch of me to give to Homeland Security or something."

"I didn't . . . I don't . . ." Christ, getting his feelings mixed up in this had been the furthest thing from his mind. He sighed, stared up at the ceiling, then pulled her into his arms and held her there. "I don't fuck anyone out of pity, Vivi. When I take a woman, it's because of one reason and one reason only—because I want her."

And he did want Vivi, wanted to lose himself in her, wanted to forget all the shit going on around him.

CHAPTER
10

Rowan was still seething long after she'd started the IV drip of antibiotics for Julia and made sure the woman was as comfortable as she could be. She'd brought the rest of the family some food and drinks and then she'd gone looking for Doc J, who'd conveniently disappeared.

Again.

Missions of mercy, her ass. Doc J was a mercenary—she was as sure of that as she was of her own name.

None of this added up and the sense of foreboding was so fierce she could practically taste it.

The camp was eerily quiet—the family only added to the mystery. The woman was dying, dammit, but had come here, where there was limited assistance for her condition, rather than seek medical help in one of the larger cities.

Rowan's frustration mounted as she walked around the small area that made up the clinic, feeling oddly safe despite the fact that she no doubt wasn't. The .38 she carried helped in that regard, but the near pitch black, save for burning candles, gave the entire place a surreal feeling, as if she'd walked into a time warp.

She'd attempted to remain in her tent after checking on Julia one last time for the night, tried to read one of the books she'd gotten at the airport and had finally thrown it down, her mind far too busy to concentrate.

She'd missed dinner, but Doc J had left her some food, covered with *For Rowan* written on a paper towel next to it in the small kitchen tent. She walked along, balancing the plate as she chewed the rice and beans and bread. The food was better than most of what she'd had for the past years and it would fill her.

She was nearly done when she entered the main tent. The African woman sitting in the corner looked up and nodded when she walked in. She was sitting across from the patients, sewing together some bright fabrics, a small child sleeping next to her on a few pillows on the floor.

Rowan had pulled her hair off her neck, was as used to the heat as anyone could be, but still wished she'd grabbed a shower before wandering around.

She'd do so before bed—would at least fall back to sleep refreshed. Now she glanced around this main room. It housed six beds, three on each side, and right now two of them were filled with sleeping patients. There was a separate area, both treatment and triage room, that was sparse with amenities, but clean.

She'd learned that, most of the time, basic was better. She was a better medic because of the stripped-down conditions. Forced to use her common sense and rely on her instincts, she'd discovered that she could do as much good in a battlefield with a bag as in a fully stocked ambulance.

Now she left and put the plate back in the kitchen, washing it with the remaining hot water. It was only then, as she looked out the window over the sink, that she noticed the other building, unlit and partially hidden by trees, as if abandoned.

A combination of curiosity and boredom got the best of her and she found herself headed in its direction, her instincts screaming.

It was probably nothing more than extra room for emergencies or whatnot. At least that's what she wanted to believe. But something was pushing her to check it out, and she knew she wouldn't rest until she did.

Rowan knocked. Nothing. Didn't expect the door to be open, but it gave when she yanked. She stepped inside . . . and her knees almost buckled. Pausing, she glanced over her shoulder and then closed the door behind her.

Row upon row of weapons lined an entire wall. Add to that, shelves filled with ammo. RPGs. A launcher. Supplies that didn't have anything to do with the running of a medical clinic.

"Holy shit," she muttered, walking over to get a closer look.

She ran her hand over the steel and metal. She was no stranger to weapons, and wouldn't have been surprised to find a few here. But this...this was akin to a store. Was Doc J selling these?

Why else would he have this many? There didn't appear to be so much unrest that they would need to be prepared to fight an army.

Coming here might have been a big mistake. Her stomach hurt. She'd eaten too quickly, needed a shower, and now she'd discovered that this place was...what? A front for training mercs for hire to the highest bidder? Looking at this cache of weapons, her imagination went wild.

She shouldn't be in here at all, should get out right now. Granted, they hadn't locked it and no one had declared it off-limits to her.

"What are you doing?" a low male voice demanded. A voice that wasn't Doc J's.

She whirled around, right into a hard chest, her hand going to yank her gun free. Before she could do so, her arms were restrained with ridiculous ease and she fought the urge to try to kick away, because she instantly recognized that the man was trained.

"Who are you?" she asked instead, attempted to keep her voice level and calm—and nearly succeeded.

"I'm the one asking the questions, since you're the one breaking and entering." The voice was low—much calmer than hers—and slid over her like a cool breeze.

But he released her and clicked on a lantern, bathing the room in soft light. She stared into the face of a man taller than Doc J, with skin tanned golden and dark eyes that snapped with anger.

She'd never felt so tiny in her life. He was broad enough

to be at least two of her, if not more, and she was well aware that she was standing there, mouth open, gaping at him.

He wasn't as impressed with her, if his stoney expression was any indication. "I'll ask again—what the hell are you doing in here? This is a restricted area."

"I was looking for supplies so I could restock the treatment room," she lied.

"These aren't the kind of supplies you need." His hand wrapped around her wrist, a grip meant to hold, not hurt, and she put her own hand on top of his.

"I can see that for myself. Shit." She tried to catch her breath as her hand remained on his, because it was like touching fire, a shock to the system she hadn't felt since . . .

Since forever. Since 2001.

It was the heat. Her nerves. Maybe even shock, because there was nothing nice in this man's eyes, not the way he looked at her, but the attraction was undeniable. "Who are you?"

He pressed his lips together, like he wasn't going to answer, then said, "Tristan. I work for Doc J."

Tristan had a rifle slung across his body in a manner that might look careless to the casual observer, but she knew the man was anything but, with that weapon. His reflexes were sharp, his tone commanding.

Years of rules and regs, blood and guts, feeling sexless and oddly sexual at the same time while being outnumbered by men and under what felt like their constant scrutiny had taken their toll.

Tristan's eyes raked over her. She felt naked standing there, surrounded by ammo.

She also felt incredibly hot and bothered, like she should

throw herself at his mercy and then beg him to take her right below the AKs.

He blinked, hard, and she wondered if he was reading her mind, because she could've sworn that something passed between them besides snarling and harsh words.

Finally, his grip eased on her wrist and she pulled her hand away quickly, rubbed her wrist where he'd touched her, and for a second a look of concern washed over his face. At least it was there until she asked, "What is all this?"

"You were in the Army, figure it out, little girl." His tone was that of boredom, like she should grow up and deal with it.

"I need to speak to Doc J about all of this—I didn't sign up to work as a mercenary."

He laughed, like she'd told him the best joke in the world. "Sweetheart, you're not going to be trained as a merc. Trust me, we don't need that from you. And you need to stay away from places you don't belong. That's how people get hurt."

"Are you threatening me?"

"I'm teaching you a universal truth."

Just then, a stuttered cry made him turn his head sharply and she followed suit, to hear a woman's scream, followed by a child's. They were calling to someone, using the local language, which she hadn't had a chance to even learn cursorily.

But the panic in the calls was unmistakable and without thinking she ran in the direction they came from, aware of Tristan beside her, keeping pace even though she knew he could easily outrun her.

Obviously, he refused to let her out of his sight.

She skidded to a stop at the open door of the main tent, because the woman and child had gone silent, were looking at the floor in fear.

She followed their eyes to the dirt, where a puff adder held court. Slow moving, non-retreating and deadly, it was already rising, hissing and puffed out, ready to attack.

"Don't move," she mouthed even as Tristan readied his rifle. She had no doubt he could make the shot, but there was a better way.

She yanked her hand down and grabbed the machete she'd noted leaning against the side of the tent instead. Moved closer and lopped off the snake's head in one swift blow. Cleaner and safer all around, if you were willing to take the chance.

Calmly, she handed the machete to Tristan, who was now looking at her with a combination of anger and lust so pure it nearly startled her.

"I thought you were from New York," he said.

"Next time, don't think so much," she threw back.

"What's going on in here?" Doc J stormed in, looked between her and Tristan and then to the floor. "Damned snakes."

"I need to speak to you," she said to him, noted that Tristan's face tightened, and she swore she flushed again, head to toe, before she marched out the open door.

This time, she walked in front, forcing Doc J to follow her. Stopped several feet away when he said, "Rowan, I don't have time for your breakdowns."

She whirled back to Doc J, fighting the urge to hit him. "I saw the goddamned weapons. What the hell is going on here?"

Tristan had joined them, watched her so intently it made her even angrier.

"If you're helping terrorists—" she continued until Doc J held up a hand.

"I'm not. I was in the Army, Rowan. I love my country." He paused, and then, "Why would the Army refer me if they thought I was involved in terrorist activity?"

"Why don't you tell me, explain what all of this is? Because now I'm in it. Guilty by association."

"We service the locals and visiting missionary families. A port in the storm."

"You lied to me about what this place is."

"For you, this place is exactly what I told you it was."

"Then who uses those weapons?"

"The men I train and send to other missions around the continent." Doc J paused. "Rowan, you can't tell me you didn't suspect we were more than a clinic."

She had, yes, and couldn't figure out why knowing for sure what she'd suspected was throwing her off the deep end.

The threat of violence? The fact that it could have terrorist ties, even though Doc J denied it? "Why wasn't I told outright?"

"Because you're not here for that purpose. You're here to work in the clinic," he said calmly. "You can leave anytime you'd like."

"Now would be a good time," she countered, was surprised when he simply nodded and said, "Tristan will get transport ready for you."

Tristan.

"Why him?"

"He'll be the one driving you to Freetown."

She rubbed her wrist again where Tristan had touched her. Tristan watched her do so and then he walked away from both her and Doc J.

"How long has he been here?" she asked finally.

"Tristan?" Doc J's eyes flicked over to the man in question and back to her. "He's been with me for three years."

"He's a volunteer too?"

"Something like that. We served together in the Army. He came here after his discharge and stayed on."

"He's not friendly."

"No, never has been. I don't see it changing anytime soon." He brushed his hands off on his khaki-covered thighs. "I wouldn't worry about it."

"I don't plan to," she muttered with a glance at Tristan's back. "I don't plan on it at all."

Zane knew they had to hold their position. It was part training, pure instinct and the will to fucking live all rolled into one split-second decision.

They couldn't outpace the men for much longer, not with Liv barely slogging through the wet jungle floors. She didn't know E&E, and even with his help, she'd put them at risk without meaning to.

It was better that she hadn't known the men had been tracking them. Tension made people freeze and move clumsily. Imminent danger tended to scare the shit out of them. Adrenaline could give you wings, but not stealth.

When she finally became aware of the threat, her body went stiff against his.

Soldiers or DMH? He knew she wanted to ask, but would also know it didn't matter. Both were men with guns and out for blood.

An ambush was the only way to end this. It would be loud and ugly, but better than him going up against a group of heavily armed men. Again. Because two times in as many nights would be pushing his luck and he didn't do that any more than necessary.

But it meant leaving Liv behind.

He slid a gun into her hands. "Don't think, just shoot. And wait for me. No matter how damned long it takes, don't you move, Liv. Promise me."

She nodded as she whispered a "yes" and he kissed her softly, leaving behind a promise of his own. And then he turned and took off, before he changed his mind.

Immediately, he pushed Liv from his mind—ruthlessly bringing himself back to his training, his focus only on the men.

Looking behind him could get him killed.

But that didn't mean he could avoid going backward completely. No, he needed to double back, then circle around the route the men were taking—not nearly as silently as they should have been. He could hear their rustle, but he supposed since they had the big guns and more power, they didn't need to be quiet.

Or so they thought.

Working quickly, he emptied his pockets, because there was always shit in there that could be useful in any situation—duct tape, a staple, a wire . . . a detonator.

A trip wire wound around the detonator and attached to two bushes across a footpath would make for a nicely improvised IED. He stretched it taut, moved away quietly, and then he started to make some noise, because he needed the men to mark him as *it* and play follow the leader.

He shot at them—a shot in the dark, as it was, although he hit at least one. Took off into the brush and shoved through a smaller passageway, so as not to disturb the trip wire. The AK fire behind him had him moving fast, and these men knew this land better than he did. It was all he could do to stay twenty feet ahead of them, until they reached the trap.

The explosion hit sooner that he thought, slamming him to the ground, face-first. His forehead hit the dirt as the blasting continued. And then there was nothing.

The thrill of being closer to activating her father's software safeguard was nowhere near as heady as the thrill of being in Caleb's arms, or the small shudder that went through her at his insistence that she remain there, despite her protests.

He'd denied her earlier, but now that same hot look was back in his eyes, and this time there was no mistaking the way he felt. And when he brushed her cheek with his palm, Vivi moved into it, the feel of the rough, strong hand oddly seductive.

His hands were capable of anything—and everything. And she wanted them all over her.

She heard him whisper, "*Vivi,*" his voice tight, a note of pure want in the sound.

Feeling bold, she moved to press her lips to his, closed her eyes with the flutter of anticipation in her chest . . . and heard the click of his gun.

For a brief moment she wondered why he simply didn't walk away from her instead of pulling out a weapon . . . and then she realized with horror that Caleb sensed a threat, and it wasn't her.

Which pretty much derailed the whole safe house concept in her mind.

Slowly, she pulled back, barely daring to breathe. His eyes were trained over her shoulder and she felt him guiding her behind him and she gladly obeyed.

"We need to go. Grab what you can—get to the garage." His lips barely moved, the words hardly registering as sound, and yet she understood.

As quietly as possibly, she collected the computers and the cords and headed out to the garage.

Cael had already opened the door and declared it clear, which made her feel marginally better as she got inside the dark car and closed the door as softly as possible.

She secured the computers in a bag she found on the backseat, put them on the floor behind the driver's seat, and then she crawled behind the passenger's seat and braced herself.

She watched the clock in order to keep herself calm. Five minutes and thirty-two seconds passed before Caleb was in the driver's seat, throwing gear over her head into the back, pulling his weapon.

It was only then she noted the cut above his eye and the bruise on his cheek.

"Caleb, my God . . . are you okay?"

"Fine. I'm fine." The words were ground out in a decidedly *not fine* manner, but he was talking. Breathing. Angry.

Considering the situation, all good signs. But it meant

that there had been men already inside the house, which was not.

"Do you know how to shoot?" he asked her. "Be honest."

"My father believed strongly in the right to bear arms."

He handed her a Sig Sauer, the metal cool against her sweaty palm. "I don't think you'll need it now, but just be ready."

She nodded, throat too dry to trust.

"We're out of here." He gunned the engine, jerking the wheel, and she felt the truck skim along the side of another vehicle, which must've been attempting to block them in.

She didn't want to think about what a close call it was—because they weren't out of the mess yet.

The squeal of tires, the long scraping sound of metal crunching against metal again, and suddenly the resistance she'd felt was gone—the back of the truck fishtailed and they were free . . . moving fast enough to make her stomach lurch.

"You okay?" he asked, and she nodded before he turned his attention back to the road. "Stay down for a little while, let me make sure we're in the clear."

"They had to find us through the IP," she said, more to herself than to Caleb.

"It's protected."

"Who knows where we were?"

"My CO. My team." He was dialing Gray as he spoke. "Gray, we were found. What the hell happened?" He listened for a while—a long while—and her stomach twisted as she watched him grip the steering wheel so hard his knuckles turned white.

He muttered a few choice words from time to time,

asked, "What else?" several times, but she didn't get any other information from his side of the conversation.

When he finally hung up, he remained silent for ten long minutes—she knew because she watched the clock on the dash with a growing sense of dread.

"Gray thinks our post security was hacked. They got in and looked into safe-house security. Got the address. Saw the lights go on, so to speak."

"You think it's part of this whole DMH thing?" she asked, and he nodded.

"If they've got someone on the inside watching safe houses, they know when one's in use. It was like shooting fish in a barrel." He glanced in the rearview mirror and realized that blood was dripping down his forehead to his cheek. "Shit."

"Here, let me." She climbed into the passenger's seat, ignoring his earlier order to stay down. She wet a paper towel with bottled water and then pressed it gently to his forehead, making sure not to block his vision. She held it there for a few minutes until the bleeding seemed to stop and then she dug into the first-aid kit he'd told her was in the glove compartment and found a butterfly bandage.

"Thanks," he said as she returned to the backseat. "Listen, my guys ran the names you gave me. The first two guys checked out fine. But Dale—one of my teammates checked on him, and he hasn't been seen for a couple of weeks. Not by his landlord or anyone at the college. He's not answering his cell and his apartment's pretty bare."

Her heart sank. Could she be responsible for something happening to him? "So he disappeared, like the lawyers?"

"Can't be sure of a connection. Is there anything else

you can tell me about him? Does he have another house? What about his parents?"

She tried to think back on what she knew of Dale—to see if she could use twenty-twenty hindsight to discover any clues he might've unwittingly left her. "I don't know anything about him, really. He said his parents had been killed in an accident on a dig. His father was also an archeologist—his mom just followed him to help with the recording and the paperwork associated with his finds. He said he was an only child. And he loved poker—he played twice a month, some really big game with friends of his from childhood. I never met them, though. But these were serious games—high stakes. He loved playing, said he was really good. I know he hated to lose."

Cael glanced at her and then back at the road. "Who doesn't?"

Ace didn't give anything away when his cards were dealt because he hated losing more than anything else on earth, be it poker or business.

DMH was born at a poker table much like this one, so the weekly games continued to this day. Part game, part meeting; many secrets were revealed at the table—and they did not leave it.

But now, the newest empty seat mocked them, highlighted their failures.

First Jones, a man who'd been with DMH from the start, who was killed by a member of the elite Delta Force, a man named Kell Roberts, last year. And then Kieran, who'd been too young and green to be invited to the table, but who'd had a damned promising future and a brass set of balls.

Either they were getting sloppy or the military operations were getting better. Technology was DMH's best friend and worst enemy as it grew bigger.

It could easily be their downfall if Ace couldn't get Vivienne under control . . . or terminated.

"Are you in?" Elijah snapped his fingers and Ace fought the urge to reach across and break his wrist.

"Always."

Cards were dealt and now was the time for concentration.

The blind risk. It was Ace's favorite move because it tended to throw the others off their game, but these men knew him too well to try it too often. Elijah was hesitating, his dyslexia getting the better of him, the way it did when stress was high.

Ace tried to temper his impatience with Elijah and his well-hidden disability, but the chink in the man's armor had always been obvious—and a source of great worry— to Ace.

He'd put everything on the line for this organization, lived life undercover in the States for six months setting up his new life, and another six dating Vivienne Clare after her father died. He left himself open to the possibility of being spotted and seized by various organizations, including Homeland Security, while she attempted to finish the program he needed.

When it became apparent she wouldn't be able to, he'd had no choice but to steal it out from under her. That was a month ago, and he still hadn't been able to get rid of the safeguard.

"You've never gotten over the fact that Vivienne was smarter than you," Elijah said.

Ace didn't let his expression change, but Elijah would still know he was seething. It was the benefit—and the problem—of having grown up with the man.

They could take each other down in the space of mere hours. The only thing stopping them was the fact that DMH and its success hinged on both of them functioning together. Each man sitting at this table held a card the others didn't know about—it would take all of them putting in their codes into the computer at the same exact time to unlock things like bank accounts and other private information.

A safeguard of their own set in place so neither Elijah nor Ace nor the others would get too big for their britches—and to make sure they couldn't unseat one another without exposing DMH.

Keeping it true to the cause, they'd said when they'd decided to take DMH overseas, away from the constraints of the U.S. government.

Already, the buzzards circled. Smaller terrorist groups who wanted more than their share of the pie.

Getting bigger meant attracting more attention from everyone—FBI, CIA, Interpol, the military.

"How is the security program?" Elijah asked finally, in the middle of a hand, in order to throw Ace.

"We're still working through the safeguard."

"You should've taken her at the same time you took the software," Elijah said flatly.

Of course Elijah was right, but Ace did not want to involve yet another female—another female prisoner in DMH. After what happened with Olivia, they realized that women were far too big a risk, far more resourceful than either man had given them credit for. Besides, there was no guarantee Vivienne would've agreed to help him fix the program, if she even could.

She would be an asset to DMH if she weren't so damned honest. He'd assumed, wrongly, that she had more than a little of her late father's conspiracy theorist inside of her, that she would be interested in helping DMH eventually. That he could turn her.

He'd barely been able to get her from frigid to warm in bed, and he'd given up on everything else. The fact that he couldn't figure out how to finish her father's program and fix the safeguard situation made him even angrier. "I'll get her back."

"How?" Elijah's eyes were heavy-lidded—the man always looked like he was resting, but Ace knew that would be severely underestimating the man he'd once called friend.

"I've got men on it."

"We've both screwed up..." Elijah started, and Ace could only nod and fold his hand. "We need more money," he continued, with a finality that indicated the topic would soon be closed. "With the loss of the Morocco clinic, we've been compromised. Going forward, I refuse to let DMH depend on the damned winds of fortune and on every terrorist intent on jihad. We want them to come to us, not the other way around. I didn't bring DMH this far to have it dependent on others. Now is the time to make the move toward total independence, to show the other organizations that we're the ones to come to if they need help."

"It's already blown up in our face, so to speak," Ace reminded him. "I've taken partial responsibility—I will get Vivienne. I've also hacked into the medical databases we need, but it's not going to be as easy as you think."

"It never is," Elijah agreed, put down his spread of cards to expose a winning hand. "It never is."

Olivia waited, holding her breath for long intervals, out of both fear and necessity. It was so quiet—too much so, at a time when it shouldn't be.

Again, Zane had left her alone, melting into the jungle with ease. Again, there were men after her.

This situation would repeat itself over and over until DMH was stopped. Or until she was dead.

And if this was because she'd saved a baby.... how could she regret that?

The air was thick, the humidity worse now that they were closer to the sea. She wanted to take in a deep breath but her lungs felt like wet rags.

She wiped her palm on the inside of her shirt and did the same with the butt of the Sig, moving it out of position for mere seconds.

Her grip was too hard. She loosened it a little, told herself to concentrate.

Her senses should've been dulled by fatigue and fear, but instead, everything was heightened. Fear ate at her... the thought of being alone again erased her calm, until her emotions were frayed beyond the point of quick repair. All the emotion she'd been forced to shove down for the past months was rising to the surface.

Shitty timing, she had to admit. She brushed the tears impatiently from her cheeks with the back of her free hand, the other still clutching the gun, pointed in the direction Zane told her to.

Zane. His face flashed before hers, those blue eyes holding secrets of their own, deeper than those of the all-American boy he resembled. There was something harder about his face, sharper in his expression. Maybe it had to do with the military training, and maybe not.

She continued to wait, shifted as quietly as she could, the pins and needles in her legs driving her crazy, the silence more so.

And then the burst of gunfire, which made her wish for silence.

Yelling. Shots. Smoke.

Her heart beat fast, her eyes watered and her mouth went dry. She jumped at an explosion—too close for comfort. The ground shook beneath her for a brief moment and she remembered too late to cover her ears.

She held the gun tight, pointed outward to face a still-invisible enemy. Waited so long that she felt sore. Her head throbbed from tension.

Earlier, she'd wanted nothing more than Zane gone. Now she waited for his return with rabid intensity.

She wouldn't hear him come back if he did. *When* he did. All she could do was sit tight. Be helpless, again.

She wondered if there would ever be a time she actually felt in control—or actually would be—and realized that it wasn't going to happen for the foreseeable future.

She counted the seconds because it was all she could do. When she realized it had been nearly half an hour of silence, panic set in. She smelled smoke, heard groaning—or maybe it was her imagination, or an animal, but all she could think of was Zane hurt and she was sitting here doing nothing, when she could be helping.

He told you not to move.

Yes, well, she'd been told a lot of things in her life. Didn't mean she'd listened to all of them.

Crawling out of the brush, she could barely see her hand in front of her face. She put the safety on the gun because she was so jumpy, she didn't want it going off accidentally. Hands stretched out in front of her, she began to walk in the direction of the smoke, bumping into trees she feared were people, tripping . . . and then she realized just how turned around she was.

Stupid. She was stupid for moving. But she had to find him . . . Did she dare call his name?

No.

God, what if she was alone here? She choked back a sob—barely—turned in a desperate attempt to backtrack, when a hand clamped over her mouth, arms held her tight, and she cursed herself for not thinking about watching her back.

She slammed her elbow back hard once, again, flailing against the person who held her. And then the ground seemed to give way under her feet. She heard Zane's muffled curse as they went down together.

They rolled at a sickeningly fast pace, a tangle of arms and legs, his body absorbing most of the impact. The fact that she couldn't see anything made it all that much worse and the dizzying spins wouldn't stop.

Somehow, Zane managed to shift them so they were no longer rolling but traveling legs-first down the hill. When they hit bottom, his feet stopped them hard, while they remained holding each other tight.

She could barely breathe.

"Liv, you all right?" he whispered against her ear. She couldn't speak if she'd wanted to, so she nodded and hoped he could tell.

"Catch your breath," he continued, gave her a few more minutes to do so, and then pulled her away from him the face. "Are you hurt? Anything broken?"

"No, I think I'm okay," she whispered. She would be sore as anything tomorrow, as she already ached, but mercifully, all her bones seemed intact. "Oh my God, the gun . . ."

She felt for it where she'd shoved it in her pants, but Zane's hand was already there, taking it away from her.

When he spoke again, his voice lost the edge of gentleness and became full-on steel. "You're lucky it didn't go off and kill us both. Dammit. What happened to don't move until I get back?"

"I thought you were hurt, I wanted to help."

He cursed softly—a string of them put together; they would've sounded fluent and beautiful, if only they weren't directed at her behavior. "Look, I know you think you're, like, Super Doctor, able to leap tall buildings and survive all alone out here, but I've been doing this a little longer than you. When I say stay put, I mean it. Out here, I'm in charge, and you need to listen to stay alive. Got it?"

He hauled her to a full standing position and she processed his words for a minute, felt the fight coming back into her body. "Leave me alone."

She jerked out of his grasp and nearly fell again. He stopped her from doing so with a strong hand on her arm, said, "Calm down."

"Don't you tell me what to do. Don't you even try. I don't need to be directed or forced." She heard the panic in her voice and was thankful for the total blackout as much as she hated it, because he would've seen the shame in her face otherwise, at the sheer helplessness she felt.

For all she knew, he might be able to see it anyway.

When he spoke again, his voice still held a tinge of anger. "I'm not DMH, Liv. I'm not your warden. I'm telling you what to do because I know combat better than you do."

"Stop acting like you know me so well."

"But I do." Zane's breath was warm against her ear. And while his hand eased from her arm, his body remained close, as if aware he was actually holding her upright. "I know you so much better than you think. You're scared as hell, and you're strong, but right now I wouldn't trust you to tell me which way is up because you're so damned turned around."

She attempted to struggle away from him but couldn't—he held her fast against him. She was shaking, her anger not softening in the least. Irrational maybe, but that's the way it happened these days—it was always unexpected. "Let me go, Zane."

"I would, if you really wanted me to." His arousal pressed against her hip and she realized that she was somehow, inexplicably, turned on, despite everything else at the moment.

The pull this man exerted over her was incredible, despite her best efforts to throw him off track and push him away. Tenacity and intelligence fueled him, and she let his free hand roam between them until it stopped at the front of her pants. "I want you to."

"And I want you to trust me."

"I can only trust myself." She instantly regretted the words, but any attempt to take them back would be futile.

Besides, he already knew, judging from his next words, which were a rough growl against her cheek. "I know you think I'm some fucking pathetic puppy dog, following you around, believing whatever you say, taking you wherever you want to go, but there's a hell of a lot you don't know. And you're severely overestimating my damned patience."

The hard column of his sex thrusted against her, as hard as his voice sounded, and it all made her shudder with need. She wondered if he wanted her to beg, couldn't read his face, and so she attempted to read him with her hands. Traced his lips with her fingers, let them flutter along his cheekbones, across his nape, while he remained rock steady in front of her.

She never should've agreed to his plan, should've taken off on her own.

You never would've made it out of the jungle alive.

Ten minutes ago, she was worried for both their lives—and now he was safe and in front of her. And pissed, but so was she. And somehow she still couldn't help the way she melted to him when his mouth captured hers.

She wondered if she would always relent this easily to

him, and then wondered why she was actually thinking about an always with a man she'd known for all of a couple of days.

"Mad at you," she managed, her voice breathy and not in the least indignant.

"So mad at you . . . so freakin' stubborn," he muttered as he yanked down her pants without pretense or gentleness—pulled a leg up so it wound around his, opening her up for him. To him.

Her mouth opened in a wordless moan as his fingers found her, wet and willing and ready for him.

They were out in the open, completely obscured by darkness. She could only hear the rasp of his breath close to her ear, could only concentrate on the touch of rough fingertips circling her sex, playing the swollen bundle of nerves with just enough pressure to make her squirm wantonly against him.

The aches and pains from the fall faded as he braced her against a tree, her shirt providing protection against its roughness.

She wondered if he knew she was desperately trying to see his face, to make sure it was still him, which was so silly, because she recognized the touches, his scent, all threatening to bring her to that sharp edge of pleasure right here, on what seemed to be the edge of the earth.

There was something about the jungle that made everything more sensuous, more dangerous. Zane was equal parts of both, about to take her in the middle of nowhere, and she willingly relented.

"Zane, please . . ."

"Please what?" he asked, his voice still fraught with anger.

"Please take me. Here. Now."

"Like I was going to give you the choice," he growled again, and at his words, her blood ran desperately hot.

He was inside her then, sheathed by her sex in one long, hard stroke—she was practically climbing him, her arms wrapped around his shoulders as his hands steadied her hips, rocked her against him in a fast rhythm that caused her to lose her breath again, although for a much better reason this time.

"You like that, little one? Like me filling you, taking you?"

She wanted to answer, but found she was past the point of making anything but incoherent moans.

"Take me, Liv...that's it...you're going to take me with you when you come."

God, he wanted her, all of her, and she got the sickening feeling that he wouldn't stop until she'd revealed all her secrets to him—and right now, that was all she wanted to do. Wanted him to know everything...wanted him to still want her, despite it all.

CHAPTER

11

Olivia held him inside her with the grip of a velvet fist, her breath coming in fast gasps against his neck. Having her back against the tree gave him more leverage to take her, pour his frustration and his need into making her feel good... as if sex could somehow make her trust him.

"Zane, yes," she whispered, the sound lost amid the high-pitched jabbering of the wild dogs that roamed in packs, the low snorting of the hyenas, the wild chatter of the monkeys above them, all of them signaling that the jungle was teeming with life and fraught with dangers he wished neither of them could comprehend.

Despite the danger—or because of it—she was slowly relinquishing her secrets to him, but this wasn't only about her. No, he'd started to spill his own secrets—and he already regretted it, was pissed that she'd forced it out of him so quickly and efficiently.

Why couldn't he keep it together around her?

A brutal hunger lunged through him, made his blood boil. Fuck, he burned for her, no matter how hard she tried to shove him away.

She didn't want him to go—he knew that—but she made him fight for every inch of ground he gained.

He wished he didn't understand that technique as well as he did. Wished that wanting her didn't make him stupid... wished he hadn't fallen in love with her somewhere along the way.

But he had. And her whispered words against his ear made his cock throb inside of her. As much as he wanted this to last, it wouldn't—not out here. He was too wound up and she was slick—tight and welcoming at the same time, pulling him over the edge as she came, contracting around him, squeezing him so tightly his orgasm slammed through him, nearly taking him down to his knees.

A desperate groan ripped from his throat and hung in the darkness as the orgasm ran through him like an out-of-control freight train, pounding through his body with a force so intense he lost his breath. He held Liv tightly, as if she was the only thing keeping him on his feet, his pulse hammering.

He pressed his forehead to hers, not sure what to say—if there was anything to say. Jesus Christ, they could still be in danger and he was buried deep inside of her, a woman he'd sworn to protect.

"What you do to me," he said, and immediately her hands went to his cheeks, brushed his too-hot skin.

"What you do to me," she murmured in response. "And I like it, Zane. I . . . might even be fal—"

She halted the thought but she'd put it out there.

She'd want to know everything about him—and telling her could be the best thing he could do. Or the worst. Either way, the cat was already too far out of the bag to think about crawling back in.

Zane lifted her as though she weighed nothing, carried her for what couldn't have been longer than ten minutes as light rain misted around her face.

He placed her down and she heard rustling, the pop of a tent opening and then the sound of a zipper. With a hand on her lower back and another on her neck, he told her to bend down and crawl inside, but she couldn't.

Instead, she panicked. Breath came in short spurts and the darkness held a million secrets, none of them as pleasant as they'd been when Zane held her.

"I . . . can't," she managed to choke out, her voice sounding thin and reedy.

"You have to." His tone wasn't threatening and she believed him, knew shelter was the best option now.

She pushed back against his hands. But he held her firm. "Liv, stop—it's dark, you can't run away. You need to go inside the tent for shelter."

But she couldn't see, only the black, gaping maw of the unknown in front of her. "Not . . . yet."

His grip eased a bit. He still held her but didn't try to push her forward. The ragged gasps began and she sank to her knees completely. His hands remained on her, more a grounding than a guide. Sweat beaded her upper lip. She hated this so much.

"Liv, honey, it's okay." One hand moved to the back of her neck, cool and comforting, the other rubbed her back. "No one's going to hurt you on my watch. Do you understand? No one."

And then she heard a click as he turned on a small penlight, used it to illuminate the tent in front of her. She bent down and looked inside—small, apparently waterproof.

Safe.

And still, she stood in place, taking deep breaths. Safe, and so small. A few moments longer, the rain coming down harder. Although partially shielded by Zane's body hovering over her, she knew she had to go inside.

"I'll be with you," he told her.

There was nothing inside the tent to harm her—she knew that, and still the logic fought with the panic that clawed at her insidiously from inside.

Zane's hand rubbed the back of her neck. She wasn't sure how long they remained like that, the sounds of the jungle echoing loudly in her ears.

"We can stay out here if you want," he told her finally.

And with those words, the fear eased. She smiled a little, told him, "I'm okay now. It's always like this for me at an entrance, and then I get over it."

"Why?"

"Because I lived," she said simply, knowing he couldn't possibly understand until he heard her whole story. She took a deep breath and crawled inside, the slide of the nylon cool beneath her palms.

She moved over as he pushed against her, heard the

zipper again, and then a low light filled the space. She rubbed her hands together, still felt clammy and not quite herself—but who would be in this place?

So many new places to enter in so few days—you'd think it would be enough to get her over some of her phobia.

She realized that the tent was under the protection of a deserted lean-to, not well built at all, but once Zane had slipped the tent over it, it was at least dry, a shelter from the rain.

"It's elevated, so we're in no danger from the mudslides," he told her. "We can't go farther now. We'll wait it out and still be able to make it in time. We're not getting picked up until closer to daylight."

It was just after ten—seemed as though much more time had passed since they left the safety of the small house. Lightning accentuated the low light, and it was only then she noted the bruise over Zane's left temple, the scratched cheek, the blood on his lip.

She reached out to touch his face gingerly as thunder boomed over them. "What happened out there?"

"Let's just say that my head's taken a beating since I met you."

There was a bump under the bruise, a cut too. She reached for her bag, which he'd piled up behind him, and he moved to let her reach it.

"Did you lose consciousness?" she asked as she grabbed for the antiseptic.

"Yes, but not for long," he admitted. "I've worked through much worse."

She pressed the gauze to his forehead. "It must hurt."

"I don't have time to think about it."

She didn't say anything else as she put a butterfly bandage on the cut and cleaned the other wounds. Finally, she made herself ask, "Was it DMH?"

He shook his head. "It was about the baby. They were wearing the same gear as the men who came to the house for him."

That could mean the baby was still safe. Most likely, she'd never know, and all she could do was be grateful for that. Could simply remember the happiness on Dahia's face and the warm beat of the infant's heart against her chest for that brief time.

She'd already all but admitted to the issues she had surrounding the first kidnapping. He was one of the few to see her pause at the entrances and he hadn't asked, had such patience when it came to her.

She was so impatient with herself for not healing more quickly, couldn't understand it. "I know you think I'm being unreasonable about all of this. But I can't be kidnapped a third time, Zane. It would break me."

"I won't let that happen."

He spoke so fiercely that she almost believed him. But he'd found the picture and the article, and he must have done his research after that. Read about what she'd endured. He had to know now that lightning could indeed strike twice.

"Do you want to hear about it?"

"You don't have to tell me . . . unless you want to."

"Besides the police, I've never really talked with anyone about it."

"I can see it not being your favorite topic of conversation," he offered.

She licked her bottom lip, thought about the psychiatrist's office. She hadn't talked much—instead, she'd drawn pictures of what happened, terrible pictures that went frame by frame, over a three-month period.

But she'd refused to speak on it.

She'll talk when she's ready.

She'd never been. "It was classic, textbook serial killer stuff. I took a shortcut through the park at dusk—I was late coming home from my friend's house and I didn't want my mom to be mad."

She'd done it before, cutting across the darkened park through the bike trails. She knew them like the back of her hand, loved running through them when there was no one else around, her feet pounding the pavement in her worn-in Keds, wind pushing her along.

And then she tripped, fell so hard her knees burned. When she looked down, she realized she'd ripped the already worn patches at the knees, which her skinned knees now showed through. There was a lot of blood and her eyes had teared up, but she bit her lip. She had to keep going.

The rag pressed across her face before she had a chance to haul herself to her feet. She smelled something—horribly sweet perfume—and the next time she woke, it was dark and she was getting sick all over herself.

When she went to wipe her mouth, she realized her hands were tied behind her back.

"I would've died if he'd gagged me," she reflected now. "I guess he realized that."

God, the fear could still cut through her, sharper than any knife.

When the trunk opened, she saw an outline of a man, but

it was so dark. She was happy to have some fresh air, but that was short-lived, because he grabbed her roughly and hauled her over his shoulder.

She struggled—screamed even—and the only response was a soft chuckle. She scrambled off his shoulders a bit, tried to stiffen herself so she couldn't fit through the open doorway, because all she saw was blackness . . . no way out.

The doorway to hell.

It hadn't worked, and she whacked her head on the side of the door frame for her efforts. And she was carried into the darkness, her stomach roiling, her head hurting so much she didn't think she could stand the scent of the man another second.

"Shhhhh, stop crying. He doesn't like when you cry."

The words were hushed, urgent, coming from the corner of the room she'd been dumped in.

"Who are you?"

"I'm Erin."

Olivia moved like a snake, on her belly, to get close to her. The other girl was tied to a chair, and when Liv got close enough, she could smell Erin's fear. Or maybe it was her own.

"We've got to get out of here," Olivia told her.

"There's no way out." Erin sounded exhausted.

"How long have you been here?"

"I don't know."

"She'd been there for a month." Olivia wouldn't learn that until later. A week of starvation, and things Olivia forced herself not to think about.

She brushed away the tears that threatened impatiently. She'd shed so many over that poor girl, and she wasn't sure it would ever be enough.

"When he took me into that cabin, I knew...I knew I wasn't getting out alive. And every day he let me live, I wondered, *Is it money? Are my parents not paying?*" She paused and pictured it, the dirty floor, heard the scamper of mice, felt insects crawling over her.

It had been filthy inside that cabin—the stench alone had told her so, but when the police showed her actual pictures, she'd realized just how bad it had been. "There was garbage piled everywhere, he was a hoarder...I guess people were part of his acquisitions. He was...spooky. Scary. Like, he was Halloween all the time," she said, because the nine-year-old part of her brain still viewed the man who'd hurt her that way. It was easier to compartmentalize him, to think of him as crazy and disturbed, when really she knew that people like him lived all around her without incident.

He never touched her—it was always Erin he took, and Olivia would try to hunch her shoulders enough to cover her ears. When that didn't work, she'd turn away from the sounds of pain and press one ear to the floor in a futile attempt to lower the volume of fear that accosted her.

"He would drag me out of the room a few times to read my tarot cards," she said, pictured the long hair, the sharp, beaked nose, the row of brightly colored cards spread like a ribbon of death across the table. "He would read tarot cards all the time—to predict my future, and Erin's too."

And on that day, the day that would forever stand out more horribly than the others—the days that simply spun together like a sticky web she could never quite extricate herself from—she finally learned why Erin screamed whenever she was with him.

Looking back, she was grateful Erin had never answered any of her questions.

He placed the cards down, one by one, as usual, never looking at her. And after the last card went down, he looked up, stared at her, his eyes glowing from the light of the single dingy candle.

Her senses were already on overload, and they'd shut down almost immediately. She was past hunger, past fear . . . past everything.

"This isn't right, not right," he muttered, scooped the cards up and placed them down again, then repeated that four times before saying. "No death here . . . no death for her. Not right."

No death for her.

It hadn't comforted her in the least.

He looked up at her again, his lip curled into a snarl. "No death, just trouble."

She stopped for a second, didn't tell Zane what happened next, didn't want to hear herself tell that part out loud, when he'd grabbed her off the chair and hurt her. Because in her mind, she'd gotten off damned easy. "That's when he hurt Erin—killed her—because he didn't like my fortune. And then I knew, when he started hurting her, the other girl, who'd been there longer than me, I knew I'd be next."

She'd spoken so fast she was out of breath, but that didn't stop her, the crescendo of the confession cascading until there was no way for her not to continue.

"And he hurt her so badly. She couldn't run. She could barely crawl. There was no way we'd make it far. And he would do the same to me and then there was no chance at all for us, and so I ran. And I didn't look back until I got to the small gas station two miles away." Her breathing was riotous, the way it must have been then, fear and adrenaline racing together—except this time, she was able to say what she wanted to, because she was looking at Zane, and there was no judgment there. "He killed her as soon as he found out I'd left. And so, especially when my claustrophobia rears its head, I have to think about the fact that I lived because another girl died."

The look on Zane's face after she finished speaking said it all.

Zane had been watching the entire scene play out in Liv's eyes, had watched her withdraw into herself as she told him the story. But now she was quiet, and he had to tell her she'd done the right thing. Because she had. "Liv, you were thinking—you were smart. Your plan was good."

"It didn't help the other girl, did it?"

"We save who we can. You didn't escape unscathed."

"No," she said quietly. "I took some scars with me."

She lifted her shirt and pointed, and he stared at the tattoo again, the dark swirls, the colors, and all he could see was a mix of colors and a pretty cool tattoo. "Come closer and I'll show you."

He did. She took his finger and traced it along one part, noting that he immediately felt the deep indent that wasn't visible to the naked eye.

He looked up at her face as she traced it again, and she saw the realization bloom in his eyes. "It's a letter. *T.*"

She nodded and moved his finger over a bit and traced a second letter with him. *R.*

The third, *O*.

"Jesus H. Christ." His voice sounded hollow, his eyes dark with horror as he realized the word *trouble* had been carved into her. "He did this to you. That bastard. That's what he did to you . . . what he was doing to Erin."

She nodded. His free hand clenched into a fist, but she noted he didn't move his other hand from her tattoo, simply placed his palm flat there as if he could magically make the scars beneath it disappear.

"There was no way to explain the scars," she said. "Doctors kept saying, *They'll fade as you grow,* but they didn't. My mom wanted me to have a skin graft, like the plastic surgeon suggested, but I had to wait until I was older anyway. And I decided that I'd get this done instead to cover it. Not for me, because I know it's there. I'd always know it's there. It seemed to be so important to other people that I get rid of it. I thought this was a good compromise."

"Your parents figured, out of sight, out of mind. And then you went and put it on display," he said. But he saw why it was her mark of survival, what drove her.

"I never told my parents, the police or the psychiatrist what he said about me."

"Why?"

"I told myself that it was because I didn't want to believe what he said. But all along, I felt it . . . knew he was right. It wasn't over. And if I close my eyes, I'm back in the cabin, tied to a chair, facing the table and watching his scarred hands work the tarot cards. Telling me that I wasn't going to die now because I had more trouble coming for me in the future."

"Liv—"

She didn't stop, couldn't, he guessed. "He told me other things too. Things that have come, true. I've lived my whole life trying to be about science and the logic behind it; I didn't want to let his truth override that plan. And as much as I tried to tell myself he was wrong, that it was all hocus pocus bullshit, a way for him to justify his insane belief that he was killing because it was all in the cards, I could never shake the feeling that he was right. And so I armed myself. Prepared. And I was ready, did what I had to do. And now you want to drag me home and I'm not ready to go yet. I need to put this behind me, come to terms with it before I go back."

Her tone was plaintive, her eyes glittered with various emotions, ranging from hate to fear, but most of all what came through clearly was that she wanted him to understand . . . and to leave her here.

Wasn't that what he'd wanted all those years ago? No doubt. Still, he was grateful that no one left him behind.

"Come here." He enveloped her in his arms, tightened them when the sobs came. "You need to let it go."

"Are you able to do that, to let all the bad things go?" she asked, her face buried in his chest.

"I'm trying my damned best."

"I fight and fight. And I'll be damned if that's not going to make a difference." Her voice echoed fiercely in the night.

"Running isn't the answer—you know that. You didn't deserve what DMH did to you. This isn't a punishment because you escaped, because you think you didn't run fast enough. You have to know that."

She wasn't sure what she knew anymore. The edges of her life had blurred, until all she wanted to do was erase the memories and start over someplace new, where no one knew anything about her.

Make up for the pain she'd caused.

"You've made up for enough." His voice was gentle, but it still startled her, because she hadn't realized she'd spoken out loud. "My past fucked me up too. Maybe together we can let it all go."

Could they? "You know everything. And now you expect me to say, 'All right,' I'll follow you to Freetown. And I've come farther with you than I'd promised myself I would—so much farther than I thought. But just because you know—"

"Doesn't mean you'll make things easy on me, right?" he finished. He didn't give any indication as to whether he agreed or disagreed with what she'd said. Simply kept his eyes on hers, his expression neutral, and she was beginning to feel like a prisoner of war. "Tell me something I don't know."

That I could fall in love with you. That a part of me already has, and damn you for that.

But she didn't have the courage to say any of it out loud, and so she said nothing, leaving their fragile peace somewhat intact for the time being.

Cael was drawing again. This time, it was Zane's face, although it wasn't a recent version. No, this one was aided by the memory of an eleven-year-old boy walking into the Scott house with the world's biggest chip on his shoulder. On his face, a mix of fear and bravado, all mixed together into the sneer he'd given both Caleb and Dylan when Mom and Dad had introduced them.

This is your new brother—he'll have his own room and you two will share. Enjoy!

God, that had sucked.

He stared down at the sketch now—Zane's face in the photograph from Africa retained all that bravado, but none of the fear. It was still there, but the man never let it show. Couldn't.

Shit.

Cael threw the pad aside, ran his hands through his hair and closed his eyes for a second.

He sketched whenever he felt out of control, not a feeling he enjoyed, especially when the fucking world was falling apart around his ears.

He'd been at the new safe house with Vivi for a little more than half an hour—they'd driven for three to get here and he'd made the executive decision to tell no one the location. He refused to let Vivi use the computers. Internet connections were spotty at best out here anyway but that had never been an issue before.

No, this was a family cabin, deep in the backwoods of North Carolina—off the grid and pretty much unused since his parents died, although someone had been keeping it up. If he had to guess, he'd lay bets that it was Zane.

Vivi had looked as though she was in a fog when they walked in. She sat down on the couch across from him, and the next time he looked up, she was asleep.

Too restless himself to sleep, he went to the kitchen to grab some food, even though he wasn't all that hungry. In the middle of heating what Caleb was pretty sure would prove to be a crappy frozen dinner, Mace called.

"Give me some good news," he told his teammate.

"We pulled some prints," Mace said. "Compared them to the ones Kell and Reid ran first. The guys who broke in were wearing gloves—they left nothing new. There were another set of prints besides Vivienne's, though. We didn't get a hit on them, until I sent them to our friend at Homeland Security—he told me they belong to a guy named Ace."

Caleb knew what his friend would say next, but prayed he wasn't right.

"Ace is one of the major DMH players. And before you say anything else, you need to know we found the fingerprints in pretty intimate places—inside the fridge...on Vivi's headboard. From the evidence, it looks like she was involved with one of the founding members of DMH."

He wanted to punch the walls, but controlled that impulse. Instead, he forced a deep, calm breath. Took some more, and wondered what the hell Vivi had been involved in.

"You still think she's innnocent?" Mace asked in a voice that told Cael his teammate did not.

"Yes."

"Cael..."

Mace hadn't spent time with her. His natural distrust often clouded his instincts—and granted, in their line of work, sometimes that was for the best.

But not this time.

"Noah wants her turned over to the FBI. Now."

"Then pretend you didn't get in touch with me."

"You're going against a direct order, for some chick who

might be involved with DMH? Jesus, Caleb, what the hell?" Mace sighed when Cael didn't answer. "You got any solid proof that she's not in with them?"

"No."

"I suggest you get some. Noah's going to want it. And don't let her back on the computers. She's done."

Cael was about to ask Mace when he'd started issuing direct orders, but before he could do so, Mace was asking about Zane.

"Beyond getting his picture taken by a DMH operative?" Cael couldn't keep the anger out of his voice, but both he and Mace knew it was masking fear. And it took an awful lot to scare him these days.

Mace was silent for a few seconds and then, "Someone's been in his apartment. Riffled through his shit—I can't tell if they took anything or not. Most likely, they're just looking to see if he's left Africa yet. Want me to tell Noah we need to go in—now?"

"Dylan's headed to him."

"Dylan doesn't have enough manpower."

"Don't underestimate him, Mace. He's got contacts everywhere."

"So does DMH. It would be a brilliant move for DMH to erase one of their own and let Vivienne infiltrate us to see what we know, to plant fake intel," Mace said, voicing what Caleb had been reluctantly thinking.

Yet . . . "There was no guarantee we'd go after her."

"Maybe they expected Homeland to get to her first?" Mace asked. "You still believe she's not working for DMH? That she's not a damned good actress?"

Cael didn't regret a damned thing he'd done up until

this point, knew that if you wanted to win it all, you needed to be prepared to risk it all. And when it came right down to it, he was the one who could get the truth from Vivi—and he would. "I'll take care of this, Mace. Trust me on that."

"With my life," Mace said before hanging up.

Cael glanced toward the bedroom and wondered how much Vivi would spill to him now that she was tired and secluded. Wondered how much of a prick he'd have to be to see if she'd been telling him the truth all along.

Julia was in pain and Doc J was dealing with other people who'd come into the clinic that morning, and even though Rowan planned on leaving, there was no way she'd sit there and not make Julia as comfortable as possible.

Despite her ire, she had to admit that Doc J was doing a good job here. They had a stockpile of IV antibiotics and shots and an OR for visiting doctors. So they actually were doing medical work at this camp.

What was she here for—her medical skills or because she could handle a gun, and herself?

Probably a bit of both.

Dammit, she'd dealt with much worse, hadn't been shaken. So Doc J's clinic housed weapons, and no doubt offered more than a simple safe haven. She'd been a soldier, used a gun, seen people flourish under the kind of services he was providing.

Why she was looking for an excuse to leave bothered her, kept her tense and irritable—and made Doc J steer a wide berth around her.

Now, back in her tent, most of her things shoved into her bags, she assumed that Tristan wouldn't be taking her into town in the middle of the night.

She'd showered after she'd packed, the cool water refreshing her, and she remained covered by the single towel she'd brought with her.

The feeling of physical need was an indescribable ache, a jolt of desire unable to be stuffed back inside with a cold shower or a good night's sleep.

Even an orgasm by her own hand wouldn't get the feel of Tristan's body from hers.

She'd worked among men like him for years now—strong, capable, handsome. Men in uniform who could turn a girl's eye with a smile and a nod.

But she'd never reacted to one on the purely physical level she had with him.

She dug out the small bottle of tequila, courtesy of Shelley, a friend she'd left back in Iraq.

For those days you really need it, Shel had written, and today was certainly one of those.

Shel had even given her a glass, salt and a lemon, which admittedly had seen better days by now. Rowan tossed that aside but rimmed the small shot glass with the salt.

She downed the first shot, didn't flinch as she welcomed the hot burn. She downed a second one just as quickly, and when the towel unwrapped and pooled around her lap she didn't bother to pull it back up.

To completely obliterate herself, it wouldn't take much, she supposed. It had been a long time since she'd gotten drunk.

She poured the next one, took a small sip and let the salt

mingle with the warm tequila on her tongue before swallowing. She licked her upper lip, paused as a slight breeze came through the opened window, stirring her body like a lover's touch.

As if she'd called to him out loud, Tristan barged into the tent, without a knock or an apology, his demeanor unchanged from earlier, an unresolved anger still burning in his eyes.

"I'm ready to drive you back to Freetown," he said, his jaw clenched, and she knew that had to be a lie—no way would they travel this time of night.

He stared at her bared breasts—his erection, obvious through his pants, did nothing to hide it—looked at her with a blatantly carnal lust that made her want to rip off his clothes immediately. And still, his eyes remained cold somehow, despite all that heat radiating through them.

She said mildly, "You're not going to try to stop me from leaving?"

"No." He hooked his fingers in his cargos. "This place could save you, if you let it."

"A place that trains killers." She shook her head. "And I don't know if I need saving."

"We all do. And we train men to protect missionaries and other vulnerable people visiting this region," he corrected her, the truth of his words written plainly across his face. "We do good things here."

"Good for you. But I'm fine the way I am."

He didn't argue. Instead, he pulled his shirt off and started toward her. His pants were unbuttoned by the time he got to her. Wordlessly, he yanked her up roughly by the shoulders, and the towel was history. She was bared to him, and all she could do was murmur, "What are you doing?"

"Saying good-bye." He dropped his pants. The only light in the tent was a small kerosene lamp, but it was enough for her to see him fully.

Then his hands wound around her waist, pulled her close to him, her body brushing his.

They'd barely said hello, and she wasn't sure if she was coming or going. All she knew was the feel of his mouth on hers, the way she gave in to his touch.

There was no going back. She'd barely been able to go forward, and yet here she was, the future naked in front of her.

"I haven't done this in a while," she murmured when he pulled his mouth away.

"I'll make sure you don't forget anything."

The laughter bubbled out then—part tequila, part pure joy at being in a man's arms again and feeling like she belonged there.

The laugh faded into a soft moan when his tongue ran down the side of her neck and up behind her ear, as if he was tasting her. His strong hands held her waist firm, his erection jutting hard into her belly, her ass pushed against the flimsy card table, which would never hold both their weight.

But he had something different in mind, sank to his knees in front of her, spread her thighs open impatiently, and she felt herself tremble as she anticipated that first touch.

She knew it would feel like a lick of fire.

His tongue found her wet cleft, dragged along her folds and then concentrated on the tight knot of nerves, sucking it until the tension built to an unbearable level. It felt incredible.

Her hands gripped the edges of the table, her body straining toward his caresses. He penetrated her with his fingers, his tongue. Her clit tightened and she shuddered toward release against his mouth, unable to hold back the near scream that erupted from her.

Her legs began to buckle in earnest as the orgasm shot through her—she was still in the throes of it when he picked her up and laid her down on the cot.

He stood over her as she watched through her haze. He was big everywhere, his cock jutting out toward her, thick and heavy.

The cot sagged under their combined weight, but she didn't care if it collapsed as long as he remained on top of her, spreading her open. She couldn't protest when he entered her, stretching her with a pleasurable pain. And then he took her with a brutal hunger that threatened her sanity as she continued to contract through the aftershocks. There was no way she could come again this soon, but a second climax ripped through her without warning.

"Tristan . . ." She said his name at least three times in a row, if not more, although she sounded completely incoherent to her own ears. It must have triggered a response in him because he bucked wildly above her. He jerked through his release, his muscles taut, a low growl drumming from the deep recesses of his throat that vibrated against her.

When his gaze met hers again, for a brief moment, she swore there was no ice in his eyes.

CHAPTER
12

She wants out the first chance she can. But first, you have another pickup.

Doc J hadn't looked happy when he caught up with Tristan earlier and told him that Rowan planned on taking off—a new record.

When Tristan slipped out of Rowan's tent now after sleeping next to her for a few hours, she hadn't made mention of leaving again. Why she'd affected him so swiftly—and so deeply—was something he hadn't stopped to consider last night when he'd stomped into her room like a caveman and acted like he was freakin' claiming her.

But he had done it. There was no denying either the urge or the act.

Shit.

He'd go grab the doctor and some guy who was protecting her first and then attempt to get Rowan to town by dark if she still wanted to go. If that didn't work out, she'd just have to wait until morning.

Or forever.

Jesus, what the hell was wrong with him?

He slid into the old Land Rover, which remained hidden from view of the road by the building that housed the weapons. The car had been a pet project, born of necessity; one he'd started when he first arrived, working when things were quiet. He'd refurbished quickly in order to have more reliable transport than Doc J typically used to go into the smaller villages, which were easier to reach than the town.

He'd gotten farther than expected because the weather held out and parts had come in, all a fucking miracle, he'd told Doc J, who'd merely smiled.

Whether or not the man's prayers worked—well, hell, Tristan wouldn't question. It wasn't worth it. But he did like to call Doc J *old man* to drive him crazy, because it seemed only fair.

Tristan had come here immediately following his discharge from the Rangers. No, it hadn't been that simple. Doc J had sent for him because he'd known Tristan had nothing at home to go back to. Nothing and no one, and that was the most dangerous situation for any man to find himself in, especially one used to combat.

He'd planned on the Army being his whole adult life. Counted on it. And when that rug had been pulled because he'd gone against direct orders, he'd shut down hard. Took a dishonorable discharge to avoid court-martial and all the bullshit that went with a trial. He'd allowed himself to be shuffled here by a well-meaning sergeant who'd felt bad that Tristan had taken the brunt of the punishment.

It had promised a lot of solitary time, which Tristan hadn't minded. He'd never liked making connections. Those he'd made during his early childhood and teen years had nearly cost him his life. When the military provided an escape from that, it became another affiliation he'd been uncomfortable with.

The training for long-range reconnaissance he'd received with the LRS unit had proved invaluable out here, and the solitary, spartan lifestyle suited him more than he'd ever have believed when he was younger and thought he needed the world and its riches at his feet to make him happy, to make him a man.

Doc J had given him a second chance—something Tristan knew he deserved—and he also knew the man would never make him feel indebted.

We're here to help people in need, Doc J had first told him.

Most people thought Doc J was deeply religious. Tristan had wanted to laugh at both the man's conversion and his assertion that the help was only in the religious sense.

Men of God weren't supposed to lie. Tristan guessed there were still some things even God couldn't beat out of a former Ranger. Furthermore, Doc J continued to hold true to that assertion, never mentioning to outsiders either the arsenal of weapons or the men scattered throughout this continent utilizing said weapons, who were there to *bring help and consolation to the weary and chronically unprotected.*

Yeah, Doc J could give a mean speech when he was

feeling inspired. And Tristan hadn't been inspired in a long damned time.

Rowan's last words to him floated through his mind now. *Don't think so much.*

Yeah, thinking was the last thing on Tristan's mind, thanks to her.

Jesus, touching her yesterday in the weapons storage tent had burned. He'd gone under the hose to cool down, stayed there for ten minutes, wasting precious water in an attempt to cool the throbbing between his legs. And it hadn't worked worth a damn, because all he could see was Rowan's face, a pretty, aristocratic blonde who would never look at someone like him if she were back in the real world.

She'd walked in all long-legged and blond and slim, like she could be walking on a runway or holding court at a society ball.

Not that he'd ever been to one, but hell, he'd seen pictures.

And she wasn't headed to a dance—she was here instead, dusty and dressed down... and ready to break his heart.

No, he'd been there, done that with a rich girl a lifetime ago, and it hadn't ended well.

He was nowhere near that place—and this world was too real for his taste most of the time.

So real that he was sure he should be convincing Rowan to get the hell out of here instead of planning ways to make her stick around.

There had been other women, sure. But not many had wandered through here, and none of them had stayed.

Missy had lasted longer than most, but for both of them

it had been much more about scratching an itch than having a future. She'd moved on last year and he'd missed having a warm body to lie next to, but they'd had nothing in common beyond their military backgrounds.

It hadn't been enough. Then again, what did he and Rowan have in common?

You know nothing about her, except for the fact that the two of you go off like firecrackers when you're together.

Who's to say that wasn't enough? She might've repacked her bags and readied to leave yesterday, but hell, she'd unpacked them first. He'd checked after she'd first arrived. His own were still packed, as if he was ready to take off at any time. To where, who the hell knew.

She'll heal and move on. He'd seen it happen a hundred times and he'd never really cared before as much as he'd been jealous that it had happened so easily for them.

We all have different paths, Tristan—some just take the long way around, Doc J would say, and Tristan would sneer, but secretly he hoped the old man was correct.

For Tristan, peace was always an uneasy level of truce in his head. The voices of the past telling him he wasn't good enough and never would be, the voices of the future telling him to move on.

It was the voices of the present he damn well needed to figure out, and they sure as hell hadn't spoken a single word to him . . . not until last night, when he'd laid with Rowan.

At least an hour had passed before Zane gently shook her, said, "Hey, Liv, we've got to go meet our ride."

The tent flap was unzipped, allowing a breeze to come

in. The rain had stopped but it was still dark, and thanks to his quiet yet insistent words, Olivia sat up and immediately missed the contact with him. She'd fallen asleep curled into a ball with her head against his thigh. It appeared he'd remained up and alert, his gun drawn. Her eyes felt swollen from crying—her throat was dry, and so she took a few long sips of water from the canteen he pressed into her hand.

She wondered if, one day soon, all the alloted tears would be gone and she wouldn't have to endure the gut-wrenching sobs or the smaller, uncontrolled trickle of tears down her cheeks anymore.

She'd known that sleep was a hot commodity and that had forced her to take advantage of any downtime they had. But it was more than that—the intimacy between the two of them had grown so much in the past hours, threatened to overflow the small space.

Threatened to completely overwhelm her.

Why she'd told him everything, why he treated her like none of it mattered, was something the logical part of her brain struggled with. She certainly wasn't ashamed of her past—she was a survivor—but she'd never expected a man to be okay with all of it too.

And either Zane was putting on a damned good show, or he accepted it, all of it—and her.

He rubbed the side of his head absently while staring out into the darkness, waiting for her to get herself together.

"How's your head?" she asked, moved to check his pupils using the penlight. Decidedly a concussion, but he presented fine.

"I'll be okay—this has happened before," he mumbled,

but he was definitely hurt. "We've got to go. No one's come through because the rain was steady, but we need to get to the road to catch our ride."

He slid out of the tent first, grabbing both their bags as he went. He seemed to disappear into the darkness and she crawled out quickly. He immediately rested a hand on her shoulder and she took a breath, then held the penlight so Zane could disassemble the tent. And then he dragged both their bags to his shoulders and took the light from her. "Ready to go?"

"If I said no?"

He gave her a small smile. "I'd tell you, tough shit."

She didn't know him well enough to be able to say he was kidding or not, but she suspected he wasn't.

Without another word, Zane turned off the light and guided her through the darkness. Her hand on his belt kept them close, and she walked through the heavy brush, refusing to think of anything else but one foot in front of the other.

An hour or so later, when she tripped, he shifted the bags to his sides and helped her climb onto his back and he carried her the rest of the way, stopping only when they got close to the meeting place.

He let her climb down and moved a few steps ahead to view the road. Then he motioned for her to follow and in less than a minute, they were there; an old Land Rover waited for them, lights and engine off.

Relief made her knees go weak. She couldn't take another step, even though maybe twenty separated her from the car. Dawn was breaking—finally, she could actually see.

They'd made it here just in time.

She should be running to the car—and the man with the rifle standing beside it, since they represented her freedom to stay here, to not return home with Zane.

Instead, she turned to Zane, buried her face against his chest. The things he'd already done for her...because of her.

For love, you had to be willing to risk everything. She didn't know if she'd be able to do that, but she'd already risked a great deal. As had Zane.

She raised her head and looked him in the eye. "I don't know who I am anymore."

"Your experiences haven't changed you—they've just solidified who you are."

If they could stay here, not face anything, they'd never have a shot. Could never give the fledgling relationship a chance to grow.

"There's never really been anyone for me...not like you. There's never been someone important. But now is not the right time."

"I figured you'd know better than anyone that there's no right time. If it works, it works." He stared at her with a gaze so commanding she shivered and then he motioned for her to walk with him to the car.

No one had ever pushed her like this. Ever. It both thrilled and scared her and she had no choice but to follow his lead.

Zane's back was up the second he met Tristan, had recognized himself behind the man's semi-mellow greeting as he'd given both Zane and Liv the once-over.

This was no regular volunteer. And Zane knew he was headed to a clinic that was anything but run of the mill.

He wasn't sure whether to curse or celebrate—but figured a little of both never hurt anyone.

He shook Tristan's hand, only to be greeted with, "You both ride in the backseat."

His car, his rules, even though it rankled Zane. He didn't answer Tristan, just grunted as he slung the bags into the third seat, then ushered Liv into the middle one.

Then he turned back to Tristan. "What route are you taking?"

"The fastest," Tristan told him. "I hope you got rid of whoever fucked you up."

"I took care of it."

"I'll get you to Doc J's safely. Just don't backseat drive."

"Don't give me a reason to," Zane told him.

Tristan grinned and Zane slid in next to Liv, who began to examine him like he was goddamned dying. She fussed over his damned head, which he had to admit, still throbbed like a mother.

But her hand was cool on his forehead and the air-conditioning in the truck actually worked, so all in all, not a bad experience.

"Sleep. I'll wake you, okay?" she told him.

It was an offer he didn't want to refuse, couldn't afford to. And so he did, in spurts, the movement of the car keeping his guard up somewhat, Tristan's music—hard rock—ringing in his ears. Liv's hand on his thigh...his covering hers.

More than once, he noticed Tristan glancing at him in the rearview mirror, once mouthing, "whipped," at him.

More than once, Zane gave him the finger, and Liv looked between the two of them as Tristan laughed at him from the front seat.

"Asshole," he muttered, closed his eyes again and mentally thanked the asshole for knowing how not to hit every bump in the road.

He wasn't used to any of this—traveling with a woman, having a woman taking care of him. He'd never made dating—or romance—a staple in his life. It was all sex and partying and bullshit and he'd never really expected more. Wasn't sure he wanted it, although he certainly held up his parents as guides.

Both sets of his parents had worked together. Lived and died together. For someone like him who'd spent so much time alone, the thought of being with someone for the rest of his life fascinated him.

The picture of Liv burned a hole in his pocket. During the time after she was first taken by DMH, he hadn't been around to help Dylan look for her. He'd had to focus on his missions, but he could feel her, never lost faith that she was alive.

Liv's parents hadn't thought it strange that he was looking for her so intently, that he'd sat with them, at their dinner table, listening to stories about Liv and looked at her picture and realized with a peace he'd never experienced before that he was on the right path to where he needed to be.

It was odd. And romantic.

Fucking whipped.

He grit his teeth and attempted to catch more shut-eye for the remainder of the trip, which didn't take long. Doc J's camp was maybe two hours from the ports at Freetown, yet it was worlds away. Quiet, almost peaceful, especially in the early morning hours.

It didn't stop Zane from scanning the area to look for anything suspicious, the sudden burst of sun slashing through his head like a knife.

"That's Doc J," Tristan said to him and Liv when they pulled into camp, nodding his head in the direction of the man in cargo pants and a tan T-shirt, with a definite military bearing, headed their way. Tristan didn't say anything else before ambling off in another direction.

"Zane?" The man asked before introducing himself to them. "I'm glad you made it safely. Looks like some trouble found you along the way. I'm guessing you won?"

Zane nodded. "Thanks for putting us up."

"No problem. Army?" Doc J asked Zane, who pressed his lips together for a second before saying, "Navy."

Doc J's lips quirked. "We all make mistakes, son. I'll still pray for you."

He moved his gaze toward Olivia, as if attempting to judge just how much to tell her.

She broke the awkwardness by admitting, "I know how Ama died. And why."

"Ama chose her path, knew the risks. She was a good woman." He paused, and then, "She told me about you."

"So my visit isn't a surprise."

He shrugged. "I can put you two up for as long as you need."

"I might stay on . . . for a while," she blurted out, and it was all Zane could do to bite back a snort.

"Like I said, it's not a problem." Doc J eyed her steadily and then shifted to look at Zane.

If Doc J noticed Zane's anger, he didn't show it. Instead, he asked Liv, "After you put down your things, do you mind taking a look at some of my patients?"

"I can do that, sure," she answered, and Doc J pointed them in the direction of a stand-alone tent.

"You guys can stay in there—sparse but clean."

"Thanks. And I can look at some patients right now," she offered, not looking in Zane's direction.

Doc J said, "Why don't you start in the main tent first?"

Olivia nodded and Zane watched her walk across the compound, the stubborn set of her shoulders making his teeth grind.

Whipped.

"So, this camp," Zane started without any pretense, because he didn't have any time left for bullshit. "What's the deal?"

"Missionary and light medical care. We help those who can't help themselves."

Doc J was damned good and if Zane wasn't born and bred suspicious, he might've bought the company line. "You're getting Olivia involved in something and I need to know exactly what that entails. And don't think for a second I buy that *We all have our own path we need to follow* bullshit."

"I happen to believe it," Doc J said. "Look, I'm in the business of helping. It's as simple as that."

"You can't help without funding."

"True." Doc J motioned for Zane to walk with him. After they got out far enough to see the road, he said, "We're muscle for hire, yes. But what you see here, this is real. I train the men and women who come to me—mainly former military—to take care of other missionary clinics throughout Africa. And then I send them with the weaponry to do so. The local government, if you want to call it that, doesn't know what I do here, they've never suspected that we're anything more than what I tell them we are. I even pay off the soldiers that come around a couple of times a year so they continue to think we're scared of them, just like a lot of the local businesses do. If any get too pushy, I take care of them and make sure no one finds them here. It's a win-win."

"I asked who funded you. I don't give a shit about the rest." That wasn't completely true, of course. Having trained men for hire in the vicinity possibly put them in more danger than they'd been in before, despite Doc J's insistence that it was done in secret. Zane was certain the soldiers were sent to sniff around the Americans far more than he was comfortable with. The only plus was that there would be more guns to fight with.

"It's a private company with no ties to terrorism at home or abroad," Doc J said.

"How do you know that for sure?"

"It's funded by some former Army buddies of mine."

"Mercs."

"They help me, I help them." Doc J paused. "The doc's not in good shape mentally."

"She's getting better. I'm trying to get her to go home ASAP."

"And you're hoping I can talk some sense into her?" Doc J raised a brow as he spoke and Zane nodded.

"I want you to tell her to get the hell out of here. She's in danger. She's putting your whole operation at risk."

"It's always at risk. I offer a haven to anyone who wants to stay. Ama was a good friend. You want Olivia out, it's your job to convince her."

"You don't understand who's after her."

"I know who's after her, trust me on that. Word travels fast. And, like I said, she's not the only one bringing danger here." Doc J nodded toward one of the back tents Zane assumed was used for supplies. "I've been hiding a family for the past five days."

Zane's gut tightened. "A family?"

"Mom, dad and two kids—a boy and girl, eight and ten," Doc J confirmed. "Tristan's going to get the kids to town. Would've already, but it's been crazy around here."

"Missionaries," Zane said quietly, and Doc J just nodded. For a long while, Zane didn't say anything. Couldn't trust his voice—or his temper. Because there were kids . . . as young as he'd been.

"Mom's dying and she knows it," Doc J said, finally breaking the silence. "Randy—the father—does, but the kids don't."

"What about getting her better medical care?"

Doc J shook his head. "Won't matter. She wouldn't survive the trip. I'm assuming Olivia will confirm that."

Doc J had been doing this long enough to know, Zane supposed, but still, he'd seen Liv work some magic.

"What about the father?" he asked finally, hands stuffed in his pockets, refusing to meet Doc J's eyes again.

"He wants the kids to stay with Julia until the end. He thinks it's too dangerous for them to travel now anyway— the soldiers have been threatening the parents with hurting the kids for months. They spoke out a little too much against the current government to a privately run newspaper, which was seen as incendiary, and now they're all wanted for questioning, including the kids."

Yeah, sounded about right. The soldiers didn't like anyone teaching the people under their control that there was another way, that they might not have to live under oppression forever.

Zane scrubbed his face with his hands. "None of this can end well."

"It ends how it's ordained to. The best we can do is try to do what's right."

"I'll get the kids to safety," Zane said.

"I can't ask that."

"You didn't," Zane said sharply. "I can get them to the harbor—I've got people meeting me."

Doc J looked at him. "Then what?"

"I'll get them to Morocco, to the American embassy. From there, they can go home." Zane paused. "I know they don't want to, but it's the best thing. Best if you tell Mom and Dad that too. Not that I give a shit what they think."

"They've got a calling."

"They shouldn't drag children into it. That's not fair." Zane heard the fierce anger in his own voice.

Pull it back, man. "Forget it. Look, I'll take them to Morocco. Get the parents on board." He turned to walk away, heard Doc J say behind him, "I'll try, Zane. I'll do my best."

Zane nodded, stopped, but didn't turn around. Trying their best was all anyone could damn do these days. Of course, doing his best wasn't nearly enough to cover the debt of those kids who'd been left behind when he was rescued . . . but it was better than nothing.

"You have to let them know those kids could be in danger with us," Zane told him.

"I'll tell them." Doc J paused. "I'll also tell them you're capable of combat, despite being Navy."

As Zane finally walked away, he knew the only thing left to do was let his brother in on the plan.

Yeah, and let Liv know as well. Shit.

He had cell service here, since they were much closer to Freetown. Dylan answered on the second ring, sounding less than happy. To his credit, he managed a "How are you" before he lit into Zane about not calling sooner.

Zane let him run on for a few minutes, because there was no real way to stop him, and he wondered if both Dylan and Cael still saw him as that feral eleven-year-old who'd come to live with them.

"... not listening to me," Dylan was saying when Zane refocused.

"I've got some extra cargo," he said. "Two kids. Going to Morocco."

"I'm not running a camp, Zane."

"They're kids of some missionaries who got in trouble."

He heard Dylan blow out a sigh, and his brother's voice was much less harsh when he said, "Fine. Just fucking get here. We can't hang out at the docks forever."

"I'll be there tonight."

More cursing. And then, "If I don't see you by 0100, I'm coming in to look for you."

Zane hung up without answering, wondered if he should just fucking stay here with Liv and see what played out. It would be easier than dealing with all the shit they both needed to face when they hit the real world again.

It was then he noticed Tristan was sitting behind him, not looking like he cared one way or the other about the conversation he'd just heard one side of.

Instead, he held up a bottle of beer in Zane's direction, and Zane accepted it, saying, "It's Happy Hour some where," and sat down on the ground next to Tristan, put his back against the building.

Finally, Tristan said, "If she stays, we'll take care of her."

Zane was well aware of how hard his hand tightened around the bottle, kept his eyes straight ahead as he heard himself say through gritted teeth, "Olivia's not military trained. And I don't think she's got a desire to become a mercenary, so what would she do if she stayed here, besides be in danger?"

"What are you planning on doing, dragging her out of here caveman-style?"

Zane was about to say something—or better yet, throw something at the man who'd annoyed the hell out of him for the past several hours—when he caught Doc J out of the corner of his eye; he was staring toward the road, but there was no sign of approaching visitors.

Then, about a minute later, a car pulled off the road and into the compound, carrying two soldiers. Or locals dressed as soldiers. Wouldn't matter, as both groups tended to use assault rifles, and to use them with an alarming regularity.

"I'll handle it," Doc J said, to both Zane and Tristan, then walked to the car. Zane glanced quickly over his shoulder, assuring himself that Olivia was still out of sight.

"They've been sniffing around more than usual lately, looking for the missionaries." Tristan's lips barely moved as he spoke, his expression unconcerned. It was all for show, of course, and Zane took the same stance. "They know we're more than likely to help a family like that."

"Will they search?"

"They know they'll have to come in with guns and a show of force before Doc J would even think about it. They respect the man—as much as they respect anyone. But holding them off for much longer isn't going to happen."

Zane took a sip of the beer Tristan had handed him as the time stretched endlessly. In Zane's book, patience had never been a virtue.

Finally, Doc J walked away from the soldiers, who hesitated a little too long before getting in their car and driving off.

"What's up?" Tristan asked.

Doc J looked grim. "There's talk of a reward offered for the capture of an American doctor. What better place to look for her than a clinic?"

"I didn't think anything traveled that fast around here," Zane muttered.

"You'd be surprised how fast when it involves money. And from what I'm hearing, this is serious money," Doc J said with a shake of his head. "And since there's also money involved for catching Julia and her family, they're not leaving many stones unturned."

"And we've got all the elements for the perfect storm headed our way," Tristan finished, then took a slug of his beer. "Clear enough for you, squid?"

"Yeah, I'm clear." Since both of his brothers were Army, Zane was more than used to hearing insults that were really more a show of competitive camaraderie than anything negative. "Did they mention DMH?"

Doc J shook his head no, but DMH had the kind of money to throw behind a bounty like this one. Zane wondered if he and Liv been tracked here. DMH tended to send in their men individually. One could easily be lurking near—he needed to make sure Liv stayed the hell out of sight.

Needed to get her the hell out of this place. "They didn't mention me, but DMH knows she's traveling with an American military man. I have to get Olivia to Freetown now."

Tristan looked at Doc J, who shook his head.

"No car available until Tristan gets back from his scheduled visit to the nearest village. The supplies he's going to carry today are lifesaving. The village is on the verge of a typhoid epidemic—saving them saves us as well. Besides they're watching. Leaving now is like sending a beacon."

Zane fought the urge to pace. He didn't like being trapped here but he'd been just as complicit as Olivia in that happening.

Doc J put a hand on his shoulder. "Taking you all out now is asking for trouble. Those soldiers will be hanging around for a bit. Waiting a couple of hours, letting them think we're doing business as usual will be to all our benefit. Besides, you fit right in—they think you're another one of my recruits."

"That's actually the best goddamned news I've heard today," Zane said, and Tristan clinked the neck of his bottle with Zane's before they both drained their beers in a small show of solidarity.

———

Vivi had slept for hours. When she woke, the blinds were drawn and the room was dark and she was pretty sure it was daylight but it was still disorienting. She heard Caleb moving around in the other room and she decided to take a shower before she faced him.

When she emerged from the bathroom, she walked right into him. He was glowering. It was a face she hadn't seen on him since . . . well, since she'd first met him.

Seemed like a long time ago. She kept forgetting she barely knew him.

She put her hands up to hold the towel in place but he was right there, hands on her shoulders, his big body hovering over hers.

He could easily overpower her—this was more of a power play, she knew; what she didn't understand was, why.

His look was predatory, reeked of distrust, and she forced herself to remain calm. She'd done nothing wrong. "What's going on, Cael?"

He won't hurt you. He will not hurt you . . .

There was steel in his bearing, and his words were ground out. "Tell me about your involvement with DMH."

"What are you talking about?"

Instead of answering, he took her by the upper arm and walked with her out to the living room and into the small kitchen. Grabbed a chair and shoved it at her. "Sit."

She did. He reached into his pocket and pulled out handcuffs, used them to bind her hands behind her, around the back of the chair.

This was humiliating. Scary.

There was no way out. The one man who she thought

believed her, replaced by the man who now looked at her with complete distrust.

Would he question her for hours, forcing her to try to remember anything and everything about Dale, a man she now realized she'd barely known?

He pulled her head back with a hand twisted in her hair, his face so close to hers. "Now's your chance, Vivi; tell me the truth."

"I don't know what you're talking about. I've been telling you the truth."

"We dusted your house for fingerprints. We found yours, of course, and your dad's. And more."

"Of course—my house was broken into," she said. "You were the one who told me that."

"Those men didn't go into your refrigerator. Or your bathroom," he said. "The fingerprints we found belonged to a man named Ace. One of DMH's major players. His fingerprints were also on your headboard."

Her cheeks heated with shame and anger. "If I'd literally been in bed with a member of DMH, I think I would've known."

He pulled his phone out of his pocket and showed her a picture on the screen. "Who's this, Vivi?"

"That's Dale."

He smiled, but it was not a friendly smile at all. "This is Ace—that DMH major player I mentioned. So I guess you were in bed with a terrorist after all. The only thing left to find out is whether or not you knew it."

She stared at the picture of Dale as everything came together in her mind. No way, no way, no *freakin'* way. The man shunned cell phones and never checked his e-mails.

Dale Robbins noted technology. But this other man . . .

Dale, or Ace, or whoever the hell he was, had been the only other person inside her house since her father had died, till yesterday. The only one. Unless she'd been hacked, but she would've been able to detect that. What she wouldn't have known was if someone had simply copied the program off her computer. "Dale—Ace—stole the program from me."

"So, your boyfriend works for the group who's rumored to have stolen your software. Or maybe *stolen* isn't the right word? Maybe you offered it to them after your father died."

"I didn't."

"Suppose I told you that we've got him in custody and he says you're part of DMH."

"He's lying," she said flatly. "If you've got him, that means you're close to stopping DMH, and maybe this nightmare will end."

"Unless DMH rescues you."

She swallowed hard, tried to read him and failed. "I was just trying to do the right thing—I couldn't pay InLine back, so I needed to fix my father's program. I had no idea it was copied."

Caleb leaned in predatorily, lowered his voice to a growl. "Your story about poor, little, innocent Vivienne is wearing thin."

"Why would I sell a program to terrorists?"

"Because, in the end, maybe your father's distrust of his own country made you vulnerable to DMH's reach. Maybe Ace whispered things in your ear, convinced you to help him. Maybe the sex wasn't really bad at all . . . maybe you liked it. Begged for it."

"I didn't." Tears rose in her eyes; her throat was so tight it felt as though it was scalded. "I didn't know who Dale was. I thought he was an archeology professor. We never talked about my father's jobs, or mine. I never saw him near my computers. I never saw him do more with technology than check his phone messages."

"I'm supposed to believe that story? No one's that innocent."

"I was. And I was lonely. You're the first man I've been more than remotely interested in."

He jerked back, his breath coming out in a hiss. "Don't."

"It's true." It was. And if she couldn't convince him, what would happen to her?

What would happen to her anyway? And the joke was still on her, because there would be no one around who would care about that either.

He wanted to hear something that would confirm his suspicions about her. Wanted to get everything out of her, wring her dry, until she was slack and weeping. She would not give him what he wanted. He was looking for a confession—a weakness.

She would give him nothing. If he wanted to break the fragile strands of trust between them, he could do it with one harsh word. And he did—with too many for her to count. He knew her entire life story, in far more detail than she cared to remember, which reminded her that the government had indeed been following her family since her father's firing.

"Please, I don't want to do this," she said, but Caleb didn't let up for a long while. Questioned her about her early years, repeated facts about her life back to her to wear her down, trip her up, exhaust her mentally—about her in fifth grade, still wearing pigtails, and again when she was ten, and then twelve, when her father lost his job and her mother left . . . the memories rushing back to her with a startling clarity, as if her heart was ripping open.

She was so exposed, in more ways than one.

"In ninth grade, you had a chance to leave your father. To find something better, but you didn't. Maybe you've got more conspiracy theorist in you than you care to admit."

Ninth grade. She'd dyed her hair for the first time that year—pink stripes—and she'd gotten an immediate suspension and an order to dye it back to her blond color. Her mom was long gone, and her father remained at home working on the next big thing. He'd isolated himself, his unemployment had run out and he'd applied for welfare for them, which wasn't nearly enough to cover expenses, but he refused to move.

Her face was wet. Despite her refusal to break down, her body had turned traitor, emotions overflowed, and when she opened her mouth, to her horror a sob escaped.

What was she guilty of? Would they go through all of this if she was innocent?

But she was. "You can't blame me for my father's choices. You can't blame me for something Dad did—for who he was. You have to believe I had nothing to do with this. You have to believe me, Cael. You just have to. Please. I'm so tired of trying to go it alone, you have no idea."

"And so you found a group to take you under their wing, to make you a part of their family." He spat the last word, and she shook her head.

"No!"

"You've turned the FBI down twice—once right after your father died. The second time, two months ago."

"Yes, because—"

"You don't trust the government. Makes you a perfect fit for DMH."

It did, for sure. Her skin crawled at the thought that she'd literally been in bed with a terrorist. "I am not part of DMH. Give me a lie detector test. Throw me in jail. My story won't change."

"Because you're loyal."

She laughed then, a sharp, biting sound. "I was once. I won't make that mistake again—at least not easily. When I was fourteen, a social worker came by the house. The school had given her reports that my father refused to come in for parent-teacher conferences. I was failing out of school because my father was retreating deeper into his theories, his paranoia, leaving me to fend for myself. I was working a paper route until I was able to work in a small shop near our house, where the owner was willing to pay me under the table. I didn't have time for school—I only knew that Dad was fading and I needed to take care of myself, and help him. That woman came into our house and acted like she knew exactly what I was feeling, said to me, *Honey, I can make sure you get put in a good home—a neat, clean house where you have someone who cares about you.*" She paused. "You asked why I stayed. It was because I was too loyal to leave him. Stupidly loyal. I risked everything for someone who would never have done the same for me. And I won't make that mistake again. Ever."

It came out more fiercely than she intended, and it hurt to say it, to utter those words, to admit that the isolation that had taken hold of her father still had her in its grips. Her breathing was harsh and tears ran down her cheeks, but she was no longer sad. The anger had taken hold and if she'd been free from the handcuffs, she'd be kicking and punching and fighting for her life right now.

Caleb stared at her, his expression still unreadable. "If you're fucking with me..."

"I know who I am, what I've done. There's nothing you can do to me that's going to make me tell you anything but the truth. And you've heard that already. I'm done proving myself to you. I don't owe you anything."

He was on her in seconds. "You damned right you owe me if you're involved with DMH. They're after my brother."

"I have nothing to do with that. I would never..." Her voice broke. She didn't want it to, wanted to stay strong, not weep like some shrinking violet. "If you don't believe me, that would be the worst. I don't care what everyone else thinks. I know how it looks. But I thought you were different. I thought..."

I thought you cared.

She closed her eyes to stop the tears, and when she opened them again, Cael was half kneeling in front of her.

"You're here without authorization—my career is on the line for you, Vivi. Do you get that?"

"I'm telling you the truth."

He dropped to his knees, stayed there for a long moment in which she felt as if her life as she knew it hung in the balance.

She didn't want the old life back—and if the new one included jail, or worse...

Finally, he leaned forward, rested his face against her thighs, his breath warm.

His hands came up to cup her hips. And then he looked at her, his voice sounding as raw as hers when he said, "Goddammit, I believe you. I shouldn't, but I do."

Relief coursed through her body, replaced quickly by confusion when Cael didn't release her.

Instead, his hand traced her breast—and she was aware of pushing against his hand, wanting more, not caring that she was still handcuffed, completely at his mercy.

It didn't matter, especially not when his mouth captured hers and then pulled back a long moment later.

"Vivi." His voice was thick, husky, unrecognizable from the man who'd been so in control before this. He was unraveling, taking her along for the ride. "I'm risking everything here."

His hand trailed the enticing curve of a breast—she wasn't big at all, but he looked at her breasts like they were perfect. Her nipples were taut through the thin towel and his hand sought the tender flesh inside the barrier.

When his fingers closed around a nipple, she started. She wasn't used to this kind of attention, the slow savor of her body, and he'd be the one to make it all better for her, at least for tonight. And then he was pulling the towel open, exposing her. Her face flushed, but there was a swell of confidence upon seeing the desire, plain and clear, in his eyes.

His mouth sought a nipple, tugged it between his teeth, rasped it with his tongue, and she arched toward him, the handcuffs jangling as she did so.

The sound appeared to bring him back to earth. He

pulled his face away and cursed roughly. Pulled the towel back around her even as she told him, "No. Don't stop. Don't you dare stop now. I'm risking everything too, Cael. *Everything.*"

He didn't react, looked like he was made of stone, except she heard him suck in a harsh breath when she said, "I want you to take me. Right now."

"Don't you say that unless you mean it. I already warned you not to fuck with me."

"I want to take it as far as we can go. Make me not scared."

"I'm the one who made you scared in the first place. Christ, I just handcuffed you to a chair and accused you of horrible things."

"I'm not afraid of you."

"I noticed. Why is that? Because most people are."

"How can I be scared of someone who saved my life, twice. Someone who looks at me the way you are right now." She glanced down, and saw the erection straining his pants.

"Once we start..."

"I'm not going to want to stop," she finished. "Please."

Dale had stripped her of her virginity—of everything, she realized now. And after that, she shouldn't want to trust anyone—ever. But Caleb, she felt safe with him now... and hot, and more than a little bit wicked. "There's been no one for so long... there's been no one ever like you."

"And you still think you're innocent?"

She nodded, because she was, in so many ways. "All I did was sleep with the wrong person. He used to tell me I was so innocent, he was afraid he'd scare me."

"I'm going to scare you, Vivi," Cael promised, his voice low and rough, his eyelids heavy. "And the last thing you're going to be thinking about is your ex."

He flung the towel to the floor, pushed her legs open as her face flushed, grew even more so when she realized what he was going to do.

His head lowered to her sex. The first lick from his tongue set her ablaze and she let out a keening cry, a sound she'd never heard herself make. She felt herself flush when Cael pulled back, demanded, "Tell me what you want, Vivi."

God, she couldn't...she knew, but saying it out loud..."Cael...please..."

"Please what? You want my tongue inside of you again, licking you until you scream?"

Her toes curled and her breath escaped in the form of a small gasp. It was all she could do to nod, to say, "Yes...I want that. I want...you."

His mouth quirked to one side and he conceded, burying his face between her legs again, the unbearable pleasure intensifying as she was unable to stop him from doing what he wanted to her.

It was exactly what she'd asked for, and he'd been right—she was trembling. Dale had never done this—no man had—and when his tongue slipped inside her, over and over, she wasn't sure she would be able to handle the loss of control.

She tried to move forward, but the restraints held her, bit into her wrists when she tugged. He was murmuring against her wet heat now, telling her how beautiful she was.

He wasn't the least bit embarrassed. And she closed her

eyes, let him splay her open more, jolted as his tongue danced along the tight nub of nerve endings until it was an exquisite torture, until the coil in her belly tightened...

Until she couldn't stand it anymore, and then, just then, her body let go with a ferocity that shocked her. The climax tore through her, blindingly white hot, and she slumped back, unable to focus on anything but the pleasure she felt.

She was vaguely aware of being freed, of being carried. And then she was on the mattress with Caleb.

"Let me take care of you," he urged, his body solid and unforgiving against hers.

She drew in a low, stuttered breath. All she could do was nod, because if this was what came from fear, she needed more of it.

Cael pinned her hands over her head as his cock rubbed her wet cleft. Watched Vivi as he moved deftly over her, her thighs spread by his, the flush of orgasm a fine dusting still on her skin.

He knew if he brushed his lips against her neck, he'd feel the nervous tick of her pulse beneath the creamy skin, and dammit, he needed to be put out of his misery.

He tangled his fingers in her hair, pulled her close as his lips sought hers. She sighed against his mouth, a soft flutter of pure contentment that cut straight to his heart, and he knew he was goddamned toast.

And he didn't give a damn.

Right now, a part of her was using him to exorcise her boyfriend and her past—and most of him didn't mind. But the sharp sting of jealousy told him he would need to erase all those memories from her mind—and quickly, long before this night was over.

He hadn't ever shared his bed with the ghosts of former lovers and didn't expect to start now.

When he broke off the kiss, he felt her trembling under him—nerves, anticipation, the bliss from the orgasm fading as she realized he would make good on what he told her.

Her lips were swollen, bruised from his kisses, and he liked that, liked the thought that he'd marked her.

Pretend it's her first time, treat her that way, his mind said, but his body insisted otherwise, wanted her with a primitive need that bordered on the edge of pain.

There would be no easing into this with her—he would take her with a fury that was threatening to scare him as well, the kind of fear that could drive a man wild.

And he wouldn't be sorry for anything he did.

"Too late to change your mind," he told her, enjoyed the stain of embarrassment on her cheeks, because it had been too long since a woman had been that pleased and innocent at the same time. Maybe never. "You're all mine. Any way I want you."

"How . . . do you want me?" she asked hesitantly.

"Do you really want to know? Or do you just want me to show you?" he asked, stroked his tongue over one nipple and then the other, enjoying the way her body surged up toward him.

Right now he wanted action, not words, and so her breathy "Show me" made him curl his fists and bite back the urge to take her that instant.

He'd already pushed aside any thoughts of direct orders, but not danger. No, the woman spread before him was far more dangerous than any firefight or tango he'd encountered, and the fear burned in his belly, made him burn all over with a desire he recognized and invited.

You're letting a woman lead you around by your dick.

And it felt damned good.

She was watching him intently. "I won't betray you, Cael. I couldn't. You saved my life. The only way I can repay that is with my loyalty."

Giving that to him meant more than giving him her body—he knew that, and he treated it with the reverence it deserved.

"I want you to know how good fucking feels...how I can make you fly." He licked a path down to a taut nipple, her skin a mix of honey and spice under his tongue.

While she might be innocent, she tasted like sin.

He saw the desire in her eyes. Her sex was warm, hot, and as his fingers played with her slick folds, her hips bucked up off the bed. A second and then third finger joined the first he'd slid inside of her and her mouth opened as he twisted them for her pleasure, but only a jumble of incoherent words came out.

He suckled a nipple hard as he stroked her inner walls, his thumb massaging the hard nub of her clit as she tried to simultaneously escape from his touch and move closer. He let her ride his hand until she was ready to come, stopping when she was right on the edge, her protests covered with another hard kiss, even as she struggled to get her wrists free from his grasp.

He let her hands go and they immediately wrapped around him, one on the back of his neck, the other sliding down to his shoulder and then farther, her short nails raking him, demanding he do more, and oh yeah, she was ready.

He couldn't wait any longer either. His cock demanded release, needed to be hugged inside her slick sex, and God, she was so tight. Her nails dug into his shoulders, the sharp sensations of pain biting his skin, bordered on pleasure as he sank into her slowly.

"Caleb . . . my God . . . please." She writhed under him as if to drive him in more deeply. He didn't want to hurt her but he wouldn't be able to hold off much longer if she kept moving like that. And while he wanted to lose control, he hadn't lost his mind completely.

"I've got to grab protection, Vivi," he told her, rose to riffle in his bag for his *never leave home without them* stash of condoms, rolled one on quickly and walked back to her.

Her hair, blond, blue-tipped, was splayed on the pillow, her body wanton and waiting for him, her eyes lit as they raked his body up and down.

"You're a hell of a lot less innocent than you think," he told her.

She smiled, welcomed him back on top of her with open arms, and he plunged inside of her, as deeply as he could. She arched against him, moaned incoherently and wound her legs instinctively around his waist.

"That's it, Vivi. You just hang on for the ride," he murmured. His balls tightened as he pulled out nearly all the way and pushed inside again, hitting the spot that made her cry out with pleasure. So much pleasure he could barely stand it, burrowing his face against her neck to breathe her in, to hear the groans vibrate against his skin.

He held her legs open—she grabbed the headboard for support and met him stroke for stroke, a rhythm that shook the bed hard, that made her moans loud enough for neighbors to hear . . . if they'd had neighbors.

And when she climaxed, she pulled him along for the ride and he came in a heated rush that made his legs shake and his mind go refreshingly blank.

When he surfaced, he realized he was still inside her . . . and still very much erect. "We're so not done, honey. There's so much more."

Her hands twined in his hair, tugged him to her breast, and yes, she wanted more too.

CHAPTER
13

Rowan's head pounded, her, body hurt, but it ached in all the right places. For a few minutes, she hugged the sad pillow she'd brought with her from Iraq and let the aftershocks of the night wash over her.

Tristan was gone when she woke, sticky from heat and embarrassment.

He probably had notches somewhere. As Rowan washed herself under the thin trickle of water in the shower, her head still throbbing from too much tequila, she wondered if she'd been one of the fastest women to throw herself at him. Too much of everything, despite the pleasant soreness between her legs that told her otherwise.

She had to admit, he'd satisfied something inside of her,

because that gnawing, gut-wrenching feeling of being empty was gone, replaced with ripe satisfaction.

Who said she couldn't sleep with him when she wanted to? She was a grown woman, with no one to answer to. If having sex with him was wrong . . . well, there was no one but her conscience to tell her so.

Right now, conscience was the last thing on her mind.

Okay, yes, technically she'd had sex with a co-worker. It was no longer against rules and regs for her, because there didn't seem to be any in this camp, except for *do whatever Doc J asks.*

Of course, she couldn't do that blindly. At least not for long.

She put sunglasses firmly in place to hide her bloodshot eyes and the guilty look she was sure Doc J could see in them. She was also pretty sure that if she looked at her own face in a mirror, it would still bear evidence of the unmistakable flush that only came from good—no, great—sex. But she didn't let that stop her from heading to the main tent and assessing the new patient who'd come in at some point during the night, an older man who was restless from fever.

Doc J was next to him. "Malaria," he said. "I've started the quinine."

She checked the dosage on the bag and adjusted the line. When she looked back at him, he had the briefest hint of a smile on his face.

"I guess you're staying."

"I'm here, aren't I?" She walked over to the cabinet and gathered the supplies with one hand, held them close to her body with the other. "Have you checked on Julia?"

Doc J nodded. "I was up with her most of the night. She's getting weaker." He paused and then told her, "We've got some new visitors. Tristan picked them up this morning."

"Are they sick?"

"No. One of them is a doctor—I'll have her look at Julia, but..." He trailed off with a shrug and she noted the look of helplessness mixed with anger on his face.

Good to know he felt the same way she did.

"You know, I was born a healer," he said without further preamble. "My mom was part Cherokee, daughter of a shaman."

"But you never went to medical school."

"School wasn't my favorite place. I wanted to see the world, you know? My mom taught me about natural medicines and cures."

"And that gets you by here?"

He shot her a look. "Usually, the visiting medical personnel, like you, get me through."

"Oh."

She wondered how much he knew about her time with Tristan. Wondered if she should care.

There had been men—other soldiers in Iraq and when she was on leave, despite the rules, because they were all lonely or horny or scared. She didn't mind when a few of them called out another woman's name—a wife or a girlfriend's—when they came. Their names certainly hadn't been on her lips either. Those men were nameless, faceless, interchangable hard bodies—mere substitutes for one man and one man only.

It was what it was, and hey, fighting it had done her no good.

"Why didn't you take the Army up on their offer of medical school? Or the RN program?" he asked.

"Why don't you worry about your life and I'll worry about mine. If we don't discuss our personal lives, we'll get along fine."

"This place—this entire operation—is personal to me." His voice wasn't raised, his expression didn't change but she felt the strength of his words blow through her like a hurricane. "I'll ask anything I want."

His smile was unexpected after those words. "You're a tough one, Rowan. I know that. But you don't always have to be."

She wanted to tell him that he knew shit, but somehow she had a feeling that wasn't true at all. His next words proved her right.

"I came here after the Army. I went into the Army to escape a gang war. It was the only way out for me, because I refused to testify against them, but I couldn't go on like that. It was senseless. And I was young and stupid—fought my way in, looking for a family. Now I make sure I give these boys—men—a way out." He turned and lifted his shirt to reveal an old tattoo that covered most of his back. "I was going to have it removed, but I'd always know, so what's the point? For me, it's not so much about escaping my past, but about moving forward. Are you ready to do that?"

"I don't know."

"Then be careful with Tristan. Because he might be. And he's come too far to have anything happen to push him back down again." Doc J tucked his shirt back into his cargo pants and gave her a nod.

Obviously she hadn't been able to hide her feelings for

Tristan. Or maybe he'd spotted Tristan leaving her tent—or entering it. Or maybe Tristan told him everything.

"Speaking of, why don't you find Tristan—he could use some help," Doc J suggested.

"Sure." *Great.* She pushed out the door without another word to Doc J.

How could Doc J have known? Tristan didn't seem like the type who would brag about his sexual escapades, but then again, how well did she know either of these men?

And why did she still want to?

Without really trying to seek Tristan out, she stumbled on him when she walked out of the main tent, must have been drawn to him as if he was a magnet.

She decided to face the potential embarrassment head-on. "You left without waking me. Avoiding the uncomfortable morning-after routine?"

"I'm not avoiding you. You were asleep and I had work to do, and that starts early," he said with a scathing glance at her, so different from the words he'd murmured against her neck, her breasts . . .

Her face flushed because she realized she was staring between his legs. She quickly shifted her eyes and he said, "Are you here to help or not?"

She'd been all but ordered to, and so she bit her tongue and followed him to the water pump. There were several empty jugs scattered around and he said, "We have to boil the water before we use it."

It was amazing how intimate you could feel with someone in bed . . . and how quickly that faded to the whole *we're total strangers* thing in the light of day.

Light of day was kicking her ass.

She stood, her head throbbing, and handed him jug after empty jug and he filled them, one by one. The day was rainy and overcast. No drops fell now, but the bareometric pressure was wreaking havoc with her hangover.

She could try, she supposed, to have a conversation with him, one they might've had yesterday, before they slept together. Or afterward, if they'd stopped the hot sex part long enough to, like, talk.

"So, how long have you been here?" she asked, because, hey, no time like the present.

He took a jug from her, their hands touching just long enough for her to know that the chemistry flying between them was stronger than she thought.

He stared at her, his body damp with sweat and still somehow not unappealing to her at all. "Long enough."

He had a knife strapped to his arm, but she didn't see any kind of gun, holstered or otherwise, on him.

He didn't need a weapon—he was one.

Although he hadn't said he'd been Special Forces, she knew he was, because she'd met men like him before. But this one, he was so . . . raw. Maybe it was because they were out here and everything was stripped down, but she could see the lethal beauty of his stance. Could appreciate the magnificence of him.

Wild and incredible. "Are you a missionary, like Doc J?"

He snorted and told her no, but she knew that, had wanted to see if he'd admit he was some kind of mercenary.

"So you're not a missionary, you say you don't believe in God, but you're out here in the middle of nowhere, working for a missionary." She crossed her arms, waited for him to brush the questions off, could already tell the man was a master at ignoring everyone and everything with that infuriatingly calm manner he had.

That had only come undone when he'd been in the throes of his own orgasms—she hadn't been able to take her eyes off him in those moments.

"I have my reasons," he said after a few minutes of silence, and then turned away, and she should've known. This wasn't high school and it wasn't the real world and what had she been expecting?

"Well, that clears everything up." She grabbed two of the filled jugs and began to walk them toward the main tent.

"Rowan, wait," Tristan called. But she didn't stop, tripping through the red dust, her arms aching. The tears were ready to spill as easily as the water that sloshed around the open plastic.

But he wasn't letting her get away, had run up beside her and was taking the jugs from her hands. "These are too heavy for you."

She let him take them, and then he told her, "I came here because I lost everything at home. There's nothing left there for me. I found a home in the Army, and then that was taken from me too. I have nothing except this place."

She almost sagged at the weight of his confession, because it was brutal and beautiful at the same time. Because it was hers as well, and because he'd told her something about himself. Maybe more than he'd admitted to anyone. For now, it was enough, and still she pushed on. "Did you find what you were looking for?"

"Sometimes." He shrugged. "At least here, Doc J gets it."

"He seems to understand."

"He's a lost soul himself, and that's better than having a fucking know-it-all shoving Bible shit down your throat, right?"

That got her to smile. She wished he had too, but he moved to continue on his way with the heavy jugs.

"I didn't mean to sleep with you like that," she blurted out.

"Funny, I did," he called over his shoulder.

She tried not to stare at him as he sauntered away but it was no use. Who could she blame? The heat? Her hormones? Stress?

You wanted him—it's not a crime.

She went back to the pump and grabbed a single jug this time, walked it over to where he was and ignored him muttering that she was stubborn and would hurt herself.

"I'm fine. I'm strong," she told him.

"Agreed on both counts," he said. "Are you staying?"

Was she? She hadn't unpacked yet—was still trying to figure out why the fact that this was a training ground for mercenaries bothered her so much...or maybe why it didn't shock her more. Time in the military had not softened her feelings about the need to serve and protect her country. "Yes."

"Why? For me?" Tristan asked, and she stared at the sleeve of tattoos on his arm, the way she hadn't given herself time to last night.

"No," she said. "And yes."

He gave a low snort. "Not a bad answer."

"Do you have sex with all the new people who come through here?"

He crossed his arms, leaned against the outer beam of

the tent with an easy stance. "Most of the people who come here are men."

"But not all." So she had an answer. Or thought she did anyway, until he moved, cupped her chin with his hand so her gaze met his.

"It was different with you, Rowan."

"Why?" she asked, because maybe he had the answer for both of them. Because there was no way she'd been able to figure that one out for herself.

"I couldn't not have you," he admitted. "Again and again. I knew from the first time I came inside of you that once wouldn't be enough. And I never thought I'd say something like that. Being with one woman hasn't been in my nature for a hell of a long time."

He seemed slightly annoyed by that and more than a little confused.

Yeah, well, join the club, she thought as she headed to Julia's tent. It was a place she was pretty certain Tristan wouldn't follow, and right now she needed that space.

Julia was dying. Olivia knew it when she walked into the room. Unless this place morphed into a city hospital with a full transplant team, the woman wouldn't make it through another night.

Julia knew it too, but there was no peace in her face. Angst riddled her features and her husband's, who kept the children occupied while Olivia talked with her.

"The kids don't know," she whispered. "I know you won't have good news for me."

"I'm sorry," Olivia told her quietly. "I wish . . ."

Julia closed her eyes so the children wouldn't see her crying if they looked over at their mom.

Olivia didn't understand why Julia was here though, instead of the main tent, why the whole family was crammed into this tent with a single window and cramped space with no amenities.

Unless . . .

A chill ran down her spine. If Doc J didn't mind taking her in with all her baggage, he wouldn't be against doing the same for others.

Before she could whisper to Rowan, the EMT she'd met moments earlier when the woman had walked in on her examining Julia, the door opened. She looked up to see Doc J entering the small space with Zane, saw Zane looking around the room, assessing the situation.

Granted, by the taut look on his face, he'd already been apprised of what was happening here and appeared to be in full mission-ready mode, and her stomach clenched because she wished she knew why.

She backed away from Julia's bed slightly as the men walked over, making the space even more crowded.

"Julia, this is the man I was telling you about," Doc J said, and Julia turned her head toward Zane, who'd bent down in deference to her.

"Take my children out of here, please." Her voice was still low, her words making Olivia's heart lurch.

Take my children out of here.

She stared at Zane. His eyes looked flat, his face devoid of expression, which was something she didn't expect at all.

But still, he nodded, ground out a "Yes, ma'am," stood

and left the room without another word to anyone or a look back.

Julia focused on Olivia now. "He's with you?"

"Yes."

"He'll do what he says?"

"I've never known him to go back on a promise." It was the most honest thing she could say, based on close personal experience.

Julie swallowed hard. "My sister, she'll be waiting in Morocco. Doc J got a message to her."

"I'll fill them both in on all the details, Julia," Doc J said quietly.

Still, Julia reached out, gripped Olivia's wrist. "You'll be with them too? Please? They need to leave soon."

Soon. That wasn't something Olivia had prepared for. But how could she refuse a dying woman anything?

She couldn't. But thankfully, Julia let her off the hook by closing her eyes and drifting into sleep. The simple act of talking had exhausted her, and Olivia knew the time for all of them was running out fast.

"Why would you help me like this?"

Ama wiped her forehead with cool water. "Because that's what I was put on this earth to do. No use arguing with the Lord."

Olivia wanted to make some rude remark, about God not giving a fuck what happened to people, but she bit it back out of respect for the woman currently keeping her off the streets. Literally.

As if Ama sensed this, she smiled briefly. "Doesn't matter if you don't believe. I have more than enough faith for both of us."

She had to, because Olivia had thought that escape from the clinic was the final move for her, wasn't sure she could keep pushing ahead but knew there was no way to go back to what she'd had before the kidnapping.

"You hide behind your work," Ama continued.

"You don't?" she shot back.

Ama took a sip of her tea before answering. "Of course I do. How do you think I recognized it so easily in you?"

And when Olivia couldn't stay anymore, when the community began to ripple with the rumor that a man was asking questions about an American doctor, Ama gave her the tools she'd need to survive day by day. Mapped out a route for Olivia to follow, gave her money. Got her a driver to take her to the first safe place.

Olivia had stayed there three and a half weeks, helped the women in the village and felt as if she could stay forever. Until she'd gotten word about Ama.

That's when she'd begun to run in earnest and she couldn't stop now, no matter how many promises Zane made to her.

She glanced at Julia again and then at Randy, a man who was losing the woman he loved, and she wished she could open herself up to love as easily as other people—though, in her heart, she knew that she somehow had. And that scared her more than DMH and her past combined.

Tristan was standing by the old car when Rowan left Julia and went back outside. For a second, she got the impression he was waiting for her and then she shoved that thought away as he pushed off the passenger's side door and began to walk around the car away from her.

It was only then he called over his shoulder, "We're burning daylight—let's move."

"Where?"

"Village a few miles down the road needs vaccines and antibiotics. You'll come and do that. Let them meet you. Unless you were lying about wanting to stay, in which case I'll take you to Freetown."

It was more than part dare and she accepted it, got into the truck without a look back.

The windows were already rolled down, a rifle on the backseat. He had a pistol on him too. There was also a wicked-looking knife sticking out of the broken glove compartment and she was pretty sure he had other weapons on his person although he'd taken the knife off his arm—and put on a shirt—but she didn't bother asking about them as he got in and gunned the old engine.

He drove out of the compound smoothly, the engine running better than she'd anticipated, but the roads themselves hadn't changed since the other day. If anything, they seemed to be more treacherous, thanks to the recent rain. So she held on and tried not to think about his close proximity.

Tried, but didn't succeed. She snuck a glance or two his way, his profile just as handsome, his big hands holding the wheel effortlessly—and how did she fall this far, this fast, in lust? "Are you sorry about last night?" she asked finally.

"No," he answered tersely. "But I'm sorry about your husband. I meant to tell you that earlier."

The way Tristan said it, she knew it was less about the

death and more about the way he'd died—and the people behind the act. The familiar ire, tightness in the expression of the men and women in the military who wanted to make sure it never happened again, those who blamed themselves as if they should've seen it coming.

"It was a long time ago." She noted the look of surprise in his eyes. "What? Did you think I'd fall apart when you brought it up? I may be screwed up, Tristan, but I don't break down anymore. It took five years, but it stopped."

"You cried last night," he told her.

She opened her mouth to protest, to tell him he was wrong, but she couldn't. It came rushing back to her like a bad dream—how long had she been lying to herself that she was over it?

And last night, once the tears came, she'd feared they'd never stop, remembered trying to muffle them against the pillow, Tristan's shoulder, but there had been no mistaking the sobs that made her throat ache.

God, Tristan must've thought . . . what? That she was a crying, drunken mess who slept with men hours after meeting them.

He should've rolled away, gotten off the cot and left her there.

Or taken her out of there, the way she'd insisted.

She was so confused, didn't know what she wanted anymore. But instead of driving her out of camp, Tristan had simply folded his arms around her so her face was buried in his chest. He'd stroked her hair. Murmured something—her name maybe, and words she didn't recognize.

But he hadn't told her to stop or that it would all be

okay or any of that crap people said when they didn't know how to help.

"I came here to find peace—Doc J told me I could find peace. How can I do that with weapons? With danger?" she'd asked him finally, when the tears had dried and she'd been too tired to care about much more than the fact she'd found a safe place to land for the night.

"There's always danger, Rowan. Even when you're at peace, that doesn't go away. Sometimes, it makes it better."

God, she wanted to bury her head in her hands, didn't want to look at him...didn't want him to remember all of that. "Sorry," she managed to mumble, her face heated.

"You were pretty wasted. I wasn't sure if you'd remembered," he explained.

She didn't have time to respond before Tristan cursed. One look in the side mirror showed the soldiers coming up fast behind them, faster than they had yesterday, and she braced herself as Tristan sped up so they could drive into the main part of the village and then he braked hard.

"Got to keep it business as usual—can't arouse suspicion," he told her, and her belly tightened. "Let's go—just get out and walk to the back of the truck like all of this is normal."

She hesitated. He leaned across the seat to grab his rifle, his voice brushing her cheek. "I'll protect you, baby."

"I'm not your baby," she said through gritted teeth right before she slammed her way out of the car—and then realized, dammit, he'd gotten her pissed off on purpose. Show no fear and all that shit.

It was better than crying all over him, she supposed.

She grabbed the antibiotics from the back of the truck

even as the soldiers approached, telling her to halt. Tristan stepped in easily between her and the men. "We're going in."

"We must inspect your packages first," one of the soldiers said.

She turned in time to see Tristan's hand curl into a fist and then unclench.

"Maybe we can avoid that?" He held out his hand for the soldier to shake, and she caught a flash of paper hidden in his palm before the dark hand clasped Tristan's.

The soldier turned his eyes to hers. "Do you know what we call him? *Padi.* Friend." The man laughed, his teeth white against the darkness of his skin, and if he hadn't just called Tristan a friend, she might consider him handsome. But there was a cruelty behind his eyes, something she had yet to see from the Tristan.

The soldiers backed off then, got into their car, and Rowan was grateful to see them leaving in the opposite direction of Doc J's camp as this tiny village they'd entered began to come back to life.

"Why do they call you friend?"

"He thinks we're the same," he said.

"Are you?" she asked, and waited, but he didn't answer that question. "Do you always pay them?"

"It's their way of life. It's how they survive. It's going to take a hell of a lot to change that," he said as they were suddenly surrounded by children—and women—all of whom seemed to be talking at once to both her and Tristan.

"Wetin yu nem?" A few of the children asked and Tristan told them, "Her name's Rowan."

One of the women smiled as she looked between

Rowan and Tristan. Said something that made the other women giggle and Tristan simply shake his head.

It was obvious they believed she and Tristan were together.

She thought about protesting, but what would be the point? There were worse things than being the subject of local gossip and, if anything, it seemed to make the women flock to her more easily. That was a plus. And as she gloved up and doled out shots to crying children and their parents, she took in bits of information. Watched the men crowd around Tristan as he helped them with their cars and various other pieces of equipment.

He seemed to know them all, which made sense since his permanent residence had been in the area for the past few years.

"You like him," one of the women said, smiling, and Rowan tried to keep the flush off her cheeks as she said simply, "He's very nice."

The women spoke fast to one another in Krio and Rowan barely caught any of the words, but she was pretty sure they were talking about Tristan. "Do you know him well? Tristan?"

Two of the women nodded, and the one who appeared to be the leader of the group said, "He's been here a long time. He's very respectful. Are you his girlfriend?"

"Me? No." She avoided the woman's eyes as she prepped another syringe. "Does he have a lot of girlfriends?"

The woman smiled and shook her head.

"Does he help you here a lot?" Rowan tried to ask casually, not sure why she was going this route with women she just met.

"He's here all the time. He helps us when he can."

"Does he talk to you, about his past?" she asked, and the woman simply looked at her, and Rowan knew she'd crossed a line. "Sorry, it's just . . . he doesn't talk about himself much."

"No, he doesn't."

The women rounded up the rest of the children for the vaccines, and after Rowan was done, she caught sight of the woman she'd spoken with talking to Tristan. She wanted to tell herself that she'd just been making conversation, but she'd been stupid asking about him. Especially when he didn't appear to fully trust her as yet . . . This would no doubt make things worse. But she wasn't used to working in the field with people she didn't know much about—combat made bonds happen fast.

What happened last night had bonded her to Tristan. She wasn't sure if he felt the same way at all.

Zane found Olivia sitting in the doorway of their quarters, staring into the mess of jungle the camp was carved into, her posture tense.

He made sure not to sneak up on her, which he would've been able to do easily, because she wasn't paying attention, and because he was damned good at it. So he cleared his throat, and she turned her head.

When she did that, he crouched next to her, staring into the thick foliage. She didn't move, turn to him or say anything.

Shit. Seeing Julia must've gotten to her. Coupled with

not knowing what Julia had been talking about at first, well, no doubt she was back to being shocked.

One step forward, two steps back . . .

"You didn't know about the family, why they're here," he said after a few moments of silence between them.

"No. I only knew Julia was sick. When she asked you to take the kids, that's when I realized there was something much bigger at stake."

"Yeah, Doc J's housing a lot of danger in his clinic right now." Zane shook his head. "If they don't get out of here soon, they could be found and arrested. Nothing good will come of that, and that's why I agreed to take the kids with us to Freetown."

She nodded, turned to him, and he saw her eyes were red. "I hate that there's nothing I can do for her. She's too far gone."

"What if we got her out right now?"

"She wouldn't make the drive—never mind a boat ride."

"Helo?"

"I'm assuming that would bring the soldiers."

"I'd stay behind to deal with them." He sounded defensive, stubborn, even to his own ears, but if this could help Liv, he'd do it.

"It wouldn't matter, Zane. If it could I'd be fighting like crazy to find a way to save her. You know that."

He didn't answer. Did he not believe her, maybe? Did he doubt her skills, the way she'd been doubting everything about her training, her oath. "I wish I could make it work."

"I know."

"I can't do it, Zane. I can't go with you and Randy and the kids."

"Because you don't want to save them?"

"Because I do." She paused, caught her breath, the vehemence of her statement. "If they're with me, they could…"

"I'm with you and I'm still alive. Maybe you're not as cursed as you think. Or maybe it's just a convenient excuse you use to keep everyone at arm's length."

"So what's yours?" she shot back. "I haven't heard you mention anything about past relationships. Or do you only fall in love with photographs?"

She regretted her words as soon as they came out of her mouth, but there was no taking them back.

He stared at her for a minute, hurt flashing in his eyes. "Yeah, okay, I've never been in love before, that's true. I didn't think I was capable of it. And then I heard your voice. I just felt something when I heard your phone message to Skylar. When I went to your apartment, that sealed it."

"Why?"

"You were alone, like me. Like you were waiting for someone to come along before you fixed things up. And then I found you, and you're right—you weren't just like your photo. You were so much better. And you don't think I understand that you worry about your past coming back to haunt you? Trust me, I know what that's like—more than you think."

"So tell me, then," she challenged.

"You already know more about me than most."

"I'm sure that's supposed to make me feel warm and fuzzy inside, but it doesn't."

"I'm getting the kids out of here. You want to come, you come. If not, I'm sure Doc J will help you work your way around Africa and let you run in circles all you want." He turned to walk away, his shoulders set, and she wanted to go after him, to tell him not to leave her behind.

But he would. He'd cut the rope and let her hang herself and she deserved it. "We're not exactly the safest port in the storm," she called out after him.

"We're all those kids have. Randy's not going. They think the kids have a better shot traveling away from them," Zane explained. "And I agreed."

He was no doubt right, knew far more about smuggling people to safety than she did. The past months, she'd relied on her instincts and they hadn't always been in her own best interest.

But being able to help the kids brought her back to where she needed to be, took the focus off her and put it onto the kids. And still, her stomach ached from stress. No matter how much she resisted, she was slowly being pulled back into the reality of what happened to her, and what lay ahead.

She was pretty sure the blood had rushed from her face, but Zane ignored that, continued laying out the plan. "Tristan will get me and the kids to town and on the boat. To Morocco. Julia's sister is waiting there to take them to safety. Randy will join them as soon as he can."

It was too much, but she would do it, despite the sickening pit in her stomach. But if they failed . . .

You will not fail.

Zane didn't think in terms of failure—she was pretty sure of that, would tell her not to let her past affect her future.

"Talk to me, Liv. Lay it on me," he urged.

She did. "I'm going with you, okay? I couldn't make the promise to Julia, couldn't say it out loud. But I can't refuse a dying woman."

"So you're doing it for her, then?"

She shrugged, didn't know if she would've ever gone with Zane as willingly, no matter how badly she did want to follow him. He knew... everything. And part of that horrified her. "I'm scared. Scared to go back, because that means moving forward—again. I don't know how to. I don't know if I can put it all back together again, Zane." The words poured out, a hot rush of confession, but surprisingly there were no tears this time. No, she could almost hear the resolve in her own voice... yet she wasn't sure what that meant, if anything.

Maybe Zane's strength was just rubbing off on her. And when he left...

Who says he's going anywhere?

"So it's not all about DMH, then."

"No. It's about me... about how things will change. How people will treat me. Never mind the possibility of witness protection."

"I'll stay with you."

"I don't need a crutch," she said, and instantly regretted it.

"The last thing I want to be to you is a crutch, Liv," he said tightly. "If that's how you see me, I guess it's better that I know now. But it doesn't change the fact that you need to go someplace safe and deal with all of this. I'll be there while you explain to the government what you did, what you know, and then I'll leave you the hell alone."

That was the last thing she wanted, but her pride—

stupid, stupid pride—wouldn't let her say anything except "okay."

But he wasn't done. He pulled her close, told her, "You didn't come this far in your life not to make it all the way. You and I both know you won't quit now, no matter how badly you want to," before releasing her and starting to walk away.

He was right. Damn him for knowing that—for knowing anything about her at all.

Damn him for possibly being the best thing that ever happened to her.

Anger and fear balled into a small, vicious pit that burned inside her belly until she thought she couldn't stand it any longer. She'd lived with it for six months already—had lived with it once before as well and wondered if it would ever go away.

And while she wondered, Zane turned back and began to speak, his words surprising her and finally snapping her out of her anger.

"You keep pushing me away, Liv. And if that's what you want, I'm out when we get you to safety," he told her.

She knew, despite everything, that's not what she wanted at all. And even though the fear gripped her like a tight vise, she forced herself to catch up with him.

"It's not what I want—to push you away. I just... maybe when we get home, you'll realize that it's all too much. That I'm too damaged, and so I wanted to push you away first, before you had the chance to do it to me."

She took a deep breath and waited, because he hadn't looked at her once while she'd talked, had kept his stare straight ahead.

The only movement she'd noted was a small tic working in his jaw.

"Maybe you'll get home, heal and then realize I'm too much of a reminder of *your* bad memories," he told her. "Maybe I'm just as goddamned scared of losing you, Liv. But it's a chance I was willing to take."

"*Was* willing?"

Finally, he looked at her. "Let's just get the kids out of here like we promised."

It wasn't the answer she was looking for, but she certainly deserved it.

This time, she got in front of him, stopped him from going farther, unless he wanted to go through her. "Back in the tent, you said that you were trying to forget your past. What's that about?"

He stared at the ground, his shoulders slumped forward for just a second before his bearing was back, straight and tall, and he was looking her in the eye, telling her, "I was born in this country—near here, actually. My parents were missionaries," he started, and her stomach dropped as the pieces began to weave together. "They were killed when I was nine."

She started, a small gasp caught in the back of her throat and she knew there was so much more to the story. Zane's words echoed in her mind and for a second Olivia was actually dizzy at the possibility that he'd been hurt as a child, as she had been.

From the pain in his words, she knew he had been. How had she missed it?

Because you were too busy being selfish, wallowing in your own pain. She didn't want anyone else's pain, not when hers was so heavy, not when she could wear it like an excuse to shut out the world and try to forget it all. "Zane, I'm—"

He ignored her, continued talking over her—like if he stopped, the story would never come out. "I was stolen. Then sold. I escaped, though." The pain in his voice sliced through her more effectively than any scalpel could.

"Zane, you don't have to—"

"Yes, I do." The command was back in his voice, and she started.

"Okay."

"I've never told anyone outside of my family," he said. "But if this shows you that I understand, then I'll do it. Because you mean that goddamned much to me."

She pressed her hands together hard, her jaw aching from keeping her teeth clenched so she wouldn't tell him to forget it, that she'd stopped bargaining for anything, including her life, six months earlier.

But she didn't. Instead, she listened, as if her life depended on it, all the while trying to forget that it actually did.

CHAPTER
14

*Z*ane couldn't believe he was actually going to tell her about his early years—his past, the secret he'd buried as deeply as he could inside of him. Olivia had pushed him earlier and he hadn't done it, but now...now, dammit, she made him angry. Like he didn't understand shit.

But he did understand. "My parents were killed in a camp similar to this one when I was nine so I could be kidnapped, taken away and sold."

He wanted to screw his eyes shut and not talk about this any longer, didn't want to go into the detail that he'd fought most of his life to keep out of his psyche. All the partying and the danger and the adrenaline rushes kept the memories at bay. Letting them out could prove to be just as dangerous as DMH, and far more damaging. "I was at the new place less than twenty-four hours before I escaped. Nothing happened to me. My dad had taught me how to fight and I fought like hell to get away."

"Who bought you?"

This time he did close his eyes, tried to see who, but it was a blur. "I don't know. Could've been a nice family. Could've been a hellhole. I didn't stick around long enough to find out, and I'm grateful for that."

"You were just a baby."

He opened his eyes then. "Yeah, I was."

"Who would do that to a child." She shook her head and he knew she was thinking about Julia's children now as well.

"Children are a hot commodity in a lot of countries for many different reasons." God, he hated talking about this. Hated it.

"What happened after you escaped?"

What happened? Nothing . . . and everything. Even now, it was blurry, only coming into view in dreams occasionally, much less frequently than when he was young. He'd forced most of it out of his head so he wouldn't focus on it.

But his ability to focus was a huge part of his success in life. When he was on a mission, it was fierce. Unrelenting.

Recently, it had given him relief from the unrelenting thoughts of Olivia, which ran on a continuous loop . . . of how he needed to find her. Needed to try to reconcile the fact that Liv might never be found.

At least that's what Dylan kept telling him, and Zane would say that he understood. Dylan was more of a realist, had learned to cut his losses in his current line of work as a private contractor. But in Zane's mind, he would never accept she was dead, not until he saw a body. In his world, no man was left behind. And he wasn't simply referring to the military world.

Now he let himself think about those days on the street, when he was ten, eleven, surviving off other people's garbage, fighting for his life and living among a small gang of boys. "I lived on the street for a couple of years. Fended for myself. Barely trusted anyone. And then I was caught again. Sold again."

He'd been cleaned up, drugged and put on sale—all because he was blond and blue-eyed and fit the model of what so many people wanted in a child. American.

He'd been a hot commodity. And too drugged to give a shit. Figured it was the end of the road. Figured he'd escape the first chance he got. After all, he'd done so before.

"My parents, the ones who adopted me—they bought me."

Her eyes went wide.

"It's not what you think. They hadn't been looking to buy a child. But they were in the Sudan on a dig and they were approached about it. And they were horrified. So they paid for me, were going to turn me over to the police, but they said when they saw me ..."

"They couldn't," she finished.

"Right." He blinked hard a few times. "I wish I'd been as trusting. I wanted nothing to do with them. With any adult."

"What made you finally trust them?"

He shrugged. "Little things. They stayed in the Sudan

for months, longer than planned, trying to get me a passport. Since it hadn't been a legal adoption, they had to find someone who'd fix that. Refused to have me put into any kind of foster care while they were checked out. They got more trouble from me than they bargained for."

"I have a feeling they didn't mind."

"Probably not. They wanted me to never have to think about that time in my life again. And for a really long time, I tried. Never wanted to think about where I came from, the kids I left behind. Gave back by serving my country. But D told me not to get involved . . . that it would feel way too personal and that could never be a good thing when you're talking life or death." He paused, nearly out of breath, thanks to the way the words poured out—fast and from the heart.

"And then I came along," she said softly.

"Yeah. And I couldn't stop thinking about you. I was OUTCONUS for a month, and when I got back Dylan told me they'd lost the lead on you. That you'd disappeared."

She had, in a sense. Everything that had happened before the kidnapping—her old life—was forever gone. Some days she was sad and angry about that, but she threw herself into her newfound role with all the bravado she could muster.

Most days, it was enough. But there were times when the guilt of escaping the first kidnapping was almost overwhelming.

"My parents—I can't even let myself think about who they outbid. And what kid took my place."

"You've spent your life thinking about the ones who didn't make it out of there," she said softly, and Zane nodded. "I do too."

"Yeah, I know you do. I get it, Liv, I really do. It's just . . . shit, staying here . . ." He trailed off then. Because the time for talking was over. Instead, he pulled her close.

Because he needed. There was no way around it—he needed.

"Zane." His name, whispered, screamed—it didn't matter. It was on her lips, in her mind, branded to her soul. "I won't leave you behind. I wouldn't have before you told me, and now . . . never."

I won't leave you behind.

It had held true for both of them. They both understood that, they both knew it was the only way to survive. And the bond between them grew immeasurably in a matter of seconds, one that he was pretty sure couldn't be broken.

"Your parents—your biological ones—no one ever looked for other family members?"

"I guess not—at least not at the time. I couldn't even remember much about life with my birth parents, never mind extended family—it's all bits and pieces. The shrinks I saw said that's my mind protecting me from details that could hurt me—both the good stuff and the bad. I mean, I know they were killed. But to be sure, I checked—or rather, my adoptive parents did. They made sure." His throat tightened as he remember Ann Scott's face when she came into his room and told him for sure they were gone. "And I was so angry and sad . . . but mostly I was relieved that I got to be angry and sad. Because if I'd found out they were alive, I would've wondered why hadn't they found me. Had they even looked? Because if it was my kid, I'd go to the ends of the earth for him." He paused, glanced at her. "I was twelve. I wasn't rational."

"I think you were. Then—and now." She leaned down and kissed him. It was meant to be gentle, comforting, but it went to wild and out of control in seconds, when he pulled her tight to him. His tongue played with hers, and they kissed until they were out of breath. Her hands twisted in his hair like she didn't want to let him go, that fierce hunger rising between them.

He pulled away from her. "I can't leave them behind. Can't. Won't. You either. Do you understand, Liv? I'll do whatever I have to."

"I get it, Zane." She'd kept her fingers threaded through his hair, pulled his face to hers so their foreheads touched. "I wish you'd told me sooner."

"I wasn't going to tell you at all."

"Why?"

"You have enough burdens. You don't need mine."

"You didn't need mine either, but you took them anyway."

He didn't say anything to that. All he wanted to do was lay her down on the ground. Strip her clothing off slowly. Lick. Taste. Spread her and take her until she screamed. Bite the sensitive flesh at the base of her neck and brand her as his own.

And she seemed willing. So much so that she looked like she ached for him—and right now that was more than enough incentive for him to forget everything else going on around them and lose himself in her.

Halfway back to Doc J's, the sky opened up. Tristan swerved the car off the road because there was no fucking way they were getting through until the deluge stopped. It wasn't safe or smart—not that anything he'd done over the past twenty-four hours had been either of those things.

He didn't want to be trapped with Rowan, but there was no getting around it, unless he wanted to swim back to the clinic. Which honestly, wasn't a bad idea.

He turned the car off and opened the back windows a little, even though the rain would come in. It would get way too hot in there otherwise.

He'd been furious from the time he'd ushered her into the car and she damned well knew it.

Finally, she spoke. "Tristan, I didn't mean—"

"To ask the locals about me?" He paused. "I've known you two days. I've known people for years and never told them shit about my life. Because I didn't want to, because it was none of their business. Because I didn't want them to look at me any differently. But hell, they always looked at me differently."

"I wouldn't have."

"You already do."

"Maybe that has nothing to do with what you've done in your past," she said quietly, and for a second his heart almost stopped at the power of those words, because maybe she was telling the truth. "Tristan, you were in the military. I know that you had to do things."

"You mean kill, right? Yeah, I did—before the military and after. I'm no saint, Rowan, and Jesus and Doc J and all the missionaries in Africa aren't ever going to heal my soul and get me into heaven. I know that and I don't care—I'm not looking for redemption from them."

Or from you. But he didn't say the words out loud—

couldn't—and so he cursed loudly and slammed his fist on the steering wheel, stared straight ahead as the rain sheeted the windshield.

Doc J hadn't missed a damned trick, had asked him that morning, "What's going on between you two?" and then held up a hand. "Forget it. I'm not your mother."

"Thank God for that, because you'd make an ugly mother," Tristan had shot back, and Doc J's face had broken into the first smile Tristan had seen all day.

Yeah, Tristan had it bad, and Doc J knew it; he had it bad enough to know that spending tonight alone wasn't going to happen. So he might actually have to put some work into this . . . whatever it was.

Because this woman made him want to beat his chest. Bay at the moon.

This woman made him want to spend the night, wake up in the morning and do it all again.

A capable woman was the biggest turn-on. And, as he'd just discovered, his greatest downfall, because he'd stopped thinking about anything else but her. For the first time in a long time, he didn't care.

All he'd done on the drive back from Freetown was think about her. Worry what would happen to her when the soldiers came to shake the clinic down. Women didn't fare well in this place, and she was too stubborn to recognize that arguing and protesting wouldn't do any good.

Even though he knew she'd be safer leaving, he didn't want her to. Planned to convince her not to by going into her tent again and taking her, hard and fast and then more slowly. When he regained some of his composure, he'd tell her she couldn't leave. Lay it on the line.

He just hadn't been planning on revealing any of that right now. But things happened faster here—everything was more intense than it normally would be, and that included bonds. And secrets, they seemed easier to share in this place, typically because you never thought you'd see the person again.

Or you didn't have to share them because they wouldn't be around long enough to matter. But Rowan, despite her earlier meltdown, she would stay. He could feel it, the way he always knew rain was coming, days before it actually did.

"You don't scare me. Not in the way you're thinking," she said after a few more minutes of silence.

"Yeah?" He turned in the seat so he faced her. "You should be scared, Rowan. Because I want to do things to you that I'm sure you've never done. Never even thought about doing. I want to take you in ways you can't begin to imagine . . . in ways I know you've never been taken."

Her mouth opened, then closed.

He got close enough to put his lips on her neck, to feel the hammer of her pulse against them. "You let me take you last night—will you let me again, right here?" His fingers brushed her breast, her nipple already stiff. Her breath came in quick gasps and she nodded as the car shook, thanks to the wind.

He had her trapped against the seat. And could tell she liked it.

Dammit, the woman had no sense at all, didn't scare easily.

Made him as hard as a rock. In a second, he could've had the seat reclined, his body covering hers, her hot sex bared to him, with his cock buried inside of her; the car would shake harder than it was from the elements, and he wouldn't even have begun to be sated.

She was so goddamned willing to let it happen. Was actually letting her hand wander between their bodies in order to get to the zipper on his cargoes.

Let her, his dick insisted.

Instead, he pulled back, told her sharply, "We can't do this. You should just go home. Find a nice investment banker—"

Her breath caught hard, and shit. *Shit.* Her husband...

"Sorry."

"That's okay. Dan *was* an investment banker. I never felt like I fit in my family. I always went for jobs that had me working with my hands and my brain at the same time," she explained. "Dan understood that. Accepted it. Marrying him made me happy, and it made my family happy, so it worked out well."

"You did it to make your family happy?" The anger crept into his question before he could stop it.

"I could never have married someone I didn't love. I don't have it in me to fake it."

There was definitely nothing fake about Rowan. He was sure of it. But then he'd thought Janie had been on the up and up.

She was a seventeen-year-old girl, asshole. And he'd been a surprisingly naive seventeen-year-old gang member who should've been smarter and steered clear of her neighborhood.

"You don't belong here. You should go home before you get hurt," he said.

He was daring her to stay, daring her to deal with him—and really, he wanted her to fail, because he was scared.

He might be more scared than she was. Tristan knew he was so far from measuring up to anything she'd had that he shouldn't even bother trying.

"What were you like before you came here, Tristan?"

"If you knew me then..."

"You're not the same person you were."

"I'm the same. My loyalty just lies with someone different these days."

Her hand went to his biceps, her palm cool on his hot skin. "Tristan—"

He shrugged off her hand. "I'm not looking for a pity screw, okay?"

"You think I'm sleeping with you out of pity?"

"No, I think you're slumming and it's hot and exciting but you'll get tired of it and end up with someone who belongs in your world."

"I don't have a world anymore!"

"You can't make *me* it, then. You can't."

"Who hurt you, Tristan? Who the hell shredded your heart?"

Was it that simple? Probably. He'd always found the more uncomplicated truths the most important. "Just a high school love gone wrong. I thought she was it for me... she was using me because I was good in bed and a nice *screw you* to her family."

"Why?"

"I was poor. The bad boy. In a gang." He shrugged. "Such a fucking cliché, and I fell for all her pretty words."

"And you'll never do that again."

One look at Rowan and he knew he already had. "I've got enough troubles without falling for someone."

"Like what?"

"I've got a dishonorable discharge that follows me around. I took the fall for someone else—and so for the second time in my life, my name's shit." Just like Janie's family treated him...just like they'd told him he'd turn out.

Her parents had tried to ensure that. "Look, you really want to know all this? Here goes—Janie, the girl, accused me of theft. And rape. Really, she just needed to get out of what her family considered a scandal, with her all-important reputation intact. So you've got the classic good little rich girl takes up with poor boy who lives too close to gangland for comfort. Who do you think the police believed? Hell, even my mother believed it."

Jesus, he still sounded so bitter, even today. He needed to let that shit go, because all it got him was pissed, but maybe laying it all out there for Rowan would help somehow. "It was the night before the prom. I'd borrowed money, gotten a tux and a limo. Bought her flowers. I still couldn't believe it. I was going to show up at her old man's mansion and prove that I could be good enough." Even now, shame flushed his face. He'd been so young and stupid. "And then, just as I was getting ready, the police showed up. Said Janie had accused me of raping her, and robbing her family, the night before. They had my fingerprints."

He'd been at the house the night before, yes. His fingerprints were everywhere...and his DNA was inside her. They'd had consensual sex while her parents were out, but Janie didn't—wouldn't—admit that.

"Her father came to me, told me he'd drop all the charges if I stayed the hell away from his precious baby. Said he couldn't afford to have any half-breed mongrels messing up his lineage. Said my kind would try to get her pregnant and take all her money."

Rowan's eyes widened. "He knew you didn't rape her."

"He knew. But this was an effective way to get me out of the picture and scare the shit out of her." He scrubbed his face with his palms as if he could scrub away the memories. "I loved her—that was all I knew. And she sold me out, which I get. Well, now I do. It got me on a better path than I was going down. I enlisted right after that, and I haven't been home since."

And then, years later, when all that was behind him, another sharp and swift betrayal by someone he trusted. "On a mission in South America, my commander got a direct order for us to pull out of a firefight and return to the LZ. Our team knew it was the wrong decision, that we couldn't pull out of the town or most of the people left alive wouldn't be for much longer. Lots of women and children who we were defending against a local drug lord's men. But apparently, Army Intelligence had gotten a new lead for us, said to leave the town and move on. The commander was my friend and so I stayed behind, disobeyed the order. He was supposed to help me out of a court-martial—I stayed behind so he wouldn't get in trouble and lose his rank. The aftermath shouldn't have been as bad as it was, but hell, it *was* bad."

Apparently, his team had missed the drug lord and everything got twisted around on Tristan—he'd been the one who'd insisted on staying behind and refusing the order. The one who held up the team as they'd tried to reason with him.

At least that's how it was laid out to him by his Army-appointed defense lawyer when he found himself in the brig.

He'd taken the rap, accepted the punishment and found himself alone again. To this day, he was still angry with himself that he hadn't fought back, but a big part of him had known that fighting that system, with only his word against his commander's, would be a losing battle and could've cost him much more. Beyond that, he'd lost someone he'd thought of as a friend.

He wondered if all of it was part of a larger pattern, if it was something he'd consciously chosen or if it was as simple as the universe enjoying crapping on him.

But he knew there were many people who had it worse than he did. "So there you have it—how I get screwed over when I trust someone."

"You would've been okay if it had just been the girl. But when you were accused of ignoring a direct order and no one believed you didn't, it brought it all back," she said with a quiet understanding.

"You'd think that realizing that would make it all better, but surprisingly, it doesn't."

"You feel how you feel. Who's to say it's wrong?"

Rowan hadn't said anything he'd expected, didn't act like he'd expected—why was it so easy with her? He'd been with women who'd lived through their own forms of tragedies and they'd never connected to him like this.

With Rowan, it felt real. But it had also felt damned real on all those summer nights down by the lake when he'd held Janie tight and they'd talked about a future together, about how she wanted out from under her family's thumb.

She'd never gotten far. He'd learned she'd married the son of her father's associate, in a big society wedding. And he'd never let himself even think about getting serious with another woman.

"I would never do that to you," she breathed, and shit, had he really said all of that out loud? The heat must be getting to him—or maybe he had malaria or something. "And Doc J doesn't think your name means shit."

"Out here, it doesn't matter. If I wanted to go home, it would."

"Do you? Want to go home, I mean."

"I haven't known what I've wanted for a really long time." But that was the biggest fucking lie he'd ever told, and he'd told a lot in his day.

He wanted to feel the way he had at seventeen—in love, the world in front of him.

He also never wanted to feel the pain of rejection again—not the way he'd gotten it from his mother and the Army, and not the way he'd gotten it from the person who'd told him she loved him most in the world. "I was raised by my mom. I put her through hell, disappointed the shit out of her—I know that. And when I went into the military, I wrote to her . . . she never wrote back. She died a few years ago. I couldn't even bring myself to go home for the funeral. I don't think she'd have wanted me there anyway."

"So this is home for you, then?" Rowan asked. She was looking for all the answers, and he'd never had many to begin with.

"I don't know. I'm just looking for peace, Rowan." It

was the best answer he could give her. He'd let a hell of a lot go—some anger still threatened to boil over at times, but he blamed a lot of that on the fact that he was ripped away from his job, hadn't walked away the way Rowan had. It was easier to do here, in a lot of ways, but he still hadn't been able to escape the noise inside his own head. And yet, he'd forgiven himself for a lot of things—had to, or he'd have gone crazy. "You ask too many damned questions."

"I know," she said softly. "I do that when I'm tired. Scared. Angry. Don't you ever get that way?"

His mouth quirked to one side, the closest to a smile she'd seen since he'd gotten angry with her. "All the damned time. The trick is not letting it show."

"I don't know if I want to learn that trick."

He swallowed hard as he nodded in silent agreement. Without further pretense, he was pushing her seat back, taking off her clothes as the wind rocked the car gently, and yes, this was what she wanted.

Last night hadn't been the first time since her husband had died, but it was by far the best—and the only time it had meant anything. She didn't tell Tristan that though. Didn't have to. The cocky man seemed to know that—and more—and she'd spent so many years playing it close to the vest that being this open, this fluid in his arms shocked her. Worried her.

But when his hands moved over her body, all of that disappeared into a fierce, rushing need. It was almost brutal in its intensity. And beautiful.

The man on top of her was also beautiful. Bronzed. Amber-colored eyes. Hard-jawed, stubborn, protective as all get out, as evidenced by his stance with the soldiers earlier.

Living in fear was something she'd promised herself she would never do and she had nearly caved in to it yesterday. If she stayed here, there would always be danger—and maybe that was okay, since she was ready for it now. On that horrible September day, she hadn't been.

"You think too damned much, woman," he breathed against her ear, and she opened her mouth to reply, but her retort became a loud moan instead as his mouth tugged her nipple between his teeth and his fingers moved between her legs, stroked her with a mastery that made her writhe against the leather seat.

Her lips curved in pleasure, a small, contented moan escaped and she realized that, as of yet, she hadn't seen Tristan smile. Then again, she hadn't smiled all that much in past years, and any laughter had been born out of relief rather than true happiness or humor. But she wanted to see him smile.

No, she wanted to make him smile. Wanted to make him murmur her name again, over and over, until she knew he was lost in the pleasure haze.

"You're so beautiful...so beautiful," she told him, unable to stop herself from calling this broad, strong man such a thing, but it was the only word that fit him right now.

She had no idea that's all it would take, but after a second, he smiled, brilliantly, the shine reaching his eyes, and she simply melted.

There was no going back. She hadn't felt this much like a woman in years. And she liked it.

His hand trailed along her bare skin, his palm somehow cool despite the sweltering temperature. She stretched out, nearly purring with contentment as his hand traveled lower still, dipping between her legs, making her shiver for an entirely different reason than a cool palm.

"Tristan." His name on her lips, she turned into him as her hips began to sway against his. "You. Now."

His arousal was rock hard against her belly, telling her that now worked for him as well.

He balanced deftly over her on the entirely too small space of the seat, her legs swiftly enveloping his, her sex cinching his cock like a delicious vise. She was going to lose it fast, and she needed him to do so as well, to spiral off that cliff with her, to come so hard he saw stars.

When she heard him cry out her name with a hoarse groan, she closed her eyes and let herself go.

Vivi's heartbeat was a steady drum in her ears as she writhed against him, the aftershocks of the orgasm leaving her unable to remain completely still.

It had never been like this—never. She'd had no idea what she'd been missing curled up with her stupid laptop.

"Did you just compare me to your computer?" Cael asked and she managed a weak laugh as she lay boneless against him because she hadn't realized she'd spoken out loud.

"Kind of. But it's a compliment really."

He muttered something under his breath and she hoped she could stay in bed with him like this forever. Forget the rest of the world existed and keep the hard-muscled bulk of this man's chest pressed to her.

She was incredibly, wonderfully sore in all the right

places, and she propped herself up to study his face, as if trying to memorize every feature, even trailed a finger along a cheekbone, his jawline, tracing a path down to his shoulder.

He responded by cupping the soft mound of her breast and fingering a still-taut nipple, which made her smile. One of her legs was thrown over his, and even though they'd been making love for what seemed like the better part of the night, neither appeared wholly sated.

With Caleb, she felt as if she could go a lifetime and never be. Nor did she want to be, and based on her current situation, that might be a problem. Because with DMH looking for her, her lifetime could be considerably shortened.

God, she was tired of problems.

As she thought this, his phone began to ring. He didn't move from next to her while he grabbed it. For a few seconds, he stared at the screen, and then he finally answered with a "Caleb Scott here."

So official.

She watched his face go expressionless, but not before she caught the tic in his jaw right before he sat up and turned his back to her.

He was getting reamed by the person on the other end of the phone, kept his bearing stiff, his shoulders straight, and she knew she was responsible for this. When he spoke again, he kept his voice calm and controlled. "Vivienne Clare's safety is my responsibility. I'm making an executive decision in order to do my job effectively. I'm sorry if that doesn't work with your plans, but you put me in charge of this mission, and as far as I'm concerned, it's not over yet."

He closed his cell phone and placed it on the night table again, waited a long moment before he lay back down on the bed next to her.

"I wish you didn't have to hear that."

"I wish you weren't in trouble because of me."

"Vivi, with my job, I'm always in some kind of trouble. It's like being a criminal, except most of the time, I'm on the right side of the law. And you're thinking too hard—so just tell me what you're worried about."

"I want to ask you what you're planning. What's going to happen to me. But I don't know if I actually want those answers. I'd rather spend our time pretending that none of these problems exist."

For DMH, she was someone easy to pick off. Inconsequential. She should've been an easy hit. Would've been too, if Caleb hadn't kidnapped her from her house.

She wasn't a warrior like Caleb, didn't know how much longer she could power through like this.

"We can pretend none of it exists until we get the all clear from my CO," he said, and she didn't push. Instead, she splayed her fingers on his chest and stared down at them.

"Vivi, we'll figure this out."

"Sure we will." She looked up. "Will Dale—Ace—find out that I know who he really is?"

"We'll try to keep that from happening."

"How can I be sure he'll leave me alone?" she asked, but she wasn't really expecting an answer, because there wasn't one.

"I'll make it my life's work to see that he doesn't come anywhere near you ever again," Cael said fiercely.

Her eyes shone. "Thank you, Cael. For everything. No matter what else happens, I'll always have that."

"What's going to happen is that we'll figure all of this out. I promise." He tugged her wrist gently. "You're too far away. Come closer."

She didn't bother to protest—instead, she moved into his arms, pressed her lips to his shoulder. "You make me feel warm all over."

"Just warm? I'm going to have to be more effective." With that, his fingers slid between her legs, massaging her clit, stroking her sex, making her nearly burst into flames and float away that very instant. "I'm supposed to be comforting you."

"You are, Cael," she murmured as her palms trailed along his shoulders and then down his back. "You have no idea how much you are."

His entire body shuddered when her hand wrapped around his erection, thick, heavy and smooth.

Any doubts she had about not being skilled at sex faded as he gazed at her with open desire and the word *more* on his lips.

The rain had let up significantly. Rowan shifted against him, their skin sticky from the heat and the sweat, and Tristan didn't give a shit, wished the storm would last forever.

It was all good now, but when he started the car and drove away from this moment in time that had turned out to be a fantasy come true, it could all dissipate like the storm.

It had before, so easily. One minute, his heart was so full he was pretty sure it would burst, and the next his dreams had instead, and he'd lost it all.

"We've got to get out of here. There's business to attend to back at Doc J's," he said, and she nodded and moved away from him.

They dressed quickly and he started the car and pulled back onto the road. The flooding wasn't terrible but it would be slow going and he stared at the road like it held all the secrets of the universe, and for a while there was just silence between them.

Finally, Rowan asked, "The kids are leaving in the morning?"

"If the soldiers stay away that long. Plans around here change at a moment's notice." He didn't want to say much more. But he did. "Doc J wants you to go to the next village and stay there until..."

"Until it's safe," she finished for him. "You've both told me that never happens."

"These are extraordinary circumstances."

"Will you try to sell me a bridge next?"

"Rowan—"

"I'm not leaving," she said firmly. "When you take them, Doc J will be alone. I won't let that happen."

He found himself about to tell her that he didn't want her around if there was trouble to be had, realized he had no business telling her what the hell to do and wondered why that bothered him.

"It's nice to have people who worry about you. I know people did in Iraq, but I was still so lonely," she said, more to herself than to him. "Lonely...and cold. No matter what I did, even in the goddamned desert, I was freezing half the time. And now..."

She paused for so long that Tristan thought she wasn't going to continue. But then she did. "I can't think about you without feeling warm. After two days. How is that possible?"

He didn't know how to answer her, because he had no goddamned idea how or why his thoughts were consumed with her. Fuck, the entire ride to and from picking up Olivia and Zane was filled with music so he didn't have to talk to either of them, could keep the feeling he had from being with her alive by letting it run rampant through his brain.

He swore he felt tears come to his eyes, which made no sense. He hadn't cried in years. Iceman with frozen innards. Nothing bothered him. Not the war, this country... his past.

But her past, yes. She'd gotten through with a single touch and he knew Doc J would tell him that was a miracle. "What made you get out if you didn't want to go home?"

He could ask that question even though they barely knew each other, could do so because they were so damned similar he felt as if he already knew why.

"It wasn't anything specific. It was all just too much one day. I was fine when I went to bed, and then the next morning I felt like I couldn't do it anymore. But I did—had to—for another seven months, six days and twelve hours."

He didn't comment about her not knowing the minutes. Instead, he said, "Makes sense to me. I'm not sure you should feel great being on my wavelength, though."

She laughed. It was a wonderful sound, one that cut through the tension and the fear and made him feel human.

"I wouldn't mind if...you, ah, came to my tent again," she told him.

His eyes glazed with a look she recognized easily now—lust. Want. Need. "I'll take you up on that invitation, Rowan, if that's really what you want."

"If that's what you want," she said quietly. "Because I'm not that girl who hurt you." It wasn't hard to read his thoughts now, he supposed, especially since his fists had tightened and his entire body had tensed, and she continued, "I'm not that girl any more than you're my deceased husband. I'm scared of being left by someone I love, could love, yes, but I'm willing to take the chance, no matter how crazy it seems or how fast it happens. You don't get many opportunities like this in life. And if it brings us some peace..."

It had brought him peace already. Forty-eight hours and he felt better than he had in years.

Sometimes you need to lose the fight to win the war, Doc J told him once, and for the first time, Tristan understood what he meant. "Coming to your tent is what I want," he told her, and they didn't need to say anything else as they drove along the flooded roads toward Doc J's.

CHAPTER

15

Zane brought Liv to Julia and then he went to the main tent to talk with Doc J and Tristan, who'd just returned with Rowan, to time the plan, to figure out if the camp would be safe or not.

Not that it would matter—Doc J wouldn't leave Randy and Julia here unprotected.

"There's no way you can convince Randy to come with us?" Zane asked, knowing full well that he'd never want to leave Olivia in that situation, but children...

Doc J shook his head, and then Zane's phone began to ring, forcing him away from the meeting. Their plans were settled anyway.

"Hey, Dylan," he said when he answered. Hell, he

hadn't been checked up on this much since he was twelve, and maybe not even then.

"Don't tell me you're not coming," his brother warned.

"We'll be there. Everything's on track," Zane assured him.

"Yeah, on track," Dylan muttered, and Zane knew something else had happened, but stayed silent—it was better to wait his brother out than push.

"I had Gray check into the e-mail and IP that received your picture," Dylan said after a moment's hesitation. "It wasn't encrypted. And was DMH for sure."

"Tell me something I don't know."

"They were able to trace you. They know your name. Where you live. How's that for something you don't know, brother?"

Fuck me. He'd been hoping his files were more secure than that, but DMH seemed to be able to get into more and more places they shouldn't be. "I'll sort it out when I get home."

"Okay, great, so you're a one-man show now," Dylan said tightly.

"You should get this, Dylan. You put everything on the line for Riley. Every damned thing," he told his brother fiercely.

Dylan had no answer for that, could only say, "I'll see you in Freetown, brother," and cut the line.

Shit, he hadn't wanted to argue with Dylan or dredge up any shit from the past. But Dylan and Riley *had* worked out, worked together doing dangerous jobs in dangerous places for dangerous people.

The fact that DMH had their sights set on him was

problematic, something to be reported to his CO, Saint, for sure when he returned home. It wouldn't be the first time a special operator's face had been known to the enemy, and it wasn't always the kiss of death to a career.

But the threat of death would hang over him a long time.

Shit, it had been a long day—thankfully, it was finally coming to a close. They'd take the kids out during the day, with Tristan driving and the rest of them hiding in the back so it would all seem to be an innocent trip to town.

Once in Freetown port, it would be easier to evade and escape.

The rain had begun again, danced along the rooftops, lighter than it had been in days... and the sun was out in tandem, a final show before dusk.

He heard laughter—a child's, followed by Liv's—and looked out to see Liv and some of the local children who hung out around the camp while their parents worked, dancing in a circle, holding hands, eyes raised to the sky as fat raindrops splattered their clothes.

Liv looked calm, very much at peace, as though the children's chanting song had released something for her.

Her eyes met his and her smile grew wider. And then the children in the circle were urging her to move to the right, to keep dancing. He scanned the edges of the open compound where, despite everything, children played. Danced. Laughed. Because they didn't know yet how bad things could get... or maybe because they did.

Resilient. A word he'd heard his parents whisper about him in the beginning, when they didn't know he was listening. But he'd had to stay sharp, to know what they were planning—to keep him, take him back . . . ship him to another family even.

Getting comfortable, even moderately so, took years. He wondered if he was simply meant to be alone.

With his SEAL team, he could work together for the common bond of survival. He'd recognized that necessity early on and learned it well. But apart from that, he could never see sharing his life with anyone else. How could he tell Liv everything, explain it all?

No, sharing his life with anyone had been, up to this point, unthinkable. But with Liv, he saw something in her that he both recognized and feared . . . and that was the possibility of having something completely normal. Love. A relationship.

Whether or not she saw the same thing in him, it was too soon to tell. But he wanted her to with a fierceness he'd never felt before. It made him restless, like he was burning with fever, and he welcomed the sensation because he knew it was real.

I t felt good to belong—to this group, to the world. Maybe the rain and sun could cleanse her so she could forgive herself.

If Olivia could love herself, she could let Zane love her.

If she could love herself, she could love Zane back. Which was crazy, since she'd known him all of three days. But he'd learned more about her in that time than she'd told people she'd known for years.

When it's right, it's right, Olivia, Mom would say, knowing that falling in love meant revealing—and reconciling—the past.

Zane was trying to do that too—together, they could help each other. She was sure of it.

She saw him watching the dancing group for a while, his arms crossed, a small smile on his face. When she motioned to him, he didn't hesitate, walked into the circle.

She heard the tinkling laughter of the children falling all around her, falling the way she was—falling, spinning, so familiar . . . except this time she had a safe place to land.

She reached out a hand to Zane and he took it, pulled her away from the circle in order to dance just with her.

The children re-formed the circle around them, continued to sing while Zane moved with her as if they were alone.

He smiled. "It's nice to see you playing."

"I was always all work and no play." Play was dangerous—once upon a time, it had gotten her kidnapped and almost killed.

"I was the opposite," Zane said. "Or at least I put up a damned good front."

"It's amazing, the things we do to fool ourselves." Her voice was soft, her grip on his hand wasn't. "Having someone else know, it feels good. It lifts the burden."

He gave her a brief smile, but his eyes were far away. It reminded her that neither of them was healed.

"What happens when we're home and things are normal?" she asked.

"I'm willing to take that risk to get halfway to normal," he told her. "Because when being here like this starts to feel that way, it's a problem."

"Yeah, a problem," she echoed, with his lips on hers, and she knew he'd been called worse.

Still, she couldn't help but wonder what would happen if they stayed, if she could convince him to give her one more week. Month. Year.

But she realized that didn't matter. She and Zane were like little kids, standing out in the rain and dancing, recapturing joy they'd lost during their childhoods.

Right now Olivia felt more alive than she had in a long time. Maybe confession really was good for the soul—certainly, she felt as if she'd done that more times over the last days with Zane than she had in forever.

And when the dark fell and the children went to their parents, she found herself walking inside the tent, more quickly this time, with less panic than she'd felt in years... maybe ever, despite the fact that Zane wasn't already in the tent.

The rain began to intensify again. She was worn out, and had finally realized it, as if the past days of running and stress had caught up with her in these moments.

Spending time with Julia hadn't made things any easier. She was a brave woman, and Olivia wanted to help her, wished she could.

She lit the two oil lamps as the darkness seeped across the sky, and kept the door opened halfway for a breeze. She was about to lay back on the cot and close her eyes when a movement at the door caught her eye, and then Zane's broad shoulders filled the space.

He waited, half in the tent and half out, his hair wrapped in a bandanna, shirt off, feet bare and pants hanging low on his hips. His eyes glowed, a blue like the Caribbean Sea with black-rimmed irises, the knife strapped to his left arm and the rifle slung with a loose band around his chest.

He looked wild. Feral. Amazing.

His eyes took her in and she felt naked sitting inside in the dark, so much so she needed to check to make sure she'd actually put clothes on. A slow smile slid across his face, the now familiar one that turned her inside out, and she wondered if he could read her mind.

In the freedom of the dark, her body felt heavy, ripe with lust. She wanted him to join her on the cot, but he didn't. Instead, he remained leaning against the doorjamb as the rain continued its steady drum, a low rumble of thunder accompanying it.

"Come finish the dance," she said, her voice a husky whisper, and she wondered how it was possible to want someone so much without breaking in two from the need.

He came to her then, stripping, so that by the time he was on her, he was naked. And more than ready to dance. "I'm not finishing anything, Liv. Not even close. You should know by now that this is just the start."

It had been over twenty-four hours since he'd heard from Dylan.

If Caleb could get his hands on his brothers—hopefully both at the same time—he'd hug them to the point of strangulation in order to make his point that they needed to stop scaring the ever-loving shit out of him. He couldn't reach Gray or Mace and didn't want to know what Noah was thinking right now.

"Can I borrow some paper?" Vivi asked, and he handed her the pad on the table next to him.

She flipped through looking for a blank sheet and then stopped.

"Is that your brother?" she asked, and he looked down at the paper where he'd been drawing as he thought about any and all options.

He'd come up with surprisingly few, given how skilled he was at getting people out of dangerous situations, but it was a hell of a lot different when family was involved. Reason went out the window.

He could bite back his worry if necessary, if he thought Noah would send him out—but realistically, his boss would send Mace or Gray or both, and that was only if he was assured they could take out some of DMH in the process.

It could also get Zane in a shitload of trouble with his own CO for taking on a black ops job, and Zane loved the Navy, loved his job.

Cael couldn't take it away from him. "This is Zane, the youngest."

"The one who's in trouble?" she asked softly, and he nodded, then flipped the page.

"This is Dylan, my older brother."

"He looks like you."

"Zane's adopted," he said. "He came to live with us when he was twelve."

"Are they in the military too?"

"Zane still is. Dylan was. Now he does private work."

"Was your father in the military?"

"He was. Then he got out and he and my mom traveled the world in search of adventure and treasure, in that order.

After Dylan and I were born, they took us along. They slowed down a little after Zane came along, but never grew out of that wanderlust."

"You traveled out there." She made a sweeping motion with her hands. "I traveled in here." A tap on the side of her head with two fingers. "My dad didn't like to leave the house, and in the end, he left me a with a lot more debt than I thought. And then having someplace to live seemed more important than traveling." She turned the conversation back around to him pretty quickly as though she was happy to be the one doing the interrogating this time around. "Your parents must be so worried with the three of you having such dangerous jobs.

"My parents died when I was still in high school. Dylan had graduated, and he enlisted so he could send money home to us. Our parents led an expensive life, ran themselves into debt. No life insurance. Dylan never told me that, but I eventually found out." Cael shook his head. "I drifted between keeping Zane in line and wondering if I belonged in the Army, because that's where generations of the men in my family ended up. In the end, I decided I did."

"Are you happy?"

He shrugged. "I don't know any other way now. It's ingrained in me. Gives me a sense of purpose."

"You like helping people."

"I'm good at it," he corrected.

She shifted, avoided his eyes; the conversation reminded them both that this was supposed to be a mission, not anything more. And yet, he couldn't deny that there was much more going on between them.

They had chemistry. That's what Gray would call it. Mace would tell him he was horny and to get over himself. Dylan . . . well, Dylan straddled a moral line—the same one he had when he was in Delta. You couldn't depend on the military to draw that line for you—you had to do so for yourself, know how far you'd go.

Dylan's line had always been more fluid than Cael's— right now Cael was angry but grateful for that.

There was nothing left to do now but give in—let Vivi help him fight, the way she wanted the same from him.

The rest would figure itself out.

He played with the ends of her hair, the blue tips on blond hair looking better on her than he could've imagined. Different, like her, but she wasn't some flighty thing the way he thought she'd be.

She wasn't anything like he'd thought she'd be. She was scared, yes, but she was still fighting for a new kind of life than what she'd had, and seeking comfort.

Now he'd seek it from her as well.

"You're really worried about Zane, aren't you?"

"Yeah, I am." He put his arms behind his head. "I'm always worried about him."

"He's in danger?"

"He's in love. Same thing."

"Why is it so hard? Love."

"The good stuff always is, I guess." He watched as she traced invisible patterns on his chest with her forefinger. Suddenly, she was no longer involved in their conversation, and he watched in fascination as she began to murmur to herself. He caught numbers until she pushed away from him absentmindedly, naked, and grabbed the pad, turned to a blank page and began to work some kind of equation, which no doubt only made sense to her.

It was close to dawn when Zane woke her with a kiss on the back of her neck. She'd nestled against him on the narrow cot and in turn he'd wound himself around her protectively—she'd had a few hours of solid sleep, not plagued by tossing or turning.

Surprising, she thought as she pulled on her clothes and washed up with the basin of water Zane brought in for her, since they were taking the kids to Freetown today. Although they'd been lucky so far in that there were no signs of either the soldiers or DMH finding the camp, Olivia knew that luck wasn't enough.

Zane was prepared though, and they would make the trip with Tristan. The plan was to get to the port during the late morning hours—less suspicious and a better time to blend in.

"Ready?" It wasn't really a question, because Zane was already out the door with their bags. She followed, noting he was wound so tightly that she felt the tension vibrate with every step she took toward the tent where the family stayed.

She knew Rowan would be inside the tent, as would Doc J and maybe Tristan, although he usually remained outside patrolling while the others met. The family remained in the supply tent and the rest of the plan would hopefully fall into place today.

By that afternoon, they'd be on a boat headed toward Morocco—closer to Elijah, and ironically, closer to safety.

As they approached, Rowan came out the door. Zane

broke away from Olivia, telling her he needed to talk to Tristan and she continued on until she got next to the other woman.

"Rough night, I'm guessing," Olivia said, and Rowan nodded. "Anything I can do?"

"I've been keeping her as comfortable as I can, but she's been refusing a lot of the pain meds so she can be awake to talk to the kids," Rowan explained. "They're almost ready. It's just . . . I couldn't watch, you know?"

She gave a small shrug and Olivia noted her eyes were red. She didn't want to imagine the good-bye scene playing out in the tent either.

With a low rumble, Tristan brought the truck around, with Zane in the passenger's seat. They waited inside, their heads together, no doubt going over contingency plans.

Doc J emerged from the main tent and walked over quickly to join Olivia and Rowan. He carried a bag with him, which he handed to Olivia. "Food and water, for you and the kids," he told her. "The local women fixed it."

"Thanks. That's great." She paused. "With Tristan coming with us . . . doesn't that leave you all unprotected?"

"What do we look like, chopped liver?" Doc J pointed between himself and Rowan. "We're fine. We can handle anything."

Rowan smiled a little at that, until the door behind her opened and Randy ushered Jimmy and Jocelyn out. "I've got one bag between them," he told Olivia, who shouldered the light canvas tote easily. "I can't thank you enough for this."

"You don't have to," she told him, noting that Zane had

come forward to lead the kids to the car. Randy caught her in a quick hug, as did Rowan.

The backseats of the old Land Rover were collapsed, and there were several large burlap sacks marked Grain in there. Plus, three empty sacks.

"You don't need to get in them unless I say so," Tristan told her in a low voice. "The three of you need to stay down back there, though. Checkpoints pop up at any given time and place, and I won't take a chance of you guys being seen."

She nodded. "Do the kids know?"

"Yeah, I told them," he said gruffly. "I'll try to make the ride as gentle as possible, but we've got to make time."

The sun would be fully up in another half hour. For now, the eerie morning light made her shiver and as she said her good-byes to Rowan and Doc J, she also said a quick prayer for their safety.

She hadn't prayed in a long time because it hadn't done her much good. But for them, the risks they took, she would.

"Liv, we'll be fine," Zane told her, helped her inside and she got herself as comfortable as possible next to the kids.

The atmosphere remained tense. She didn't want to look at the kids, to see their eyes swollen, their expressions heavy with the knowledge that they wouldn't see their mother again.

She was surprised when Jocelyn curled up against her, but she gave her a hug, reached out to hold Jimmy's hand. He didn't refuse it.

"We're going to be okay," she told them, because there was nothing else to say... because she finally believed it herself, and the more fiercely she did, the truer it would be.

They nodded silently because they wanted to believe

her, but the atmosphere would remain tense until they reached freedom.

She had to be right this time. It had to matter.

They would make it to the harbor and beyond. She'd made Julia that promise.

"Will my father come for us?" Jimmy asked finally. Somehow, his question echoed in the silence of the car, and Olivia knew Zane had heard it. She was grateful not to be able to see the pain in his face, but she heard it in his voice anyway when he called back, "He will. I'll make sure of it myself."

At his words, the car jerked with a sharp tug and hit the open road, grinding along and dragging all of them closer to their future.

With Doc J and Randy's help, Rowan moved Julia to the main tent. It would be much easier to keep her comfortable there, and she'd be able to get air and light.

"The kids . . . did they get out?" Julia kept asking, and both Rowan and Randy continued to reassure her that they did.

By now, Zane should have them to Freetown. But hours passed and there was still no sign of Tristan.

Rowan paced outside the main tent nervously, where neither Julia nor Randy could see her; waited alone because Doc J had insisted on sending the women who worked here away, along with the children.

She was grateful for that. Would be more so if she didn't have the horrible foreboding that came with waiting for an imminent attack.

At this point, Julia was the only patient in the room. Randy was sitting next to the bed. He refused to be separated from her now.

What if the soldiers come for them? she'd asked Doc J earlier.

Doc J had said to her, *We greet them like nothing's wrong. We have nothing to hide, because there's nothing here.*

She'd asked about the weapons and he'd shrugged. *Like I said, nothing to hide.*

She hadn't thought they'd had much time to do any preparation, but Tristan had snuck out of her tent while she slept at some point, crawled back to her hours later and said he'd had some things to take care of.

Obviously, he'd been planning just in case the soldiers came back with reinforcements and it made her feel better. Marginally anyway, because she was straining her neck trying to look down the road for any sign of his car.

"Stop worrying." Doc J came up from behind her.

"I'm not," she protested lightly, and he shook his head.

"Here." He handed her some homemade bread with jam spread on it. "You haven't eaten and you're making me nervous walking around like GI Jane."

She laughed in spite of herself. She'd been holding the rifle Tristan gave her the way she'd been taught by several Special Forces soldiers who'd spent time in and around the camp hospital in Iraq. Although she'd never been considered front line, she knew that in so many ways, she'd always been exactly that.

She was ready for this. There was a time to heal and a time to protect. If necessary, she would take a life to save the people in this camp.

Now she put the safety on and let the rifle hang from the strap over her shoulder instead of holding it, and she accepted the food, her stomach growling in appreciatory anticipation.

That feeling soon turned to unmitigated dread when she saw a blur of a figure running into the camp from the outskirts.

Doc J saw it too, and before either of them could move too far toward him, the young African boy was in front of them, panting, "They're coming, they're coming."

How far he'd run to deliver the message Rowan couldn't tell.

"Who? From where?" Doc J demanded of him, his hand firm on the boy's shoulder to steady him.

He pointed from the way he'd just come. "Soldiers. Many...six, at least. From that way. They're not far behind. Stopping...at...every village."

Doc J took the water bottle from a pocket on the leg of his cargo pants and handed it to the boy, stared over his head at Rowan.

The boy drained the bottle quickly, handed it to Doc J, who told him, "Thank you. Go, now. Stay away from the camp, understand?"

The boy nodded, took a few deep breaths, as though preparing for a race, and then he was off, cutting through the back of the camp, probably in an attempt to avoid the soldiers.

She and Doc J would not be that lucky.

CHAPTER
16

Tristan waited with the car at the edge of the market-place while Zane walked everyone through the bustle around Freetown's harbor. He spotted some lost and lonely kids—the kind he'd been—immediately. Could differenti-ate them from the kids at the market who were with their parents, by the look of sheer panic and determination in their eyes. He thought about grabbing some of them, tak-ing them on the boat, taking them to random missionary families and telling the missionaries that *these are the ones you should be saving*.

But it would simply be moving them from one place to another with no one to lean on.

Maybe some of them would be saved, like he was. Right

now, he was saving the two he could—and for the moment, it would have to be enough.

He smelled the strong brine from the sea. If he stayed long enough, the salt would lightly coat his cheeks and he would taste it for hours. The waves were stronger here than just twenty feet out, but the waters could be deadly. He knew that now—had known it then too—but he hadn't realized then they weren't only deadly because he couldn't swim.

When Zane had entered the military, he'd chosen Navy—and the SEALs—because of the water. Because he remembered feeling trapped as a young boy, being that close to the fresh, inviting blue-green waters off the dock of Freetown and wishing like hell he could dive in and leave everything behind.

He'd seen those waters as his only chance for escape, and so the second he was able to, he took swim lessons, spent more time in the water when they went on vacations— surfed, swam, sailed. And when it came time, and Cael thought he would go Army, Zane let the Navy lure him right back into the water. His escape route, sometimes the only one. The only place he could truly be free.

His body responded to the water close by. If the port had been quieter, he would've been tempted to strip and dive in for just a few minutes, to let the lull of the current soothe him into a trance, a place where none of this shit existed . . . where he was at peace.

But this time, he wasn't alone, and the fear would only drive him to do a better job—he knew enough to harness it, knew that fear let you know you were alive.

Fear was a damned good thing.

Dylan didn't wave, didn't do anything out of the

ordinary, but he'd spotted Zane. Riley had too, and Olivia was close to him, the kids pressed to their sides, and in another twenty feet they'd all be closer to safety than they'd been in a long while.

When they got to the boat, Riley took over the kids, and instead of cursing or throwing orders, Dylan grabbed him in a headlock of a hug.

When his brother let him go, Zane saw that Riley had gotten the kids on board and out of sight already. She waved to him briefly before disappearing below to the cargo bay.

"You okay?" Dylan asked.

"Fine, I'm fine." He paused. "Get them out of here, okay?"

"You're getting on this ship, Zane. Cael will have my ass if you don't."

"Their mother's dying. Their father stayed behind—I have to make sure he gets out. I have to." His voice was low and controlled but even that couldn't stop the emotion from bleeding through, cutting a path through his brother's resistance faster than a heat gun through steel.

Dylan sighed and then asked, "Does she know?"

He glanced to where Liv was, already on the ship, watching the exchange. "No."

"You're going to be the one to break it to her. I don't need another woman trying to kick my ass." Dylan paused. "You're going to need some help."

"I have help waiting."

"We don't leave for another few minutes—they're still loading," Dylan said finally, his only admission that he was consenting to Zane's plan. "Talk to your woman."

Zane caught Liv's eye, motioned for her to come back down the plank to him, which she did. When she got close, she asked uncertainly, "Is everything okay?"

"Yeah. The boat's just taking on last-minute supplies," he assured her, and the tension around her eyes eased a little bit.

"I can't swim."

He smiled but it faded quickly. "I thought about that so many times back then when I couldn't swim either, stared at the water and wondered what would happen if I just jumped in."

He looked at her, his eyes bright. "It would've been sink or swim. Either way, I'd have been out of hell."

An eleven-year-old having to make that decision . . . she wanted to say she couldn't imagine what that must be like.

But she could. All too well. They both bore the marks of survivors, and without saying anything further, he tugged her to him and kissed her, a long kiss that made her knees weak and her body flood with heat. She twisted her hands in his hair, pulled him closer . . .

Until she realized he was saying good-bye.

"No," she said against his mouth, pushed at him until he backed off.

The look in his eyes told her that her instincts had been correct. "Why? You pushed me to leave and I am!"

"For the kids," he insisted, and she didn't understand until he continued, "I have to make sure their father gets out of here safely. The kids will be safe, you will be safe. I have to give them something to make up for the loss of their mother."

And she got it. What could she say, except grasp at straws? "Doc J and Tristan said they'd take care of that."

"It's more about me. I can't sit back and let what happened to my biological parents and me happen to Randy and his kids. Not when I have the means to stop it."

"What means?"

"Tristan's waiting to take me back. I spoke with him earlier."

Such fierce determination in his eyes. Such love. The only thing she could do was give him one last kiss before she accepted Dylan's hand and boarded the ship.

What's the plan?" Rowan asked Doc J after she'd spent a few minutes of internal panic. The soldier in her stiffened her spine and bucked up.

"You wait inside with Julia. Get Randy into hiding."

"And you're going to take on six soldiers all by yourself?"

He eyed her coolly. "They bleed like everyone else, don't they?"

She knew better than to question a former Ranger, a fact she'd found out from talking to Tristan. But still, she didn't move.

Finally, he pulled an as-yet unlit Molotov cocktail out of yet another side pocket of his cargo pants. "I'll shoot the tires, then the gas tank. And then this. When they're running, I'll shoot them."

"You're not even going to try to reason with them?"

"I'll try, Rowan. But they'll want to search the camp."

"If you kill them, more will follow."

"Not if no one knows they were killed here. Go now."

She couldn't ignore the command in his voice and did as he asked. At her urging, Randy took a rifle and hid among the brush at the far end of the camp. She waited until he was out of sight before turning her attention to Julia, who was mercifully asleep.

She didn't remain that way for long, opened her eyes at the sound of the rapid fire that broke the still air. And then there was shouting, more shots fired.

Rowan fought the urge to cover her ears, looked over and saw that Julia was cyanotic.

No, not like this. Not without her husband near her.

She put down the rifle and blasted the O_2, urging Julia's head up slightly to facilitate breathing. "Come on, honey... you can do this."

The morphine drip was taking its toll on her. With the oxygen mask fully in place, Rowan reached to turn down the drip of the IV and then propped Julia up on another pillow, all the while aware of the battle going on around her.

It shouldn't be going on this long. Unless...

She turned in time to see a soldier slam into the room, speaking rapidly in Krio, then shouting and pointing between her and Julia.

Her rifle was still under the cot.

Bare hands in the air, she was shoved back against the wall viciously, the breath knocked out of her momentarily. The soldier's gun was aimed at her chest and then it moved to Julia, who'd begun to revive. Rowan saw the fear in the woman's eyes.

"Please, she's dying," she said, and the soldier whipped

his attention from Julia, put his hand around Rowan's neck and pinned her against the wall.

She put her hands on the soldier's, tried desperately to pull it away, choking and watching in horror as the man's rifle pointed toward Julia. There was movement on the other side of the door, and the soldier called, "She is here. Come get her—we will bring her to the jail now."

When no one came into the room, the soldier released his grip to turn and check the door. Rowan doubled up, coughing, dragging air into her lungs, and it gave her enough time to pull her own gun, hold it to him.

His back remained to her and he was curiously still, but only for a moment. And then he fell backward toward her and she fought the urge to reach out and catch him, instead, letting him hit the ground hard.

She saw Tristan standing in the doorway and looked to see a knife sticking out of the soldier's chest.

"Are you okay?" he asked.

"Yes." Her voice was hoarse but it could've been much worse. "Doc J?"

"Shot in the leg. He's all right." He bent down and pulled the knife out of the dead soldier, and then hoisted the man up. "I've got to hide the bodies. I'll be back as soon as I can."

"You're going to do that alone?"

"I have some help with me. I'll send Doc J in here—try to get him to let you take the bullet out."

With that, Tristan was gone. She turned back to Julia and saw that her color was deteriorating fast.

"It's okay, Julia," she assured her. "Randy, come out. It's

all right now." She wasn't sure he heard her, until the back door opened and he rushed inside, knelt by Julia's bedside.

It wouldn't be long now—and Rowan stood by the door, giving the couple their privacy but staying close enough in case she was needed. She heard Julia's murmurs, Randy's rough sobs, and she wondered if this was better, being able to say good-bye, or if it always felt as if a part of you had been ripped off with no warning, no matter how much actual warning you'd been given.

No matter what, you suffered with the loss. A gut-wrenching, aching void that one day, hopefully, if you're lucky, could be filled again.

She looked up to the ceiling and knew her husband would understand about Tristan, would want this, and she said a silent prayer of thanks. If he hadn't loved her, and loved her well, she'd never want to find that feeling again.

When she opened her eyes, she realized tears coursed down her cheeks, saw Randy standing by Julia's bedside, holding Julia's hand and refusing to let her go.

She wasn't gone yet, was staring back at Randy, smiling.

Rowan had been gone a long time, but in these moments of chaos, she realized with a stunning clarity that she'd finally been found.

The boat wasn't exactly built for comfort. It was a freighter, smelling of fuel and God knows what else, but it was supposed to be safe transport.

She'd watched the woman Dylan called Riley help hoist the kids onto the boat. Then she accepted her help in climbing aboard . . . had been waiting for Zane to join her.

It wouldn't happen, and without looking back, she accepted Dylan's help getting onto the ship, and in seconds he was next to her on the deck and the crew was untying the moorings from the dock.

Dylan Scott was a dangerous man. Zane was as well, but Dylan was so different.

"Go below with Riley," Dylan told her, then leaned in and whispered, "None of the crew knows about the children. Keep it that way."

She would.

The first thing Riley did when she saw Olivia was hand her a small yellow pill. "Dramamine," she explained. "Even if you don't normally get seasick, this trip will change that."

Olivia took the pill with a sip from the bottle of water Riley had also handed her.

"I already gave some to the kids. They should sleep most of the trip," Riley continued. Olivia saw the bunk hidden by some trunks, the kids under blankets.

Upon closer inspection, Olivia noted that they were already asleep—the combination of the medication and the stress of the past days taking its toll, no doubt.

"They've been through so much already," she whispered, more to herself than Riley.

"So have you," Riley told her, handed her a cell phone. "It's secured. Call your parents by pressing 1. They have a secure device as well."

She didn't wait for a further invitation, did what Riley had said and heard her mother's voice for the first time in over six months, and then her father's, and they were all crying. There was relief in her parents' voices, but it was mixed with fear, even when she assured them that she was okay.

She wondered if they'd heard the fear in hers. "How are you both?"

"We're fine, Olivia. We've just been so worried," her mother said, and her father interjected, "We know you can't tell us where you are. Just please . . . keep calling. Please."

"I will. I promise," she said, saw Riley motioning for her to wrap it up, and so she did, telling them she loved them and hearing it in return.

"Thanks for that," she told Riley when she handed her back the phone. The tears were too close, her voice thick with them held in.

Dylan joined them, told her, "We've got food."

"I'm not—"

"You need to eat. I can't deal with you fainting from low blood sugar when we dock again."

"So being bossy is a family trait."

Dylan didn't answer but Riley smirked, told her, "Wait until you meet Caleb."

Zane had waited until the boat was safely out of the harbor before he left with Tristan, new weapons in the back, plenty of cash to throw at anyone who tried to stop them.

They'd gotten back to camp just in time, had heard the AK fire when they were down the road, and Tristan drove like hell into the shitstorm, Zane hanging out the window, providing cover fire.

He'd seen Doc J go down, picked off the soldier who held the rifle on him before he could do further damage.

Taken care of another while Tristan ran toward the sounds of shouting in the main tent.

Now Tristan piled the bodies into the soldiers' own truck. "There's a nice drop-off about a mile from here," he said. "That's where they're headed."

"I'll drive behind you," Zane offered but Tristan shook his head.

"We don't want anyone spotted around the truck. I've got a few friends, locals in the next village, who'll be happy to do the job. I'll walk back." He climbed into the driver's seat and backed the truck with the dead soldiers down the rough road, away from the clinic.

Doc J sat propped on his elbows on the ground. "Bullet went straight through. I'm fine."

"Yes, you're fine. You didn't ask why I'm back," Zane said as he helped him up and took his weight against him, moving with Doc J slowly, toward the main tent. The man still had a Molotov cocktail in his side pocket.

"I'm guessing for Randy."

"The kids are on the ship, they're fine. But they need their father."

He and Doc J met Rowan at the door of the main tent. When he looked past her, he saw they'd moved Julia there for comfort. It was light and airy, and although the breeze still carried the smell of gunpowder and blood, it was an infinitely better place for Julia to be.

She tried to sit up in bed when she saw him, and Randy stood quickly.

"Julia, Randy, please, it's okay," Zane started, quickly drowned out by Randy's demanding, "What's wrong? The kids . . ."

Zane raised his voice. "They're on a boat to Morocco with Olivia and my brother. They're well protected. I promised you."

Randy muttered a prayer and Julia sank back against the pillow, her face unnaturally pale. "Thank God," she said. And then, "I'd like to speak with Zane alone."

Zane was as surprised by anyone at that statement—and honestly, it was the last thing he wanted to do. But he couldn't refuse her, and so Rowan and Randy helped Doc J back outside, with Rowan grabbing supplies to dress Doc's wound.

Zane stood by Julia's cot uncomfortably, his adrenaline still running too high from the firefight to stay truly still, but he tried. "You sound better."

"Rowan lightened up on the morphine. I'd rather feel the pain and be awake for the short time I have left."

He nodded, shoved his hands in his pockets.

"I'm glad you came back for Randy."

"I didn't come back for him—I wanted to make sure the kids have their father." His words were blunt, but she wasn't offended.

Instead, she said, "You don't believe, do you?"

"I believe in some things."

"I don't know why you do what you do, but I thank you for saving my family."

Zane felt the anger rise, hot but not wholly unexpected. "I don't know why you do what you do when you have kids. Why you drag them into your choices."

She blinked. "Are you looking for a deathbed confession?"

"Sorry, forget it," he said roughly.

"No, it's a fair question. It must seem risky . . . stupid, especially now."

"My parents were missionaries," he told her. "They weren't as lucky as you, and I wasn't as lucky as your children."

"I've grown up in this life," Julia said. "It's all I know. I followed in my parents' footsteps. Serving like this, it's what I do."

"Children don't have a choice."

"My sister chose not to do this work as an adult. She's been in the States since she went there at sixteen for boarding school." She paused. "Our work is dangerous. But so is everything in life—you can't make choices based on fear."

He knew that, agreed with it, and still . . .

Not your parents, not your problems. In a way, he'd absolved himself with this trip, best he could do to alleviate the nagging guilt of all those other kids left behind.

This family wouldn't fracture completely on his watch. "I don't have to take Randy right now. He wants to wait with you."

"You'll let him do that?"

"I won't be able to stop him."

"Do you . . . have any good memories of Africa?"

He snorted softly.

"You must have some, Zane. I know my children do, and I'd hate to think that this would erase years for them."

Catching snakes with the local children in the riverbeds. The tall grass, the freedom. Space.

When he'd first moved back to the States with the Scotts, he hadn't realized that he'd been lucky. He now understood why they traveled so often—they were seeking the same space.

"School wasn't school here, it was more like...life. Lots of reading. Hands-on learning. Everything was different."

"I can see you here, running wild," she told him. "You seem to belong somehow."

He was more comfortable here than he'd thought he'd be, even with the missionary family close by and in danger. It was as if the old instincts came back...as if they'd never left. He knew what to do, how to act. "There were some good times. In truth, I didn't know anything else until..."

Until the day of the massacre. That's what it had been, what his memories told him, fogged though they were. Until that point, he'd been another child running free and wild, loving his parents.

"What were they like?"

"I don't remember that much about them," he said honestly. "Almost like I stopped myself from remembering because when I was captured and sold, and then hiding, I knew it would hurt too much to think about them."

"I'm sorry, Zane. This must be bringing back such bad memories for you."

"It's making new ones too."

"Olivia," she said softly.

"Yes, Olivia." He paused, and then, "You should be spending this time with Randy, not me."

Julia simply nodded, and Zane called out Randy's name, walked past him as he left, not looking back at Julia again, not wanting to be thanked. He'd never understand what she was doing—would never accept her answers.

Zane wasn't convinced by Julia at all. It wasn't that easy,

never would be. The only thing he could do was take comfort in the fact that he'd gotten the kids—and soon, their father—out.

Julia had been beyond saving. Hell, maybe they all were—but that wouldn't stop Zane from trying.

The boat ride had been rough on her and the kids, but Olivia watched them reunite with their aunt at the American embassy in Morocco, from the safety of the car while she waited with Riley.

Dylan had driven her and Riley to the airport then, even though she thought they'd be staying in-country to wait for Zane.

"Too dangerous for you" was all Dylan said, and she wondered if she could do this, board a plane away without Zane by her side.

No choice, sweetheart.

At least the plane taking them back to the States was a private one. And still, she had to pause for a second before boarding, even as Dylan radiated impatience behind her.

She couldn't be rushed though, although the time was shorter since it was daylight. And when she finally climbed on board and buckled in, she actually felt some of the dread of leaving Zane wash away.

He'll be fine.

"Zane will be fine," Dylan told her, as if reading her mind. "Trust me. I wouldn't have let him go back otherwise."

"I don't think Zane would say you let him do anything,"

she said, and for the first time since she'd met him, Dylan laughed, albeit a short, barking one.

"Tell me what's happening with DMH," she said to him. "Does the CIA know about me—where I am now?"

"The CIA's been trying to catch up with you for a while," Dylan told her. A straight shooter like his brother, he didn't hold anything back. He was lean and dangerous, for sure, but when he looked at Riley, he seemed like a different man. "They'd like to debrief you about DMH. And they want to offer you protection, of course."

She shook her head upon hearing the last part. "I don't want anything from them in return for sharing what I know. Zane said he would . . . you would keep me safe."

Dylan simply nodded, giving no clear indication as to what he thought of her plan. He wasn't in the bodyguarding business and neither was Zane—she knew that, wondered how long it would be before Zane had to return to work.

Where would that leave her?

"If I went into some kind of protection—I mean, I've seen it on TV. Is it really like that?" She directed her question to Riley, who'd handed Olivia a cold Coke Light.

Different name, same slice of heaven. She drank while Riley answered.

"You'd start over—new state, new name. You couldn't practice medicine or do anything remotely related to that field. You couldn't talk to your parents again. Or Zane. Or us—for your own safety as well as ours." Riley paused and Olivia let the weight of that settle over her. "Witness protection is a good thing for a lot of people, but it's not easy. And, after all of those precautions, you're still not going to feel any safer inside. I know that's what you're ultimately looking for. If there were some way to do it, I would give it to you."

She appreciated the frankness of Riley's answer. Even though she didn't feel ready at all to go back to practicing medicine, she also couldn't see herself giving it up. "Will DMH ever be eradicated?"

Dylan and Riley glanced at each other. "Realistically, no. But we can do enough damage that the key players will be gone and you won't be in the line of fire any longer, if we're lucky," Dylan said.

She was suddenly nervous as hell about meeting with the CIA. Would they believe her? Help her? Blame her for the bombing of the clinic and call her a criminal? "Will one of you be with me when I talk to the CIA? Or can I wait for Zane?"

"The agents would like to hear everything from you sooner rather than later—it's in your best interest to do so expediently," Riley explained. And then her demeanor softened. "It'll be a good way to pass the time while you're waiting for Zane—or else you'll sit at home and drive yourself crazy."

Riley sounded as if she'd had some experience in that area. She supposed anyone who'd fallen for a dangerous man did.

CHAPTER
17

Tristan drove Zane and Randy back to Freetown after Julia passed. It had been a dangerous mission for all concerned, more so because it left the clinic vulnerable—down a man, Doc J had said.

Rowan had asked him for one of the AK-47s from his closet to hold on to, and he obliged her willingly. Grinned a little but didn't bother to ask if she knew how to shoot.

Now it was well past midnight, and she sat with the lantern on the small steps of the main tent, waiting.

Relief swept over her when the old Land Rover chugged into the camp. She noted that Doc J limped right over, knew he'd been waiting and watching too, even though he'd played it much cooler than she did.

Later that evening, she listened to Doc J and Tristan arguing about relocating the clinic as she dressed Doc J's wounds again.

"We're not moving," he said stubbornly.

"They'll come back now, all the time," Tristan argued.

"So let them. And you, enough fussing," he said to Rowan, then pushed up from the chair, and limped away. "And don't come into my tent to check on me tonight."

She watched out the open door until he'd gotten inside his tent and then said, "The old man's tough."

"Tough enough that he'd kick your ass for calling him old." Tristan shook his head. "And he's just fool enough to put himself in the middle of six men and win."

"Lot of that going around," Rowan said. "I don't see it ending anytime soon."

Tristan snorted. She could still see the remnants of the deadly weapon he was in his eyes, the glint of fire that sparked when he'd killed the soldier who'd threatened her. "We're okay," Tristan said.

"I'll worry though—about Zane and Olivia."

"Doc J will keep in touch with them."

God, it had been a long day. Long week, long year... and watching Julia die with quiet dignity had been both uplifting and horribly depressing.

Now the camp was quiet; it remained to be seen if the regular workers would be back tomorrow. But Doc J and Tristan, they were constants.

Tristan might be a loner but, like her, he was trying to reach out, to look for more.

He was stretched out on one of the cots like a lazy lion in the sun, but she knew he missed nothing. The tension coiled in her belly, the way it had before a firefight in Iraq, and she couldn't help but scan the borders of the clinic, looking for trouble.

"We're okay for now," Tristan told her. "I'd know."

" 'For now'?"

"That's all we've got, honey."

She stretched in her seat, a yawn escaping. She felt dustier than usual. "I need a shower."

"Give me a few minutes," he told her. When he returned, he guided her into her tent, where he'd set up an old oil lamp that threw a gentle glow over the room. There were fresh sheets on her cot. Flowers. And an old beach chair in the middle of the room, near a porcelain bowl and jugs of water.

"Here." He handed her a towel.

"What are you doing?"

"You going shy on me all of a sudden? Come on—strip down."

She pulled her clothes off and wrapped the towel around herself so the chair wouldn't cut into her. When she sank into it, he poured some of the water into a big pitcher and she took it from him, planning to douse her hair with it, because that would have more water pressure than the shower, but Tristan took it from her.

"Lean back," he said. "Let me."

"I can take care of myself."

"Yeah, you've proven that. Now, can you shut up and lean back?"

She thought about protesting, but instead did what he'd asked, lowered the chair nearly flat so her hair was over the basin. He tucked a towel under her neck for her comfort and then soaked her hair, careful to keep the water off her face.

Then he used the small bottle of shampoo—travel-sized—and gently worked the suds through her hair, massaged her scalp.

At first, she kept her eyes screwed shut. When she opened them, the rapt concentration in his eyes floored her.

"You're beautiful, Rowan."

She didn't know what to say, because it had been so long since she'd felt that way.

But as Tristan slowly washed her hair and dried it just as gently with a towel, so that a riot of long, damp waves tumbled over her shoulders, she felt beautiful.

And then the smile broke through—his, that rare and wonderful thing that she wanted to wake up to every morning.

It had taken a long time to get to this place, so the speed in which this thing between them happened shouldn't have surprised her. She'd been slowly healing inside, and when the right man had shown himself, she'd been ready.

It was like being hit by lightning—painful, startling and very disconcerting, and when she came to, she'd definitely seen stars.

He rinsed her hair clean and then he slowly unwrapped the towel from around her, proceeded to run a washcloth along her body, in the sexiest sponge bath ever. She watched him soap up her breasts, her belly, move the cloth between her legs as his gaze heated her to boiling.

This was pleasure she'd forbade herself, convinced herself she didn't want—and now realized she couldn't live without.

Without warning, he picked up another jug of water and poured it over her body, soaking her skin, rinsing away the day—the past—with his hard flesh against her. And when they made love on the old, creaky cot, she knew she'd somehow found home.

It had been forty-eight hours since Olivia had been brought to this safe house in upstate New York. Forty-eight hours straight she'd been awake. She hadn't been this sleep-deprived since her residency and that wasn't exactly self-inflicted.

This was. And there was only so far she could pace around the safe house—at least not without driving Dylan and Riley crazy.

Too late, she figured, since they were camped out in the living room pretending not to watch her pace and worry.

Dylan was as worried as she was—she knew that. The only thing keeping him from going back for Zane was her and the kids.

Riley had offered to go, but Dylan had refused. Said they needed to stick together.

All Olivia could do was tell the CIA what she knew—several times. And what she'd done to escape—several times. Dylan had stayed in the room with her, and she swore she heard him growl when they asked her a question he didn't like.

How he had the authority to stay in the room with her and the agents, she had no idea, and when she'd mentioned it to Riley, she'd simply said, "They owe him this one."

Olivia was grateful for that, but she couldn't help wishing Dylan would leave her and go searching for his brother. Immediately.

In the end, the CIA told her to stay where she was, that they needed time to decide a few things on their end.

"It means they don't know what the hell to do with you," Dylan told her with a shake of his head when the agents left. "You're valuable, to both DMH and to them—you've given them a lot of intel that will be helpful in making a big dent in the DMH machine. It's a matter of how they handle it now—and how they'll want to protect you."

"Do you think they'll prosecute me for the clinic bombing, since Americans were killed? And they said that extradition to Morocco is always a possibility."

Dylan gave a noncommittal shrug. "I think they're trying to scare you into not running. Honestly, I can't see them doing anything but saying that it was self-defense and, in my opinion, a fucking public service, and not revisiting it again."

His phone rang and she crossed her fingers and hoped like hell it was Zane on the other end. Dylan didn't stay in one place while he talked, but paced, so she only caught a few words like *visas* before he hung up and was back in front of her.

"He's on a flight home," Dylan told her, and for the first time, he looked half-relaxed. "He's fine. The father's fine, kids are fine."

She felt dizzy with relief. Literally, she guessed, since Riley and Dylan were by her side within seconds.

"Doctor needs to take care of herself better," Dylan said.

"Olivia, you need to eat something and then get to bed."

"But I want to be awake when he comes in," she told Riley.

"He'll kill me if he finds you an exhausted wreck," Dylan countered. "He won't be home for hours. He's in the air. Eat, then sleep."

She complied—ate a sandwich, and took a shot of whiskey to help with sleep.

Going to her bedroom, Olivia lay down on the soft mattress, the softest she could remember since the new one she'd bought for her apartment over six months ago.

Her eyelids were heavy and she knew fighting sleep any longer wouldn't work. And so, still wearing Zane's T-shirt, she hugged the pillow, drew her legs up and let herself drift into slumber.

In her slumbering state, she dreamed that Zane was next to her on the mattress, his body cupping hers. She snuggled closer into the pillow, the whiskey Riley had given her doing its job. Because in her mind it was Zane's hands rubbing her hip, lingering over the tattoo on her belly, sliding down in between her legs.

She heard herself moan softly as her thighs parted and talented fingers dipped into her core. She opened her legs more, shifted to her back and the fingers were joined by a warm tongue rasping against her already wet sex. Her fingers tangled in thick hair as she writhed against his mouth, cried his name, although she couldn't be sure if she'd actually called it out loud, because the dream had turned so real.

She was coming, hard, pressing against the mouth and

the fingers that held her captive, and then she was coming again, one orgasm toppling over the other until she was covered in a thin sheen of sweat and utterly drained.

She stretched like a contented cat, the orgasm warming her from the inside out. What a way to wake up...she could most definitely get used to that...except she'd been awake for most of it, and it was nowhere near morning.

"Are you still upset that I didn't leave with you?"

She smiled into the pillow at the sound of his voice, a rough whisper against her ear. This was no dream. He was here, a heavy, warm body pressed to hers—impossibly here, and he'd done what he'd set out to do.

Her part of this journey wasn't over, but they were close. So close. "I was worried," she admitted.

"I'll make it up to you." He still smelled like the sea, and she turned in his arms to taste the salt on his lips.

"I thought you just did."

"Not even close," he murmured against her mouth as her hands roamed his body. From anyone else, that would be a signal that she wanted him. With her, Zane knew she was in doc mode, checking him for injuries.

He didn't bother telling her he was fine, just lay back and let her see for herself. "We ran into a little trouble with soldiers at the camp."

"I see." There were scrapes that had been tended to— bruising, a flesh wound on his thigh. He'd need more antibiotics. Maybe Dylan could get her an IV so they could make sure an infection wouldn't even think of starting...

"I heard you spoke to the CIA." His words broke into her mental doctor's inventory.

She nodded, glanced at him. "It wasn't so bad."

He snorted. "Yeah, right. It's always a walk in the park talking to the feds."

"Your brother helped. I'm just glad you're here."

His arms wrapped more tightly around her. "I'm here, Liv, just like I told you I'd be."

"Julia?"

"She died not long after I returned to the camp. She knew the kids had gotten off safely."

Zane had kept every word of his promises. Every single one, and not just to her. "Randy?"

"He's okay. Devastated about Julia, but physically he'll be fine. And he's already with the kids and Julia's sister. I made sure they were on the damned plane with me."

"That's what took so long."

"The embassy has a different way of doing things—I got a little impatient and my brother's teammate helped me pull a few strings to get everyone out of the country. The kids didn't have visas to travel—and these days that can pose a problem when trying to get into the States."

"You did such a good thing, Zane." She rubbed some of the bruises along his chest lightly, then moved down to lift the bandage on his naked hip and inspect.

"I stitched that myself," he told her proudly, and she rolled her eyes. "What? There were hours to fill."

"Not a bad job."

"Are you done?" he asked finally, his patience waning. "Because I'm tired, sore and dirty."

"And alive," she added. "And no, I'm not even close to being done."

She tugged him on top of her and he eagerly shifted into

that position, was hard against her belly, which thrilled her. "You don't seem tired."

"Not when I'm around you." He didn't sound sorry at all and she could see the soft glow in his eyes, the absolute, unvarnished desire. "Any regrets?"

"Not a single one," she whispered against his mouth, eager for his body to find comfort inside of hers. She took comfort in his weight, the feel of the warm flesh pressing hers down. He was grounding her, with every word, every touch, and she wondered if he realized it.

His tongue played with hers, a sensual, demanding kiss that kept her mind to only him. And she could think of nothing better.

Her need had quickly become frantic again and she sought release by rubbing against him, as if they were teenagers making out in the back of a car in the heat of a summer's night, stealth the most important thing next to pure, unrelenting pleasure.

"Zane," she whispered as she thrust up, and in one long stroke, he was inside her to provide the sweet relief she sought . . . the relief they both needed.

For a moment, he didn't move, simply filled her, his eyelids heavy with lust, a small smile on his face. "I've been thinking about this since you left on the boat. Wanting this."

And then he began to move, pressing her into the mattress so she could gain no quarter from his thrusts.

She didn't care, hooked her legs around his lower back and let him take her hard and fast, her sex still hot and wet from her earlier orgasm. Her hands trailed over his shoulders, now slick with sweat as they moved in a rhythm that rocked the bed against the wall.

Neither cared. Zane didn't take his eyes from hers, his face a fierce mask of need—and somehow, of peace. And she knew she wouldn't be able to hold out much longer. Didn't want to when she was with him, because she knew it was far from the last time he would have her tonight.

And he knew. "That's it, Liv...let go." His hips moved deftly and he bent his head to suck the delicate skin by her collarbone, and her climax came with an explosive burst that nearly tore her apart.

G ive me some good news, Gray." Caleb ran his hands through his hair and looked toward the bathroom, where the shower was running. Through the half-opened door, he could see Vivi's shadow behind the nearly sheer curtain, and he forced himself to look away.

She'd been working all night on her father's software, had been so sure of the breakthrough, he'd let her on the computer. When she was done, she'd asked him to email Gray back the program, with the flush of success on her cheeks.

She'd fixed it. And hopefully, that would be enough to get both of them out of some major trouble.

"It's done. The safeguard's in place. If DMH is stupid enough to try anything at the power plants, we'll stop them. We might be able to track their location too," Gray said. "Of course, that's only a small part of their operation. They've been hacking into hospital databases too."

Organs were a major source of income for DMH, one that funded their other terrorism schemes. Chatter claimed that Elijah was getting tired of outsourcing, relying on different countries to help him in his quest to be a major threat to the United States. With money of their own, DMH could finally have all the power they'd wanted.

A dangerous game. Cyber crimes were on the rise—and the thought of DMH hacking hospital databases, targeting vulnerable patients . . .

"They lost their biggest and most profitable clinic in the bombing, and they've probably had to cut down on the transplants at the other clinics for now, to avoid detection. The clinics are their biggest moneymaker—they needed a way to make up for their lost funding."

"Looks that way. Shit, they're hacking faster than the FBI can keep up with them."

Cael knew how easy it would potentially be for DMH to shut down the electrical grids. Blow them out, because the parts would take weeks to get, since they were all out-sourced to China and Japan, thus causing enough chaos for them to do God knows what.

That had happened already, although on a much smaller scale, in Brazil. Two blackouts of unknown origin, thought to be the work of hackers who'd never taken any credit for the mass confusion in the media or in any intelligence chatter.

It could very well have been DMH. Dry runs for something much larger and far more insidious.

The shower stopped and he caught a glance of a towel and a flash of skin.

The good thing was that Vivi would no doubt be cleared of the mess—and her conscience would be cleared as well.

Where she would go from here though, he had no idea.

But the United States needed someone like Vivi on their side. If he couldn't convince her to give the FBI cyber crimes division offer a chance, he wasn't sure anyone could.

"Noah needs to speak with you," Gray said, giving no indication as to whether Cael was in a shitload of trouble or not.

It was a pretty safe bet that he was, regardless of the fact Vivi had done what she was supposed to. "You can put him on the line," he said.

Gray hesitated and then said, "Vivi really pulled it off. Thank her for me."

"Will do." He waited through the silence, heard the rustling in the background and then, without prelude, Noah began to speak.

"Vivienne Clare is free to go," he said, and although it sounded like goddamned good news at first, Cael knew that, somehow, it wasn't.

"Free to go where, exactly?" Cael asked. "Ace—aka Dale Robbins—and his merry crew are still out there, looking for her. She's still in some serious risk."

He'd lowered his voice so Vivi wouldn't hear and he waited for Noah's response which, yes, he could've predicted.

"There has been no change in her status, but she's no longer a person of interest," Noah said, and Caleb was glad he wasn't there in front of him.

"What the hell does that mean?"

"You know damned well what it means. Cut her loose and get your ass back to base."

"And where the hell do I send her? She can't go home."

"Homeland Security and the FBI are looking into it."

Cael laughed then, a bitter sound that he knew would carry into the next room, and so he bit it back. "That could take fucking forever, Noah, because they're dealing with national security—she's their lowest priority. The FBI's too. You and I both know that the post is the safest—the only—place for her. I'll bring her in with me today."

"I can't compromise the entire post for her."

Just what he hadn't wanted to hear—and what he'd known his CO would say. "Noah, give me something."

"The FBI would still take her. But I have a feeling Vivienne Clare would still stubbornly refuse to get on board with that."

"Yeah, well, beyond that fact, you got what you wanted from her. Now she's completely on her own." Cael knew that getting in his CO's face like this was way beyond protocol.

Noah's voice remained impassive. "Like I said, Homeland's working on it. The FBI's been notified as well."

"And until they get off their ass and do something?"

"I know she's screwed, but there's nothing else we can really do for her. And while you can stick with her for now, in forty-eight hours I'm going to need you mission-ready."

"I'm bringing her to post, Noah."

"Caleb, cut her loose. You've gotten attached—that's obvious. And it's not a good idea."

"Then give me another option."

The click of the line being cut was Noah's response. Cael cursed and hung up, knowing that calling back for more would be fruitless.

He was surprised when the phone rang again, then saw it was Dylan. Dylan, not Zane, and he cursed and looked at his watch at the same time he answered, saying, "Tell me you have him."

"He's fine. He's back in the States, with the doctor."

With the doctor meant still in danger. This day had gone from shit to worse, and Cael wondered if he could take Vivi to Mace and then get on a damned plane and get all of this figured out. "Dylan, if you're lying to me..."

"He's fine."

Cael still couldn't bring himself to fully exhale. Zane home on U.S. soil was exactly what he'd wanted. "Tell him to give me a call."

"Yeah, I'm sure that's on the tippy top of his to-do list, Cael."

Caleb snapped the phone shut. One worry taken care of; another, still a big problem, with no solution in sight. At least not an easy one.

He sketched a picture of Vivi, smiling, the way she had been that morning after they'd made love, for what seemed like the thousandth time, because he couldn't keep his hands off her. The thought of being mission-ready sounded damned good and horrible at the same time—he never thought he'd be sorry to leave a woman behind when the call came in.

Especially a woman who was still in as much trouble as Vivi. But hell, he was in so much trouble already, so what was a little more?

Your goddamned career.

He sighed heavily. Noah had already let one transgression go—and the fact that Cael had disobeyed a direct order to bring Vivi to the FBI was a big one. Now, reading between the lines, Noah had given him the go-ahead to stay with Vivi for another couple of days, but that was all.

It was time for Cael to get his ducks in a row.

Vivi had dressed quickly, was listening to music using his iPod, didn't hear him call her name at first. He glanced down and saw she was listening to "Thunder Road" by Springsteen, her foot tapping in time with the music, eye closed, lost in some kind of daydream.

There was certainly magic with her in the night, so yeah, Bruce knew what he was talking about.

He tapped her shoulder lightly and she jumped. Smiled and then it faded when she saw his non-poker face. Back to serious, Army business. Maybe it would go easier that way.

"What is it?"

"I just heard from my CO. You're free to go."

"I'm free to go," she repeated. "To what?"

"The Army thanks you for your service."

"That is such bullshit and you know it." She jerked the earbuds out of her ears and stood, her eyes flickering with anger. "Unless you've taken Ace into custody?"

"Rest assured, it's being worked on. We can drive you to—"

"Where?" she challenged. "In the past forty-eight hours I've been shot at, threatened, kidnapped by the Army—although I guess that's better than the alternative, because I'd be in DMH's hands—and now you're telling me that threat isn't eradicated, that there's nothing to stop DMH from coming after me, but I'm free to go."

He nodded, because what else could he say? Her shoulders slumped, the argument nearly gone—he should be glad, but he wasn't.

She looked up at him, eyes wide, voice soft. "Cael, don't do this, not to me. Please."

"I'm not the one doing it, Vivi."

She swallowed. Stopped arguing, because she wouldn't beg—he knew that about her. "Fine. Where will you take me?"

"There's a safe place you can stay in the meantime."

"Then take me there."

"It's my apartment," he told her, after she'd turned her back to him and begun shoving her borrowed clothing into her borrowed bag.

She dropped what she was doing and went over to him. "That's going to get you in trouble again, isn't it?"

"I don't give a shit. We'll figure something out." There was no way around it—Vivi Clare was staying in his life, for now, and the relief that spread through his body told him he'd made the right decision.

CHAPTER
18

In the middle of the night, Zane drove Olivia from the first safe house to another one, a few hours away. It was still in upstate New York, but Dylan and Riley thought it best that Zane and Olivia not remain in one place for too long.

The second one was a good-sized house in the middle of a suburban neighborhood. Like the first, it was private and well furnished—actually, neither had been anything like she'd pictured a safe house to be. "I thought safe houses were tiny and dingy."

"Most are. Dylan and Riley set this place up as a safe house for themselves and the people they help," Zane explained.

"Who do they need protection from?"

He shrugged. "Depends on the day."

She wasn't sure she wanted to know more about Dylan and Riley's business—more than she already did, that is, because she'd had an up-close-and-personal view.

She stared out the tinted—and, from what Zane said, bulletproof—window. The house was alarmed to the nines, Zane was armed, there was a rifle near her . . . and she still couldn't settle in.

She started to make some grilled cheeses for both of them, assembling them and putting them in a pan on the stove to cook. Zane had been through his own personal hell and he didn't deserve her falling apart. He'd always partially put her back together—the least she could do this time was fix herself.

Suddenly she felt his hands on her shoulders. "Want to talk about it?"

She put her cheek against his hand. "I want to talk about anything but."

"The CIA will put the intel you gave them to good use."

"Yes, and they could hand me over to the Moroccan government to be indicted for the bombing."

"That's bullshit, and they know it. Like Dylan said, those CIA agents are just making sure you've told them everything, Liv. And you have, so try not to worry."

"I have to—they're coming here tomorrow."

Dylan had forwarded the safe house intel to the CIA agents who were following her case with DMH, and he'd just informed her that they'd be paid a visit by the CIA at this new house tomorrow.

"Okay, but we have the day and night to ourselves, right?"

"I guess."

"Maybe we can have that piece of normal we talked about in Africa, then?"

She smile. "I can handle that." She flipped the sandwiches and plated them. "I like your brother. He's nice."

He snorted. "Yeah, he's a real sweetheart."

"He was worried."

Zane sat on the counter and took the grilled cheese she handed him, took a bite and chewed thoughtfully for a few moments. "My brothers have worried about me since I came to live with them. Since I became part of the family. It wasn't easy integrating, you know? But I remember the time when I was twelve and my parents took me and my brothers on a trip to Disney. And look, they were like, big-time adventurers, you know? And they went to Disney. For me, mainly, although Dylan and Caleb loved it too. I have pictures of them wearing those stupid Mickey Mouse ears. Was planning on bringing those out when it could embarrass them most." He smiled at the memory. "It was so goddamned normal. I couldn't believe it."

She scooted up on the counter next to him. "My first back-to-normal moment came on my birthday, about eight months after the attack. I hadn't gone back to school, hadn't seen my friends—didn't want to either. I wanted to be someone else. Anyone else. And I begged my parents to change my name. I didn't want to be the girl who was attacked for the rest of my life. But they wouldn't change it. They told me I needed to be proud of who I was. But they took me out to dinner an hour away. And we sat in the restaurant and no one recognized us. No one pointed. For that night, I was me again."

"Normal."

"Normal," she agreed softly. "And safe. Times like that are some of the best memories."

"My father built me a tree house," Zane said. "Right outside my bedroom window, it was my escape route if I ever needed it. I always had a way out. And it was all mine—my brothers stayed out of it, like they knew I needed something of my own." He blew out a breath and then laughed. "They probably knew everything. I just didn't realize it until much later, when we finally talked about it."

She pictured Zane in that tree house, waiting, watching, looking for a reason to escape and finding none. Sometimes, that could be more frightening than actually finding something to run from. "I didn't have a tree house. My room felt safe enough for a long time, though. I came in long before it got dark and slept with the light on. And then one day, there was this dinner my parents were having with some friends, on the back deck. I was the only kid and I was out in the hammock reading, and I didn't realize that it had gotten dark and that I was reading by the outside lights. Or maybe I did and just didn't care, but I was outside for an hour after dark and I forgot. For that hour, I forgot that I was supposed to be scared of being alone, of the dark . . . of everything. And I can still remember how happy I was that night." As she spoke, he'd reached down for her hand and she squeezed his. "I feel that happy now. I never thought I would get that feeling back, so I held on to it, just in case it never happened again. But it did."

"You don't have to hold on to this moment that tightly, Liv," he said, and she froze until he continued. "There will be moments like this every damned day. I want them to become so regular to you that you forget they're supposed to be such a premium. I want you to be this happy every single day."

"With you," she whispered.

"With you." He tightened his hand on hers. "I feel safe with you, Liv. So safe."

She wondered how long metal doors and bulletproof glass could hold them so securely, and decided she didn't want to know.

She finished her sandwich, let go of his hand and hopped down from the counter in an easy movement. "I'm going to do some laundry. I never thought I'd be so grateful for running water."

"I'll help," he offered, and she cocked a suspicious eyebrow at him. "What? You've never heard of a guy doing laundry?"

"Not when someone else is offering."

"Yeah, well, you don't need to be so suspicious. Maybe I like doing laundry."

She shook her head and went to collect the clothing, brought it into the small room off the kitchen, where he was waiting.

Naked.

"My clothes need to be washed," he said innocently.

"You just put them on a few hours ago, and they were clean," she pointed out.

"I tend to get dirty fast." He shrugged, opened the washing machine, let her put the clothes in as he turned the water on. "You do too, you know."

"Is that right?"

He was tugging at the hem of her shirt, pulling it over her head, and she didn't bother protesting. Her body had begun to respond the second she'd seen him naked. Her sweatpants—actually, his sweatpants, which she'd borrowed—went to the floor. She hadn't bothered with underwear and his eyebrows lifted approvingly.

She poured in the detergent and he closed the lid. Then he lifted her up and placed her on the cold machine, pressing her thighs open as he did so he could fit between them. His mouth traced a path along her neck, his hands sought her breasts. Her nipples grew taut under his touch and she wound her arms around him, pulling him in closer, her ass tilting off its perch so his erection could rub against her sex.

"I should've known you had ulterior motives," she murmured as the spin cycle began to rock the machine under her thighs in a satisfying, vibrating motion.

"Want me to stop?"

"No."

"Good," he said against her neck. "Because laundry's so underrated."

She had to agree.

Olivia woke to an empty bed and cold sheets and she wasn't nearly ready to let Zane out of her sights for long.

It was quiet in the house, so much so that she almost freaked out, until she realized that Zane was out in the garage. He'd propped the door open slightly and she saw him rustling with in the large combo fridge and freezer that looked industrial, a screwdriver sticking out of his back pocket.

And then she noticed the water leak that spread across the floor.

She sighed with relief, glad he didn't see her in a near panic. She headed for the shower, took a long, hot steamy rinse and dressed quickly.

He'd let her sleep late and the CIA was due very soon. If she was lucky, she'd grab a meal before they came.

"Hey, Liv, you around?" Zane called, and she walked out of the bedroom, realizing her chance for food was gone for now, as the CIA agents in charge of her case were walking in behind Zane.

"We'd like to speak with Olivia alone," she heard the man she knew as Agent Blane tell Zane, who looked at her as if to check her response.

"That's okay. As long as you're close," she told him with a smile.

"I'll be right in the garage," Zane told her. He waited a beat, looking between her and the agents, and then went out to the garage again.

Zane hated leaving Liv alone in there with the CIA agents. Dylan had been allowed to stay with them because he knew the female one, but it had been a favor not extended to his youngest brother.

Zane could listen at the door easily enough, but Liv would tell him everything later. And she knew enough to come grab him if they leaned too heavily on her.

And dammit, the fridge was still leaking, despite his best efforts to fix it, and although it was something minor compared to everything else, it was bothering the shit out of him.

He hadn't had a hell of a lot to do around here to work off excess energy while Liv had slept, and so he'd taken to tinkering with it.

He was on his side, penlight between his teeth, trying to see underneath to the motor, when the dart caught him on the side of the neck.

He reached up and yanked it out of his skin, but it was too late. Whatever drug the metal point had been laced with took effect almost instantaneously because even as he tried to stand, his legs buckled under his weight and he found himself back on the floor.

He could hear and see everything but couldn't move a damned muscle. Wondered how the hell these men had gotten into the garage.

One of them one bent down toward him, whispered, "This one's for Kieran," and showed Zane his own picture on a cell phone, the one taken in Kambia by the man Zane killed, and he knew.

DMH had been there the whole damned time, hiding behind the other distractions—the soldiers, the missionaries. He'd lost focus and he'd promised himself he wouldn't do that again.

There was nothing he could do about it now but memorize the faces, the voices of the men standing over him. Whoever they were, they didn't think Zane would live long enough to hunt them down.

But he would. He had no doubt about that.

———

For a moment she considered following Zane, asking him to stay despite the agents' request to speak with her alone.

But then the door closed behind him, and Olivia forced herself to focus on the two people in front of her, a man and a woman—Agent Blane and Agent Pearl.

"Please, come sit down." The female agent motioned to the small dining table that had its own nook in between the kitchen and the living room. The wood floor was chilly on Liv's bare feet and she tucked them under her as she sat across from them.

"You're going to have to keep moving a bit if you want to do this on your own, Olivia," Agent Pearl said, her voice soft, which belied the spine of steel Olivia knew she had. She'd seen the look in the agent's eyes when she'd described what she'd gone through at the hands of DMH, and Olivia knew she'd want this woman on her side in a fight.

But the truth of her words stung too much for her to deal with effectively right now. "I know that."

Agent Pearl nodded. "What happens when Zane Scott needs to report back for duty in five days if he doesn't want to run the risk of being AWOL?"

Olivia stared down at her hands, hands that had once gotten her through the toughest of days and allowed her to face down her demons by losing herself in helping people. No one had talked to her about getting back to that. "I'll figure something out with Dylan Scott."

Agent Blane simply took notes, his expression pleasant enough as he did so. And still, Agent Pearl talked about safe houses. The possibility of a trial when they caught up with

Elijah or the other major players for DMH. Using her information to stop DMH's black market organs.

"That's my top priority," she told them. "Was the information I gave you helpful in that regard?"

Agent Pearl clasped her hands together. "We can't share that with you, Olivia."

"Right, suddenly it's all classified when I want to know what's happening with information I gave you that could get me killed." She rubbed her head, the throb behind her eyes sudden and sharp. At the same time she heard the garage door go up.

Zane. God, she needed to talk to him, got up and headed toward the door before the agents could stop her.

She realized later that this was her biggest mistake, especially once the door opened and the tear gas hit her square in the face, filled up the room so fast there was no place to run.

The last thing she saw was the empty garage...and then Elijah's face.

The scream that rose up died in her throat as her head hit the floor.

Vivi had been in Caleb's apartment less than twenty-four hours—twelve of those alone, but that was okay. She pulled on one of his sweatshirts and crawled into his bed and she felt safe.

She refused to think that it would be a short-lived feeling, but when Caleb came into the bedroom with a serious look on his handsome face, she knew something was very wrong.

She used the remote to turn down the TV—she'd been watching old episodes of *Law & Order*—and waited for him to talk.

He didn't at first, just sank down on the mattress next to her. He wore jeans and a T-shirt, not his fatigues, and more than a five o'clock shadow dusted his cheeks.

She forced herself not to reach out and rub the scruff, or to kiss him, but even so, she couldn't help moving closer to him. He responded by pulling her into his arms, resting his chin on the top of her head.

"We've got intel on DMH," he said finally, and she swore she heard a crack in his voice before he continued. "They might have Zane."

She moved so she could see his face, sat up straight, grabbed his hand. "You need to go, Cael. Go find him."

He nodded. "I hate leaving you this soon, but I don't have a choice."

"You can help me and your brother by going. I trust you to get the job done. I know you can do it." Her tone implored him to go but she realized her hands gave her away, because they held the front of his shirt, the fabric balled in her tight fists.

"Noah knows you're here. He's not happy about it, but he said he'll make sure you have money, that you're okay until I get back," he said, and she nodded—and held his shirt tighter for another long moment before releasing him.

He got up then and riffled around his drawers, packing gear into an Army green duffel while she watched. Weapons were lined up, the discarded ones got locked in a steel case, which in turn was locked in a closet. He stripped, and redressed in his fatigues—jungle greens—and laced up his heavy boots.

All she could do was watch, growing colder by the second.

He'll come back. He will come back.

When he was done packing, he turned to her, slinging his bag over his shoulder. "I wish I had more time."

"It's okay."

"Vivi, you should seriously consider the FBI's offer," he told her.

"I was waiting for you to bring that up."

"I wasn't planning on it, but with this . . . I can't be here to protect you all the time. And letting you just sit around wasting your gift with computers is a fucking crime," he said fiercely, enough to make her start. "If you join the FBI, they can protect you and you can help them. I know you have a problem with trust, I get that. But I think it's time you let go of the past a little, for your own good. For our own good. Trust and loyalty can be a really good thing."

"I can't promise, Cael. But I'll think about it." Because deep in her heart, she knew he was right.

He motioned for her to come closer. She did, wrapped her arms around him, wanted to say so much, but the only thing that came out of her mouth was, "You'll come back for me when it's over, right?"

His voice was tight when he said, "Try to stop me, Vivi."

She wanted to make him swear to it, as ridiculous as that sounded. "It—this—might never be over."

"It doesn't matter. I'll help you any way I can, make sure DMH can't touch you." He paused. "It's like this a lot, you know. Me having to leave suddenly. I can't get in touch with you. It could be a while."

Translation: Secret missions would happen often and she'd need to decide if she could deal with it. Long absences where she wouldn't even know how he was could easily break a woman.

He was digging in his pockets. Handing her keys. "For the apartment. Check the mail for me. Bills are paid online automatically, so you'll be okay."

"Are you sure about this? About letting me stay here?"

"Yes. Because I want to come home to you. And trust me, that's never happened. I've never said it to any woman."

She believed him. And so she palmed the keys and held them tight.

"I'm coming home to you, okay?"

He would. His eyes held a promise that made her sure enough to let go of his shirt and touch his cheek instead. "Go, Cael. Go now."

A fierce kiss and then he walked away, without looking back. The way it had to be. The only way it could be.

CHAPTER
19

Elijah had both of them now, right where he wanted them. He'd carried out his part of the deal, even though Ace couldn't be damned to carry out his, since Vivienne Clare was still alive and well. Granted, so were Dr. Olivia Strohm and Zane Scott, but that wouldn't be the case for long.

No, not long now at all, at least for Zane. Olivia... maybe she deserved another chance, although this time it would be under his total manipulation. He fingered the syringe that held the second dosing of drugs he would administer to her shortly, watched her sleeping at his feet on the floor.

So beautiful. He'd let her run, and run she had...but

she could never escape him. He'd told her that before, but now she'd truly know.

She's in love with the SEAL, Ace had told him earlier, after they'd made the trip to dump the man off. Ace had given him an idea for Zane, and Elijah was beginning to learn how truly effective torture was as a method to instill madness.

She'll forget him soon enough, he thought to himself, looked down at her and smiled. Sooner than she'd think.

Olivia cursed the fact that the drugs made her hands shake, pressed her palms together hard as she pushed herself off the cold cement floor in a dizzying attempt to get the medication out of her system quickly.

She wasn't tied down, but she was locked in. Once she was steady enough, she moved around, trying the door and then simply pacing and jumping around a little. Sweating it out had helped her escape the first time. Her naturally quick metabolism and non-addictive personality had helped as well.

She knew how lucky she was.

Lucky. She laughed, the sound a harsh echo in her ears.

God, she wanted Zane to have the same kind of luck. She knew that, no matter what, neither of them would ever be the same if they survived all of this.

Then again, both of them had lived through worse.

Trouble. Most definitely.

When she'd woken earlier, she was confused, but she'd still known it wasn't Zane touching her, not the way the fat hand mauled her breasts while a sweaty, smelly palm clamped over her mouth, holding the chloroformed cloth in place until she'd slumped forward, unable to remain conscious from sheer will alone.

She hadn't been out long—she knew that. The sun had still beat down on her in the back of the moving car where she had been tied and was recently yanked from to be put into this dark room...unless a full twenty-four hours had passed.

Frantically, she checked her arms for needle marks and found only one.

Good. Now she had to figure a way out of this.

"You called for him in your sleep."

The voice, so familiar, made her snap to attention. Her blood ran cold when she looked across the room and saw him—Elijah, the man responsible for all this, the one who'd had her on the run.

He would not win. "How did you find me?

Elijah laughed. "You're assuming we ever lost you."

She chilled at the thought that she'd never been truly free of them. That DMH was both vicious and patient, and now they'd taken the man she'd fallen in love with from her. And would maybe even keep her alive, to do God knows what for them.

She thought back to the predictions made when she was still a child—predictions from another madman—wondered when she'd realize she wasn't in charge of her own fate. Never had been.

What Zane would say to that she might never know. But he would never forgive her for refusing to fight, for giving up.

Without him though, she didn't think she had the strength to try.

Elijah knew who she was thinking about, if not what But he wasn't stupid.

She wished she'd kept Zane's gun closer, or one of his knives . . . wished so many things. "What do you want from me?"

"Sadly, nothing. I did, of course, but you're of no value to me now that you've spoken with the CIA."

"They'll never let you get away with this."

"With kidnapping you again? They will. They already did. Those agents you met with are dead. The rest is incon-sequential. Black market transplants are a small part of our operation."

"You're an evil bastard. Screwing with people's lives like this—"

"Save it. Your passion bores me."

"Then let me go."

"I have a better plan. I can still have you, but without the mouthiness. You had it good with me, Olivia, you just didn't realize it. Now you will, and it'll be too late to do anything about it."

He stood and walked over to her. She saw the needle, at-tempted to get up and stop him, but he was too strong grabbed her and sank the needle into her arm. "This will make you pliable. Before long, you'll do anything I want Anything anyone wants."

He let her go and she fell like a limp rag doll to the floor She knew he'd lock her in here again, the way he'd done countless times before when she was his prisoner.

She could still hear his laugh echoing in her head as he stood over her. He would continue to drug her into sub-mission until she was nothing but a shell, succumbing to his way of controlling her . . . and she could think of nothing worse.

It took a great effort, and concentration, but she managed to spit out, "I'd rather die."

"That could be arranged."

At the sound of that voice, Elijah grabbed her roughly off the floor and turned with her in his arms.

A tall, handsome blond man with a very large sawed-off rifle pointed at them waited in the doorway.

"This doesn't concern you at all," Elijah said.

"That's where you're wrong. All of your mistakes concern me."

Elijah's grip was strong, holding her up because she certainly couldn't stand on her own—the drugs had numbed her so badly she could barely feel her legs.

She smelled the fear, being this up-close and personal with him—no doubt it was partially hers, but it was also him—he was definitely worried about this other man.

Granted, so was she, but the loopiness kept the panic down, allowed her to float outside her body, an observer wondering how this one would end.

"Be reasonable, Ace. DMH is nothing without me," Elijah said.

"At one time, maybe so. And it took a while, but now that I've finally accessed all your personal files, I know all your secrets." The blond man smiled and a chill went through her at the dead look in his eyes. "You know what they say, three can keep a secret if two are dead."

"You killed Marty?" Elijah asked, his voice shaking slightly.

The blond man shook his head, said, "Not yet. You're

first," and came forward with two fast shots—she didn't even have time to scream. She remained frozen as she felt the heavy hand on her shoulder begin to pull her backward. She shifted, lurched forward to avoid falling and managed to turn in time to see Elijah slump to the ground.

In his forehead, two perfect entry wounds.

He was dead but any joy for that was short-lived when the handsome blond man grabbed her roughly by the arm.

"You're of no use to me, Doctor."

"Where's Zane?"

"You're about to be reunited with him. I promise."

It was a promise she wasn't sure she should want granted.

Zane woke slowly at first, and then blinked the haze away furiously.

Rounded walls. Metal floor. Ladder.

He was in a goddamned holding tank—a silo for water he thought . . . and one hand was manacled to the wall in a steel grip above his head. He was shut in this place—and completely alone.

After a few minutes of being awake, he knew he had to get up and move, in order to get the drugs out of his blood-stream as quickly as possible. He pushed himself to his feet heavily and attempted to get the feeling back in his bound arm.

It tingled painfully, but that wasn't nearly as bad as what he figured the future held for him.

He looked up to see if it was day or night, but the opening at the very top had been closed, so he couldn't tell, which meant he had no idea how long he'd been out, or if he was very far away from where he and Liv had been staying.

Fear coursed through him, more fiercely than adrenaline could. He had no choice but to keep it together, because his mental strength was his most important asset right now.

He would do that for himself. And for Liv. God, had they grabbed her too? She hadn't been in the car with him—he would've known, would've seen her. But they'd moved him quickly off the garage floor into the vehicle and they'd sped off within minutes of shooting him with the dart.

He pulled at the chain, having already realized that was useless but unwilling to give up that easily.

He'd been stripped down to his boxer briefs and a T-shirt, so there was nothing on him he could use to pick the lock. He searched the ground around him in vain for a loose nail or screw, the walls, found nothing.

No, they'd swept the place clean.

So basically, he was screwed. Either they'd keep him here until he died from exposure, or starvation, dehydration, or—the big *or* that he felt gnaw at his gut—at some point they'd turn the goddamned water on and let him drown in here.

He eyed the ladder—it was at least fifteen feet away, but he noted that the bottom piece was rusted at the bolts.

That could come off the wall—how, he didn't know, unless . . .

Jesus, he didn't want them to bring Liv here, but she was his only shot now. Unless she hadn't been captured. Even then, it would take her and Dylan and Riley longer to get here and help him.

He leaned against the wall for a second, forcing himself back to calm. Panic never helped sort anything out, and he wouldn't succumb to it now. Better to conserve his energy in case one of the men who captured him came close enough to fight.

The thought was a good one, because the door across from him opened about twenty minutes later, by his calculations—trying to keep track of time was one of the methods they utilized in training to remain calm and in control.

All control was nearly lost when he saw the man who'd stood over him earlier, now carrying an unconscious Liv in his arms.

He moved as if his body could follow through to her, ended up at the end of the chain growling like a rabid dog.

It made the man jump a little and he was glad to have some modicum of success. And then he laid Liv down on the ground, about nine feet away, just frustratingly out of Zane's reach if he stretched all the way.

"She wanted to see you again," the man said. "Hope she wakes up in time."

"There are people tracking you," Zane told him.

"Not fast enough." Then the man was gone, slamming the door behind him.

"Liv—Olivia—you need to wake up," Zane told her, his voice loud and firm. A few seconds later, he repeated his request, even as he heard the squeak of metal being turned and the sound of pipes rattling against one another.

The water came in slowly at first, from a pipe close to the door. And then it started gushing from several others.

Zane looked around and realized with a sickening clarity what the man's plans were.

He had to wake Olivia if there was any chance of getting either of them out of here alive.

O livia..."

She heard her name, over and over. He always did that, called to her and then giggled as she squirmed closer to the wall in an attempt to escape the sounds. Another way to torment her, to make her hate the sound of her own name.

And she was cold, so cold all the time. She wanted to curl up in a ball, to try to get warmer, but her body wouldn't cooperate. He must have put something in her water—and she'd had to drink it, because she'd been feeling weaker.

"Olivia, wake the hell up."

The man with the eerie voice never used the word hell, *only forced her to live in his own personal one. She was shivering now, teeth chattering...floating.*

The freezing cold surrounded her, so frigid it hurt.

"Olivia."

The voice...it wasn't his...wasn't the man with the tarot cards...but it was familiar.

"Olivia, wake the hell up."

Zane!

She turned and nearly breathed in a lungful of water. Sat up, coughing, and realized she'd almost drowned in less than four inches of water.

But more was rushing in. She looked at the pipes across

the way, with water rushing from them at an alarmingly fast rate. She would drown, she thought, wrapped her arms around herself in a ridiculous attempt to warm up, because she was already soaked to the skin. The water from the pipes above splashed her and she moved away, nearly tripping over her own two feet.

"Olivia, focus on me."

Zane.

She turned and saw him, standing against the wall, one wrist shackled to it, so he was helpless to do anything but talk to her.

"Are you okay?" She sloshed through the water toward him. Put her hands to his face.

"I'm fine. But we're not going to be for long. So listen to me—do exactly as I say."

She was staring at him. The drug haze was hard to fight, despite the dash of hard, cold reality.

"Olivia, listen up—you need to do what I tell you to. Understand?" His eyes met hers, and in that horrifying moment, she realized exactly what would happen if she didn't.

And still, she couldn't move. There was no way . . .

I won't survive this a third time. I told him I would break . . .

"Can't, Zane . . . can't . . ."

When he spoke to her again, his voice was hard, almost unrecognizable. "I guess Elijah was right. He told me you'd never be able to do this, to save me. That you were weak."

She felt weak, but the words made her angry. "Shut up."

"Truth hurts, right? So was the *I won't leave you behind* speech a bunch of crap? Should've known you wouldn't be able to save yourself."

She stared at him—his eyes were hard, unforgiving...
cruel even. "What do you want from me?"

"I want you to stop feeling sorry for yourself and help us
get out of here. If you can't do that, then I hope you're prepared to watch me die. Because you can get out—climb up
the damned ladder and get out of here."

The ladder. She looked at it and back to Zane, and then
realized his wrist was shackled. "None of this is good."

"No shit," Zane said through gritted teeth. "Can you
climb to the top and open it? Quickly? Look for something
that can break this cuff?"

She went all the way up, her muscles protesting. When
she got to the top, she pushed the hatch. It gave, enough to
let her know it wasn't locked, but she was nowhere near
strong enough to push it open herself.

"Come back," he called. "And don't look down—
concentrate on putting your hands in the right place, feel
for the rungs with your feet."

When she reached the bottom, before she jumped into
the water that was more than puddling on the floor now, he
said, "The ladder—some of the bolts are rusted."

"But then how will we get out of here?"

"Let's worry about one thing at a time."

"Good point," she muttered. They'd worry about the
but then after she'd freed Zane.

She jumped down into the now calf-deep water, noted
that the ladder was really two separate pieces, the one closest to the bottom was the one that was rusting.

With the water rising rapidly, she'd have to work fast
while she still had leverage.

She gripped the rusted metal with both hands and

pulled, put all her weight into it. Shook the damned metal so hard it made her teeth knock together . . . and nothing, nothing was happening. "This won't work," she called out.

"Then DMH wins. If you're comfortable with that, I guess I'll have to be too," he responded.

His goading made her want to punch him, but instead she pulled harder at the ladder.

Bastard. Hitting nerves left and right with his zings. She turned back to the metal, not wanting to look at him, yanked so hard her back lurched and her teeth ached because she was grinding them together from the effort. Her fingers were bloodied and raw, as were her palms, but still she shook and pulled at the rusted metal, and finally—finally—after what had to be ten minutes the ladder began to pull away from the old bolts. She attempted to pull at the bolts themselves. One turned easily enough for her to get it out, but the other one was too tough, and the top two too far away for her to get to without climbing on the now unstable ladder. And the water was rising rapidly around her.

No choice. If she got close she could manually unscrew it. Tenaciously, she steadied herself and got one of them loose. The ladder shifted, throwing her backward into the water.

Thankfully, she'd held on, and she used the now-moving ladder to haul herself back to her feet, sputtering. She coughed the water up and out, gagged, breathed. For a second she stood there, waiting to hear Zane say something else to her. Anything.

"I know you can do this, Liv." His words were spoken with a quiet, calm strength, and she knew he had all the faith in the world in her.

It made tears come to her eyes and it pulled her focus back to where it needed to be—on the ladder, not the rushing water.

They would make it.

One wrenching yank and she fell into the water again, the ladder free and smacking her in the face before she went under.

Learning to swim really might've been a good thing.

Thankfully, she felt her foot touch the ground and she pushed herself up with a clumsy series of splashes.

In another time and place, Zane would no doubt laugh at her. For now, all he said was, "We need to teach you to swim. Put that on the *normal* list."

The freezing cold was already affecting her. She moved sluggishly toward him, wading through the water—which had a surprisingly strong current to it—dragging the metal ladder behind her.

She pushed the ladder to him and he positioned it behind the bolt holding him to the wall. "We'll try this first. Otherwise, I'll have to deal with a broken wrist. Hold here, and when I say *go,* bear down on the ladder as hard as you can. Full weight."

She did, heard a creak, but all it seemed to be doing was bending the ladder, not the piece of metal holding Zane's chain fast to the wall.

"Shit. Okay, once more." Repositioned, and again, failure.

"Okay, here." He moved the ladder's lower rods inside one of the chain links. "We're both going to bear down."

It was the link closest to the wall, but still. "Zane, your wrist—"

"Will heal. Push down—*now!*"

His words didn't leave room for argument. He groaned viciously as the link broke, no doubt breaking his wrist along with it, and they both went into the water.

He hauled her up swiftly and she coughed and pointed to his wrist. "Broken?"

He shrugged. "Doubt it. I've had worse. Come on."

The water was up to his chest now, and he kept her head from going under as they made their way to the remaining ladder.

"I'm going to get up there. When I get a grip, you grab my leg and hold on."

He bobbed, jumped and missed. He did it again, and again, and finally he reached over and ripped the T-shirt off her body, leaving her in a tank top. He tore the sleeve off the shirt and wound it around his palm, twisted up the rest of the fabric in a long rope and held on to it as he tried the jump twice more.

On his third attempt, he caught the rung, and she watched him pull himself up with one fully working hand, the other arm wrapped around the rung with sheer will.

"Grab my leg, Liv. Grab and hold."

She tried but a sweep of water knocked her hands off the wall where she'd been furiously palming it to keep from going under.

Don't panic, don't panic.

She reached her hand up and saw a blurred image of his leg and she grabbed for it, made contact with his foot and held on for dear life.

"Get a better grip," he called out. "Both arms, wrapped around my calf until you can grab a rung."

Her hands slipped and she went down hard, under the water. She found the bottom and pushed away. She broke the surface with a huge gasp, her lungs filling gratefully. She reached for the wall, put her palms out in an attempt to hold on to something, watched Zane.

He'd hauled himself up a bit, used his weaker arm to wrap around the bar while he tied the shirt tight to his leg with one hand—a slow process as she bobbed along in the water—and then he moved up a rung to get a better grip.

"Grab the shirt, Liv. That's it, both hands. Now hang on, okay?"

"You'll have to pry my hands off the damned shirt when we're done," she assured him.

A rough hoist hauled her partially out of the water and then there was another jerking one a few seconds later, and the rungs were in her grasp.

"One hand on the shirt, the other on the rung, okay? And push up—help me bring you up a couple more rungs."

One by one they climbed in a precariously swinging motion, with the water rising to meet them, and she was hanging on with both hands.

Stubborn refusal to let DMH win forced her to use all her upper-body strength to pull her weight to a place where she could just get her foot onto a rung of the ladder. And then Zane was hauling her by her tank top up and up, until she was even with him, between him and the ladder, and they were moving upward slowly. Together. Painfully.

Step by step, they got there until the air rushed at them. Her head cleared the opening first.

"Go on, Liv—get out."

She did, scrambled on hands and knees, turned to

watch him do the same, his wrist swollen and red, held against his body. "I'll wrap it."

"Don't bother."

The voice came from the darkness in front of them, the voice of the man who'd dragged her here and locked inside.

When she looked into Zane's eyes, she saw the calm focus there. The promise. And she knew she wouldn't have to worry for much longer.

CHAPTER
20

It was the same guy who'd taken Zane from the safe house and brought him here. And now he'd pay, just like Zane had promised.

Zane pushed Liv behind him and waited. This guy got off on torture—simply shooting them wouldn't be enough. No, he'd want to draw it out—and Zane was banking on that. "Like I said, you're not going to win this one, Ace."

The pale light came from a lone bulb on the side of the tank, positioned upward. It currently highlighted the surprise in Ace's eyes.

"I figured that Elijah would underestimate you. I don't make those kinds of mistakes." Ace shook his head. "It

would've been more fun to watch you drown, though. T
know that she got to watch you die first, realizing that i
was all her fault."

God, the guy really got off on this shit. His eyes glaze
talking about torture.

Zane heard Liv's sharp intake of breath. And then shot
rang out overhead—not from Dylan, because Dylan woul
not have missed. No, they were coming from farther away
but they split Ace's attention for a second, allowing Zane t
charge at him, tackle him with a full-body slam.

Ace's gun clattered away, and yeah, that was good. Zan
could do this, wring the guy's neck with one good hand an
the rest of his damned body.

"Get down, Liv," Zane told her, and she would have . .
except the gun was kicked to the side, ended up on the edg
of the platform of the silo, and she could reach it if Zan
could keep Ace away from her.

I͟t wasn't an easy fight. Ace obviously had military-lik
training in hand-to-hand combat, and Zane was no doub
starting to feel the effects of the early stages of hypother
mia. She knew she was.

Olivia crawled, still unsteady, toward the gun.

My God, she was half-frozen and so weak.

Zane, thankfully, didn't appear to be having that prob
lem at all because he was fighting as if he wasn't half-frozer

It had been sheer will that had helped her get the ladde
freed. She would harness that again.

But the men were rolling, precariously close to her, an
to the edge of the tank, from which there would be at lea

a sixteen-foot drop, if not more. She caught the handle of the gun and she pushed away from the hand-to-hand combat, barely avoiding a boot to the head.

Ace appeared to have the upper hand, had Zane down on the ground, holding his throat. She tried to get the gun to work, but her hands were shaking so badly that even if she got it pointed in the right direction, she wouldn't be capable of aiming toward Ace only.

Then he made the fatal mistake of looking at her and smiling. Before she could react, get the gun up, Zane's hand went up, the flat of his palm slamming Ace's nose upward, and the man knocked back hard. One kick and then another and another and Ace flapped his arms wildly to regain his balance, and lost the fight.

Olivia heard his scream on the way down and winced at the crushing sound his body made when it hit the earth. And Zane was taking the gun from her, telling her, "We've got to keep going. Come on, stay with me."

Her body felt made of lead, her head all floaty and dizzy, and she recited the stages of hypothermia in her head to try to remain as clear as possible.

She followed him, one foot in front of the other, down the endless steps to the bottom of the tank.

She was about to ask, *Now what?* but the sounds of police sirens interrupted her.

"Must've heard the shots. Most likely there are hunters in the surrounding woods, but they were damned lucky," Zane said. "Come on, let's get closer to the road and get ourselves rescued."

———

Liv had refused her own ambulance, rode with him all the way into the next town as they shivered under blankets and the warm IVs that infused rapidly into both their hypother mic bodies.

Zane pictured Tristan saying, *Whipped,* and realized, re leasing a resigned sigh, that he didn't give a shit.

She'd refused to leave him when they set his wrist a well—it was a small fracture but a bad sprain and it wa turning colors fast. Wouldn't leave him during both thei exams and—probably because she was a doctor—the hos pital personnel allowed it.

Zane didn't blame them—he wouldn't refuse her any thing either—not now, not ever.

He was toast.

"You know, you're more hypothermic than I am," he commented. "Maybe I should be fussing over you."

"Not in your nature." She smiled from where she wa curled up in the next bed.

"Wanna bet?" He peeked around the curtain the EF staff had pulled and hopped out of bed and moved towar her. He'd snagged a pair of scrub bottoms to go under hi hospital gown, because the walking around bare-asse wasn't something he enjoyed.

Hell, he hated the whole hospital thing...except fo Liv. And so he slid next to her on her bed. "Can you get u out of here?"

"We have to be cleared."

"You're a doctor. We're fine."

"Are we really?" she asked, and he knew she was talkin about much more than hypothermia.

"Yeah, really. It's over. Elijah's gone. He won't bother you. Ace too. And the rest of DMH is fragmenting. My brother Caleb actually got called away on a mission because there's major intel on the line about where the last main player of DMH is hiding out."

"God, I hope he finishes them off."

Even so, she knew that there were so many more groups like them.

"So what happens now? Normal?" she asked from where she'd snuggled against his chest.

He was nearly done with leave from the team, although his wrist would keep him out of action for a little while. The brutality of the training kept him sharp. Battle-ready. He liked that, the feeling of always being on the razor's edge with the knowledge that, if necessary, he could take on any-one and anything.

The other side of the coin was that it kept Zane very aware of his own mortality. Strangely, the balance worked well, reminded him that life was too short and had once kept him partying pretty damned hard.

Dylan kept him working on black ops missions in order to keep him out of trouble, and in its own odd way, it had worked well.

"Before this I lived alone, worked a lot and partied a whole lot more. And I took both very seriously," he said.

"And now?"

"Now I think I can handle both if you'll join me." He paused. "As long as I know you'll be okay when I have to go away with the team."

"I don't know if I can practice again. I'll have to go be-fore a board, I'm sure."

"The CIA will help clear that up, Liv. You need to get back to doing what you love."

"You're that confident, huh?"

He pulled her up so she was looking into his eyes. "All I've ever known is this. Warrior. Survival mode. Everything I do is based on me surviving whatever it might be that crosses my path, no matter the obstacle. I've been in that same mode for so long, I don't know if I can be anything different."

"I thought the same thing about me," she said softly. "But you showed me that it doesn't have to be like that—not all the time. I think we'll always be survivors, but we won't be as..." She searched for the right word.

"Desperate?"

She punched him lightly on the chest and he turned serious again. "I feel like I fell in love with you before I even knew you. And then I met you and..."

"I wasn't what you expected," she finished for him.

"You were better."

"You were pretty damn good yourself," she told him.

"Is that why you hit me in the head with a frying pan—to stop me from leaving?"

"Zane—"

He cut her off with a kiss and she gladly accepted it, melted into his arms. When he pulled away, he murmured, "You saved my ass today."

"And the rest of you."

"Yeah, that too."

"No man left behind, right?" she joked weakly, holding on to him for dear life.

"Not for either of us, ever again."

It was a promise—she knew that. Zane had come through on every single one he'd made to her, even the ones she hadn't been so crazy about at first.

And it was a promise she would make sure they both kept.

EPILOGUE

It had been a month with no word when Noah called Vivi in to see him. She'd taken a cab onto the post and, wearing a badge declaring her an authorized visitor, walked past security toward the building the guard had pointed out to her.

She wasn't an authorized anything else when it came down to her own life, although she had been contacted by the FBI and Homeland Security. She was still in danger until they decided that enough of DMH had been eradicated, and it was better for her if she remained off the radar, which meant staying away from her house and her bank accounts and credit cards. It wasn't forever, they assured her, but couldn't tell her when it would be safe enough for her to resurface. They hadn't offered her protection beyond that advice though, and she knew she'd be in big trouble without Caleb's generosity.

Noah had simply been a stern voice on the other end of the phone line, checking in with her weekly, never mentioning Caleb. Now she would get to meet him. She knocked lightly, jumped at the sharp "Enter," that followed.

Noah was taller than Caleb, leaner, but not much older. His face was tanned, his blue eyes so light she wondered if they turned translucent in the sun.

His countenance was unsmiling, and she wondered if that ever changed. She noted no wedding band, no personal pictures in the office, and realized that most of these men could never wear their personal lives on their sleeves, if they could even have one.

"How have you been?" he asked gruffly, as though being nice was something he had to actively work at. It definitely didn't appear to come naturally to him.

"I'm doing okay."

"Good." He passed a large envelope across the desk. "Sit down. This is for you. Open it."

She did what he asked, opened the envelope and saw that it contained cash—a wad of it. Internally, she sighed with relief, because money had been tight. Cael had left her some, but she was running out quickly because of the little things, like food.

She'd taken to wearing Cael's sweats quite easily, though.

There were also keys. A passport and a social security card with the name Vivienne Simmons on them. "I don't understand."

"Your last name is proving problematic. Getting you off

DMH's radar is challenging, and ultimately, the FBI thinks the name change will help. Along with this, they've got a deal for you."

"I'm listening." She picked up the keys and held them, wondered what they were for, because moving out of Caleb's apartment wasn't something she'd planned on doing.

"You'll be given a new identity. Since the agency's convinced you had nothing to do with DMH's theft, they can do that easily. But they want something from you."

"What?"

"Your computer skills."

She nodded, her throat tightening. It would all come down to this, she had known that. And she'd spent the last month going over the pros and cons.

In the end, she'd come to the conclusion that, when asked again, she would say yes. Not so much for her, but for her and Caleb. Otherwise, staying together would prove problematic for both of them. And she wasn't prepared to let the best thing in her life disappear because she was too proud, or too scared of her past. "What are these keys for?"

"To an apartment in Washington, DC. You'd have to relocate there for a while if you decide to go through with this."

So she had some money. A small apartment, a new last name and a social security number. Small consolation to be able to keep her own first name, but it was something. And an opportunity to utilize her skills under protected circumstances. "It's a good offer."

"It is," Noah agreed.

"I accept."

"I figured you would. There's a phone number in there—call it. Agent Parr will tell you what you need to know."

"What about Cael?" she asked uncertainly, wondering if Noah would tell her anything. If he even could.

"I'll give him your new information."

No indication of when that would be. But she simply nodded and headed to the door.

"You're a brave woman, Vivi. I want to thank you personally for your help."

She paused, hand on the doorknob. Her shoulders straightened at his words and she could feel a flush of pride stain her cheeks.

"Thank you," was all she could trust herself to say before she exited the office, then the barracks, and the cab, and finally, she entered Cael's apartment.

Only then did she allow the tears to come.

She could leave now, start over in a new place with a new life...without Caleb. Or she could stay here and sleep on Cael's pillow and breathe in his scent, his strength.

His T-shirt came to mid-thigh, reminding her of how big he was. His clothes were folded and hung neatly. Like when she first arrived, the apartment was neat and clean... but comfortable; the couch and chairs were meant for relaxation, as was the bed.

No, nothing austere and soldierlike about them, she thought as she crawled under the sheets and pulled the comforter up around her.

You'll be starting over without Cael only for now. He'll be back. And then...

And then.

If you loved
PROMISES IN THE DARK,
don't miss the next book in Stephanie
Tyler's red-hot Shadow Force series

IN THE
AIR TONIGHT

Coming from Dell in
Summer 2011

Read on for a sneak peek inside . . .

CHAPTER

1

The gun was pressed to the side of Paige's bare neck, the cold barrel barely registering against her skin. She'd gone numb. Her hands gripped the beefy arm across her throat. It was close to choking her, pulling so hard her feet were nearly off the floor.

She tried to balance on her toes, but Wayne was moving backward, dragging her into the bowels of the ER and away from security.

The smells accosted her. Stale air. Rubbing alcohol and air freshener. Fear and death. No matter how well it was cleaned, those odors would never cease, embedded into the hospital as surely as they were into her senses.

In the background, she heard the cacophony—sirens and the screams of the patients and her co-workers—heard someone trying to reason with the man who'd taken her hostage.

"Mr. Wallace...Wayne, please, you don't have to do this."

Jeffrey, please—put the gun down—don't do this.

The echo in her head threatened to take over everything, even as she told herself fiercely that this wasn't the same situation—that the man holding her wasn't her brother and that none of this was remotely personal.

Less than an hour ago, EMTs had brought in Cindy Wallace—she'd been beaten and at first insisted that she'd fallen down stairs. Paige had worked here long enough to recognize the signs, the excuses, the fear etched into the fine lines in the woman's worn face.

After a few moments alone with Paige, Cindy had admitted her husband had been abusing her for years. She hadn't offered up much more than that, but it had taken Paige only one touch with a bare palm to know the full story, her gift of psychometry working overtime—and she'd called the social worker down immediately. And the police.

And then she'd put on exam gloves so she wouldn't have to feel more of Cindy's pain.

But she hadn't realized the extent of Wayne Wallace's anger, hadn't taken Cindy seriously enough when she told her that Wayne had gone so far over the edge that he would do anything not to be separated from her.

The police had still been searching for him when Cindy was brought in. And while Paige had been so intent on taking care of Cindy, neither woman had noticed Wayne sneaking into the curtained area.

They'd noticed when he'd grabbed Paige and held the gun on her.

"I'm not leaving here without you," Wayne was saying now as he dragged her, Cindy following along, until they reached an empty room where he herded them both inside, ordering Cindy to shut the door behind her.

Time and space shattered inside Paige's head when the door closed—everything slowed down to the point of nearly stopping and her heart throbbed in her ears.

You've done this before—stay calm.

And suddenly she was fourteen again: the ER was the high school cafeteria and the man doing the shooting wasn't an overweight bully who abused his wife—it was her brother, Jeffrey, and he would make headlines for the school shooting.

She forced her mind to the present. One wrong move—by anyone—and things could get ugly fast. Especially because the police were here—she'd heard their calls to Wayne to answer the phone in the room, which he ignored. Cindy was screaming at Wayne, the three of them trapped together. Paige wished Cindy would be quiet, wished everyone would shut up and stop talking.

But nothing ever stopped in the ER—especially when it was a matter of life and death.

If she could get the examination gloves off her hands, she might be able to help herself. Or she might make things worse, but there was no way this could end well anyway. She refused to let it drag on for hours.

Her gift was both a blessing and a curse—sometimes

both at once. She'd been using it for as long as she could remember—inadvertently when she was a child. Later, when she'd begun to dread its intrusion, she'd taken to wearing gloves or pulling the sleeves of her shirts well past her fingertips as a defense. She'd even gone as far as to tattoo symbols of protection on the insides of both wrists, although they didn't seem to be much help at the moment. She was alive, yes, but the symbols were there more to keep the evil she touched from invading her.

This time, it might be the only way she would survive this.

Sliding her hands along his arm as if trying for a better grip, the latex began to roll off her palms. Halfway off and the images came through—ones she didn't want to see. Broken bones and blood and screams nearly shredded her with pain . . . and this was all a part of Cindy's daily life.

Shoulda killed the bitch when I had a chance.

God, was there anything Paige could see that could help her?

"You beat her yesterday and again this morning," Paige said, her voice hoarse and breathless, and the grip went slack for a second before tightening.

"Shut up, bitch."

She tightened her own grip, letting her hands take in the violence and pain that threatened to shatter her. It was why she worked a job where no one thought it odd that she wore gloves all the time. "You lost your job again yesterday. And you were so angry that you came home to Cindy, tried to have sex, and then you hit her when you couldn't get hard."

Wayne shifted suddenly so he faced her, but before she

could move away he had her by the throat, his fingers wrapped hard around her neck, closing her windpipe. Her only recourse was to grab at his wrist with both hands, but his was unmoving. He was remarkably strong—and dead inside. That's all she saw—anger and death—no hope, no love.

Nothing.

She was light-headed. She opened her mouth but no words came. He pointed the gun at Cindy as he slowly took her entire supply of air away.

"Leave her alone, you pathetic asshole." Cindy's voice had gone from near hysterical to calm, and Paige recognized that tone. Cindy had decided she had nothing to lose.

She would egg her husband on until he killed her.

He keeps getting out on technicalities. His dad's a cop. They always let him go, she'd whispered in response to Paige's earlier questions about pressing charges.

"You don't tell me what to do. If you'd listened to me, the way you're supposed to, this never would've happened." Wayne's voice was furious, full of guilt and blame—all things she recognized.

"You can't get it up, and I can't wait to tell everyone about your limp dick." Cindy's words were as deliberate and malicious as her husband's fists had been to her face.

They did the job, because Wayne released Paige by slamming her body against the nearest wall. She hit her head hard against it and fell to the floor. From there she saw Wayne lunge forward to squeeze his wife's throat, tighter, until Paige saw Cindy's eyes bulge and her face turn reddish purple. One of the officers, who'd come through the curtain

when Wayne crashed the bed Cindy had been on to th
floor, wouldn't let Paige up, no matter how hard she fough

Then one of the doctors came in, armed with a syring
With the help of the officer trying to subdue Wayne, th
doctor jammed the needle directly into Wayne's neck.

Finally, the medication worked its magic, shattering th
insanity, and everything went mercifully quiet. Wayne's bi
body slumped down on top of his wife's prone one, and
didn't matter anymore. Cindy was gone, Wayne would g
to prison for murder, and Paige was back in that awful tim
in her life when everything had suddenly turned from goo
to bad.

The entire situation had taken an hour, but it ha
seemed like seconds passing.

"Ma'am, it's over." One of the police officers was a
tempting to help her up from the floor. She wanted to sta
there, on the cold linoleum, to curl up and sob, but he
pride wouldn't let her. At least not in front of strangers.

She stood and let herself be led through the crowd to
cleared curtain. Her breath came in harsh gasps, part
from fear and partly because she'd been held by her neck s
tightly. She would have bruises there by morning, as we
along her side where she'd landed when Wayne had tosse
her. Her body ached, her head throbbed, and her nerve
were worn down to the nub.

In the hallway, she was vaguely aware she'd passed b
doctors, nurses, orderlies, heard their murmurs of concern
She didn't want any of it.

Finally, the officer escorted her behind a curtain wher
Carole Ann, a woman she'd known since she first starte

working here, was waiting for her. She was the charge nurse in the ER and dealt with the stress of the job easily. She didn't play favorites and she was an excellent nurse. She was also the one person Paige had given her personal information to, although she would hesitate about calling her a good friend. Paige had shared her cell phone and a few meals with the woman—the barest periphery of her life. And yet, it was far more than she'd done with anyone in a long time.

"I'm fine," Paige insisted to Carole Ann now, but her barely there voice said otherwise.

"Yeah, I'll let you know when you're fine," Carole Ann said with a smile—an old joke of theirs, as that was one of Paige's first words to her when they worked together.

She sat patiently as Carole Ann examined her. She knew the bruises on her throat were already showing, no doubt a deep purplish red. "I failed her," she said finally. Quietly.

Carole Ann crossed her arms and shook her head. "Paige, you were almost killed by this guy. He was out of control. There was nothing you could've done."

Nothing you could've done, honey—no way for you to know what your brother was capable of doing.

They all said that at first, until their pain hardened into anger and the town began pointing fingers at Paige's parents, at Paige.

No one would ever be friends with her if they remained in that town. As it was, no one wanted to be her friend as soon as they found out who she was. Except for her stepbrother, Gray—her fiercest protector. Her best friend.

Her heart surged with loneliness because Gray was

gone. This time he wasn't coming back the way he had al
the other times he'd went off on a mission for Delta Force

He'd died three months ago. She hadn't been informed
until two weeks earlier, when his body had finally been re
leased with no explanation as to why it took so long to be
told of the tragedy.

Gray's body had been sent to her stepfather, Joseph—
Gray's father—out in Arizona, and she'd flown out for the
burial, staying in his one-bedroom townhouse. God, that
had been depressing. Joseph was in a wheelchair, attached
twenty-four/seven to an oxygen tank because of advanced
emphysema.

Everyone close to her was either dead or dying.

"She started drinking again," Joseph had said about her
mother, who died a year earlier. They'd visited her grave
after Gray's service. "It was always so hard on her. You un
derstand that, right?"

She did. Although it always bothered her that her
mother didn't seem to think it was hard on Paige. But all of
their lives changed that sunny May afternoon, and now her
older brother, Jeffrey, was in a maximum-security institu
tion for life.

"Maybe you should take the time you've got coming,"
Carole Ann suggested as she wrote Paige a prescription for
pain pills and gave her a shot of a steroid to shrink the
swelling in her throat. "Take a vacation. They're going to
force the issue anyway—make you visit the shrink."

She knew that Carole Ann was probably right. Getting
out of here and taking some of her accrued vacation time
would be a nice way out for both the hospital administra
tion and the reporters who, like vultures, were outside in

the parking lot for the duration of the incident. "I don't know where I'd go."

"Someplace not as heavy. Which is any damned place but this hellhole."

She couldn't explain that she needed to be here, to feel the heaviness. Instead, she stared down at the stars on her inner wrists and wondered if they protected her from anything at all. "Thanks, Carole Ann. I'll think about it."

"Good. Go home and rest. I don't want to see you back here for at least forty-eight hours and I'd prefer a week." Carole Ann used her best nurse's-orders tone before she stepped away from Paige and headed back to work. Business as usual.

The dizziness had stopped, her throat still ached, the hoarseness would take days to go away, but she hated being treated like a victim. She wasn't, in this case—Cindy Wallace was. And so she slid off the exam table and headed out to the main part of the ER.

It was still quiet—too much so—and tension bowed the air as she walked out of the exam room and toward the main information desk. It was usually bustling, no one staying in place for very long, but they'd stopped taking patients and now all she saw were people's backs as their faces remained glued to the television mounted on the wall above the station.

She saw the hospital front, and pictures of the Wallaces flashed on the screen. Next was the picture from her ID badge, looking humorless and sallow. She grimaced a little, but if that was her worst problem . . .

It wasn't.

Her face was on the news—a younger version—that

same file photo of her at sixteen that the press had used over and over again when the school shooting first happened.

She knew the one they would show next—the one of her wearing a bloodied shirt as she was being escorted out of the school . . . and then her kneeling on the pavement.

There had been a recent school shooting. Whenever that happened, it was inevitable that Jeffrey's name would come up as sure as Columbine. It did this time especially because of the new lawyer and his transfer to the mental-health section of the prison. They claimed it was just as secure as the prison itself, but she'd worked with her share of psych patients and, in her opinion, they could be far more devious than regular criminals without being obvious about it. Often underestimated, they could appear catatonic and still steal your keys to the ward.

It's prison, it's different, she repeated to herself.

Her brother and what he'd done was her secret since she'd moved here to this large New York hospital. She was twenty-six and she still looked slightly haunted, some might say, but the anonymity was something she craved . . . something she needed as much as air.

Even though she used her stepfather's last name, it would be easy enough to tie her to the horrible tragedy that occurred. It was so far in the past for most people that she'd thought, by now, she was safe. But she of all people should know better. She would never be safe from any of it.

Still, the news report signaled the first time anyone had found her since she'd gone off to college. She'd kept her identity hidden, cut her hair short and died it darker, wore glasses even though she didn't need them, and made up a fictional background that basically left her an orphan.

She wore her hair long and back to its natural blond again now—and no more glasses, since she was old enough not to be recognized as the girl she once was. But as of today, her security was gone.

The entire staff was glued to the television. One by one, they'd turn surreptitiously to look at her, to try to see the resemblance between her and that young girl in shock. She could see the questions in their eyes—and she understood.

Everyone wanted to know what it was like to live with evil. She would do anything in her power if she could only forget.

Carole Ann snuck her out of the hospital, but a few members of the press followed her home.

Paige, do you have any comment about your brother's transfer?

Paige, are you going to allow yourself to be interviewed for the new book on your brother's crimes?

Paige, after all these years, are you ready to talk about what happened?

She shut the front door without a word to them and locked herself in her apartment. The press continued to knock on the front door until her landlady threatened to call the police on them.

Paige didn't bother to open her door to thank her, didn't want to face her landlady's questioning eyes. No doubt she already knew.

Exhaustion covered her in a sudden, debilitating wave. She felt as if she'd been on the move since the murders.

In the beginning, before Jeffrey went on trial, it had

taken exactly fifteen minutes before the first news crews camped out and seven days before the first hate mail showed up. There were news articles and magazine covers and books that all tried to make sense of what had happened, all asking, *How could the parents not have known?*

Anonymous death threats and accusations followed, resulting in six moves in that first year until the trial was over and many people felt as though justice was served. Then some of the parents of the murdered teens had wanted to bring Paige's parents up on criminal charges, but that hadn't happened. Still there were civil suits, and even though there was never a judgment found against Paige's family, the trials had still drained them physically and emotionally and bled them financially.

The saddest part of the entire ordeal was that neither Paige nor her parents blamed any of the victims' families for anything they did. Their own guilt was too deeply imbedded in them to do so.

Now that guilt became so all pervasive that she didn't leave her apartment. She wrapped herself in her quilt and stayed in bed. But nearly forty-eight hours after she'd left the ER, once the press had finally left her alone, she got a phone call from a man whose name she recognized from the recent newspaper articles.

"I'm writing a book about your brother, and I'd love to interview you," the man said after introducing himself as Adrian Weiss, and her skin began to crawl.

"Don't you ever contact me again," she whispered, her voice raw as if she'd been screaming for days. But really, that had only been inside of her head.

"Don't you want your side of the story told?" he asked.

"I'm interviewing the victims' families and friends, and I think your point of view would be invaluable."

She hung up on him and unplugged the land line. Mind made up, she packed as much as she could into two suitcases and figured the rest she could call a wash. She'd miss the landlady, a widow who often dropped homemade cake and cookies off to Paige, especially around the holidays.

Yesterday had been Christmas Day—she had the half-eaten apple pie and a plate of ham and mashed potatoes to prove it. Mrs. Morris had been kind enough to simply knock and leave them outside the door, as if she knew Paige still couldn't face her.

She'd lived here two years, a tidy, furnished, one-bedroom apartment in the borough of Queens, close enough to Manhattan to get back and forth to work easily without the ridiculous rent. She'd bought herself a new mattress, a small TV stand, and some kitchen utensils in all that time, preferring take-out and extra shifts at the hospital.

The most valuable things—the photo albums and Gray's medals and letters—those she packed up and dragged down to the car with her, but not without checking first to make sure that no one was hanging around. But it was dark and she appeared to be alone in the small driveway.

She hoped her old car could make this trip to the Catskills. Sometimes it barely made it across town.

She wore the thickest sweater she owned and still wasn't warm enough. She suspected she never could be. She jacked the heat up as high as the small car would allow and ignored her own racing pulse and butterflies in the stomach. Two hours of highway driving left her on the two-lane road that would lead her to the small town named after a cow, and she realized that her head felt clearer up here.

Or maybe she was light-headed from the change in altitude.

Fingers tapped the wheel as the truck in front of her car lumbered slowly along. She peered at the sky and then turned off the radio, tired of hearing how the early-for-the-season snowstorm would be the worst of the century.

She hadn't called ahead. Mace—Gray's best friend—wouldn't know she was coming. Better that way. She'd always believed that the element of surprise was most effective—based on her own experience and hatred of surprises, she could say that with firsthand certainty.

But if she ever wanted to find out what happened to her stepbrother, she'd have to speak to his teammate.

The army wouldn't tell her anything. She'd waited for his friends to show up at the memorial service, but none of them did. It would be up to her to find them, and this seemed the perfect time.

Everything happens for a reason, her mother used to say, and Paige wondered what this reason was, why Gray was taken from her . . . why her face was plastered on the news.

Gray had always told her to go to Mace if anything ever happened and he wasn't around. *Mace will take care of you.*

She'd met Mace once, when she lived in Chicago. Gray and Mace had stayed at her apartment overnight—they'd been on leave and traveling to California for vacation. She could still hear Gray introducing him.

Hey, sis, this is Mace. He's motorpool, like me.

Translation: He's Delta.

She'd been on her way out to work the night shift, but Mace's eyes had haunted her the entire time. He was broad and handsome and seemed to take up the entire apartment.

She'd hated him on sight. Maybe because he was handsome. Cocky. An asshole. And she'd labeled him all of that before he'd even opened his mouth.

When he'd spoken to her, it was all one-word answers.

She'd had to work that evening, so spending time with him hadn't been an option. But the next morning the men were there later than she'd realized. She'd come in from work after having breakfast out with some other nurses on the night shift and dropped her stuff by the door. The pocketknife sat on the table next to the keys and jackets, and she picked it up, assuming it was Gray's.

It hadn't been. The images of fear came spiraling through the metal before she could stop them. She'd wanted to throw the knife down, but she couldn't. She saw a young boy. Saw fear and mistrust—and the words *trust* and then *escape,* over and over again.

The man this knife belonged to had been through hell as a child. And suddenly she was glad she'd been working last night. Even though she understood tough childhoods, she didn't need to take on any more than she had.

But that hadn't been the end of their encounter.

She'd walked in on Mace, sleeping naked in her bedroom—in her bed. She'd given him and Gray her room, despite their protests that they'd be fine on the couch.

Gray had been in the shower.

She'd wanted to tear her gaze away from Mace but hadn't been able to for a good long while. Although she was used to seeing the human body on a regular basis, she remembered having never seen anything so exquisitely male.

In those four years since she'd seen him, she'd been with a handful of men, none of whom really mattered. No, she'd never been able to shake Mace from her mind, and, to be fair, she hadn't really tried.